Bad Boys
in Kilts

Bad Boys in Kilts

DONNA KAUFFMAN

B
BRAVA

KENSINGTON PUBLISHING CORP.
http://www.kensingtonbooks.com

BRAVA BOOKS are published by

Kensington Publishing Corp.
850 Third Avenue
New York, NY 10022

All Kensington titles, imprints and distributed lines are available at special quantity discounts for bulk purchases for sales promotions, premiums, fund-raising, educational or institutional use.

Special book excerpts or customized printings can also be created to fit specific needs. For details, write or phone the office of the Kensington Special Sales Manager: Kensington Publishing Corp., 850 Third Avenue, New York, NY 10022. Attn. Special Sales Department. Phone: 1-800-221-2647.

ISBN 0-7582-1199-6

First Kensington Trade Paperback Printing: March 2006

10 9 8 7 6 5 4 3

Printed in the United States of America

This book is dedicated with love and a wink to my sister, Kathy.

Acknowledgments

I'd like to take this opportunity to thank those who helped me with this book. To all my Scotland contacts, the usual lot of suspects, once again, I couldn't have done it without you. To my sons for putting up with the crazy hours and for keeping Dominos on speed dial. To my mom, to Kat, and to Jill for being my constant lifelines to sanity. I'm pretty sure it's working, but let me have the fantasy if it's not. You know I'm always here to return the favor. To my agent and champion, Karen Solem, who has steadfastly been there for me this past year in ways I will never be able to fully repay, thank you, thank you, thank you. And lastly, but very importantly, to Kate Duffy, my wonderful editor, whose unflagging support and enthusiasm reminds me every day why it is I write what I do for a living. Thank you all!

Contents

BOTTOMS UP

Chapter 1

"This place isn't big enough for the both of us." Kat Henderson wiped her hands on the already grimy rag hanging from a loop on her coveralls. She glared across the cobblestone square as Daisy MacDonnell flipped the OPEN sign over in the small stationery shop that sat catty-corner to the Hendersons' own motor-body repair business. "Call me Daisy Mac," Kat mimicked, remembering how Daisy—all perky American perkiness—had introduced herself several weeks back upon taking over the place for her late aunt, Maude.

Of course, if that sign in the window was the only thing Daisy was flipping in Glenbuie, Kat would have been first in line to welcome their newest resident to their small, eastern highland village. Every male in all of Tayside, it seemed, had been panting after the Yank since the moment she'd stepped out of that hired car.

"Come now," her father urged. "Enough of that. Hand me that wrench. This bastard is being a stubborn stick in the arse if ever there was one."

Kat absently handed over the wrench, her thoughts still on the American interloper.

"If you ask me, I say you go over and befriend the enemy," her father said conversationally, between grunts as he tried to loosen whatever it was that was stuck now. Given the condition of the old Cooper he was working on, it wouldn't surprise Kat if the whole undercarriage was permanently welded together with ancient axle grease and decades worth of dried manure. Only Hinky Thomas would think a Mini Cooper capable of being used as a farm vehicle.

"Make nice with her? Why on earth would I do something like that?"

"Do you a sight more good than standing here, shooting fiery beams of hell through her front door, that much I do know."

Kat muttered something under her breath, and reluctantly pulled her gaze away from Maude's shop. She took the wrench when he waggled it back up at her, then handed him a rag when he asked for one.

"You can't blame the lads for sniffin' about now, either," he went on. "Of course they're going to do a bit of ogling and the like. She's a might bit younger than most of the single lasses about town, yourself excluded. She's not hard on the eyes, and besides that, she's—"

"Fresh meat. I know, I know, you don't have to tell me."

Alastair Henderson rolled out from under the car and looked up at his only daughter. "I wasn't going to use quite that language, but aye, you've hit squarely on it with that observation. She'll be a challenge to them for a bit, then the dust will settle. More than likely she'll take up with one or the other, and all will return to normal."

"She can have all the rest of them, but why did she have to set her sights on—" Kat's rant ended abruptly as she spied the object of her lust strolling affably down the opposite walkway, stopping just in front of—"Och, the ruddy bastard! Already staking his claim. And in broad daylight, no less. Cheeky wanker."

"Such language. Yer sainted mum is surely rolling her eyes in the heavens, hearing you talk like that." Her father reached up and snagged the dangling tool from Kat's hand before she dropped it on his head, then rolled himself back under the car. "And I sincerely doubt he's in there doing anything other than chatting her up. Although God love him if he could swing something more at half past eleven in the morn—"

"Papa!" Kat kicked the trolley he was lying on with the toe of her boot. She scowled when he chuckled. "It's not funny. I'm in pain here. Your only offspring's heart is bleedin' and you're wantin' to raise a toast to the man's sexual prowess."

"What better reason to raise a glass, says I," he responded, completely unrepentant. "At least it gives the rest of us poor sods some hope."

Kat shook her head. "Incorrigible, the lot of you." Although she was certain Brodie Chisholm had had more than a toast raised to his prowess. Which was well documented in these parts. And those a bit abroad as well, if rumors were true. And they likely were. She'd known his charming self all her life, as well as most of the girls he'd spent time honing those skills with. None of whom had been her. Something, of course, she'd been fine with. After all, she was more to him than any of those backseat crumpets would ever be, and proud of it. She'd much rather be his valued friend and confidante than chance losing the special bond they shared for a brief peek at heaven.

Not that she'd ever had the opportunity to turn down the invitation.

"You wouldn't have us any other way," her father was saying. "Your mum would be quite disappointed in me for spendin' as much time alone as I have these past ten years and we both know it."

Kat had nothing to say to that, because her father was right. Her mum made him promise on her deathbed that he wouldn't wallow in grief and be a burden to their only daughter for the remainder of his days. In fact, what she'd said was, *Find yourself someone to care about and do it before you're too grizzled for anyone to find ye' charming.*

"And," he added, "she'd have no patience for the way yer still caterwauling about over Brodie Chisholm all these years later."

"Shh," Kat warned, looking over her shoulder. As if Brodie could actually overhear them from across the square. "I'm not caterwauling."

"Mooning, then."

She glanced across the street, wondering what was going on behind that closed door. "I'm, uh, I'm merely looking out for the best interests of a good friend. After all, what do we really know about her other than she's Maude's great niece, come from America to start a new life. For all we know, she's running from a husband and a brood of children. Or . . . or worse. Maude never spoke of her."

Her father rolled out just far enough to give her a look of reproach. "Maude never spoke much at all about anything in her personal life. Kept to herself, that one. And you'd do better to simply own up to your role in this and stop trying to pin it on some innocent bystander."

Kat huffed out a sigh. "Okay, fine. So I had kind of a crush on him that summer after I finished my sixth-year highers, before Mum passed, when we were, what, seventeen? That was over ten years ago. We were solid friends way before then and have been ever since. So, am I wrong to worry that he'll get caught up in some passing fancy with the American? Honestly, how do we know she's not here on some whim? Thinking it a lark to take on her inheritance herself. As if running a shop in a small highland town is a game to be played at."

"And you know all this about our newcomer because you've sat across from her so many mornings over tea?" Her father wasn't much for sarcasm, and even now, his words were laced with affection.

Kat's cheeks grew a bit pink. "I'm only sayin' that he might want to be a bit more circumspect, is all. Until we know what she's about."

"And I'm sayin' that it's a sad day when a Henderson wants something and doesn't go after it. I've the patience of a saint, which is a good damn thing considering this son of a bitching bastard is about clapped out and I promised Hinky I'd find a way to keep it going. But even I'm about out of patience with you on this matter."

"I didn't come running to you for advice now, did I?"

"I'm just sayin' that I don't know why you didn't play your hand when you were the only game in town. No, ye go faffing about until another woman shows up, making all the lads come sniffin' 'round, then ye start mooning over what might have been and lost chances and the like." He rolled out from under the car. "There are no lost chances, only missed opportunities. And you know what I always say about that."

"Opportunities are the chances you make for yourself," Kat repeated with him. She tossed the rag at him as he sat up.

Her father dabbed the rag to his forehead, blotting off the beads of sweat but leaving a bigger smear of grime behind. "You can pull the wool over everyone else's eyes, Kat-o-mine, but no one knows ye like your papa. You and I both know you've wanted Brodie Chisholm for so long that you grew comfortable with it, accepted it for what it was, thinking at some point perhaps you'd press for more. Now there's someone who might compete with you for that spot in his heart and suddenly you're all concerned, claiming you're looking after his best interests. All I'm saying to you is that for once, you might want to look after your own."

Her father was right and they both knew it. "You think I'm being silly." She gestured at herself. "But look at me, Papa. Daisy is as fresh and pretty as her name. I'm—"

"Solid as a rock and the best damn thing going in this town," Alastair answered automatically.

It was silly, but his instant and unwavering defense made her eyes water a little. She quickly recovered by glancing back across the square again. Brodie was in there right now with Daisy. And here she was, just standing in the shadows, watching. Knowing, as she'd always known, that this one would be like all the rest, just another passing fancy for him. Only this time she wasn't so sure. Daisy might not be a true Glenbuie villager quite yet, but she wasn't some tourist passing through town, either.

And Kat knew she wasn't the only one feeling the changes that came with time. Brodie came from a strong family, as did she, each of them with ties to Glenbuie that went back several hundred years. Despite his playboy ways, he'd want his own family someday. Had said so to her more than once, hadn't he? Of course it had been in that dreamy, can't-imagine-it-now kind of way, but the longing was there nonetheless. She understood it as she'd begun to feel that same longing a wee bit herself.

Her father was right about another thing, too. A Henderson didn't sit idly by and let others take what was theirs. Shamed as she was to admit it, it would serve her right if Brodie found the one who settled him down, and Kat hadn't done anything to let him know she fancied herself as that woman. It was supposed to be her. That it was always supposed to be her.

"Thanks, Papa," she said, "your defense is well noted and appreciated. It's only that I can't help but think he's had plenty of time to notice me in that way, and he's never once so much as hinted at it."

"Brodie Chisholm might enjoy playing as much as he enjoys laboring, but the lad is anything but an idiot. Hagg's Pub was never so profitable or popular when the old cuss ran it. Brodie's a scamp and a scoundrel for certain, but his heart is fully meshed with Glenbuie and all who reside here. It's that love and respect for his past that auld Finny Chisholm instilled in all his grandsons that makes Brodie good at what he does. Hagg's is now the heart and soul of this village because Brodie has made it the heart and soul of this village." He pushed to a stand and moved beside her. "Your heart runs just as deep and true, lassie. He knows that. It's why ye have that special bond between you that you do." He leaned down and bussed her forehead, then favored her with a wink. "You should have more faith."

Kat leaned into him, pressing her shoulder against his, but her gaze shifted back to the door of the stationer's shop. "I have faith in a lot of things," she said after a moment or two. *But my ability to attract a man, especially one who is all man like Brodie Chisholm, isn't one of them*, she thought, not putting her biggest fear to words. Knowing her father, she didn't have to, anyway. He was the only one who saw past the tough-as-nails, tomboy exterior to the vulnerable woman beneath.

Proving the truth in that, he gently chided her. "So go clean yourself up and walk over there and buy a card or something. Give you a chance to size up your competition, and something to use to get a little attention."

"Buy a card for Brodie? It's not his birthday and the closest holiday is months off."

Alastair sighed and looked up to the heavens as he shook his head. "Where did we go wrong, Maddy mine? Our girl has not a speck of the romantic fool in her."

"A fool is exactly what I'm afraid I'm going to make out of myself."

He was grinning broadly as he looked at his daughter. "Och, lass, where love is involved, you not only have to be willin' to risk looking the fool, you have to embrace the inevitability of it. Cupid forgives those who make fools of themselves for love, you know. As do the targets of his arrows . . . if they're worthy."

Kat knew when she was beat. So she did the only thing she could do. She turned the tables. She snagged the rag from her father's hands and snapped it playfully, a devilish smile ghosting her lips. "So why havena I seen you at Maude's shop, buying a card or perhaps a few posies for Miss Eleanor?"

She had the distinct pleasure of watching her father's already ruddy complexion turn a far more serious shade of red.

"What I do and who I do or don't buy posies for is my own particular business," he blustered, snatching the rag back and turning once again to Hinky's recalcitrant Cooper, which still awaited his magic mechanical touch. "Don't recall asking for your advice either," he grumbled.

"And there ye have it, my point exactly. But that didn't stop you—"

"I don't go mooning about over Eleanor Walth, daydreamin' about things I'm too afraid to go after, when I'm supposed to be working."

Kat batted her eyelashes and folded her hands under her chin. "Would that explain why ye almost burnt the place down the other night then? When you forgot to take the water from the stove after a certain someone stopped in to see about getting her brakes fixed? A double entendre if I ever heard one, ask me."

"No one is asking you. And you can forget I ever mentioned anything. If you want to go on standing there and watching from the sidelines while that Yank snatches what you want right directly from under your nose, without even so much as making an effort after it, well, then I suppose you deserve the heartache you claim to be havin'. I'll leave you to explain in your prayers to your sainted mum, why you're content to let her see her one and only not so much as lift a finger to go after what she wants."

"Don't play Mum into this to distract me from my topic," Kat said, partly to tweak him and partly because his words now were having a far bigger impact on her than his loving defense of her had earlier.

"I'll stoop to whatever means necessary," her father said, wholly unrepentant. "How do you think we Hendersons come to still be here, three hundred and a quarter years after first setting foot into Glenbuie?"

Kat mouthed the words with him, so often had she heard them, then leaned over and bussed him loudly on his still-red cheek. "I'm going to head down to Plough's for some sandwiches. You want your regular?"

"When don't I?" he said gruffly, but then he tugged at one of her braided ponytails. "Bring me an extra orange cream while you're at it."

"When haven't I?" she shot back, glad they were back on even footing once again. She loved her father dearly, didn't know what she'd do without him, but he knew her all too well. And she knew she'd chew over his comments far longer than she'd chew on one of Plough's hard rolls. Which was saying something.

She went into the small washroom in the back and scrubbed at her hands, her thoughts already running back over their conversation as she let herself out of the side door of their corner shop a moment later . . . only to bang directly into the subject of that conversation himself.

Chapter 2

Brodie grabbed Kat by her shoulders to keep them both from going down on the cobblestones. "Have to love a woman on a mission," he told her with a laugh, as she tugged free from his grasp.

"Aye. Going to Plough's."

He stepped aside and waved his arm in a courtly fashion. "Never stand between a woman and food, I always say."

"And you always say the sweetest things," she retorted, batting her eyelashes in a cynical fashion before pushing past him.

She took two strides before he snagged one of her braids and tugged on it, making her turn back. "What's wrong with you? A little engine trouble?"

She glared at him before flipping the braid over her shoulder, pointedly out of his reach. "You might say that."

Now he frowned. Had he missed something here? "Am I in trouble? You're not still fashed because Pitts beat you at darts the other night? Everyone has an off night—I told you that. And I know he's been a bit of a sod, gloatin' as he does. But I still say if you'd just listened to me, and balanced the weight further back on the—"

She shrugged out of his grasp. "It was a game. I'm over it. Besides, we both know I can get back what's mine the next time he gets paid. Now, if you don't mind—"

She went to push past him, and again he tugged her back, knowing it would just rile her further and fine with that. Seeing as he had no idea what he'd done to earn her ire in the first place, he was willing to risk a little wrath to find out what was going on.

She glared straight through him as she blew the hair off her forehead with a little huff. Most women staring down thirty would look silly in braids, he found himself thinking. Not Kat. They looked as normal on her as did the grease-stained dungarees she wore. He couldn't remember a time when they hadn't, and he'd known her since they were both six years old and in primary school together.

Might be it was the freckles sprinkled across her nose, the very same ones that had been there more than two decades ago. Or that fringe of blond wisps across her forehead that was forever needing trimmed, always tickling her eyebrows and making her chuff them away. Always defiant, his Kat. It was her never-say-die attitude that had drawn them together that long-ago fall day when they'd partnered up in Miss McKee's P1 class, knowing they'd met a like soul from the moment they spied the mischievous twinkle in each other's eyes.

But this chuff, while definitely defiant, seemed a bit different. It was a loaded chuff if ever he'd heard one. And he'd heard one or two in his day.

"I do mind," he said mildly. "I mind that you're snarling at me like a rabid fox, and I've yet to discover my crime. Don't I deserve to at least know what I've done to put you in such high dander?"

She cocked her head. "You're in the doghouse with at least three-quarters of the women in your acquaintance at any given moment in time, and you seem to suffer through that without much remorse. Why should one more or less matter to you?"

Brodie frowned. He knew Kat Henderson better than he knew pretty much anyone, save his own brothers. Sure, the two of them bickered on occasion, but there was always an affectionate edge. Today she was all prickly female and there didn't seem to be anything affectionate or familial about it. On someone else, he'd blame the monthlies, but not on Kat. She was too ornery to put up with something as lowering and generic as PMS.

"Alastair doing okay?" It was the only other thing he could think of that would put her in this kind of mood. He'd only just walked past the open bay door to their motor repair shop and had seen the old man's legs sticking out from under Hinky's ancient Cooper, heard him cursing up a storm. All perfectly normal, or so he'd thought. "You two argue about something?"

She planted her hands on her hips, eyes narrowed. "What makes you think that? He's been nothing but wonderful to me."

Brodie realized he'd somehow managed to cross into that netherworld of a woman's logic in which he had no prayer of exiting unscathed. Better to cut his losses now. It was a small village. If it was anything important, he'd hear about it at the pub over ales. Or Kat would eventually tell him herself. They weren't cut out to keep secrets from each other. Not important ones, anyway.

He lifted his hands, backed up a step. "Fine, fine. Sorry I asked. Ye seemed a wee bit on edge and I was only wantin' to help out if I could."

"Because that's you, Brodie, helpful to a fault." She jerked her chin toward the opposite corner of the town square. "Is that what you were doing in Maude's earlier? Helping out?"

Now he was frowning. "What in the world are you talking about?"

"I don't see any packages in your hands, so I'm supposing you weren't in there shopping. Or maybe you were, but it wasn't the kind of purchase that gets rung up at the register, if you catch my meaning."

Now he cocked his head. She did look a little pale. Save the twin spots of heat on her cheeks. "How long has it been since you've eaten? Did you skip breakfast again?"

She threw up her hands. "Fine. Dodge the question."

He hadn't even heard a question.

"I don't have time to stand here playing silly games," she went on. "Games are supposed to involve darts or a pool cue. Life, on the other hand, is serious business, Brodie. You can't just play at it."

"At the risk of angering you further, I respectfully say I have no idea what you're talking about. I went to Maude's because Daisy stopped by the pub when I was out yesterday, looking for me."

"*Daisy* is it now? And I bet she did," Kat muttered.

"Huh?" Brodie shook his head. "Did something happen between you two? You want to fill me in? Because I have no idea—"

"This isn't about what's going on between the Yank and *me*," she retorted, giving him a pointed look that only perplexed him further.

Brodie's patience finally grew thin. Women. He'd never been one to lump Kat Henderson into that confusing and oftentimes frustrating category. Not that she wasn't a woman, but she was different. A straight shooter who told it like it was and didn't mess with his head on a regular basis. He could always count on Kat. He always knew where he stood with her.

Except for right now.

At the moment, where he stood appeared to be atop a very high cliff. And he was much closer to the crumbling edge than he'd like to be. All he wanted to know was how the hell he'd gotten there in the first place. He planted his hands on his hips. "Why don't you tell me what is going on, then? I'd at least like to know what I've done to piss off her royal highness here before she lops off my head."

"Men," Kat fumed. "Everything has to be a game with you. A contest. With rules. And some kind of scoring system. And a clear winner in the end. So fine."

She surprised him then by smiling. And it was something to behold, but not for a good reason. It was almost . . . feral. She moved closer and he had to fight the urge to retreat a step.

"Let's say, then, that this is like a rousing good game of darts." She poked him in the chest, right in the heart.

"This what? What this?" He was completely flummoxed. Not that it mattered, apparently, as she went right on without so much as pausing.

"The rules of play are, she who hits the bull's-eye and sticks there for good wins the prize."

It was on the tip of his tongue to ask her what that prize might be, but at the moment, he honestly wasn't sure he wanted to know. There was something . . . different in the way she was looking at him now. As if she hadn't eaten in a very long time—which he still suspected might be the problem here—and he was a perfect steak. It just didn't make any sense.

"And just like in darts, there can only be one clear winner."

"Kat, I have no earthly idea what you're referring to. Is this still about Pitts and the dart game?"

She shook her head. "Don't be daft. I have no interest in Pitts other than taking his money. My money, as it were. I'm talking about the game of life. And I'm finally realizing that I can't win if I don't play. So I'm in." She poked him in the chest. "And you know me, Brodie, when I enter a contest, I play to win. Take no prisoners."

Come to think of it, she did look a bit on the bloodthirsty side at that moment. Brodie was torn between laughing off this whole strange mood of hers . . . and covering his bits and pieces. Ultimately, there were times when retreat was the better part of valor, and he was beginning to suspect now was one of them. "Fine, fine. Pretend I never asked."

"Oh, no. I'm all done pretending." She patted the spot she'd poked a moment ago, her smile still a bit on the edgy side. "So there you have it," she announced, sounding both relieved and, if he wasn't mistaken, nervous. "I've gone and put it out there."

Nervous didn't apply to the Kat he knew. Unless she was trying to bank a corner shot to sink a double against a tourist who'd proven to be a bit more on his game than he'd let on, Kat Henderson rarely displayed nerves of any kind. Fearless she was. Around these parts, when it came to darts or billiards, she was the shark in the pond.

"You've been put on notice, Brodie Chisholm."

He lifted his hands in surrender. "I have no doubt. Take whatever you want."

"If it were only that simple," she said with a long-suffering sigh, then pushed past him. This time she was fleet of foot and managed to sidestep his last-second grab. He thought about going after her, but somehow he doubted the real meaning behind her odd behavior would be further illuminated at this point. However, she had left him standing on the corner, literally scratching his head, purely puzzled by the whole of their conversation. And if there was one thing that provoked him, it was a good puzzle.

Then there came a round of metal clanking against metal, followed by another round of very creative swearing. Brodie smiled and walked back around the corner toward the repair-shop door. Something was up with Kat, and considering mention had been made of no prisoners being taken and the like, perhaps it might be best to be forearmed if possible. There was only one man on earth who knew Kat better than he did. Maybe he knew what in the hell had gotten into her.

"Good afternoon, Alastair," Brodie called out as he approached.

The old man's legs jutted out from under Hinky's old Mini. "Not sure what's good about it," he grumbled, grunting as more metal clanged about, the sound ringing through the small garage and echoing back again. "But I suppose it's better than not having another afternoon a'tall." He grunted some more. "Seeing as this one is like to be my last, as I'm about certain this bloody transmission is going to kill me before I manage to wrangle it into—" Another ringing blow, then, "Bloody hell!" Alastair shoved the trolley out from under the car, holding one hand in the other. "Teach me to taunt the fates, that will."

Brodie was already searching for a clean rag even before he spied the blood oozing rapidly between the fingers Alastair had clenched around his wounded palm. Brodie dragged the wicker wash basket out from under the tool rack and fished out what appeared to be something clean—clean enough, anyway—and tossed it to Alastair. "Where's your first-aid kit?"

"Just hand me some glue and some tape—I'll be fine enough."

The blood had already soaked through the rag. "So you're sayin' you don't have a kit? I thought Kat had harangued you about that ages ago. She sees this and there will be hell to pay from now till all—"

Alastair scrambled up. "Now, now, no crazy talk like that." He wobbled a little, having stood up too fast.

Brodie immediately slung an arm around his shoulders, taking the weight of the older man against him. Seeing as, at a few inches over six feet, he had almost a full foot on the man, stout of build though he might be, it wasn't much of a burden. "Let's get you over to the washbasin and see what we see."

"Hello?" came the sound of a lilting female voice from the open bay door behind them. Even though she'd only spoken one word, he had no doubt who it was. There was only one American in town with a voice like that.

"Hullo, Daisy. Just a bit of first aid going on here."

"Bloody hell," Alastair muttered. "This is all I need. Kat'll be back any moment." He shifted his weight out from under Brodie's supporting arm and stepped away. "Why don't you escort Miss MacDonnell wherever it is she needs to go. I'll take care of this. Hardly more than a scratch."

Brodie waved Daisy back. "Just a moment."

"Are you sure you don't need some help? My mother was a nurse. I picked up a few things growing up. Maybe I can help. Or go after someone for you? Dr. Frampton, maybe? I think I just saw him heading to your pub for lunch, but perhaps—"

"I'll be fine," Alastair called out. "Thanks anyway."

If he'd been striving for civil, Brodie thought, he'd missed it by a stone's throw or two. And he'd never known Alastair to be anything but friendly. Probably the pain. The cut must be even worse than it already looked to be. "Maybe we should get Frampton over here."

"For the love of all that's holy," he hissed, "get her out of here before Kat comes back, will ye? I've trouble enough on my hands today without adding a catfight to the mix."

Brodie had been trying to get Alastair to put his hand back under the water so he could see just how deep the gash in his palm was. He paused, frowned, remembering now the reason he'd stepped back around the corner. "Are Kat and Daisy at odds over something?" Of course, they couldn't be more different. But then, no woman was quite like Kat.

The American lass was open, cheerful to a fault, and exceedingly friendly. Partly, he'd felt, during the scant few times they'd had words, because she was eager to fit in with her new neighbors. And partly, he knew, because reading people was his business, after all; it was her nature to be bubbly. Nothing like her Auntie Maude, that was for certain. A more grim-faced woman he'd never had the displeasure of meeting. There had been a collective sigh of relief when the taxi ferrying Maude's only blood relation came in from the train station and Daisy had turned out to be nothing like the auld bat, God rest her mortal soul.

Kat, on the other hand, though outgoing enough, was bold and brash, bordering on cocky. But no' arrogant. The lass was quite able to back up any claim she made about herself and was quick to defend any in her acquaintance who needed defending.

She was also quick to extract retribution from those who'd done wrong.

Probably why he was a bit twitchy at the moment.

"It's more than a flesh wound," he said to Alastair, dragging his thoughts back to the moment. "You're likely to need stitches. Why don't I send Daisy off to Hagg's to get Frampton here before he finishes off his first ale." He grinned. "You wouldn't want your stitches to be all crooked."

He thought he saw Alastair pale a little at the last part.

"You're not afraid of a little mending, are you?"

"'Course not." He pried Brodie's hand off of his. "Not the first time I've seen a little blood. Just get me something to wrap around it—I'll be fine." When he looked up and spied Brodie's set expression, he relented. Slightly. "I'll see the good doctor tomorrow, aye? We've cleaned it well enough. It's hardly pumping out any fresh at all at this point."

"That's because you've got water running over it and it's compressed. Lift one finger and it'll be gushing again and we both know it." Over his shoulder, he said, "We appreciate the help. Send Frampton here as soon as you find him."

"Will do," she said, with a cheery smile and an even cheerier wave.

He gave the same in return. It was almost impossible not to be cheery where Daisy was concerned.

"You might want to reconsider that hound-dog smile when Kat gets back here, lad. No use in rubbin' her nose in it."

"In what?"

"Anyone can plainly see yer moonin' after our newest resident. No' that I blame ye, lad, she's quite a corker."

Brodie was honestly surprised. "Mooning? Me? After Daisy?" He glanced back to the spot where she'd been standing, as if looking there would help him make more sense of things. What was up with the Henderson clan this fine day anyway? They'd both gone a bit starkers. "Did you have the exhaust running at any point today?"

Alastair scowled at him, as if he were being particularly dense. "The only brain that's been clouded lately is yours. Right in front of your nose is where she is. Where she's always been."

"You've lost more blood than I thought," Brodie told him. "Here." He grabbed a clean wad of paper napkins stacked by the sink for drying hands. "Press this against your palm, and hold it tight. Daisy should be here any moment with Frampton. Why don't we sit down until he gets here." Not that Alastair looked particularly woozy now, but obviously he was more out of it than he appeared, given the gibberish he was spouting.

Of course, that didn't explain the gibberish his daughter had been babbling on about earlier. *I should have never left the pub*, he thought with a slow sigh.

"I don't need to sit down, I'm perfectly fine," Alastair grumbled, just as Daisy stepped back inside the shop.

"Here we are," she announced, ushering in the doctor.

"What have you gone and done to yersel' now, Alastair?" Frampton was from Alastair's generation and the two had not only grown up together in Glenbuie, they'd fought for the heart of the same woman. Alastair had won. But even though Maddy Urquhart Henderson—Alastair's loving and devoted wife of almost twenty years—had gone to her great reward almost a decade ago, Ben Frampton had never quite forgotten or forgiven.

"It's naught but a scratch," Alastair told him, clearly not pleased to see the man. "I told them both there was no reason to drag you from your midday meal."

"Better Daisy got him here to get you fixed up before Kat gets back and sees what you've done to yourself," Brodie reminded him.

Alastair grudgingly held his hand out for the doctor and

scowled over his bent head in the general direction of both Brodie and Daisy. "Thank you both for your concern, but I'm being tended to, so why don't the two of you move on now, enjoy the rest of your day." His grouchy countenance belied the ostensibly friendly words.

Brodie decided maybe it was better after all to let the Henderson clan sort things out on their own. "Right you are," he said to Alastair. "We'll be taking our leave."

Alastair waved absently in their direction with his good hand, his head bent and getting in the way of Frampton's efforts to see the wound more clearly.

"Those two are quite the pair," Daisy said as they exited the repair shop. "I sense some tension there."

"Long history between them. But Ben is the only doctor we have, so they tolerate each other when necessary."

Daisy nodded, looked like she was about to say something else, but thought better of it. "I appreciated you stopping by earlier. I hope you'll reconsider what I had to say about promoting the pub, but I can't thank you enough for passing along Reese's business card. You know," she added with a smile, "if his business card is any indication, he's in dire need of my services."

Brodie laughed. "The only Chisholm less inclined to spend a lot of time tooting their own horn than me is, well, any of my brothers, actually. But by all means, take your best shot. I'll put in a good word for you."

She put her hand on his arm. "Thanks, Brodie, I really appreciate it. I know I'm an outsider here, and I understand Maude wasn't the easiest person in the world. I do truly appreciate how nice you've all been to me since my arrival. You've always gone out of your way to make me feel at home at Hagg's, and that's been really wonderful. I don't take your hospitality for granted."

"Och, we're a pretty friendly bunch here. No need to get territorial, especially with a lass as fetching as yourself."

Daisy blushed quite becomingly. "You Scots are quite the

flatterers," she said on a laugh. "I still think you should give some thought to my ideas." She grinned. "I think we could make a great team."

Brodie grinned back, then glanced beyond Daisy's shoulder . . . to where Kat stood, clutching a Plough's bag to her chest.

Chapter 3

After spending the past twenty minutes castigating herself over her ridiculously foolish display with Brodie—what on earth had she been thinking?—it took less than twenty seconds for her to switch gears right back again.

She hadn't but stepped around the corner for a few sandwiches, and he was already consorting with the enemy. Again! Make a good team, would they? No one made a better team than Kat and Brodie, and she had half a mind to tell Daisy exactly that. Then she looked at Brodie and the words lodged in her throat. Did he have any idea what kind of partnership Kat really wanted with him? What would he think if he knew?

Every single one of her insecurities came rushing in, swamping her, tying up her tongue . . . and her stomach. Maybe she was a fool. Not for stating her intentions to him earlier, but for having them in the first place.

Daisy had noticed the direction of Brodie's gaze at that point and turned to face Kat. Her smile was instant and seemingly sincere. Of course, she had no idea of the turmoil she was wreaking just with her very presence.

"Hi, Kat. I was just on my way to find you."

She raised one highly skeptical eyebrow. "Really." She couldn't imagine why.

"Your father—" Brodie started, but before he could complete the sentence, Doc Frampton stepped around Hinky's

Cooper and came over to where the three of them were standing.

Her heart squeezed and her stomach clutched more tightly, but for entirely different reasons now. "What happened? Is he all right?"

"Ornery cuss, so he's fine," the doctor told her, scowling himself, as if at war between his Hippocratic oath and his personal ones where Alastair was concerned. Which, knowing full well the history between the two, he likely was.

Kat felt her lips twitch. She knew Ben took the feud quite seriously, but after all this time, she couldn't help but think what both of them needed was to down a few ales together and let bygones be bygones. "What happened?"

"Cut on his hand. Needed a few stitches. He should come get them out in a week."

Everyone standing there knew Alastair wouldn't be darkening Ben Frampton's door unless it was life or death, and even then, only if it wasn't his own. So she juggled the sack of sandwiches into one arm and stuck out her hand. "Thanks, Doc. I'll make sure he takes care of himself."

"Ale's on the house," Brodie told him as Frampton gave Kat's hand a polite shake. "Thanks for coming right over."

Frampton nodded and was gone a moment later.

"I should go see to him," Kat said, motioning to the back of the garage. "He'll be like a lion with a thorn for a few days, I imagine. You know what a baby he is when it comes to things like this." She was bordering on babbling, and she knew it. Brodie likely thought she'd lost a marble or two after her speech in front of the shop earlier. And who knew what Daisy thought of her? She shouldn't care. But a part of her wondered, nonetheless. The insecure part that was standing there in grease-stained coveralls, hair in ratty braids, nails torn and ragged, not so much as a swipe of makeup on her face. While Daisy stood there looking every bit as cute and perky as her namesake. Effortlessly so. She wondered what it would be like to have the kind of natural beauty that so easily turned heads, and the quiet confidence that came along with it.

Kat had plenty of confidence about a lot of things regarding herself, namely when it came to her abilities and skills. But when it came to things like appearance and attractiveness to the opposite sex, that same sense of self deserted her completely. Sure, she cleaned up okay, all things considered. She wasn't a total grease monkey. Before going to Hagg's for an evening of billiards, darts, and Brodie, she'd scrub herself clean, rebraid her hair, put on a clean pair of dungarees and a fresh shirt. But that was as girly as she got. No need to pretend otherwise, after all. She knew everyone far too well, and they her. What would be the point?

Aye, there might have been a moment now and again when she'd indulged in a makeover fantasy—hallucination was more like it—but when it came down to it, she had zero inclination to so much as paint her nails, much less her face. She was a take-it-or-leave-it type when it came to any sort of cosmetic enhancement. For the most part, she chose to leave it. Her feeling had always been that if she had to slap on layers of goop in order to get a man's attention, it wasn't worth getting. Men didn't have to go to all that trouble. They shaved, brushed their teeth, and combed their hair. She was willing to do that much.

Standing there now, in the face of Brodie's easy good looks and Daisy's perky perfection, however, she began to have second thoughts about her stance on all things cosmetic. Brodie liked girly-girls. Well, to be fair, Brodie liked all kinds of women. His head could be turned by an infectious laugh as easily as a pretty face. It was one of the things she liked best about him, that he judged people for who they were and not what they looked like. And yet . . . when he looked at her, she doubted he saw anything resembling a desirable woman. He just saw good ol' Kat. One-of-the-boys Kat. Best-buddy Kat.

"I, uh, I'd better get inside and make sure Papa isn't doing anything he shouldn't be," she stammered, suddenly feeling

out of her element and hating it. This was her town, her people, her place of business. It was ridiculous to feel like an outsider in any manner. "Thank you for taking care of him, I
appreciate it," she told them both, and meant it, but wanted
nothing more than to get as far away from them as possible.
Not waiting for a response, she clutched the sack of sandwiches more tightly in her fist and went inside the shop, leaving Brodie and Daisy standing there looking confused by her
abrupt departure.

"Go ahead and make a good team," she muttered. "See if
I care. God, you're such an idiot, Kat. To even think you
could get him to—"

"Hey—"

She jumped when Brodie put his hand on her arm. The
sack bobbled dangerously, clanking the soda bottles together
that were tucked inside. Brodie moved easily to take the bag
from her. "Sorry, I didn't mean to startle you. I thought you
heard me."

"What?" she said, knowing she sounded testy beyond reason and that he'd have no way of understanding why. But
there wasn't much she could seem to do about it. Hell, after
her little performance earlier, God only knew what he was
thinking. At the moment, she just wanted to crawl into the
nearest hole and hope he eventually forgot all about today.
Maybe Daisy could take his mind off of it. The thought made
her scowl deepen.

He lifted his hand from her arm, palm out in a placating
manner. "Nothing. I—I just wasn't sure—" He broke off and
cocked his head, his typical teasing smile nowhere to be seen.
A sincere look of concern colored his expression instead. "Are
you okay? You seem all jittery or something today and . . .
well, and I don't know. Just not you. Alastair seemed a little
off with me today, too. Is everything okay?"

"He thinks he's invincible and hates it when life proves
him otherwise. I wouldn't take it personally." It took what
was left of her control, but she held his gaze directly and did

her best to sound like her normal self, praying he wouldn't push this further. "I'll come around later, after we close up, and let you beat me at a round of darts. Okay?"

His expression didn't change, and she found herself holding her breath. Why-oh-why couldn't things be easier? Staring into those beautiful hazel eyes of his, eyes she knew almost better than her own, knowing they reflected a soul that was just as beautiful . . . she wished she could have fallen for almost anyone else. Anyone other than her best and closest friend.

"Okay," he said, his voice a shade on the gruff side. "But there will be no letting me win. You'll have to beat me fair and square." His lips quirked just a little, and that twinkle of mischief lit up his eyes. It was no wonder women couldn't resist him. Lord knew she couldn't.

Her heart was pounding, her palms were sweaty. It was ridiculous, letting him have this effect on her after all these years. And yet there was nothing she could seem to do about it. "I'm sure I'm up to the challenge," she responded, a smile of her own threatening. It was hard to be around Brodie and not smile. Of course, he took her statement as typical Kat Henderson bravado, not the flirting banter she wanted it to be.

His smile grew to a grin that made the dimple in his chin deepen and the corners of his eyes crinkle. He needed a haircut, too, she noted absently, his unruly mop threatening to cascade down into his eyes. She wanted badly to reach up and push the tangle of dark curls off his forehead. Wanted to trace her fingertips across his lips. Her nipples went hard and the muscles between her thighs tightened in almost painful awareness. And she wondered just how shocked he would be if she told him what was going through her mind in that moment. How badly she wanted to trace that dimple in his chin with the tip of her tongue.

He pushed the bag of sandwiches back into her arms. "Better fortify yourself, then," he told her. "You're going to need all the help you can get. I'm feeling lucky today."

If you only knew how lucky you could get, she thought woefully. "Big talk," she retorted, edging away from him, wishing like hell he'd either leave and let her get herself back under some semblance of control . . . or rip the bag out of her hands and toss it aside before yanking her into his arms, pushing her up against the nearest wall and taking her right then and there. Now *that* would be lucky. "Save it for later," she finished hurriedly, before turning tail and basically running away.

She'd made a big enough fool of herself for one day. She had no idea if she'd be in any frame of mind to go to Hagg's later or not. At the moment, she just wanted to check on her father . . . and get far enough away from Brodie so she could get her head back on straight. Not to mention various other clamoring body parts. She had to get a serious grip. And she had to do it soon.

Five hours later the only thing she'd gotten a grip on was the undercarriage of Hinky's Mini. "Bollocks," she swore as a huge glob of axle grease plopped on her forehead and oozed back toward her hair. At this rate she was never going to make it to Hagg's tonight. She'd talked herself into and out of going at least a dozen times. It was already an hour past the time they usually closed up shop, but with her father out of commission for the most part—hard to be a mechanic with only one hand—she'd taken on his project, as they'd promised it to Hinky before the end of the week. Or her father had, anyway. It was a wonder the damn thing ran at all, but to Hinky it was like a recalcitrant child who needed a bit of coddling or bullying from time to time. The one time she'd suggested that he might consider getting a new car, he'd looked at her as if she'd suggested he murder his youngest child.

"Maybe I'll do it for him," she muttered, thinking there was no amount of bullying that was going to save this rusted hulk this time. But she was also every bit as stubborn as any blasted automobile, and she'd be damned if this one was going to do in two Hendersons in one day. So, with a deep huff, she blew her hair off her forehead—the parts that weren't mired in axle grease, anyway—and redoubled her efforts. If she could just get this last part dismantled without the whole thing cracking up, she could start actually replacing parts and putting it all back together in the morning.

What felt like minutes later, she heard the tower clock across the square chime eight times. How in the hell had it gotten so late? At this rate she'd never get upstairs and cleaned up in any decent fashion. She snorted at her foolish anxiety. Like it mattered what she showed up looking like. It was just another evening at Hagg's. Not a person there hadn't seen her looking just like this or worse. Which was half the problem. She wondered if Brodie even noticed her appearance anymore.

It was early spring, generally the height of tourist season in Scotland, but Glenbuie wasn't exactly a hot spot of activity. Yes, they were known to some degree for the Chisholm family whisky distillery, which had been actively producing the locally famous Glenbuie whisky for over two hundred years. But being located on the westernmost end of the Tayside region, they weren't exactly in the whisky tour loop that annually brought tourists to the highlands in droves. And with no castle ruins of any repute nearby, Glenbuie had been more or less left to prosper on its own merits. Some time periods in history had proven better than others, and at the moment, they were just hanging in there, doing their best.

The distillery was still the main source of income for most of the townsfolk, either directly as employees of the family-owned company, or the indirect beneficiary of having a large employer located just outside of the village. More and more, the younger generation had migrated north to Inverness or south to Edinburgh, or even farther, to London and points beyond. Kat, on the other hand, was perfectly content with her lot in Glenbuie. There had been Hendersons here almost as long as Chisholms, who had held the clan seat for close to four hundred years.

The motor repair shop was the only one in over a fifty-kilometer radius, so they managed okay. And okay was good enough for her. She was happy here, living amongst the same people she'd known her whole life. She'd never harbored dreams of being a big success somewhere else. She was quite content with her modest lifestyle and the security that came with knowing she belonged. She was well rooted to the land, the people, and the town itself, its past and its future. There was enormous comfort in knowing she was but one of a long line of Hendersons who had helped shape the course of Glenbuie's history. And would continue to shape its future. Unless, of course, the line died out with her.

Her contentment ebbed, and her stomach knotted a little. Visions of Brodie, smiling and laughing as he served and sang with the townsfolk they'd both grown up with, swam through her mind. He was much like her in his beliefs, his feelings about life in Glenbuie, and his attachment to all that came with it. Why couldn't he see how perfect it would be for the two of them to continue on together?

Of course, there was that wee problem of him not knowing she wanted him like that. But honestly . . . "How bleedin' hard is it for him to see what's right in front of his charming devil of a face?"

"Kat? Is that you under there?"

For the second time that day, she startled badly. This time it caused her to yank hard on the wrench in her hand, which had the fortunate result of finally loosening the damn oil pan. Which led to the unfortunate result of gelatinous glops of crud plopping down on her face. "Jesus and Mary," she swore, spluttering.

"Oh, I'm so sorry!" Daisy bent down as Kat shoved herself out from under the car, blindly reaching for the rag, any rag, within groping distance. Daisy grabbed one from next to the tool tray. "Here," she said, pressing it into Kat's hand. "I'm really sorry."

Kat sat up as she scraped the greasy goop from her face and fringes of her hair.

"You have some there," Daisy said, helpfully pointing to Kat's ear.

Kat purposely didn't look at her for fear she'd say something she'd later regret. Why was it that the one person who, without even trying, made her feel like some kind of cretinous grease monkey, had to see her looking, well, like a cretinous grease monkey. She supposed it could be worse. She could have showed up with Brodie in tow. Not that he hadn't seen her looking her worst many times over, but at least on those occasions she had been spared the immediate comparison to Miss Sunshine Bright here.

"Right," Kat finally managed. "Is there something I can do for you?" As far as she knew, Daisy had come to town by train and taxi and didn't even own a car. So it was doubtful she was here on business.

"I, uh, I was wondering . . . how is your father?"

Kat cocked her head. Daisy MacDonnell, nervous? Not that she knew the woman all that well, or at all, really, but in their brief acquaintance, Kat couldn't recall her ever being anything but completely together, both in appearance and manner. "He's grumpy and in general being a real baby about the whole thing. Nothing that I hadn't expected. I sent him down to Hagg's a few hours ago. I imagine he has a pint or two in him now and feeling quite fine. Which suits me, as I can get more work done that way."

Daisy looked momentarily nonplussed by Kat's lengthy response. Apparently she hadn't been expecting such a frank answer to what had likely been a polite query and nothing more. Tough. Kat didn't put a lot of stock in small talk or polite queries. Ask her something and she'd tell you what she thought.

When Daisy didn't reply or, even better, wave her off and

disappear, she said, "Anything else I can do for you?" Perhaps she was a bit more terse than absolutely necessary, but she had work to do, dammit. Any chance of making it to Hagg's tonight was looking more remote by the minute. Although if Daisy was headed that way, Kat's enthusiasm for an evening out dwindled rapidly. She had no actual plan in place for getting Brodie to notice her once she was there, mind you, but she wasn't a complete idiot. Even she knew better than to play her hand while someone else held all the aces. She'd wait until the odds were at least partially in her favor. With grease currently dripping off her nose, it was a pretty safe bet that now was not that time.

"Actually, the real reason I came over here—not that I'm not interested in your father's health, I am," Daisy added quickly. "But as you know, I'm new to Glenbuie, and though I've met most everyone it seems, and you all couldn't be more warm or welcoming, I, uh . . ."

Kat had to bite her tongue to keep from mentioning that it had been the men warmly welcoming her more than anything, but then as Kat was one of very few single women left in Glenbuie within a decade of their age group, that probably would have sounded a bit too much like sour grapes. Then she noticed Daisy was twisting her fingers together, and concern for her fellow man got the better of her. "Is something wrong? Did something happen at your shop? You seem a little . . . unnerved."

Daisy laughed a bit unevenly, and Kat couldn't help but notice that even her nervous laugh was melodious. Figured.

"No, nothing like that. It's just, from the short time I've been here, I've noticed that there aren't too many of us here in town."

"Us?"

Daisy blushed. "Young, single women."

"Well, I appreciate you pointing that out to me."

"No, that's not what I meant. God, I'm so screwing this up. I wasn't meaning to offend, and I know I don't even know you, but I was just thinking—hoping, really, I guess you could say, that, well . . ." She broke off and laughed again, only this time it was more solid, if a bit self-deprecating. "Jesus, I sound like a flighty dimwit. I'm not usually so off my game—it's just that you're a little intimidating, and it's important to me that—"

"*I'm* intimidating?" Now it was Kat who laughed. "You're kidding, right?"

Daisy blew out a sigh and let her shoulders slump a little. "I am totally blowing this. You see, I was going to come over earlier today, when I saw you leave to go out for some lunch, offer to go with you, so maybe we could spend a little girl time together, get to know each other. But then I saw you and Brodie and I didn't want to interrupt anything. And then your dad cut his hand and, well—" She broke off, shrugged. "It was probably silly of me. I just—I mean, I love it here and I am really enjoying everyone in town, but I guess I was hoping maybe we could—"

"Be friends?" Kat was still trying to digest the possibility that Daisy was nervous because of her. It was to laugh, really.

Daisy nodded, smiled a little. "Ridiculous hope, maybe, since you've lived here forever and probably aren't in the market for new pals."

"Nonsense." Kat might be many things, but heartless in the face of someone putting themselves out there wasn't one of them. She clambered to a stand and stuck her hand out, noticed the grease caking her fingernails, and quickly grabbed a rag instead. "I'm sorry. I'm a total mess here."

"It's amazing to me."

Kat sent her a sideways glance. "What, that I'm constantly looking like something the cat dragged in, after dipping me in an oil pan? It's rather difficult to fix cars without touching the greasy parts. Although, it's possible, even probable that someone like you would find a way to manage it." She hadn't meant to make that last part sound so negative, really she hadn't.

Now Daisy faltered. "What do you mean 'someone like me?' What I meant by amazing was that you're a mechanic, and a very good one, to hear the people in town tell it. I can't even change my own oil. Not that I have a car any longer to worry about, but when I did . . ." She shrugged. "I was hopeless at even the most basic repair. So the fact that you can dive in there and have any clue what's what . . ." She trailed off and gave a self-deprecating shrug.

Kat felt her cheeks heat at the unexpected compliment. "I was raised with a wrench in one hand and a jack in the other. It's in my genes, I guess. I can't remember a time I didn't know how to dismantle an engine." She stared at Daisy, and though she really hated to admit it, she found it impossible not to like her. Just a little. Kat admired someone who went for what they wanted, especially in the face of their own insecurities. Bollocks. This just complicated things even further.

"And what I meant with my earlier remark was that no matter the weather, rain or shine, you always look as bright as your namesake. It's a wonder to me. I'm about as inept at that as you are at changing your oil." She smiled in response to Daisy's grin, surprised at how natural and good it felt. "Once a grease monkey, always a grease monkey, I guess."

Daisy impulsively stuck her hand out, then shook it a little, waiting for Kat to put hers there. "Come on. Grease and all."

Kat gave Daisy's perfectly manicured hand a tentative shake, but Daisy grabbed hold and pumped it properly, then smiled when she held up her grease-smeared palm. "There, now we've sealed it. I can too get dirty."

Kat laughed. "That only proves half the battle. I still don't clean up well."

"Oh, don't be so certain about that. I bet your hair is amazing when you take it down. I always thought blondes had more fun." She pushed at her own auburn, shoulder-length bob. "Mine is pretty boring."

"Shut up. It falls in a perfect, shiny waterfall." They both grinned, delighted by the easy banter between them. "And I never take mine down. It's a pain when it's loose."

"That is an absolute crime. With your skin and those eyes . . ." Daisy's eyes twinkled. "Are you close to calling it quits for the night?"

Kat looked back at the Cooper and sighed. "No, but I think I will anyway."

"Good!" Daisy surprised her by looping her arm through Kat's. "My turn now."

"Your turn what?" Kat asked, only hoping she didn't sound as alarmed as she suddenly felt.

"To prove you clean up well. When we're done, we'll head to Hagg's and let the crowd be the judge. Deal?"

Kat stood there, helpless against Daisy's relentless enthusiasm. "Uh, sure. Why not?"

And somewhere between a long, hot shower and Daisy doing her hair, then helping her pick out something other than dungarees to wear, Kat completely forgot she was consorting with the enemy.

Chapter 4

"One more, then I'm cutting you off for the night," Brodie warned.

Auld Fife was one of Glenbuie's oldest residents, and everyone knew he could put away a fair number of pints before debilitating any part of what remained of his senses. But Brodie didn't want to spend the hour after closing time seeing Fife all the way to his cottage door. Normally he didn't mind, but tonight he had other things on his mind. Most of them involving what was going on between Kat, Alastair, and, apparently, Daisy. And just where was Kat this evening, anyway? Neither she nor Daisy had shown up. Even without their earlier dart game challenge, Kat could usually be counted on to put in at least a brief appearance after closing the shop, if for no other reason than to give him a hard time and beat a hapless tourist at billiards. But here it was, almost half past nine, and not a sign of her.

Alastair had been all but nodding off in his ale an hour or two earlier, probably because he'd ignored Frampton's warnings and taken a pain pill before Kat had exiled him over here. Brodie had fed him a bowl of Marta's Thursday stew, then had one of the lads get him back across the street. Where, presumably, Kat had gotten him upstairs and into bed for some much-needed rest. Probably she'd decided to stick close for the night. Like most men of his acquaintance, himself included, Alastair wasn't the best of patients. But then, neither was Kat. Nor, he imagined, did she likely make a particularly good nurse.

He grinned as he wiped down the bar. Perhaps it was just as well he steered clear of the Henderson clan for a wee bit. Let things settle back to normal. He still hadn't the faintest clue what bee was in Kat's bonnet earlier today. Women. Love them he did, but pretend to understand them? Not a chance.

He finished cleaning, then drew another ale for one of the few travelers in Hagg's that night. He liked springtime. The occasional tourist wandered in, but mostly it was the towns-folk, all emerging happily into the sunlight after a long winter. He loved the settled pace of life in Glenbuie, the steady rhythm and flow, as dependable as the change of seasons. Tending bar might not seem the most aggressive career goal, but although the Chisholm clan holdings did require a good bit of effort by all four brothers to stay afloat, all of them were in firm agreement that happiness, not a fat bank balance, was the truest sign of success. By that measure, well, other than his oldest brother, Dylan, perhaps, they'd all achieved a great deal of success. And Dylan would find his way, Brodie was certain of it. Time had a way of healing even the harshest of wounds.

Looking around the pub, he felt such a peace within himself. Who would have thought it? The rapscallion Chisholm lad, an entrepreneur before the age of thirty, and a successful one at that. His own place, filled with all the people he loved most. Hagg's was the heartbeat of the village, located right on the square. Everyone stopped in at some point, for a pint or two, maybe some of Marta's stew or a hearty platter of fish and chips, followed by a game of darts or billiards, a bit of dancing when someone brought a fiddle. More importantly, they came to talk, catch up on the business of the day, share the triumphs and curse the failures. And Brodie was right in the midst of it, reveling in the thrum. He couldn't imagine a finer place to be.

Just then the big oak door pushed open, letting in a sliver of lamplight . . . along with the more cheerful sight of Daisy MacDonnell.

Brodie's grin widened. Maybe there were one or two finer places a man could be after all. He hadn't quite yet made up his mind about the newcomer, though some of Alastair's comments earlier today had admittedly given him pause, but in the interim, there was no denying she was certainly a fair sight to look at. And nice scenery, in his estimation, was never a bad thing. Given the number of heads that swiveled in unison as she stepped into the darker environs of the pub, he wasn't the only one. Which came as a surprise to exactly no one.

The available men in Glenbuie and surrounding parts— although the attention being paid to their newest resident certainly wasn't exclusive to the single lads—definitely out-numbered those who were already spoken for. Most often it was the occasional wandering traveler or busload of tourists who brought welcome respite to the gender drought the vil-lage had been suffering through over time. An actual perma-nent resident was both rare and welcome. For the most part. Brodie imagined there were one or two significant others out there who weren't too happy to see their men's heads swivel.

He smiled. He had faith, however, that home and hearth would win out every time. He felt a little pull inside his chest at the thought. Lately, he'd been wondering about that very thing. He had his brothers, and they were close enough, and Lord knew everybody in Glenbuie felt like family to him in one way or another. But there was something else tugging at him lately. He found himself watching the couples that came into Hagg's more and more of late, how they laughed to-gether, played together, sometimes even argued together . . . and, ultimately, left together. He thought about that a lot as he climbed the stairs to his rooms above the pub each night, after closing up. Alone.

"So, what does a girl have to do to get an ale around here?"

So caught up in his reverie, he hadn't realized Daisy was standing across the bar, an expectant smile on her pretty face. He'd also been so caught up that he hadn't noticed the hush that had fallen in stages across the breadth of the pub. Those seated at the tables first, followed by those in the back, shooting pool or tossing darts.

"What?" challenged an irritable and entirely familiar voice. "Did I grow another head when I wasn't looking? Rhys, you better snap your mouth shut before you catch a fly. And Conner, I believe you owe me a quid from that thrashing I gave your dart game last week, so the first round is on you."

Brodie stood there, damp rag clutched loosely in one hand, a look of pure shock likely etched on his face. "Kat?"

The object of his attention, and everyone else's, judging from the complete silence, turned and scowled at her apparent partner in crime. "See? I told you this was a ridiculous idea. Everyone knows I can't pull this off."

"I'd like to see you pull it off," Fife shouted, his words slurred more from the toothless grin that accompanied the offer than the amount of ale in his belly. He raised his empty mug in her direction, finally breaking the extended silence as a riff of laughter skated through the crowd.

Daisy leaned closer to her compatriot and whispered none-too-quietly, "Well, it would help if you weren't quite so surly about the whole thing."

"Surly?" She turned to Brodie. "Am I surly? Never mind," she added quickly, seeing his grin reappear. "And not a word from you about this." She motioned to the brightly colored sundress she was wearing. And quite fabulously, if he did say so himself.

He nodded easily in response, knowing once he got over the absolute shock of seeing Kat Henderson in anything other than dungarees or coveralls, he would have a lot to say about it. All good, he was thinking.

"Besides," she went on, "you'd be surly, too, if you had to dress up like this."

"Oh, I imagine I'd be more than surly," Brodie agreed, folding his arms. "I'm not big on dresses. I have the devil of a time finding ones that fit across my chest. I'll stick with the occasional kilt." He shot Daisy a wink. "My legs I don't mind showing off." He leaned over the bar and glanced down. "I'm just wondering why you've waited so long to show off yours," he told Kat, much to the agreement of the rest of the pub patrons, if the sudden lusty cheer was anything to judge by. Instead of being flattered, however, Kat turned six shades of red and clutched Daisy's arm.

"That's it, I'm out of here. I appreciate the idea and the effort, really I do. But the last thing I need is a drink. My judgment is obviously already impaired beyond recognition."

"Would you hush?" Daisy leaned closer then and whispered something in Kat's ear. Brodie could barely make out what she was saying, but it was something along the lines of, *It's working, you idiot. Isn't this what you wanted?*

Was what, what Kat wanted? And since when were Kat and Daisy bosom pals? Last he saw, Kat was staring daggers at the Yank. But before he had time to puzzle any of that out, Kat replied, "I don't know what I want, but I do know I can't go about it like this." She gestured to the flowery shift she had on, then flipped at her hair. "Or this."

That was when Brodie realized that, for once, Kat was wearing her hair down. He'd been so caught up with the dress . . . and those legs . . . Of course he'd seen it down over the years, but usually that was only when she was in the process of braiding it back up again. It was all shiny and wavy, tumbling over her shoulders and partway down her back.

"I like it," he said to nobody in particular. Both women looked at him, and he shrugged a bit sheepishly. "The hair, I mean. And the dress." When Kat's eyes narrowed, he quickly added, "Of course, I liked your hair before, too." Women. Damn, but he never knew what was going on in their minds. Here she went to all this trouble, but she was mad now that anyone was noticing? Like they wouldn't have? Somebody explain that to him.

"See?" she told Daisy, as if his comment explained everything. "Honestly, Daisy, I really can't do this. He's all yours."

"But I don't want—"

Daisy's protest was cut off when Kat made a beeline to the door, amidst a few catcalls, an appreciative whistle, and another toast from Fife. Brodie tracked every step of her departure, and was still staring, somewhat dumbfounded, for a full ten seconds after the door closed behind her.

"Well," Daisy said at length as the pub activity finally returned to its normal level of chaos. "So much for winning new friends and influencing people." She slid onto a stool and propped her elbows on the polished oak bar, sinking her chin into her hand. "I should have left well enough alone, but no."

"Ah, she'll be fine. She's been acting a wee bit off lately for who knows what reason, but she'll snap out of it. Don't take it personally." Brodie drew her an ale and slid it across the bar to her.

"Thanks. But I still feel stupid."

"Maybe if you explain what that little experiment was all about I can sort it out for you. I know Kat pretty well. Better than most, actually."

Daisy sipped her beer and seemed to think long and hard about his offer. Although what there was to think about, he had no idea.

"She looked good," he offered. "If that helps."

Daisy just took another long sip of ale. "I shouldn't have meddled," she said at length. "I mean, I've only been here a few weeks and I'm still getting my bearings. It's just, it seems like there aren't many single women my age and I thought maybe Kat and I might hit it off. I know we're a bit different—" She stopped when he snorted. "See? I knew I shouldn't have meddled."

"I didn't mean that in a bad way, but you two *are* different." Earlier today, when Kat had seemed downright bristly, had someone asked him he'd have said those two would have made an improbable pair. But then it was back to that not understanding the whims of women thing. In his experience, stranger things had happened. And he sort of thought it was nice that Kat looked to be taking Daisy under her wing.

Though, come to think of it, maybe Daisy had been doing the under-the-wing taking. He grinned at that. No wonder Kat had been so prickly just now. She was hardly the type to let others dictate to her.

Daisy sighed, took another quaff. "You're right, but we're still women of a similar age, and so I thought it might be nice to get to know her better. Maybe our different backgrounds and life experiences would lend themselves to an interesting friendship. Or something like that. And it did, sort of. Briefly. We got to talking and I sort of talked a bit about my past, then she sort of unloaded a little, and the next thing I know I'm trying to help fix her up with—" She suddenly clamped her mouth shut, then studiously avoided his curious stare while finishing off her ale at an alarming rate.

"Daisy—"

She slapped the mug down on the bar and began fishing through her purse. "I should be going. I have a lot to do if I'm going to be contacting your brother with my proposal."

"I haven't said anything to him yet, but we haven't talked since I saw you this morning."

"No, that's okay, that's okay." Suddenly she was in a big hurry to leave. Or, as she continued to avoid looking at him, get away from him.

Brodie laid his hand on her arm, stilling her frantic search for her wallet. "The ale is on the house."

"That's okay, I can—"

"Daisy."

She stilled. "Okay. Thanks." But she still wasn't looking at him.

"What's going on?" he asked quietly. Earnestly. "I really want to know."

She said nothing, then finally blew out a long breath. "I so should have just gone straight upstairs tonight." She dipped her chin further. "I promised myself when I came here that I would take things slowly, not get involved until I got a good feel for the town, the people, and here it is, only three weeks in, and I'm already embroiled in something that's none of my business."

Brodie heard the sincere redress in her tone, but found himself smiling a bit anyway. He nudged her arm with his hand. "Hey."

Her shoulders slumped a little more, but she finally looked up at him. Any other time, seeing such a hangdog expression on her usually sunny face would have bothered him, but at the moment, it just made his smile grow a little. After all, she'd only been here three weeks—how bad could the situation really be?

"I have no idea what's going on with you and Kat, but trust me, she's the most self-sufficient person I know. Given how bad you seem to feel about whatever it is, I'm sure your heart was in the right place. She'll know that." Of course, he had no idea what the hell he was talking about, but he hated to see Daisy torture herself. "Besides, Kat rarely lets anything defeat her for very long."

"I just hope I didn't make things worse."

"What things?"

She suddenly pushed her stool back. "You know, you're entirely too easy to talk to."

Brodie chuckled. "Well, I am a bartender. But you're not exactly spilling your heart out here, luv. In fact, it's rather like pulling teeth."

"If you were anyone other than you, I probably would be."

He frowned, confused. It was a feeling he was getting entirely too familiar with.

"I could use an outside opinion, and you'd probably be the best person for a lot of reasons, which also makes you the worst person."

He shook his head, laughed. "Females."

Daisy laughed a little, too. "I know I'm making total hash out of this. I'm sorry I brought it up."

"I can't say one way or the other since I still haven't a clue what you're talking about. But I've never been short on offering up an opinion on things I know nothing about, so if you can't find one that suits you, feel free to come back by and ask me. I'll do my best."

She smiled, nodded, gathered her purse, then paused, looked at him. "You are a really good guy, Brodie. If Kat knows what's good for her—" She shook her head and shot him a fast grin. "I really need to shut up now and just leave. The meddler in me must be stopped."

He leaned on the bar, propped his chin on his hands. "You do realize you've gotten me quite curious. One of the reasons I like runnin' Hagg's is because I'm nosier than an auld woman. Which makes me a good listener, too, by the way."

"I already know you are. Too good."

"So . . . ?" He let the offer dangle, and when she continued to linger and didn't immediately take her leave, he nudged a bit more. "Tell me what all this is about between you and Kat. Just because I'm a good friend of hers doesn't mean I can't keep my thoughts to myself. I won't mention this talk to her if you'd rather I didn't. But I canno' help if I dinnae know what's wrong."

Daisy sighed. Clearly torn.

"Why the dress and the new hairdo?" he asked, figuring they might as well get right to it and stop beating around the subject. "What was the point of it all? Were ye' tryin' to make her over or something? Because, you know, Kat isn't much for frills and the like. Everyone here knows her and loves her for what she is. She doesn't need all that. I mean," he turned his palms out, not wanting to offend, "she looked wonderful, as I said, but it's not her."

"But you thought she looked good?"

"Sure. Pretty lass in a pretty dress—what's not to like?"

"So you think she's pretty?"

That made Brodie pause. "Of course I do—why wouldn't I?"

Daisy lifted a shoulder. "Well, she plays with auto parts every day and spends a good amount of time every evening scraping grease out from under her nails."

"She's an ace mechanic," he said proudly, "almost as good as Alastair. Has nothing to do with whether or not she's pretty."

Daisy sighed. "Men."

Brodie laughed. "Why do I feel that we're both talking at cross purposes here?"

"Probably because we are." She tapped her fingers on the bar, a look of internal debate clear on her face. "I wish I knew you both better—I'd be better able to figure out how best to handle this."

"How best to handle what?"

"You really find her attractive?"

Brodie sighed. "Aye, aye. Why is this an issue?"

"You've known her forever. Best friends and all that. Have you two ever dated?"

Brodie's mouth fell open. "No, of course not."

"Why do you say it like that? You just admitted she was pretty. And though I've only been here a short time, I already know that you're not shy when it comes to the ladies. Is it because you think of her like a sister or something?"

Brodie's mouth was still hanging open. Was Daisy getting at . . . what it sounded like she was getting at? Because that was simply too preposterous to contemplate. "No, I don't think of her like a sister. I think of her like a best friend. I wouldn't mess with that. She's closer to me than almost anyone."

"But you don't think of her like a sister," Daisy repeated.

"No. At least, not in the way you mean. I think." Now he was really confused. And starting to be very sorry he'd pushed his nose into this business. Especially as it was becoming increasingly clear it had something to do with him. "Maybe we should both reconsider our meddling ways," he muttered.

Only Daisy apparently heard him and smiled. "You're probably right." She leaned across the bar. "So I'll just leave you with this, and you can do with it whatever you want."

"Do whatever I want with what?"

"The fact that she finds you attractive, too. And she definitely doesn't think of you as a brother."

Chapter 5

Honestly, she really did need her head examined. One minute she'd been giving Daisy MacDonnell the evil eye, and not ten minutes after her rival had extended the olive branch of friendship, Kat was pouring out her frustrations and desire for Brodie, carrying on about how she wanted him to look at her the way he looked at Daisy. Or any other woman.

To her credit, Daisy had laughed and taken the news a whole lot better than Kat might have if the opposite had happened. It helped that the only part of Brodie she wanted to get her hands on, or any other man in Glenbuie, for that matter, was his publicity business. She'd come to town ostensibly to take over Maude's shop, but in fact, she was hoping to bring her skills and talent as a marketer to the local shopkeepers.

After listening to Kat bemoan her lack of feminine wiles—she still couldn't believe she'd done that and had decided to blame it on the aftereffects of a very long day, far too much of which had been spent brooding over Brodie—Daisy had confessed that back in the States, she'd been known as something of a matchmaker amongst her friends. And though she didn't claim to know Kat or Brodie all that well, it had appeared clear to her that there was definite chemistry between the two, and that maybe all Kat had to do was get him to open his eyes and notice her in a different way. She said that most men didn't appreciate subtlety and suggested that perhaps it was time to take a more direct, more blatant path to getting his attention. It was all about marketing, really, according to Daisy.

Hence one of the more embarrassing moments of Kat's life. My God, she'd never be able to show her face in Hagg's, or anywhere else in town, for months after her little stunt last night. What the bloody hell had she been thinking? A dress, makeup, her hair hanging all over the place? Could she have looked any more ridiculous? They were probably still laughing it up at her expense.

Sure, sure, there had been that wee moment when Brodie's look of shock had worn off and he'd actually given her a once-over that at any other time in her life she'd have swooned over. But she'd immediately realized that if the only reason he was noticing her like that was because she'd had to tart herself up, then she didn't want him. Marketing be damned. But it was the truth. She knew right then that the only way she'd have him was if he wanted her for who she was.

And the only thing he wanted from the Kat Henderson he knew was a hot game of take-no-prisoners darts and a shoulder to occasionally lean on when times were tough. A friend. That's what he wanted. A friend.

She wanted him as a friend, too. She also wanted him naked, sweating, and hot for her.

"Jesus and Mary, I need a drink." A shame it was barely half past eight in the morning. She'd been hiding out down here since dawn, when she'd given up any hope of sleep. Mercifully, her father had gone off to Sudley shortly after daybreak to pick up supplies and wouldn't be back till dusk. So she'd escaped his far too keen eye . . . and any chance he'd hear about her entrance into Hagg's last eve.

She'd already finished up Hinky's car, and now she was in the office, going over the books and paying the bills. Likely as not, he'd hear about it the moment he got back, but she at least had the remainder of the day to find her balance. She supposed she should be thankful Glenbuie was too small to support its own newspaper. She could only imagine the headlines:

MECHANIC TRIES TO WIN THE HEART OF PUB OWNER BY FLAUNTING HER BITS AND PIECES ALL OVER TOWN.

Not that the village needed headlines. Word would have spread by now. Laughingstock was what she was. Though honestly, she could handle the rest of the townsfolk giving her a hard time. The only part of the whole thing that really bothered her was that Brodie was likely laughing right along with them. Not that she could blame him. After all, if someone else had pulled that kind of silly stunt, she'd be right next to him, leading the chorus. Served her right to be the butt of every joke. Stupid, stupid idea.

The things a woman did for love. And the possibility of hot sex.

Kat glanced through the sole window in the tiny office. The round patch of leaded glass was permanently hazy, but clear enough for her to make out the shop across the square. Daisy was up. Her curtains were pushed open. Kat had waited tensely to see if her newfound friend would make an appearance, or stop by the shop to discuss the previous evening's events. But, as yet, there had been no sign of her today.

Kat had thought about going over there herself, just to make sure Daisy knew there were no hard feelings. She'd certainly known better than to try to be something she wasn't. She'd just gotten caught up in the moment, and Daisy's enthusiasm. It had felt kind of good, actually. For a few moments, anyway. Her gaze drifted down the square to the corner, and Hagg's Pub. She wondered what Brodie was doing this morning. Probably sleeping in, as usual. Such was the lot of a pub owner. Her gaze drifted to the narrow, gabled windows above the bar . . . and her thoughts drifted to images of what Brodie looked like, sprawled across that huge, heavenly featherdown bed of his.

Not that she'd been in it with him, of course. But she'd been with him when he'd bought it at an auction four years back. He was a big man, sixteen stone and just shy of a full two meters, and he'd bitched so often about his feet hanging off the bed he'd inherited from Hagg, that Kat had finally dragged him off to an auction in Inverness one weekend and made him open his tight fists long enough to see what a good investment a nice, big bed would be. She didn't hold his frugal ways against him; in fact, she was quite proud of how hard he worked to contribute to the Chisholm clan coffers. It took a lot to maintain the family property, and Brodie was never one to demand much in the way of creature comforts.

But she would sure like to have him demand a few things of her in that big down bed of his. She imagined they could find all kinds of comfort, creature and otherwise, romping about in that oversized—

A light rap on the door made her jump guiltily and turn her attention away from the window and back to the books. The last thing she wanted was for anyone to find her doing anything resembling lusting after Brodie Chisholm today. Or any other one from this day forward.

So it figured, naturally, that the door cracked open and the devil himself poked his head in. "Mornin'."

It was the lingering image of him sprawled naked across white linen sheets that had her flushing clear to her roots, but there was nothing to be done about it, so she brazened it out. "You're up early."

"Looks that way. Got a minute?"

God help her, he wanted to talk about her big entrance last night. What else would bring him here so early? "I'm, uh, doing the books, although I'd rather be doing just about anything else, so by all means, distract me." Dear merciful heaven, that wasn't at all what she'd meant to say. She really needed to shut up now. Distract her indeed. Could she be any more Freudian? Of course, she could quite happily give him a long list of things she'd like him to try. All of them featuring that bed of his as a backdrop. With her naked, writhing body as the centerpiece. The mere thought of which was guaranteed to keep her cheeks flushed for hours.

Brodie stepped inside the small office, filling the room and making it almost impossible for her to even pretend to concentrate on the columns of numbers in front of her. How had she let it come to this? She'd known the man forever—she should be able to keep herself in check. Except her mind would flash on that moment in the pub last night when he'd given her that inherently masculine once-over, making every inch of her body simultaneously tighten up and go strangely weak. She'd felt every inch the imposter and had panicked . . . but none of that erased that instant where, just for a split second, anyway, he'd looked at her with the kind of male appreciation she'd never thought to see him direct at her.

She was going mad starkers, really she was. She wanted his attention, then panicked when she got it. And yet, even now the thought of having to jump through all those ridiculous hoops of girlishness just to secure that attention made her cringe. Wasn't there a way for her to get him to notice her when she was just being her?

"Earth to Kat. You okay?" Brodie leaned down a little and tilted his head to the side so he could make eye contact as she studiously continued to pretend she had a clue what was written in the columns in front of her.

"Tops," she said. "Just some of these numbers aren't adding up." Well, something wasn't adding up, anyway, though it had little to do with their accounts. "I keep telling Papa he needs to list the parts as they come in rather than just when he uses them, but you know how hardheaded he is." Which was total bollocks, but she had to make some kind of conversation. If for no other reason than to stave off the moment when he'd ask what the bloody hell had gotten into her yesterday. Which, surely, he was going to do.

"Want me to take a look?" He started to get up and reach across the desk.

Kat slapped her arms down on the book, keeping the perfectly added columns from his view, and pasted on a smile as she finally looked up. "I'll figure it out. I guess I'm just not in the right frame of mind to do simple math this morning."

Brodie's lips quirked. "What are you in the mood for?"

Kat's throat closed over. He couldn't possibly have meant that to sound that suggestive. Could he? No. It was just her imagination, still in overdrive from the whole Brodie's-bed-with-her-naked scenario she'd just been contemplating. What if she just assumed he had meant it that way and responded in kind? Would he pick up on it?

Or worse, would he laugh it off as some kind of joke?

Merciful Mary, but she could use a glass or two. And it wasn't even nine in the mornin' yet. Why couldn't she be cool about this? Daisy would be cool. She'd smile and laugh, verbally spar and parry with him, making it all look effortless and adorable, because for her it would be. Kat had never felt so clumsy and awkward in her entire life.

"Can you take a short break?"

"Huh?"

Brodie just smiled and shook his head. Shoving his chair back, he stood and extended his hand. "Come on. I want to show you something."

She looked at the hand reaching for hers and wished with all her might she'd never started thinking of Brodie Chisholm as anything other than a friend. Because so help her God, all she could do was look at his broad, strong hand, with those long, dexterous fingers of his—a hand she'd held hundreds of times with nary an improper thought—and yearn for him to put it just about anywhere on her body.

Flustered and knowing he must be wondering by now if

she'd gone completely 'round the bend, she glanced down, pretending she didn't see his hand, and slapped the book shut. "Uh, sure. No problem." She noticed the black grime coating her hands from finishing up Hinky's car earlier and curled her fingers inward. "Just let me—" She'd been about to say freshen up, but that sounded ridiculous. She was also wearing grime-covered overalls, and she doubted Brodie intended for her to rush upstairs and change clothes, though she had a sudden, intense desire to do so.

Not the sundress—she wasn't that far gone, but at least something less . . . grungy. It occurred to her that her wardrobe didn't extend much beyond that. The dress had been Daisy's. "I need to scrub a layer off," she mumbled. "I'll be right back." She scooted out from behind the desk and did her best to skirt past him without brushing any part of her body on any part of his.

With his freshly shaved face and just-washed mop of hair still damp and curling about his head, wearing loose jeans and a faded green Hagg's Pub t-shirt, he looked handsome and clean and so damn good. It made her feel even grungier.

"Don't worry about that, it's not—" But Brodie's protest fell on deaf ears, as she'd already hurried through the open bay to the small washroom on the opposite side of the shop floor.

Kat closed herself in, then braced her hands on the tiny porcelain sink. "Get a grip, lass. Yer losin' yourself here." She lifted her head and stared at herself in the mirror. Her hair was parted and plaited as usual. There was a smudge of grease across her nose, along with a giant blotch on her jaw. Great. She scrubbed at each one with the back of her hand, which only made them worse. Sighing, she turned on the spigot and grabbed a hand towel from the pile stacked on the small shelf above the loo.

As she was scrubbing her hands and face, she found herself toying with the idea of unplaiting her braids. It wasn't the same as putting on makeup or a dress, neither of which was comfortable for her. But hair was hair, right? She wore it in twin braids because it was functional, allowing her to lie flat on her back beneath a car without there being a lump under her head and neck, as would be the case with a ponytail or single braid. She'd really never thought much about it beyond that. Until yesterday.

Daisy had gone on and on about how lovely she thought Kat's hair was, what a pretty shade of blond, how thick and naturally wavy it was when she'd insisted Kat wear it down, wondering out loud why Kat still wore it in braids after work hours.

Kat supposed that was because it was still functional. She liked to play billiards, throw a dart or two, and having her hair out of her face made it easier to play, all of which she'd told Daisy. Who had promptly asked her why she didn't just cut it off then, wear it short. Too much bother, Kat had immediately replied. Her hair grew like a weed and she hated going to get it cut. It was long enough, hanging past her shoulders, that she could trim the ends of the braids when they showed signs of fraying and splitting, and it was an easy enough matter to trim her own bangs.

But she'd thought about it later that night, after her disastrous—to her way of thinking—debut at Hagg's, as she was brushing it out before bed. Maybe she was a wee bit vain, after all. Because she'd been forced to privately admit that, if she were honest, she liked having longer hair for reasons that weren't entirely practical, too. Granted, she didn't use it to her feminine advantage, but it made her feel somewhat more womanly, just knowing it was there. She was toying with the elastic bands holding the ends in place, and had just started to pull one off with the intent to unbraid it and fluff it out, just to see what kind of reaction she got from Brodie, when a tapping came at the door, making her squeal in surprise.

"What are you doing in there?"

"Hold your horses, for God's sake," she barked, feeling immediately foolish for her silly daydreaming.

She heard Brodie chuckle. "We're not meeting royalty, Your Nibs, so come on."

She decided she should be thankful for the interruption, as it had likely kept her from making a fool of herself twice in a twenty-four-hour period. "He's your best friend," she whispered at her boring, regular old reflection. "And that's a good thing. Be happy with that and get a grip."

"What?"

"Nothing, nothing," she grumbled, and opened the door, which always stuck, so she shoved at it, not thinking. It came suddenly unstuck, as it did sometimes, and slammed right into Brodie.

"Hey!" He grabbed at the edge of the door, stopping it short from smacking him on the nose, sending it bouncing back on Kat, who lost her balance. Brodie grabbed her elbow and pulled her forward again, letting the door go so he could grip her other elbow and steady her on her feet.

Kat's pulse kicked into overtime. The very last thing she needed was Brodie's hands on any part of her body, even something as innocuous and innocent as her elbows. Which didn't feel so innocuous at the moment, or innocent. What they felt like was far too close to her breasts. Her suddenly tight and achy breasts. She felt his fingers dig into her flesh a little as she continued to stare at him . . . and realized that neither of them was making any move whatsoever to disentangle themselves. His gaze remained steady on hers, those eyes she knew so well, that mouth she'd seen in every possible expression from a scowl to a hearty laugh . . . a mouth she wanted so very badly to taste for herself.

Then, as if in a dream, he was releasing her elbow and lifting his hand toward her face. Unable to stop herself, her breath caught in her throat, and she felt herself leaning in, eager for his touch.

"Here," he said. Was it her imagination, or was his voice a bit deeper, a shade hoarse? "You missed a spot." He rubbed his thumb over her nose as her lips were parting in anticipation of him cupping her cheek, pulling her face closer so he could—

And then his words sank in and she felt her cheeks go hot with embarrassment. She jerked away from him and rubbed furiously at her face, wishing she could scrub off mortification as easily as a grease spot. "Thanks," she said tersely. "Come on, I don't have all day." She went to push past him, but he stopped her by sticking his arm out in front of her.

"Hold on just a minute."

"I don't care if I have grease in every nook and cranny, okay? As you said, it's no' like we're off to see royalty."

"Just calm down and turn back around here for a minute."

She did as he asked with a defiant lift of her chin, even knowing her face was likely still red. "By all means, Inspector. We wouldn't want you embarrassed to be seen with me." She was speaking nonsense and she knew it, but her pride was wounded—her own foolish doing, of course—and, at the moment, who better to take it out on than the subject of all her foolish fantasies? If he only knew what torture this was for her.

"Just calm down for a minute, okay? What is wrong with you, anyway? "

She huffed impatiently, more disgusted with herself than anything, but stood still. "What did you want me to see? With Papa gone, I shouldn't be gone long." Though there were clearly no other cars waiting to be serviced. She stood her ground nonetheless.

"I wondered where he was. I was going to ask after his injury." He winked. "Let me guess. He's over at Miss Eleanor's café having breakfast with a side of flirtation."

Despite herself, Kat snorted a little laugh. They'd talked about her father's recent fancy before, both of them enjoying the rather sweet, blossoming romance. "He turns six shades of red when I mention his attraction and wants nothing to do with anything I have to say about it, but he's the first one to jump in with his opinions on how I should handle my lo—"

She immediately stopped the instant she realized what she'd been about to say. And who she'd been about to say it to. That was the problem with lusting after your best friend. He was too damn easy to talk to and she was too damn used to telling him everything. Except, of course, that one thing. But he knew damn well she didn't have a love life at the moment, so that would have been a might awkward . . . "He's in Sudley, actually, picking up a shipment." Better to stick with safe topics.

Brodie's smile didn't shift so much as a millimeter, but it seemed, to her anyway, that his gaze lingered on hers a moment longer than absolutely necessary. But instead of quizzing her on the obvious, he just took her arm and said, "I want to show you something. It will only take a few minutes."

She closed the bay doors and followed him out of the shop, grateful he'd let the subject drop, determining then and there to keep her mouth shut and speak only in response to whatever it was he had to show her. It quickly became clear they were heading over to Hagg's. "What do you need to show me at the pub?"

"Shh. Just be patient. I wanted your opinion before I got it, but I was at auction with Dylan, picking out a few things for Glenshire, and he was being his usual impatient, pain in the arse self, so I had to make a split-second decision." He glanced at her and his eyes were all twinkly, like they got when he was really excited about something.

They entered the cooler, darker environs of the pub, which wouldn't open to the public for an hour or two, at lunchtime. He pulled her through the tables in the front of the pub, around to the back and the door leading to the stairs up to the rooms above. His rooms.

Kat swallowed a groan. Of all the days . . . She did not need to see that big, huge bed dominating the open loft bedroom that comprised the entire second floor of Hagg's. A conversion Brodie had made shortly after taking over the place. He'd torn out the walls separating the second floor into three smaller rooms and created one huge room for himself. One part was set off as a living room of sorts, with an ancient, overstuffed brocade couch and huge ottoman, around which were stacked piles of books and magazines on every subject imaginable. There was a small counter with a toaster oven, a coffeepot, and a sink, with a shelf nailed over it holding the few dishes and utensils he needed. He had a full kitchen right downstairs in the pub, so saw no need to recreate one upstairs.

The only private area upstairs was the loo, which she happened to know he'd converted into an almost sybaritic paradise, complete with a six-foot-long, deep-sided, claw foot tub that he'd found during a rummage sale of the contents of a manor house, put on by a remaining family member too deeply indebted to keep the place an ongoing concern. Something the Chisholms knew more than a little about, as they all struggled to keep Glenshire afloat, which had been in the family for more than four centuries.

"So, how is Dylan coming along with the conversion of Glenshire to a bed and breakfast? Do you think you'll be able to open for business soon?" she asked, trying desperately to look at anything other than the huge bed she'd so recently imagined him sprawled across. Naked, of course. The more she tried to block the image, the more detailed it perversely became.

"Slowly. He's still grappling with everything that happened, you know. But it's all coming around."

Dylan, the oldest of the four Chisholm brothers, was the only one who had left the clan and the village, building a life in the city, in Edinburgh with his city-bred wife. Her sudden death had deeply affected the whole family, but none so much as Dylan himself, who finally returned to Glenbuie a changed man. While one of those changes had been his recommitment to the family concerns, no one was really certain if it was such a positive change in the long run given the other, less favorable changes grief had wrought in him.

As much as she wanted to keep Brodie talking about anything that would keep her mind off throwing herself on that bed and just flat-out showing him what had "gotten into her," talking about Dylan was not the best way to go. He turned his back to her as he went to get a box off the small café table tucked alongside the wall next to the counter and sink.

With his gaze away from hers, she took full advantage of the opportunity to look at him with all the unabashed desire that had been building up for what felt like eons now. Maybe if she just mentally played the fantasy all the way through, she could get this constant ache for him to finally dissipate. At least a little. She'd just gotten done imagining pulling his t-shirt over his head and unbuttoning his jeans, backwalking him to his feather-down bed before bracing her palms on the broad expanse of his chest and pushing—hard—when he turned back to face her, a small, carved box in his hands.

"Come here," he said, eyes dancing with delight. "Look at this."

For a short second, she was still in the fantasy . . . and his eyes were dancing because of her. Of what he wanted to do with her, to her, in that soft, wonderfully decadent pile of featherdown and white linen. And, her body achy and tight, she moved across the room toward him, her gaze locked on his.

Wondering what he'd do if she told him exactly what she was thinking that very instant . . . Or better yet, what if she just showed him . . .

Chapter 6

"I had no business paying anything close to what I spent," Brodie told her, "but I couldn't help it. The provenance on them was fascinating . . . and I knew you'd be the one to understand why I had to have them. Actually, truth be told, you're the reason I had to have them."

Kat stopped right in front of him, but her attention wasn't on the carved box, it was on him. She was looking at him like . . . well, if he wasn't mistaken, and when it came to women and this particular thing, he rarely was . . . it looked like she wanted to eat him alive. In the way every man with a pulse wanted to be devoured.

Since the moment last night when Daisy had uttered her not-so-veiled hint about the reason behind Kat's unusual behavior of late, he'd thought of little else. She hadn't been all that subtle, but Daisy was new and didn't know anybody in town all that well. He had to believe she'd been seeing things that weren't really there. Except he wasn't entirely sure he wanted her to be wrong. And then his little voice had played devil's advocate, saying that maybe it took an outsider, with no preconceived ideas, to see so clearly what he'd missed all along.

That Kat Henderson wanted him. All of him.

Looking into her eyes now, he felt his body stir. Much as it had last night, lying right there in the bed behind her, as he'd thought back over everything that had happened yesterday, everything she'd said . . . and realized that when interpreted through Daisy's assumption, it all made far too much sense. In a Kat Henderson way, anyway. But because he did know Kat better than anyone, he realized exactly what she'd been getting at. She'd thought he wanted Daisy . . . and for whatever reason, that had sparked her to put her thoughts and feelings for him on the line.

His hands tightened on the carved box. He'd told himself he was up at dawn this morning for the first time in . . . well, ever, and off to see Kat because he was anxious to show her his new treasure, one he'd planned to show her last night before commencing to play their little challenge round. But he knew damn well he could have done that when she dropped by Hagg's later, after work.

No, he'd been up early and across the square because he'd wanted to see her—needed to see her—to figure out once and for all if Daisy's assumptions were merely those of a hopeful romantic . . . or if there might be some truth to her amazing claims. The fact that his heart had been pounding since he'd tapped on Kat's office door, his palms sweating like mad, and the fit of his jeans becoming a might bit uncomfortable behind his fly, were clear indications to the conclusions he'd drawn during the wee hours of the night.

Except seeing her had only seemed to complicate things further. She was irritable and jumpy around him now, and he honestly wasn't sure what that meant. Or what he wanted to do. Well, that last bit wasna entirely true. He had a quite detailed list of what he wanted to do, each of them more shocking than the next. His gaze strayed from her, to the bed behind her, back to her . . . and he cautioned himself to slow way the hell down, think with his head and not the part of him that was growing shockingly hard. Imagining Kat Henderson. Naked. In bed. His bed.

Was he crazy?

He jerked his gaze from hers, suddenly unsure about this

whole thing. But now that Daisy had planted the damn seed in his brain, he couldn't seem to shake it loose. Did Kat want him? Really want him? Because he'd come to the very real, stunning discovery that he wanted her, too.

She tapped insistently on the box, drawing him from his reverie. "So, are you going to show me or what?"

Irritable again. Now what had he done? And why the hell couldn't either one of them just come out and ask the other about this? After all, they'd known each other forever. Talked about everything under the sun. Worst case is, she'd just laugh it off. Right? Crazy Daisy and her barmy ideas. No harm done. They'd just go right on being friends.

So why wasn't he asking her?

Maybe for the same reason she hadn't come right out and asked him. Because friends didn't constantly picture their friends naked. Or because friends didn't want to do the things to each other that Brodie couldn't seem to stop thinking about doing to Kat. And her laughing off the suggestion wouldn't stop the images flooding his brain. Or the burgeoning need filling him to the point of bursting. So maybe the harm had already been done. Thanks, Daisy.

He flipped the box open, banishing the thoughts, images, all of it, from his brain. They both just needed to get a grip. Find some common ground where they both felt comfortable. And that wasn't going to be anywhere in the vicinity of his bed.

But he knew exactly where they could go. He lifted the box so she could examine its contents, never so thankful he'd had a weak moment and made this purchase.

Kat gasped. "Oh my God, they're lovely." She reached a tentative hand to very gently stroke the antique throwing darts. "How old are they? Hand-carved shafts, real feathers for flights. But the feathers look—"

"New. They are. I had them cleaned up and refitted with new points and feathers, but the shafts are the original carved wood. The points and feathers had probably been replaced numerous times over the years anyway, and both were half rotted away. It's amazing the wood hadn't suffered much, but it had been sealed with some kind of resin."

"You had them refitted?" Kat looked at him like he was daft. "But that lowers their value, doesn't it?"

Brodie just smiled. "I didn't get them to look at, I got them to use."

Kat's mouth dropped open. "You want to throw them? But they're at least—"

"Four and a half centuries old or thereabout. The shafts, anyway. They were reputedly made by a courtier to King Henry VIII. Anne Boleyn having given him a set, he supposedly had them commissioned for her." Brodie winked at her. "Unfortunately for Anne, she lost her head before the gift was finished, and they were passed down to the courtier's daughter instead." He shrugged. "It could all be rubbish, of course, but that's the story I was told. I did get documentation from the family dating them back to at least the late 1600s, but no actual proof of the royal connection. Still, they struck my fancy and I thought they would yours, too." He handed her the box. "They were carved for a woman's hand."

She gasped again. "Brodie! I couldn't."

He just laughed when she pulled her hands away and pushed the box forward. "Go on. You're the only one who appreciates the game more than I do. When I saw them, I thought immediately of you. Look at how slender the shaft was carved. I did pick them up, and despite the longer size, the balance is amazing for something made so long ago, without the technology we have today." He pushed the box toward her. "I thought we could keep them here, on display somehow. But I wanted you to be the one to throw them."

She took the box, her hands trembling a little. "I—I don't know what to say." She carefully eased one of the trio out of the velvet lining and balanced it in her hand. "Wow. You're right. Amazing." She slowly stroked her finger along one of the feathered shafts.

Brodie was shocked to feel his body harden further, as if she'd just slowly stroked him. Damn, but this was supposed to get his mind off of those kinds of thoughts where Kat was concerned. He glanced up at her face, but her attention was riveted on the dart.

"They are works of art, Brodie." She looked up, caught him looking at her. Her lips quirked, but her cheeks pinked a little. "What are you smiling at?"

"You," he said, thinking he'd always loved looking at her. Why hadn't he ever thought of her any other way before? "You're dying to give them a toss. Come on, admit it." He groaned inwardly, thinking if she only knew what he was dying to toss. Her. Right onto that bed. "Why don't we go downstairs right now and try them out?"

She looked at the darts, then back at him. "I still can't believe you did this."

He feigned a look of insult. "You implying I don't ever do anything for you?"

"No, it's just . . . you're careful with money. We both are. And this . . . this couldn't have come cheap. You said yourself you had no business buying them. I really shouldn't let you—"

"But you will let me." He took her arm and dragged her to the door, before he threw her on the bed and did things he could end up regretting the instant he was done. Though he was having an increasingly difficult time buying that particular argument. "And I'll have ye know, I can be as impulsive as the next bloke." If she only knew the impulses he was tamping down at that very moment.

They reached the first floor and Brodie flicked on the lights in the back of the pub where the billiard table and dartboards were. The rest of the pub was left in the early-morning dusk, the only light that which slid in through the cracks of the shutters on the windows.

She moved in front of him. "Okay, but it's not even a birthday or special occasion or—"

He tugged her back around, so she faced him, keeping his

hand on her arm. "Just seeing the look on your face when I opened that box made it all worthwhile. You're important to me, Kat. I like making you happy."

And as he said the words, he realized just how true they were. He did think about her all the time. She was a huge part of his day-to-day life. He talked to her about everything, looked forward to seeing her smiling face come in the door at the end of the day, got a major kick out of watching her banter with the locals and shark the occasional ballsy tourist out of his money. In fact, he couldn't imagine life, as he knew it, without her. His goals, what was important to him, were much the same as hers. They both valued family, heritage, the villagers, more than anything else.

He had no idea why he'd never thought of her as a partner in every way before. Now he couldn't seem to shake the idea that what he'd been looking for, waiting for, had been under his nose all along. And it had taken a blimey American lass to point it out to him.

The question now was what in the hell to do about it.

Just pull her close and kiss her? What?

Daisy swore that Kat felt the same way . . . but standing right here, right now, he felt he was suddenly standing right back at the edge of that very tall cliff . . . where one right step might send him soaring to the heavens . . . but one wrong one would send him plummeting to his doom.

Too much at stake.

Then he looked at the darts. And an idea formed in his mind.

"We haven't played for stakes in a long time," he said, oh-so-conversationally.

"What?" Kat had put the wooden box on the edge of the billiard table and was lifting out one of the darts. "I can't believe I'm handling such history," she breathed, then glanced at him, such excitement in her eyes. "Are you saying you want to play for money?"

Brodie grinned as he leaned against the table and folded his arms. "Something like that."

Kat arched a brow. "Something like what?"

"Go ahead and toss these a few times, get used to them, while I figure out what the stakes should be." He already knew exactly what the stakes would be. He was about to play the biggest game of his life.

Kat stared at him for another long moment, then gave a half-shrug and turned toward the dartboard. "Okay, suit yourself. But be prepared to lose whatever it is you're going to bet."

"Now who's sounding ungrateful?" he teased. "Buy a lass some antique darts and she gets all cocky on you."

She was lining up her shot, getting accustomed to the design and balance of the longer dart body, but paused long enough to toss him a look over her shoulder. "You should know by now that I can't intentionally lose at anything. So if you were trying to bribe me with these, just so you could say you finally beat me at darts—"

"Ho, now. I've beaten you at darts plenty of times."

She smiled sweetly. "Name the last time."

"Well, it was—" He had to pause and think about it. "You know, I honestly can't remember."

"Exactly. You got tired of losing to me, so you conveniently only join in when I'm shooting pool."

"You can't tell me I don't beat you at pool."

"Oh, you do, all the time. But at least I still give you the chance."

"Are ye sayin' I'm a poor sport about things?"

She let her shrug speak for her.

"Och. Bloody females."

"Quit yer bellyachin'. I'm here to give ye fair chance to win back yer manly pride."

Brodie motioned her to turn back to the board. "Go ahead, warm up. You'll need it." One thing they also had in common—they were both competitive. Neither liked to lose. Which, at the moment, he fervently prayed would work in both their favors.

"What are ye telling me, Brodie? Have you already practiced with these?"

"I can't say how many hands have held those darts, but other than to admire them, mine hasn't been one of them. I plan to throw my own."

"Ah, now I see your angle. Think to outplay me with me usin' unfamiliar weapons." She smiled and turned back to the board. "We'll see about that, we will."

It felt good, knowing they could ride each other, tease and even taunt each other, and that beneath all of it was a foundation of trust and certainty that was rock solid. As was his body at the moment.

How in sweet bloody hell had he come to this point so swiftly? Could it be only yesterday that he'd had no earthly idea that Kat might have feelings for him that were based on the desire for more than friendship, even one such as theirs? Even more shocking was the discovery that all he'd had to do was be made aware of the possibility and his body had taken off like a rocket on a mission to Mars. As had his head . . . and, it seemed, his heart.

He watched as Kat tossed the first one, then the second, then the third. "Not bad," he claimed, as two hit the inner ring and one pinned the outside of the bull's-eye.

She snorted. "Not bad, he says." She grinned at him, a taunting grin if ever there was one, before sauntering to the board to retrieve the darts. "In fact, I won't even take the rest of my warm-up shots."

Brodie felt his body twitch hard. She was a saucy one. He'd always liked that about her. Only now he couldn't help but wonder where else that would play to his advantage. Christ, but he'd be lucky to stand upright when the time came for him to throw.

"You want to practice?" she offered.

He shook his head. "Since you're using an unfamiliar set, it's only fair that I forgo mine to even the field a bit."

She just smirked at him, as if to say he was fooling himself if he thought that would save him. He found himself grinning.

As she took her place back on the *oche*, the toe line, he surreptitiously untucked his t-shirt and rearranged it to at least make a modest attempt at covering the effect she was having on him. He was still working out the particulars of how he was going to use their game to ease her into exploring this newfound attraction they apparently had for one another as she took her first real throw.

Fifteen seconds later, she was hooting and giving a little victory wiggle with her hips. One dart in the inner ring, two darts had landed on the outside edge of the bull's-eye. "Nice," she said. "They feel really nice."

"I should hope so, seeing as what they set me back," Brodie said, knowing it would distract her. And it did.

She frowned immediately. "I told you it was too much, but you insisted. So you can't very well make me a gift like that, then complain about the cost."

He just laughed and stepped over to the wall that separated the dart area from the drinking area. He reached up and grabbed down his own boxed set of darts from the heavy oak support beam that ran overhead. "I'm just saying it's good to see I'm getting my money's worth." He lined up at the mark, and with barely a moment of preparation, let his first dart fly. Inner ring, right next to hers.

"Show-off," she muttered.

He grinned at her; then, in quick succession, let his other two fly. One matched hers on the outer edge of the bull's-eye, but the other pegged the inner bull's-eye square in the middle.

She folded her arms. "Rusty luck, I say. You never hit the bull's-eye before your second round."

"Maybe I've been practicing."

She snorted another laugh. "You've been playing since you

began workin' for Hagg at the tender age of twelve, and probably threw a few before then as well. If that's no' enough practice for a body, I don't know what is."

Instead of walking to collect the darts, he stepped over to where she was leaning against the billiard table. "Maybe I was more motivated this time."

She shifted a little when he closed the space between them a bit more than was absolutely necessary. Her pupils expanded . . . and her throat worked a bit. But she didn't shift away. In fact, her gaze seemed locked on his. "Motivated," she managed, though the word sounded a bit hoarse. "You don't even know what you're playin' for."

He stepped closer still, his grin slowly spreading. "Aye, but I do."

Chapter 7

Kat swallowed hard, which was a rare feat considering how dry her throat had suddenly become. The way Brodie was looking at her was like ... well, to be honest, it was a lot like she'd fantasized having him look at her. Which meant either the dim lighting was playing tricks on her eyes, or she'd finally gone off the beam completely and lost all sense of reality. Because, other than that brief moment when he'd stared at her legs last night, he'd never once in all the years she'd known him looked at her like anything other than a bud—

The rest of that thought vanished as he slowly lifted his hands and toyed with the ends of her braids. Which just happened to be brushing below her collar bones ... and right above her breasts. Aching breasts now tipped by nipples that had contracted with such exquisite pleasure she'd choked on a gasp the instant the backs of his fingers had brushed along her coveralls.

Coveralls. Christ. She *was* hallucinating. Because no way was Brodie Chisholm fantasizing about anything sexual having to do with her. Stupid braids and baggy, grimy work clothes, and—

Then he shocked her mind blank all over again by tugging the braided elastic from the ends of her plaits ... and slowly unweaving her hair with his fingers.

"Wha—what are you doing?"

"I won the first round." His grin was lethal. "So I'm taking my spoils."

"Spoils?" she squeaked. She'd never been anybody's spoils before. The fact that she might be Brodie's stunned her beyond comprehension.

He merely nodded and bent his head back to the task, leaving her to wonder what in the world was the appropriate reaction to something like that. Of course, what felt appropriate at the moment was to grab his head in her hands and thrust his mouth over the burgeoning tips of her breasts. But surely that wouldn't be a good idea. No matter that the mere thought of it had her pushing a deep, very heartfelt groan to the back of her throat.

"What—" The single word came out like a croak, forcing her to stop and attempt to clear her throat. "Why?" she finally managed.

He glanced up, those green-brown eyes of his dancing through lashes that were far too sinfully thick to belong to a man already genetically blessed. All the Chisholm men were. How often had she teased him about being too pretty?

At the moment, she was too busy trembling as his fingers continually brushed the front of her heavy cotton jumpsuit. Surely he knew the havoc he was wreaking? He was a master at seduction, the tales in the village and surrounding hills having long since taken on legendary status. Which gave her momentary pause. If this was a seduction, then was she destined to merely be another notch on a thoroughly gouged bedpost?

At the moment, her nipples alone would have argued for the affirmative, and all her hopes and dreams be damned. Why hadn't she thought this through? Probably because she never thought it would really happen. She wasn't entirely certain it was happening now . . . but she was a damn sight closer to anything resembling it than ever before. She had to think, which was damn near impossible when he was standing so close, touching her. Why had he chosen now to do something like this? No way could he have known what she'd been thinking. The only other person who knew was her father, and though he loved to meddle in her business, he would never—oh, no. No. There was one other person.

"Brodie?" The single word came out like a croak.

He paused in his unwinding. His fingers brushed against the edge of her jaw and the side of her neck, making every inch of her sensitive skin there tingle with heightened awareness. He merely arched one brow in response, his hands still tangled in her partially unwoven hair.

"Why?" she asked again, though with different intent. If Daisy had told him, and she'd bet the family business she had, it still didn't answer why he'd decided on this course. Could he possibly feel the same? Or was he just having fun, giving ol' buddy Kat a thrill? No, he wouldn't do that, trivialize her feelings . . . would he? She knew damn well it wasn't to give himself a thrill. His exploits might be legendary, but her very lack of the same could have drawn an equal number of tales. Not that she'd never—she had—but an accomplished, confident lover she was not. Far from it, in fact.

He went back to unweaving her hair as he said, "Because you never wear it down. And last night I found myself thinking that was a bit of a crime." He smiled at her, eyes dancing with mischief . . . and more. "So my choice for a prize this round is the pleasure of watching you continue to play with your hair all loose and wavy around your shoulders." He lifted one of the long, shimmery blond strands and let his fingers rake through it. "You should think about wearing it down more often."

"You're just doing this to distract me from my game," she said warily, finding herself hoping beyond hope that wasn't the case. That he really was flirting with her. But experience forced her to maintain a worst-case scenario mindset. She reminded herself that nothing had to happen here. Legendary conquests notwithstanding, Brodie Chisholm was also a gentleman. He'd never force his attentions where they weren't wanted. Granted, he'd likely never encountered such a situation.

This morning appeared to be no different.

"Trust me," he said, "I'll be far more distracted than you."

Well, she thought, slightly stunned by his admission. Just . . . well.

Finally done with his task, he raked his fingertips along the back of her scalp as he sank his hands into the unwoven ropes of hair and raked them all loose. She shivered at his touch, and did nothing to help him. Nor did she make any move to stop him.

"There," he said, a very satisfied, very male smile on his face. "Your turn, I believe. Second round."

If she could have snorted in laughter, she would have. He'd just discombobulated her entire nervous system—and a few other systems as well—and he trusted her to throw sharp, pointy objects? She'd be lucky if she could take a single step without sinking to the floor. Her knees were about the substance of pudding at the moment.

As if reading her thoughts, he waggled his eyebrows and added, "You win and it's your turn to take the spoils."

The very idea that she could take something from Brodie, whatever she wanted, in fact, something that would give her pleasure, was more than a little overwhelming. And her senses were already reeling.

She still had no exact idea about what was really going on here, but she knew she wasn't going to quit now, before finding out. Her natural competitive nature pushed through the fog of lust and need currently clouding up her brain . . . and humidifying other parts of her body. "Right, then," she uttered. "Off I go." She stumbled only a little on her way to removing the darts from the board, but took the wobble in stride, knowing it could have been far worse. *Fire, Kat, that's what yer playin' with here.* In over her head, to be certain. But when had that ever stopped her?

She almost choked entirely when she felt Brodie move in

behind her. "I should get these out of your way." His chest brushed against her back as he reached past her to dislodge his own darts from the board.

Och, he was a smooth one, he was. But practiced or no', it didn't seem to matter to her. Her pulse was roaring along like a racing engine, and her skin felt like she'd taken a sudden fever.

With more care than he could possibly know, she plucked each dart from the board. When she got to the last of the three, he leaned his head down so his mouth was next to her ear. "Steady hands, now." He placed his own on her shoulders, then shifted and pressed his face lightly into her hair. After taking an audibly deep breath, he let his lips brush the rim of her ear. "Have I ever told you how much I like the scent of your shampoo?"

Okay, he was definitely pushing them beyond the boundaries of their friendship. He was surely flirting with her. Or perhaps it was more. Perhaps he was trying to seduce her fully. Rocked by the absolute reality of the situation she was in, it was all she could do to stand there, absorbing his touch, while the vibrations of his deep voice sent her nerve endings into their own little lust frenzy. Any actual response was beyond her at that moment. By the time she managed to say, "I don't—no, I don't think so," he'd dropped his hands and stepped back.

She resisted the urge to fan her face, and, instead, resolutely moved back to the toe line, careful not to look directly at him. She'd waited forever for this, it seemed, but now that it was actually happening, it was rather terrifying. What if she screwed this up somehow? Where would they go from here if it proved to be a disaster? And how did a dart game come into the middle of it all?

Well, the one thing she understood was competitive sports. So if Brodie had chosen this playing field as his scene of seduction, then perhaps she owed him a debt of thanks. *Just focus on the game. Let the victory . . . or defeat, unfold as it may.* It was a pep talk she'd given herself many times. Admittedly, the stakes had never been what they were today.

She looked at the board, and took aim, uncertain for the first time if winning was in her best interest. What the hell would she take as her "spoils?" Although perhaps that concern was somewhat premature. At the moment, given her trembling fingers, she'd consider it a victory to hit the target at all. She took her stance, twirled the shaft between her fingers. She really did like the slender design of the dart body, the feel of the smooth wood. She wondered at the hands that had held it before, their stories. It was the distraction she needed to get the fine tremors in her fingers to still. She raised her hand and took aim.

The first dart sank deeply into the target, but it was the outer ring once again. Her second toss gained the same reward. Dammit. Taking her time, she took a slow breath as she lifted her arm for the last toss. When she finally lofted the dart home, she knew she'd thrown a ringer. It plunged dead center into the bull's-eye.

She hooted and pumped her fist in automatic celebration, then turned to Brodie, only then remembering where she was . . . and what they were doing. Her first two throws weren't that great, and bull's-eye or no, he could still win this round, too. She shivered quite pleasurably at the thought, thinking it might have been worth it to simply tank that round straight off. But never one to show her soft underbelly, she gave him a cocky little curtsy, holding out the sides of her baggy jumpsuit, before stepping aside and leaning against the billiard table as he moved to the line.

Brodie's responding grin was quite confident. Mr. Cock o' the Walk himself, he was. She should know better than to try and out-peacock the peacock. He didn't even pause, or try to make it look like he was worried. In short succession, he sank all three of his darts. One inner ring, one outer bull's-eye . . . and, after a brief look at her, he buried the final one so close to hers it made the feathers quiver. She was beginning to know the feeling.

"I believe that puts me ahead," he stated unnecessarily.

"I—I believe it does." She found herself pressing her weight hard against the side of the pool table, as if it might steady her somehow, or even better, swallow her whole. She tried like mad to maintain a casual demeanor, but that was a daunting task. Because this time, when he turned and moved toward her, she knew what was coming. He was going to touch her again, somehow, some way. And, in that moment of brutal honesty, she acknowledged—fire, risk, and all—that she'd never wanted anything so badly in her entire life.

Her knees were already knocking, as was her heart. Her pulse rocketed even faster, and she had to work at finding even a trace of moisture in the sudden arid environs of her mouth and throat. She was having quite the opposite problem in other areas of her body. She pressed her thighs tightly together against the intense ache building there, her fingers digging at the mahogany billiard table behind her as he stopped directly in front of her.

She'd have given anything to be able to tilt her chin just then and give him some sort of cocky come-on. But that kind of bravado was well beyond her at the moment. Mostly because she wasn't in the habit of making empty boasts . . . and in this game, she had no idea if she could back her taunts up.

"I guess I get to take my prize. Again."

She said nothing. Her gaze was locked on his mouth as he spoke. Wondering what he would taste like. She was both terrified and thrilled at the very idea that she might get the chance to find out. *This is Brodie,* she reminded herself, scrabbling for an emotional foothold. *You've known him forever. You can trust him to make this okay.*

He held her gaze as he brushed her hair back over her shoulders, then toyed with the collar of her coveralls. For all her protestations, she found herself wishing fiercely that she was dressed in something more feminine. Or anything other than her grubby work clothes.

"You know," he said casually, "I've probably seen you in these things, what, about a million times?"

Her heart sank and she wanted nothing more than for the floor to open up and swallow her shapeless, baggy self whole. She didn't even bother to answer. As much as she wanted him to want her, she knew, deep down, that if she'd had to tart herself up as something she wasn't, it wouldn't be worth it. Although she admitted to a doubt or two as he tugged a little on the collar.

He let his hand drift to the first of a long row of buttons that fastened up the front, making her half wish she'd worn the zippered one.

"In all that time, I don't think I've ever once wondered what you were wearing underneath."

She gulped a little as her cheeks flamed. He'd never noticed her like she'd noticed him. He couldn't be making that more clear. "Brodie," she choked out, letting go of the table with one hand, intending to stop him.

Then he lifted his gaze to hers. And what she saw in his eyes wasn't disinterest. Or even mild curiosity. What she found there wasn't remotely casual. Anything but. She saw an intensity of want, and need. She saw desire. For her.

"Yet, right now," he went on, his voice a husky murmur, "I can't seem to think of anything else." He slid the top button free, then another, pushing the edges apart. Her nipples were twin points of fierce need, and the muscles between her thighs had clenched so tightly together now, she might never be able to relax. He slipped another button free . . . then another.

And suddenly this wasn't a game any longer.

"What changed your mind?" she blurted out. *Don't stop him now, you bloody loon!* But whatever sliver of sanity she had left told her she'd forever regret this if she didn't understand his reasons behind this sudden about-face.

"Does it matter?" He slipped another button free. "Do you want me to stop?"

She automatically shook her head. What? It was the truth. She didn't want him to stop. She just wanted to know why.

"Then let me get on with discoverin' what treasures ye've been hiding from me all these years."

Her hand came up of its own volition and covered his. "Brodie." She heard the urgency in her own voice, and she wondered what he saw when he looked into her eyes. "Why now?" she insisted. "I need to know."

He let his fingers play through hers. "A little bird came whispering by and mentioned that maybe what I've been looking for all along was right under my nose."

"A bird," she managed, her entire body tightening as he slid his hand free and toyed with the next button down, this one between her breasts. "Or, perhaps . . . a flower?"

He paused, glanced up through those lashes. "Does it matter?"

Her heart stuttered a little. *Why had she opened her big, curious mouth?* "Yes," she said quietly, knowing why. "It matters." She forced herself not to pull away from him. To stand there and listen, and not run from the room before he could say the words that would crush any hope she had of ever getting him to love her like she loved him. If this was all a lark . . .

"Kat." He snagged her hand and held it still against his chest. "I don't want Daisy, if that's what you're asking. Do ye think I'd be here with you now if that were the case?"

"But it *was* Daisy who—"

He nodded. "But it's me who is doing something about it. I was thinking ye might want to thank her." He smiled. "I know I do."

Inside she was a tumble of emotion and not a little confusion. "But all these years and you never once . . ." She let the sentence trail off, wishing she was as confident about this path they were embarking on. However playful, it was still going to change things. "And if we . . . and I'm not . . . things won't be the same."

He grinned then, surprising her with the force and surety of it. "I should bloody well hope things won't be the same."

She wished for a sliver of that confidence.

He feigned a wounded look and pressed her hand to his heart. "I'd rather ye'd keep me about, underfoot . . . and perhaps under other more interesting things as well. I'd hoped to be unforgettable."

She couldn't help it, she laughed. "Oh, aye, ye are that, Brodie Chisholm. Ye are that."

His lips curved and that mischievous twinkle returned to his eye. "Then perhaps ye'll let me get back to claiming me spoils, and stop interrupting."

She wanted nothing more in the whole world. "I want to. You have no idea. It's just—"

"Och, so much worryin'. Of all people, you should trust me, shouldn't you?" He stopped her from finishing with a finger pressed to her lips. "Let me ask you something, then."

She nodded, moaning just a bit when it caused the warm skin of his finger to brush over her bottom lip.

"Why haven't ye said anything to me, Kat? About what you were feeling? Why didn't you approach me yourself?"

She dipped her chin then, but he lifted it right back up.

"We've always been the best of friends to one another," he said. "You could have told me anything."

"Anything save that," she answered. "I couldn't . . . I didn't want to risk . . . because I do know you. I'm not your type. I know that. Hell," she said on a watery laugh, mortified at the tears that suddenly threatened. Could she be any more pathetic? "I'm not anybody's type."

"Enough of that kind of talk." He held her chin rather firmly when she tried to duck him again. "I'll not have that from you, Kat Henderson. You deserve better than that from yourself. And I deserve better than that from you."

Surprised by his outburst, she could only stare at him. She'd never thought of it like that.

"You've been closer to me than anyone and the fact that we've stayed close throughout should tell us both something. You were smart and recognized it for what it was before me." He loosened his hold, let his fingers stroke along her jaw. "And you're not the only one with insecurities, Kat-o-mine."

She couldn't recall the last time he'd used that nickname. It felt good to hear it from his lips again, better than ever before. In that moment, the way he was looking at her, touching her, saying her name like that, she felt more intensely female, and feminine, than she had in her whole entire life.

"What could you possibly be insecure about?" she asked him.

"Love."

The single word, so seriously spoken, surprised her. "Why on earth would you be worried about that? Everyone loves you and you've got the biggest heart of anyone I know."

"I don't doubt my capacity for love . . . I just—" He stopped, as if looking for the right words. He was really serious about this.

"Brodie—"

"I've dated my fair share. More than my fair share," he blurted.

Her lips curved in a small smile. "Aye. A legend ye are, Brodie Chisholm. Which is why I find it hard to believe you're looking at the likes of me." She gestured to her grimy coveralls. "You could do a damn sight better."

His gaze found hers and locked on. "That's just it. I've dated plenty. But I haven't given my heart, or didn't ye notice? I was beginning to think maybe I wasn't meant for the long term, and I've been finding myself thinking that it'll be a lonely life for me indeed if that's the case. In fact, I've been thinking about it a lot."

She didn't know what to say to that. He was a charming rogue, for certain, and every lass in a hundred kilometers likely knew his name. Or wanted to. She'd never once thought what he was thinking, how he felt, assuming he was happy, romping through the field of available women.

He toyed once again with the buttons, and as she watched the uncertainty fill his beautiful eyes, her heart melted further. Something she hadn't thought possible. "You're not destined to be alone, Brodie," she said softly. "I can't imagine such a fate for you. You're the heart of this village. You thrive on people, on being around those who mean so much to you. You'd shrivel up without the fervor and hubbub of life around you."

"And yet . . . Have you ever felt alone in a room full of people, Kat?"

The quietly asked question caught her off guard. "I—" She paused, thinking how often she'd felt that way when looking at other couples, wondering what it was that had given them the impetus to come together, and stay together. And why that magic forever seemed to elude her. "Aye," she said softly. "Indeed I have."

He tipped her chin up. "I don't feel like that when I'm with you."

Her heart skipped a full beat, then resumed beating in double time. "I—I . . . neither do I." It was the God's honest truth if ever there was one. But so was this. "Being friends, Brodie, isn't the same as being lovers. I couldn't bear it if—"

"That's just it, Kat. I think I kept you in this special place in my heart, separate from all the playing and fooling around, because, to my mind, you were above all of that. Better than all of that. And I think now it was because I knew that fun was fun, but I'd never managed to find a way to make it more than that. Every relationship I've had has been disposable. Except this one. So I couldn't see you like that. Do you understand? I didn't. But I do now. And I want more. I want it all. And if you don't think that terrifies me, too, then you're daft. But the thing is, I trust you. If I'm ever to make this work, I can't imagine it with anyone but you."

He was looking at her with such earnest sincerity . . . and an intense desire that couldn't be feigned. It was enough to shake her right down to her toes. She'd come into this wanting to get his attention. Well, she'd gotten it, all right. But she hadn't expected that he might actually fancy himself in love with her. In the way she knew she was with him.

"And ye see me that way now? Truly?" She kept pushing, needing to be absolutely certain before taking another single step. "Because of something Daisy said? Or because I wore a dress? Because that wasn't me, Brodie, that was me being stupid and insecure and thinking that I'd do almost anything to get your attention. And now you want my hair down and I'm thinking I'm no' the woman you—" She broke off when he burst out laughing.

"You keep talking about yourself as if you're not desirable. Don't you understand? It's no' just the hair, or the clothes, that make the woman. In fact, it's almost everything else that does."

"That's friendship, Brodie. I need to know that you—"

"Desire you?" He took the edges of her coveralls and yanked her to him. "Want you?" Pushing her back against the billiard table, he pressed the full length of his body against hers. "You mean like this?"

And, without wasting another breath, or even asking her if she was ready, he kissed her. Took her mouth, and claimed it, he did. There was no slow lowering of his mouth to hers. One instant she'd been standing there, clutching the pool table as if her life depended on it.

The next thing she knew, she was clutching him. Fists in his shirt and in his hair. Kissing him back as if her life depended on it.

And maybe it did.

Chapter 8

He was kissing Kat Henderson. Like there would be no tomorrow and this was his last chance at heaven. She tasted like heaven.

He groaned when she sank her fingers into his hair, then grabbed on and kissed him back with the same fervor. How in the hell had he missed out on this for so long? Their tongues dueled, both of them seeking to gain as much of each other as possible. It was insane, the need he had for her. It should rightly terrify him, and on many levels, it did. He knew her too damn well, knew everything there was to know about her . . . except this. Which served to make every touch, every taste, that much more intense, that much more primal.

Yet he knew immediately that this was what he'd been missing all along. A connection that went so deep it was like a joining of souls.

He heard what he thought was a whimpering moan coming from her, but when she pushed him back a little, she was smiling, her cheeks flushed as she shook her head in disbelief.

"What?" he said, struggling to pull back on the reins a little. It felt like he'd waited his whole life for this moment . . . and now that it was here, patience wasn't looking to be his strongest suit.

"Us," she said simply. "What the bloody hell are we doin' here, Brodie?"

He grinned at that, at the excitement he saw reflecting so purely in her eyes. "If I have to explain that to ye, lass, we're in a heap of trouble."

She swatted at his shoulder, then gasped when he caught her hand in his and slid two of her fingers into his mouth. Desire made her pupils punch wide. Her lower lip dropped further as he pulled her fingers deeper and began to suck. He wanted to suck that lower lip of hers. Badly.

He released her fingers, letting them slide slowly, wetly, from his mouth, nipping at the soft pads just before letting go completely. Her gaze was locked on his as he cupped her cheek and pulled her mouth back to his. He nibbled at her bottom lip, making her moan deep this time, and perhaps there was a little groan of his own as she sighed and sank into him. He took her mouth again, and again. Leisurely, thoroughly. Her bottom lip was an irresistible delight, one he treated himself to repeatedly and with great indulgence. If her little whimpers were anything to judge by, he wasn't alone in the pleasure it evoked.

Her fingers curled into the hair at the nape of his neck. There was no battle this time as he continued his exploration, but a slow capitulation as she let him have his way with her mouth. His entire body was rock-hard and screaming for release, but with a clarity of sanity he was surprised he still possessed, he knew that they would both be better served by scraping together whatever patience they could find.

And take this one exquisite step at a time.

He had many firsts in his life with Kat. First fish caught. First bike ridden. First ale consumed, followed by far too many more, leading to their first time drunk, as well.

But this would be by far the most important first. He'd never forgive himself if he did anything to screw it up.

"Ye make me ache, Kat-o-mine, that you do," he whispered against her jaw. She murmured something he couldn't make out, but let her head drop back, allowing him access to the soft skin of her neck. Of which he took full advantage.

She moved against him, her hips shifting in the tight space between the table . . . and him. Now he was growling, and it was all he could do to maintain concentration on the task at hand. He alternately kissed, licked, and nipped at that place just below her ear . . . while simultaneously slipping another button open on her coveralls, and another still, until he could push the garment off her shoulders and down her arms, so the top half hung around her waist.

He didn't want to risk making her feel self-conscious again, but he had to look at her. Had to see her with these new eyes of his. He lifted his head, holding her steady with his hands at her hips, gripping the bunched-up coveralls . . . and, more importantly, keeping part of her body in constant contact with a very needy part of his.

"Och, but what ye do for a man's white t-shirt should be declared illegal, Kat."

Under her coveralls she wore a tank-style, ribbed undershirt that was so thin he could see every detail of the bra she was barely wearing underneath. She was a tall woman, but small-chested, yet what she had was cupped sweetly inside lacy little cups of silk that plumped them up perfectly for the taking. And take them he would.

His throat went dry and his fingers dug into her hips as he struggled against the need to yank her tight to him and press his now-throbbing cock into that soft spot at the joining of her thighs. Where he knew she'd be wet for him, ready for him. It cost him. Dearly. But the reward was just as great. "Ye run about claiming you don't like the frippery and such of bein' a woman, so kindly explain to me where that wisp of nothing came from."

She was blushing furiously, clearly wanting to believe he was aroused by her, and just as clearly not. She gripped his wrists, but didn't try to wriggle free. "Please, don't make fun—"

"A man never teases about something that makes his body harder than the marble cutting board atop his own bar." He tugged her just a little closer, costing him another chunk of his restraint, but wanting her to know just how deeply she was affecting him. He pressed the bulge of his jeans hard between her thighs. "That's what you're doin' to me." He shifted his gaze to the perfectly budded peaks of her breasts, just begging to be suckled, then lifted his eyes back to hers. "And it's glad I am that you seem to enjoy it, too."

Her flush crept down her neck, but her lips twitched a little. And for the first time, he saw the other part of Kat, the part he knew as well as he knew himself. "I never said otherwise," she teased. "And why is it I'm half undressed and you're still—?"

"I believe I'm the one collecting my spoils here." He pressed even more deeply into her, making her gasp and dragging a long, guttural groan from him as well. "However, if it'll make you feel more comfortable, by all means, take a little for yourself as well." He gamely held his arms out to the side, still keeping her hips pinned to the table behind her with his. "Like as not you'll take the next round anyway, seeing as I'm a little distracted at the moment."

She surprised him by reaching immediately for his shirt and tugging it up over his head. Seeing his slightly stunned expression as she tossed it over her head onto the table behind her, she smiled smugly. "When have you ever known me to take a pass on gaining an edge in a competition?" She took her time getting her fill, looking him over.

He had no idea how he looked to her, wondering if he suddenly looked as different to her as she had to him.

"You have a fine chest, that ye do, Brodie Chisholm," she said on a sigh as her gaze all but gobbled him up, making him twitch even harder.

He grinned, liking that thread of need he heard in her voice. "Aye, something we both seem to be in agreement with about the other. Speaking of which, I believe I was in the midst of claimin' my prize." He reached around behind her. She stiffened slightly when he nimbly released the catch on her bra.

"What are you about now?"

He slipped his fingers inside the edges of her tank top and slid the straps down her arms, slowly dragging the lacy silk across those oh-so-perfect budded nipples of hers. She gasped first, then moaned, grabbing the edge of the table once again for support as her knees dipped a little.

Once he'd slid the garment free, it joined his shirt on the table.

"The only feminine bit I'm wearin', and you—"

"Think you're incredibly sexy standing there with your coveralls half hanging down from your hips, those perfect nipples of yours pushing through that t-shirt, begging for my hands to cup them." Which he did, making her knees buckle a little again as he softly let his palms rub over her nipples through the thin, ribbed cotton.

"Dear, sweet Christ," she murmured, her knuckles white as she gripped the table harder.

He lowered his head, unable to keep himself from her a moment longer. He captured one cotton-covered nub between his lips and pulled it slowly, softly into his mouth. Her groan was deep and satisfied, pleasing him in a way another woman's climax couldn't even compare with. She released her death grip on the table and clutched at his head, keeping him where he was, which was perfectly fine by him.

He slid his hand up and toyed with her other nipple, making her body twitch hard and her hips drive forward. So responsive, his Kat. Every inch of his body was rigid and aching hot. He pushed the t-shirt up, needing to taste her sweet flesh. Her nails raked his scalp as he finally circled her bare nipple with his tongue. Her hips were pumping now. He skated his palm across the nipple that was still damp from the t-shirt he'd suckled it through, then rolled it gently between his fingers as he continued to flicker his tongue over her.

She groaned again and again, holding him to her breast, her back arching now. It seemed the most natural thing in the world to slip his arm around that arched back and lift her up onto the pool table. He pushed her back and climbed right up on top of her.

"Brodie," she gasped. "What—" The word ended on another long groan as he pressed his hips to hers. When he'd dragged her onto the table, her coveralls had slipped down her hips, revealing a pair of soft rose-colored bikini panties that made the pale skin of her belly and thighs look luminous in comparison.

He slid to one side of her, needing to see all of her, touch all of her. With her blond hair all wild and spread out across the green felt, her skin so alabaster pure against the dark backing, all slender legs and slim torso, she looked like some sort of fairy sprite. Which, had he mentioned it out loud, would have surely brought a derisive snort from her.

The thought of it made him grin.

"That looks distinctly feral," she told him.

"Och, but I'm a harmless bloke, merely looking to pleasure his lady."

That earned him a short giggle, which somehow turned him on more than everything that had happened to this point.

"Yer doin' a fine job of it so far," she told him on a sigh.

For all that he had her sprawled across his billiard table, in complete dishabille, he'd have thought she'd have turned shy or self-conscious. Once again, the Kat he knew peeked through. There was almost a taunting thread to her tone now. "Of course," she said, "you have me wondering just how much 'spoils' one round of darts should earn ye. And don't think I'm no' payin' close attention, as I plan to best you for certain next round."

Brodie reached across her and plucked one of the handmade darts from the table, twirling it in his fingers. "Do ye, now."

Her eyes widened a little, but not in fear. He loved that about her most. She didn't shy away from him. Never would. Their bond went far too deep.

He shifted onto his side next to her, propping himself up on one elbow as he continued to toy with the dart. "Lovely piece of art, don't you think?" Then he looked at her and winked. "The dart is quite a piece of work, too." And he got the satisfaction of seeing the pink rise in her cheeks again, even as the curiosity regarding his intentions flared to life in her eyes. Och, but she was a complexity of needs, his Kat. He was going to quite enjoy unraveling them all.

Slowly, and with great deliberation, he turned the dart around, cupping the sharp end in his palm . . . then softly twirled the feathers across first one bare nipple then the other. Both were still budded and damp from his earlier ministrations, and slightly flushed in color. Her hips jerked as her back arched deep, her sudden intake of breath coming out on a long moan as he slowly trailed the soft feathers down the line of her torso, circling her navel.

He leaned down and continued his exploration with his tongue. "Och, but a man could feast here for days," he told her between suckling her nipples, the words never more heartfelt. "And yet . . . I am drawn to the rest of the feast."

Her breath was coming in short gasps as he drew his tongue down along the path the feathers had taken. Shifting his body down, he hooked one finger in the slender strap holding her panties around her hips, and tugged. She gasped, arched again, and he could smell the musk of her. Aroused she was, which was a good thing. His boxers clung to the tip of his cock, so wet and ready was he for her. Had he ever wanted a woman this badly?

With his body, aye, perhaps, he acknowledged. But when

the power of love was behind that need, it took him to a place he'd never dreamed of approaching. The need was deep, bordering on desperate, and came from places within him, deep-as-a-well places he hadn't thought he possessed.

Possess her, that's what he wanted. Nay, that's what he needed.

Patience, lad. Handle this right . . . and she'll be yours forever. The very idea almost made him come right there. And what a waste that would have been. The smile that brought to his lips also brought with it the much-needed edge he required to continue.

As he traced his tongue along the edge of elastic that ran between her jutting hip bones, she flung one hand over her head, clutching at the far edge of the table. Her other hand came down to grip his hair so hard he was certain he lost a few in the battle. The visceral nature of her need drove him even higher. But he also resisted her urging him to move his mouth to where she needed it most.

And smiled as he looped his finger under the other strap, and tugged, freeing her to him, but binding her thighs together at the same time. Tugging wasn't going to work, so he flipped the dart and grabbed one of the delicate straps, using the sharp point to create a small tear.

"What do ye think you're doing?" she gasped, as he ripped her panties free and tossed them aside.

"Shh," he told her, then flicked the feathers between her legs, eliciting a surprised growl from her. "Lay back, let me play." He glanced up at her. "We always did have the spirit of play between us, I dinnae see the need to stop it now. No' when it might be the most fun we've had yet."

She held his gaze and almost looked as if she wanted to argue the point. That was his Kat. But then he flicked the feathers again, making her body—and his—twitch hard. And she eventually let her head loll back once again on the green felt.

"I won't leave you wantin' for anything, Kat," he murmured, as he traced his tongue from her hipbone to the fringe of her pubic hair. "That I can promise ye."

Her nails raked his scalp again as her grip tightened once more in his hair. He teased her legs apart with the feathers. "Open for me. Let me have my way."

She shifted her thighs apart—a long, keening moan ripped from her as he replaced the feathers with the very tip of his tongue, and flicked it back and forth across that most highly sensitized of nubs. Something primal within him roared as she shifted again and allowed him even deeper access.

He rose up, scraping the darts to the floor as he dragged her around so she lay on the length of the table, pausing only to fully remove the rest of her clothes and boots, leaving only that white t-shirt, bunched up above her breasts. He crawled up between her thighs, his face inches away from where she wanted him most. "Beautiful," he whispered almost reverently. "Every part of you, Kat. Lovely. And all mine." And then he buried his tongue deeply inside of her.

The sound that ripped from her was more bark than growl, her hips pistoning up, driving his tongue even deeper. He kept the rhythm, felt her climb. He slipped several of his fingers in his mouth, then slid his hands up her body and took her nipples between his wet fingertips, softly tugging them, flicking the pads across her engorged tips.

She went wild beneath him, and it was all he could do not to climb up her body and drive deep. But he wanted to taste her as she peaked. And he knew he could take her there again. She was so damn responsive to him, it was driving him insane. He skated the palm of one hand down her torso, then slipped his fingers between her thighs. She was growling deep now, raw, guttural sounds that drove him wild, her hips pumping, pressing herself into his face. As he slid his tongue up and over her wet, pulsing clit, pulling it gently into his mouth, he pushed one finger deep inside of her. She was hot, tight, and so ready. One slow slide out, and when he pushed back in, she climaxed. Hard.

He swore she almost came off the table completely, her hips jerked so violently, her back arched so deeply. She held his head with her hands, and clutched at his fingers, still buried inside her, with her body. The hot, slick folds were so wet, she could barely find purchase.

Then she was pushing herself up, reaching for him, for any part of him she could sink her fingers into, and pulling. "Come here," she commanded. Not begged. Not his Kat. His needy, wanting, and oh-so-hot-and-wet Kat.

But Brodie had other ideas. He hadn't waited all these years to discover her, only to take her like a rutting beast on a rock-hard billiard table, for God's sake. Especially when he had a nice, soft, and very big feather bed waiting for them right up the stairs.

He slipped free from her, dropping a hot, wet kiss right between her thighs, making her arch again, moan again. Then he slid off the table and, gripping her thighs, pulled her to him. "Wrap your legs around me."

"What?" She was still trying to make sense of the sudden change. Her eyes were half closed, her lips soft and relaxed.

She looked sated and drowsy and happy . . . and it was because of him. He'd never wanted anyone so much in his life. "Hold on to me, Kat." *And don't ever let go*, he thought.

"I don't want to play darts anymore," she said, the words soft and growly.

He smiled as she locked her ankles around his waist and he pulled her up and looped her arms around his neck. "No more darts."

"Mmm," she managed, "that's good." Her smile was so soft and so damn sweet, he had to taste her.

He kissed her, gently this time, tenderly. Her arms tightened around his neck, her thighs did the same around his waist, and she sank into the slow, sweet kiss with a soft sigh of contentment. He decided he wanted to hear that exact purr in his ear all his remaining days.

But if he didn't get her off this table and up those stairs, those days would be cruelly brief as he was sure he would die a certain death if he didn't have her soon.

"Come on," he whispered against her lips.

"Where?" she managed, dropping kisses along his jaw, nipping at his chin.

He didn't think he could be any harder, want her any more thoroughly. "Do ye have any notion a'tall what ye do to me?"

She laughed a little and squirmed against him, hooking her heels in as he swung her off the table and walked to the stairs in the rear of the pub. "Perhaps. A wee bit."

"Wee?" he said, teasingly affronted as he wiggled his hips right back.

"Och," she declared, pulling his mouth back to hers. "Men. Take me upstairs and ravish me properly, Brodie Chisholm. Then we'll decide who won the bigger prize today."

He made her squeal when he tossed her over his shoulder. It was the only way he had a prayer of making it upstairs. "Bottoms up."

She reached down and smacked his as he climbed.

He was grinning like a mad fool as he kicked the door open to his upstairs loft. "That could likely be a topic for long and heated debate."

She smiled and hummed against his neck. "Lucky me, then."

No, he thought, his heart swelling as he put one knee on the bed and lowered her into the pile of linen and down. "Lucky us."

Chapter 9

Kat felt drunk with power. And yet, all she'd done thus far was let him have his way with her. Not that he hadn't seemed quite pleased with that particular setup, but she needed to know their partnership would be equal. Outside of bed, she knew they were well matched, well suited. In bed . . . well, she knew he was perfectly suited for her. A wicked smile of satisfaction curved her lips.

Now, however, it remained to be seen if she could be for him, what he'd so effortlessly become for her. A partner in full. She was particularly interested in that "in full" part . . . but first things first.

He was lowering himself down on top of her, and her resolve wavered for just a moment. She was so wanting to feel his full weight on her. *Patience, Kat, patience.*

At the last second, she caught him by surprise and hooked her leg around his, rolling him to his back and sliding on top of him in the process. Not that her slighter weight could pin him down by sheer force alone, but perhaps she could persuade him to see things her way. At least for a little while.

His momentary shock was quickly replaced by a devilish twinkle as she pinned his hands to the bed beside his head. "Claimin' spoils ye didn't earn, are ye?"

"Perhaps this is part of the game, no' the prize." She

grinned. "I'll let you decide who can claim the victory when we're through and done."

"I'm no' so certain I'll ever be through and done with you, Kat-o-mine."

She smiled at that, her heart swelling a bit, but locked her ankles on his when she felt him start to move. She tightened her grip on his wrists as well. "Now, now, play fair and let me have my turn. Else how will we decide the winner?"

Brodie took a moment to consider this, then lay back, completely relaxed. "Have your way, then." He closed his eyes. "Be gentle with me."

She laughed. "Now, why would I want to do that?" She took the opportunity to flip his jeans open and drag them down and off, along with his shoes and socks. She gave a brief thought to the clothing and torn panties scattered across the billiard table and pub floor below . . . but was quickly brought back to the present when she looked upon Brodie in nothing more than his boxer briefs. She'd seen him in little more over the years, every time they'd taken a dip in the hot springs nestled in the outcropping of rocks just beyond Mr. MacClellan's gooseberry patch.

But she'd never seen him quite like this.

"Do ye have any notion of how comely you look, wearin' nothing more than that t-shirt of yours?" Brodie grinned, keeping his hands resting quite naturally next to his head. "Still a wee bit damp there in the front."

Kat wasn't sure where the moxie came from. Had anyone told her she'd be so bold in this situation, she'd have laughed them down the lane. Perhaps it was because this was, after all, Brodie, her closest, most trusted friend and ally. She'd thought it would be difficult, complicated, if they took this step. And yet it had been anything but. Aye, it had been arousing, thrilling, and downright perfect. And despite the pitch of nerves currently fluttering in her belly, she seemed to have no problem answering him with a saucy retort of her own.

She yanked the shirt over her head and tossed it away, amazed at how free and relaxed she was in her own skin. "I'm more than a wee bit damp in front, as you say." She wriggled on him a little bit. "But you're likely to know that better than I."

It gave her quite a little thrill to see him momentarily without speech. She took full advantage, once again not willing to relinquish any edge ceded to her by the opposition. Though it was getting harder and harder to see him as the opposition. When she caught his naughty wink just before he wiggled his hips at her, she thought "partner in crime" might ring truer at the moment.

"Now you're just braggin' some," she said on a laugh, then did the boldest thing she'd done yet. She slipped her hand around his still-cotton-clad erection and stroked him from base to head. "Not that you dinnae have a point there," she added, somewhat shocked herself by her action. And yet, given the way his eyes immediately squeezed shut and his hips pumped forward as he let out a long, deep, growl . . . well, she might have to consider being bolder more often.

"You're killin' me, but I find I don't mind dyin' so much. As long as you don't stop what you're doing until I draw my last breath."

She was sliding her hand up, then pulling his briefs down along with her hand, when he opened one eye a tiny slit and peered down at her, a cocky grin ghosting the corners of his mouth. "Stop taunting me," she warned him, "or I'll—" She loosened her hold a wee bit.

He immediately closed his eye and let his head press back into the duvet. "Have your way with me, then."

With his boxers off, she took a moment to stare at the full glory that was Brodie Chisholm. Aye, to be certain she'd pictured him just like this, in this very place, many times over. But for all she had a quite vivid imagination, she hadn't begun to do him justice. His body was big and rugged, muscles here, sharp angles there. He had a pretty face, that he did, but his body was more rough-hewn, owing to a life of physical labor, hoisting kegs of ale, and unloading truckloads of spirits. And, at the very moment, it was all hers, to do with whatever she wanted.

It was hard to know where to begin. It wasn't every day a girl was granted her fondest wish. She didn't want to squander it, on the off chance she'd awake to find this was all but a dream, never to be dreamt of again.

With his eyes still closed, his body sprawled there beneath her, ready, willing, and apparently quite capable, he casually stated, "Are you aware of the continued distress yer causin' me by staring at me, all the while depriving me of your wonderful touch?"

"Maybe I don't want to touch, but just look," she teased.

Brodie was known for his continual good nature and charm, and no one would say he was afraid of a little hard work. But he did things at his own pace, in his own time, his own way. So Kat was once again caught quite off guard when he moved so swiftly, she was suddenly on her back, beneath him, with her own arms pinned above her head, all before she quite knew what had happened.

He was grinning down at her. "Ye know my ancestors were fond of raiding a castle or two in their time, perhaps ravishing a comely wench here and there."

Kat laughed. "I don't know about comely, but I certainly like the ravished part."

Brodie leaned in and gently bit her chin. "You don't know the half of it yet." He tugged at her earlobe with his teeth. "And I believe it was quite clear how comely I find you, so we'll have no more of that."

It was supposed to be harder than this, she thought. Tumultuous and angst-filled as she'd been, battling her insecurities and her fear that she wouldn't be enough for him, she should have known better than that. She should have trusted him, the man she'd have easily trusted with her life. She should have known she could trust him with her heart, that he'd never do anything but take the same care of it as he had the rest of her. She settled beneath him, on that big bed, in the very place she'd imagined herself for so long . . . and felt as if she'd finally come home.

Her own lips quirked in a playful smile, and she shifted her hips beneath his, intending to tease a little, only to be hoisted by her own petard. Or his, as the case more clearly was proven to be. She swallowed a soft groan as he pressed that oh-so-beautifully-rigid length between her thighs. "I thought I was supposed to be havin' a turn."

"Turn's over. You took too long."

Now the smile came in full. "I wasn't aware I was being timed."

"Victory never comes to those who wait."

"Sure it does," she protested. "All the time."

"Not today. Today, and from this day forward, you're all mine." He stared down at her, as if he couldn't believe his good fortune.

She wanted to believe that with all her heart.

Then he leaned in, and rather than ravish her, he kissed her with such tenderness her eyes abruptly welled with tears.

"What is this now," he murmured, kissing away the moisture gathering at the corners of her eyes. "We'll have no weeping here. A bloke could get a complex."

She snorted then, making them both laugh. "Right. You haven't had any insecurities about this particular endeavor since you lost your virginity to Jolie Griffin in MacClellan's gooseberry patch."

He sighed. "We were trying to make it to the springs. What can I say—I guess the Chisholm charm wore her down."

Kat rolled her eyes.

Then Brodie surprised her by turning serious. Bracing his weight on his elbows, he released her wrists and framed her face with his hands, weaving his fingers gently into her hair. "Dinnae have any fear with me, okay? This isn't like anything before, I need you to know—"

She silenced him with a kiss. "I know," she said. "That I know. I just . . . I want to be enough for you."

He made her start when he barked out a laugh. Then he rolled to his back, pulling her atop him. "Enough for me? Since when havena' you been?"

She straddled his hips. "Since about thirty minutes ago when we got naked and you made me see stars."

He grinned. "Really? Stars was it?"

She swatted at him, then laughed as she settled her body over his. "It's important to me," she said at length, loving the strength of the arms holding her so tightly. "I need to know."

Shifting his hands to her hips, he lifted her, then slowly pushed her down onto him. He entered her slowly, keeping his gaze locked on hers as each velvety-hard inch of him pushed inside of her. He held her there, tightly. "*I* know," he said. Then he began to move beneath her. And her hips immediately found his rhythm.

They moved together fluidly, Kat gasping and Brodie groaning deep inside his chest. As she felt him quicken, felt his muscles gather beneath her, she locked her legs against his and used the leverage to ride him, to dictate the rhythm. They moved harder, and faster still, his hips pistoning into hers so hard he came half off the bed with each thrust. She gave back to him as fully as she got, matching him stroke for stroke, loving how fully and completely he filled her . . . and how well and truly she held him. She kept on until she finally took him over the edge completely, bringing forth from him a guttural shout that shook the bed.

He'd barely finished pulsing inside of her when she once again found herself on her back. "Tha' never happens," he said, still breathing heavily, his skin damp against hers. "I never finish that way, I have to be on top. How did you—" He stopped, laughed shortly, then kissed her soundly on the lips. "I should ha'e known you'd be different. You'll take from me what ye will." His face split wide with the devil's own grin. "And I'll be happy to give it to you." He gathered her to him as he slid out of her and shifted them both to their sides. "So," he said at length, stroking her hair, keeping her cheek pressed to the crook of his shoulder, "I suppose round one goes to the fair maiden."

She lifted her head slightly. "Maiden?" she asked dryly.

He shot her a wicked smile. "Fair lady, then." He tucked her head back down. "Now take your victory and don't gloat on about it."

"Like you wouldn't have."

"Och, ye know me too well. I can see where this could present me with a problem or two. I'll no' be able to charm my way out of situations of my own making, will I?"

Kat wriggled closer to him, tangling her legs with his, tucking her ankles as she settled against his body like she'd been born to fit there. "Oh, I suspect ye might be able to con me into forgiving you now and again."

He stroked his hand down her back, then pinched her bum. "I'll keep that in mind."

She pinched his nipple, making him hoot, then propped her chin on his chest. "So," she said at length, "how do you propose we . . ." She drifted off, thinking perhaps now was not the time to question their future, but as it was going to be pretty immediate, she had to ask. "How did you want to . . . you know, tell everyone?" She paused for a second. "You do plan to—"

He rolled his eyes. "Of course I do. But I dinnae think 'twill be much of an issue for us."

"Why is that?"

He craned his neck and looked over at the clock on his nightstand. "Marta's likely to be in the kitchen shortly, if she's no' already. I imagine she's found enough evidence to put two and two together and—"

Kat sat straight up and went to scramble off the bed. Brodie pulled her right back down again.

"Do you have a problem with everyone knowing I wanted ye so badly I couldna wait to even get you up the stairs? A legend you'll be."

Kat paused, then laughed somewhat smugly as she snuggled back in his arms. "A legend, you say?" She wrapped her arm around him, tucked her legs back between his, and sighed as he tipped her chin up for a long, lingering kiss.

"Aye," she said drowsily some time later. "I can live with that."

ON TAP

Chapter 1

"I've no time to spare for her, Silas." Reese Chisholm strode down the row of white oak casks that housed his family distillery's aging single-malt whisky. There was a long list of things awaiting his personal attention, and he wasn't happy about adding yet another to the queue. "I've got calls coming in about the new mash tuns and I need to make yet another attempt to track down a new supplier for—"

Silas silenced him with a clearing of the throat.

He stopped short and turned to face his floor manager. Reese had taken over the running of the distillery seven years ago, when his grandfather, Finney, had passed. But Reese had worked at Finney's side since he was old enough to reach a tap. So when the time had come, no one had doubted Reese's ability to run the place. Despite the fact that Silas had several decades on Reese in both experience and age, the two had long since come to a mutual respect for one another. Which was why Reese took the older man's quiet rebuke in stride. "What have you done to me now, auld man? My schedule is already fashed and it's no' even noon. I've no time for chitchat about some mad business scheme with the newcomer in town." He folded his arms when Silas merely smiled at him. "No matter how comely a lass she might be."

Just because Reese, second of the four Chisholm brothers, was still single past the age of thirty—only by a year!—the local elders had taken it upon themselves to throw every available female within a fifty-kilometer radius in his path. And now that Brodie had managed to find love, they'd only redoubled their efforts. He reminded himself to soundly beat his younger brother at billiards the next time they played. Then ignored the niggling thought that it had been far too long since he'd made it down to Hagg's, the pub Brodie owned and ran, for something as simple as an evening off.

"Ye work too hard," Silas told him, as if reading his thoughts. And Reese wasn't so sure the auld Gael couldn't. "Ye need to think about more than aging whisky," he went on. "You're no' getting any younger yerself, you know." Silas's eyes crinkled at the corners, that wee twinkle of his appearing in their faded blue depths. "She's a fair sight, that she is. And, well, lad, she's here. Parked in your office, pretty and fresh as her namesake. Said she'd cleared it through Brodie," he added when Reese scowled.

He began to regret less his overlong work hours and neglect of his siblings. They were all doing as he was, trying to make a go of it at their own businesses, all for the sake of keeping the family holdings together. He could hardly be faulted for being a little overly involved in the distillery, seeing as it was the largest concern the family oversaw. At least, that's what he told himself, anyway.

But he also knew when he'd been beat. Better to deal with her now and get them all off his back for a bit. He did a quick mental scan of his schedule, rearranging what he could, knowing that no matter what he did, this was going to set him back further. He gave it one last shot. "Silas, can't you just get her card or something and tell her—"

"Don't punish the messenger," he said, lifting his hands, palms out. "Besides, I've already got three people waitin' for me in my office. It's only because I had to come find you to give you those estimates that I was elected to deliver the news in the first place." His smile returned. "What harm is there in giving a pretty lass a few minutes of your time? The rest of your day will sort itself out, and who knows, might put a bit of a spring in your step."

Reese just shook his head. "Springtime. I swear, it turns the lot of you into rutting beasts."

Silas laughed. "I dinnae think that's a seasonal condition, lad. But then, what would you know of it, anyway?" He continued to laugh as he moved on past Reese and hurried around the end of the cask row, off to attend his own business.

Reese was well aware he was the long-standing butt of many a joke, all centering around his workaholic ways keeping him from having any real social life. Not that the small highland village of Glenbuie afforded much of that. But, truth be told, even when he could make the time, he wasn't much of one to gather with the locals at Miss Eleanor's in the morning for breakfast, or at Brodie's pub in the evening. Was it such a bad thing that after dealing with the details of the day, which were always myriad and typically fraught with problems, he sought out his own company in the evenings, where it was peaceful and quiet?

Tristan certainly understood that for the luxury it was, although Reese couldn't cut himself off quite to the degree that his brother the sheepherder had. Of course, Tristan did a fat lot more than tend to the Chisholm flocks. He also tended to all their leased farm properties, the crofters, too. But, by and large, the youngest Chisholm was happiest when it was just him and his flock, away from the maddening world and the people who inhabited it.

As Reese approached his office door, he allowed himself the momentary daydream of joining his brother out on the moors and hillocks for a fortnight, driving the flock down to the valley, as they had in their youth. Of course, now that he thought of it, talk between them during those long hikes had often turned to the fair lassies of the valley . . . and how they could convince them to go wanderin' with them on their way back up into the hills. That fond reminiscence kindled a quick smile, because they'd been successful, often as not. Maybe he had left behind more than one of the better aspects of being a carefree youth.

The smile lingered as Reese entered his office.

"Hello!" The young woman, who had been seated in one of the two studded leather chairs arranged in front of his desk, shot to her feet. "I'm Daisy MacDonnell," she said, extending a slender hand.

Wow, was pretty much the whole of what went through Reese's mind at that moment, blanking out everything else. For a wee bit of a thing, she packed quite a wallop where first impressions were concerned. The top of her head barely crested his chest . . . but what a head it was. She sported a face as fresh as her name, with a sprinkle of freckles across her nose and cheeks that she did nothing to hide, which disarmed and charmed him all at the same time. Her blue eyes fair to twinkled at him, and her grin was downright infectious. All of that bright, energetic loveliness was topped off by a shoulder-length swing of deep auburn hair that she'd clearly come by naturally. And that he found himself quite uncharacteristically wanting to bury his nose in, wondering if she smelled as fresh as she looked.

Wow pretty much summed things up.

Coming to the realization that he was standing there, all but gaping, he cleared his throat—and his mind, while he was at it—and took her hand for a quick shake. Given the slimness of her lithe frame, he'd thought her touch would be cool, but instead her palm was warm when it pressed against his. Delivering another little jolt.

"A pleasure to finally meet you," she gushed. "I know what a busy man you are, so it means a great deal that you agreed to meet with me."

Disarming and charming, she was all that and more. He found himself reluctant to release her hand. "The pleasure is mine," he said, surprised at the depth of sincerity there was in that standard platitude. "I can see why the lads are all panting after you." He blanched. "Did I actually say that last bit out loud?"

Twin spots of pink bloomed in her cheeks, which only served to set off that scattering of freckles even more endearingly. She slipped her hand from his as she nodded in response, her smile one of amusement. Thank goodness.

"I'm terribly sorry," he said at once, completely at a loss. Which was so unlike him, it flummoxed him even further. "I can assure you I rarely use such poor judgment, especially with a prospective business acquaintance. Or . . . well, anyone, really. I'm not one of those boorish blokes who does the whole nudge, nudge, wink, wink, if you know what I mean." Dear Christ, now he couldn't shut himself up. What the hell was wrong with him? He sounded like a flaming loon.

Fortunately she reached for and found the aplomb that had so swiftly abandoned him. He couldn't remember a time— even as a callow youth—when he'd been so quickly out of step.

"Not to worry," she assured him in her crisp Yankee accent. "I appreciate that I'm . . . uh . . . appreciated." The bit of pink still coloring her cheeks was most becoming, even as she turned—all business now—and scooped up a trim leather briefcase. "To be perfectly honest, though, I'd rather be appreciated for my business acumen." She smiled and stepped back to her chair, silently encouraging him to take a seat. "If you have a few moments, I'd love to discuss several marketing ideas I have for both your whisky label and the distillery itself."

Reese simply stood there, like a blinking fool. The remaining sliver of his brain that was still functioning finally nudged him forward, simultaneously reminding him about his overwhelming schedule, and that his game plan had been to put Ms. MacDonnell off until a future time. A distant future time. So why he moved behind his desk and took a seat, all attentive, as if he had the entire afternoon at his disposal, he hadn't the faintest idea.

Okay, so he had a little idea. He was an admitted workaholic, but he was also still a man, with fully functioning hormones, among other things, if the sudden snug fit of his trousers were any indication. Ridiculous, really, to even consider pursuing this any further. He knew that—of course he did. He had no time for flirtatious banter and even less for starting up anything more involved.

Daisy was opening her briefcase and pulling out a sheaf of papers, which turned out to be several smaller proposals, each bound separately. Very professional, he noted. Of course, having Maude's print shop at her disposal certainly made creating business proposals a little easier, but he was impressed with her attention to detail nonetheless. All he'd heard from Brodie, or his own employees who'd gotten a gander at Glenbuie's newest resident, was how attractive she was, so bright and friendly and outgoing. She definitely lived up to the hype. Made him wonder if any of the lads had made any inroads on their plans to sweep the lass off her feet . . . and preferably right onto her back.

The thought made him frown a little, though he couldn't exactly say why. It wasn't jealousy, though perhaps envy might play a bit part. Aye, he could quite easily envision tumbling her back onto his bed, all that stunning red hair of hers splayed across his dove-gray sheets, her pale skin faintly luminous in the early morning light. He absently wondered where else she might have freckles . . . and how lovely it might be to while away the morning hours after dawn, tracing them . . . with his tongue.

"I don't know if Brodie mentioned to you what I'm hoping to do here in Glenbuie," she said, all brisk and businesslike as she organized her proposals.

He knew what he'd like her to do, was his immediate thought. But then he was having a devil of a time being brisk in thought or manner, much less thinking about anything having to do with business. "No, uh, I don't believe he did." *Scintillating stuff there, Chisholm. Deep, too.* He'd definitely been off the horse far too long.

She smiled at him, oblivious, he prayed, to the completely

inappropriate thoughts he was having about the nicely tai-
lored blouse she was wearing. The way pale yellow cotton
hugged her breasts—which were small, but every bit as perky
as the rest of her—just begged a man to reach out and—

"In conjunction with taking over my late great aunt's stationer's shop, I am also hoping to offer a variety of marketing
and publicity services to the various businesses in Glenbuie
and the surrounding area." She slid the top proposal across
the desk. "Before moving here, I headed up the marketing department for a well known, high-end catalogue company in
Washington, D.C. So I've had the opportunity to work with a
wide variety of products and clients. And though the com-
mercial focus is very different here in the U.K., I think I can
be of some service to you, and the other businesses in Glenbuie, if you'll give me a chance."

More to give himself a moment to collect his thoughts, and
get them on anything other than the image of what Daisy's
perky breasts looked like naked, than because he had any interest in what she was saying, Reese took the proposal and
flipped open the top page.

Daisy leaned forward slightly, enthusiasm and confidence
radiating from her every freckle. "First let me say how impressive it is that you've kept Glenbuie Distillery a family-
owned operation for over a hundred and fifty years. From
my preliminary research, you're one of very few to have had
that kind of continued success without selling out to a corporate entity. So don't think I'm trying to tell you how to run
what is obviously a very successful operation. I just think, if
you don't mind my saying, that your approach to marketing
and publicity is a bit . . . shall we say, outdated. Or perhaps
narrow in focus is a better description. If you'll look at my
proposals, I think you'll see that there are some simple, but
highly effective ideas that you could incorporate at very little
cost to you, while providing a potentially huge boost to both
your local and global presence. The world is a very small
place these days, Mr. Chisholm—"

"Reese, please," he said automatically, forcing his gaze back to the proposal. It was that or stare at her like some entranced fool. Not that anything on the page was registering in his rapidly disintegrating brain. What was it about her that had him so gobsmacked?

It wasn't like he didn't enjoy the attention of women on occasion. Every time he went to Hagg's, Brodie's pub, which he'd admitted was rare of late, but still, on those former occasions, he'd had no problem making small talk or sharing a tale over an ale or two. Of course, most often it was with someone he'd known his whole life, and most of them were spoken for. Friends rather than potential companionship, of whatever sort he might be interested in. But there was the occasional tourist, the occasional passer-through. Although, come to think of it, he couldn't quite remember the last time he'd done more than grab a casual snog or—

"Your office manager, Flora, was kind enough to give me your brochures, both from the industrial side of your company and the public aspect as well," she was saying. "And thanks to your quite charming brother, Brodie, I have your business card. So, after looking at those, you'll see where I've made some preliminary suggestions as to what you can do to emphasize your public persona, both in the business world and in the tourist industry. I've also—" She paused long enough to put another proposal on his desk. "I've also worked up a schematic for a proposed Web site. Glenbuie whisky has zero Internet presence, and I think you're missing out on a tremendous opportunity to boost your bottom line. The investment outlay to immediate revenue ratio is very attractive. If you'll turn to page three, there is a graph . . ."

Reese listened, or pretended to, as she continued on with her excited recitation of how she was going to single-handedly drag Glenbuie Distillery into the twenty-first century. However, the details were floating in one ear and out the other. She really had the most remarkable bow-shaped mouth. He'd read about them, in sonnets and the ancient fiction of the bards, but he'd never recalled actually seeing lips that pursed together like that. Bow-shaped indeed. Sweetly tilted at the corners, with that plump bottom lip and the delectably curved upper one, her mouth managed to evoke the innocent look of a cherub ... while at the same time conjuring up the most carnal, indecent images he'd ever had the pleasure of imagining.

The very idea of watching her wet those lips before sliding them over and down the rigid length of his—Christ. He rolled his chair slightly forward so he was farther beneath his desk before shifting slightly to ease the sudden pressure of his rapidly growing, rigid length.

"Mr. Chisholm? Reese?"

It took several very determined seconds before he could forcibly banish the remarkably inappropriate images of Daisy sliding those cherubic lips over the tip of his now-throbbing cock. It took more willpower than he'd been required to exert in some time. Dragging his gaze from that mouth, he pretended to pore over the proposal in front of him. He hadn't the faintest clue what she'd said to him. "You've put a great deal of effort into this," he said, struggling to find a foothold in this conversation. And harness his suddenly out-of-control libido.

"I know this company has a long history here and that it is the lifeblood of the village in many ways. I wanted to make sure you understood that I also take my job very seriously and that I wouldn't be here if I didn't think I could provide a valuable service to you."

Reese swallowed a groan. Oh, she could service him, all right. If she had any idea what he'd been thinking these past ten minutes . . . she'd either sue him or slap him, or both. Shoot him, even, if suitably armed. He'd have no defense for it, either. Guilty, guilty, guilty. And not particularly upset about it, either.

Mother Mary, but he needed to get his mind back on his work. Which meant getting her out of here, and blessedly out of his emerging fantasies as well. "I do appreciate all the effort you've put into this, and I have no doubt there will be other businesses that will want to take advantage of you—I mean, of what you have to offer." He knew nothing of the sort, actually, and, in fact, suspected that the village shop owners would respond much the way he had. Set in their ways, it would take a lot more than one intoxicatingly perky, albeit seemingly qualified, Yank to make them consider any real change in the way they conducted business. Many of them were third, fourth, or fifth generation shop owners, as was he. And stubborn when it came to doing anything different from the way it had always been done.

Sure, as technology had advanced, he'd updated the process by which they made their whisky, but remarkably, those changes had been very few, and made only after protracted deliberation on his part. For the most part, Glenbuie whisky was distilled much the way it had been back at the turn of the nineteenth century when his ancestor, Donnghail Chisholm, had finally gotten a permit from the crown to turn his illegal still operation into a law-abiding, and profit-earning, production.

"But I'm afraid, at this time," he went on, forcing an end to this otherwise delightful but untimely interlude, "I'm going to pass on your very kind offer."

To her credit, she didn't reflect even a moment's disappointment. In fact, she looked as if she'd been almost expecting this exact response. "Mr. Chis—Reese," she amended, when he lifted his hand, "I know looking at the way you've always done things with a new slant is asking a lot, especially from someone you don't know, who is new to the area. I'll admit there were selfish reasons for approaching you first—"

"I was under the impression that you approached my brother, Brodie, first."

"Not intentionally," she said, quite sincerely. "Hagg's is easily the centerpiece of the village, and so I've been spending time there in the evenings, meeting the locals, trying to get to know everyone and give them a chance to get to know me. We had a talk over an ale, and he was asking me about what

I did back in the States, why I'd decided to pack up and move my life over here, and one thing led to another and I told him I'd be happy to work up a plan." She smiled then, and those eyes of hers crinkled at the corners, so damn lovely when combined with that splash of freckles. "He shot me down, of course. Seems to run in the family. But I'd asked about the family distillery and he was kind enough to drop off your business card." With barely a breath taken, she pushed on before he could interrupt. "I won't lie to you. I targeted the distillery right off, because I knew that if I secured any business with you, that it would make the other townsfolk more agreeable to at least hearing what I had to say. So it was definitely a calculated move. But I spent time on the proposals up front, in hopes you'd clearly see I take this very seriously and that it could be a mutually beneficial partnership."

"And I appreciate the time you've taken. I do," he said. Why was he even encouraging conversation? He should be standing and ushering her out the door, even as she raced on with her pitch. It was something he had done a hundred times over with other pushy salespeople, without a twinge of conscience for cutting them off mid-spiel. Well, one of the reasons he hadn't was the very noticeable bulge in his pants, but that seemed to finally be under some semblance of control. He pushed his chair back. "But, Ms. MacDonnell—"

"Daisy, please." She stood, too, and moved to stand directly opposite from him, with only the desk between them.

She was so petite yet curvy in that neat little suit of hers, and then there was that russet waterfall of hair—Reese immediately looked down, scooped up the proposals, and stood, before he was trapped behind his desk forever with a permanent hard-on. "Daisy, then. I really must—"

She reached out and laid her hand on his arm. His body all but leapt to attention even as his throat closed over at the unexpected contact. He shuffled the papers in his hand so that her line of vision was obstructed, and prayed like mad his body would calm the bloody hell down before she noticed.

"Can I ask you one favor?"

He swallowed hard, and wondered what she'd think if he told her the kinds of favors he'd be more than happy to extend to her.

She slid one of the proposals from his hand and placed it on top of the pile, inadvertently pushing the whole stack so it brushed the front of his trousers, making things quite worse for him. Reese had to fight the urge to sit down—something, anything, to keep her from spying his very visceral reaction to her. It was one thing to be mortified by his own sudden inability to control himself. He didn't need to further complicate matters by drawing her attention to it. *Awkward* wouldn't begin to describe the situation then.

But she seemed exclusively focused on business. Thank God. "If you would just look at the Web site proposal. It's the one thing that would be completely separate from anything having to do with the way you otherwise promote or market your whisky. As it is something completely new for your company, it's really an adjunct, and wouldn't require you doing anything differently from the way you do now. I really think—"

"Fine," he said, rather more abruptly than he intended. But she was killing him here. She smelled good, too. Wasn't it enough that something about the—the energy she emitted just by being in the same room was enough to send his other senses reeling? She had to assault his olfactory senses, too? "I will be happy to look it over." Anything to get her out of here.

"Wonderful!" she said, her smile as bright as the sun itself. "Perhaps I can talk you into letting me buy you an ale at Hagg's or something—when you have the time, of course— and we can discuss it again when you've had time to really look it over."

"Brilliant," he said absently, more concerned with keeping the stack of papers in his hand angled over his fly as he skirted out from behind the desk. "As I said, I appreciate the time you invested in this. I really must get back to work, however—"

"Oh, certainly." She quickly closed up her briefcase and followed him to the door. "I appreciate you taking time from your schedule to see me." She paused in the open doorway and touched his arm again.

Reese fought not to groan. Or, worse yet, toss the papers to the floor and push her up against the doorframe and find out just how that delectably carnal mouth of hers would taste.

"You know, Brodie says you work too hard and don't play enough."

If he could, he'd have laughed out loud at that. He wanted to play, all right. "He works as hard as any of us," he managed. "He just makes it look like more fun than I do."

Her smile widened, stretching that bowed bottom lip, making him want to sink his teeth into it in the worst way possible. He shifted slightly, pleading with his body to cooperate, and praying she didn't glance downward. "Well, I've been accused of working too hard myself." She lifted her hand. "Guilty as charged. In fact, I moved across an ocean trying to find a little balance between work and play. I'm still trying to get the hang of it. So . . . maybe we could do some business together over an ale and just make it look like play. It would be a start, anyway." She smiled again, perfect rows of white teeth emerging between lips created to drive men to their knees. "If you change your mind, you know where to find me." Then, finally, mercifully, she left.

He watched her walk all the way to the end of the hallway, and was still standing in his doorway a full minute later, his body every bit as much at attention as it had been the entire time she'd been there. "Right," he finally muttered, stepping into his office and closing the door before slumping back against it. "Of course I do." That was what he was most afraid of.

Chapter 2

Daisy paused before entering Hagg's and gave herself a last-second hair, face, and clothes check. The leaded glass windowpanes on either side of the pub doors were thick and uneven, making her reflection waver. "Which is exactly how the rest of me is feeling right about now. Wavery."

She'd debated with herself often over the past fortnight on whether or not to push Reese Chisholm into another meeting. She hadn't heard a single peep from him. Though, to be honest, she wasn't entirely surprised. He'd been less than enthusiastic about meeting with her, despite his outwardly professional demeanor. She'd had to basically shove the Web site proposal down his throat there at the end to get him to even look at it.

Getting him to look at her, however, had been a completely different matter. She shivered a little, despite the warm spring air. Even now, just thinking about the way those gray-green eyes had drilled into her, as if he was seeing right through her, made her skin tingle in awareness. Reese Chisholm gave a whole new meaning to the term *intensity*. He'd been smiling when he'd initially walked in, but from the moment he'd closed the office door, he'd been so intently focused on her, it had been all she could do to stay on point during her presentation. After meeting Brodie, who was the definition of "charming rake," she hadn't been prepared for such a deliberate sort.

Where Brodie was more the rugged hunk type, Reese was tall and lean, and even though his business wear had been a rather casual khaki trousers and polo shirt combination, he'd still come off somewhat refined in manner, almost to the point of seeming a bit stuffy. Brodie had an outgoing, engaging manner, with a brogue that thickened the more animated he got. Reese's voice was deep, smooth, almost calming in the way he spoke—purposeful, with such measured precision. His brogue was there, but it was crisp, clean . . . as refined as its owner.

And yet, she found herself shivering a bit again, thinking about it. There was definitely an air of power and raw masculinity about him that had unnerved her, and later, when she'd calmed down enough to admit it, aroused her a little, too. When she was nervous, she talked faster, became more animated, and she'd known she was doing exactly that the entire time in his office. And yet every time she made an attempt to get a harness on her nerves, his gaze would connect with hers. It had been like wrapping her senses around a live wire. Her pulse had knocked up a few beats, her cheeks warmed, something would go a bit wonky in her knees . . . and she was off to the races.

And a man like Reese was the very last sort she had any business getting involved with. Mainly because he was business. Hadn't she specifically said she was going to firmly separate church and state once she'd started over? For her that meant no fishing in the company pond. Or in the client pool, either. In her old life, she hadn't had much choice. It was like actors dating actors. Who else understood the life better than someone who lived it? She'd only dated men who were as dedicated to their careers and their overextended daily schedules as she'd been to hers. BlackBerry Socials, she'd called them, as she'd scheduled them in as neatly as she did her next power presentation. After all, it was sort of the same thing, when you thought about it.

She had always thought sex was a lot of fun and had approached the event much as she did any other project, with gusto, good preparation, and perfect timing. Her partners had found her sex-tech terminology amusing rather than insulting . . . and invariably adopted it when they'd moved on to their next BlackBerry rendezvous.

But eventually that life began to catch up with her. Antacids were a staple in her diet, her skin was perpetually sallow, her hair limp, her nails split. Insomnia was her most frequent bed partner, and suddenly life wasn't so much fun anymore. She was burning out, rapidly, and she knew it. Then the telegram had arrived from Scotland . . . and she'd taken it for the celestial sign it had to be.

Six months later, she was now a resident of Scotland. Her whole purpose in coming here was to slow down and get a life, rediscover the joy in living. It seemed she had this teeny problem with relaxing. Okay, maybe it wasn't so teeny. But relaxed and laid back simply wasn't how she approached life. How did anyone get anything done that way? Maybe it made a bit more sense in bed, but she'd never seemed to master that particular skill, either. There had never been enough time!

But that was all different now.

Which was why, though part of her new life plan was to operate a successful business—she still had to earn a living— the rest of it centered on eventually finding an easygoing, gentle, down to earth, earnest type who could teach her to slow down and enjoy the ride. Literally, if she was really lucky.

Her thoughts shifted back to Reese and she imagined what he must be like in bed. All sleek and sinewy and powerful, taking control and—she quickly shut down that train of thought. She was going to be sitting across a small pub table from him momentarily, and that was the last image she needed in her already fevered brain.

She'd tried to chalk her reaction to him up to nerves. He was out of bounds, anyway. After all, she had been quite honest with him about what taking him on as a client would do for her fledgling business idea. She was serious about making a success of herself here, and though she knew it might be difficult to convert the staid thinking of some of the longtime shopkeepers in the village, she very definitely wanted to contain her business to Glenbuie if possible. If she'd wanted her old life, complete with the frenetic pace, traffic jams, and endless work hours, she'd have sold her inheritance here and opened up shop in Edinburgh or Glasgow. But she hadn't left her stressed-out city life just to trade it for another.

"Going in or just considerin' it?"

Daisy jumped, belatedly realizing she must look like an idiot, standing there staring vaguely into the pub window. She turned to find Alastair Henderson standing behind her. "Working up my courage," she said with a rueful smile. "How's the hand?"

The old Scot ran the auto-repair shop on the opposite corner of the village square. He'd cut his hand a few weeks earlier while working on a car, and Daisy had happened to be nearby at the time and had offered assistance.

"Och, good as new it is." He flashed his palm at her, showing her the healing wound. "Tried to tell you all it was hardly more than a scratch."

Daisy happened to know it had taken seven stitches to heal the gash, but she nodded politely.

"So, I understand I have you to thank for the lovely smile my only daughter is sportin' of late." His tone was a teasing one. "Tried to tell her myself she should have made a play for that lad long ago, but oh no, she doesna listen to me, her dear father."

Daisy flushed. "Kat would have managed fine on her own without my nudge." In Daisy's efforts to make new friends, she'd sort of helped encourage his daughter into doing something about her more-than-best-friends feelings for Brodie Chisholm. "I'm just glad to see the two of them figured things out."

Alastair reached past her to open the pub door. "I'll spot you an ale just the same." His eyes crinkled at the corners as his smile grew wider. "Kat mentioned you've quite a knack for matching up folks back in the States." He opened the door and gestured for her to go in before him. "Makes a bloke wonder why a pretty young thing such as yourself isn't likewise attached."

Daisy laughed, even as her flush deepened. Where she had scheduled similarly minded, commitment-free men into her life with unerring precision, she'd also occasionally matched up coworkers. She had an eye for what worked . . . and what didn't. Marketing, after all, wasn't confined to mere products. Now if she could just figure out how to reach her new target audience . . . "You're very kind. Let's just say I tended to have a better eye for matching other people than myself."

"I see," he said, as he ushered her into the dimly lit interior. "Well, perhaps the lads on this side of the pond will treat your puir heart more gently."

His kindly spoken words took her by surprise. "I, uh— thank you." She smiled. "And . . . I hope so, too. But for now, I'm just focusing on getting my business off the ground and settling in here."

"A thrivin' business is all well and good, lass," he said close to her ear. "But it willnae keep you warm at night. This I know, all too well."

As did she, she thought ruefully, as did she. Daisy knew that Alastair had been a widower for the past ten years. The door shut behind them and she had to blink her eyes to adjust to the suddenly dimmer light. As he steered her through a small cluster of tables, a small, somewhat plump, older woman began waving at him. Miss Eleanor ran the small café off the square, and it was the worst kept secret in Glenbuie that she and Alastair had eyes for one another. Her salt-and-pepper hair was pulled up in her usual soft bun, her skin was smoother than that of most women half her age, but what drew the eye was the way her own sparkled at the sight of Alastair.

Daisy smiled at him and nudged his arm. "Maybe you should be taking your own advice."

He surprised her by winking back. "I plan on doing just that. Seeing my own daughter's happiness has spurred an auld man on to new and better things. Perhaps I owe ye an ale for that, too."

Happily surprised by the news that he was finally going to bring their budding romance into the light of day . . . or the dim of the pub, as it were, Daisy patted his arm. "Well, I don't want to interrupt your date. Besides, I'm meeting someone myself. Just business."

"Of course," Alastair added drolly, then leaned in close again so she could hear him over the din of clacking pool balls and shouts of encouragement coming from the dartboard area. "Dinnae make the mistake of believin' that old myth about mixing business with pleasure. I met Kat's mum when she came into the motor-repair shop as a young lass, looking to be hired on by my father." He sighed in remembered pride. "Woman could rebuild a transmission like nobody's business."

Daisy laughed. Alastair was quite the character. And in a village filled with them, that said something. But she had a soft spot for both Kat and her father. Gauging from the look on Miss Eleanor's face, she wasn't the only one. "I'll keep that in mind. Better not keep your date waiting."

She scanned the interior of the pub now that her eyes had adjusted. No sign of Reese. He'd better not be standing her up. She made a mental note to choose a table out of the direct line of Alastair and Eleanor's vision. She was nervous enough as it was, without their well-meaning glances. "Enjoy your evening," she told him.

"I havena forgotten the ale. We'll share one soon enough, aye?"

"Absolutely."

"Well, well. There's your date now." Alastair nodded toward the stool at the end of the bar. There sat Reese, listening to Brodie as he went on about something in his typically animated way.

"How did you know I was meeting—?"

He winked. "Small village. Big ears."

"And it's not a date," she reiterated, but Alastair was already heading over toward Eleanor. Huffing out a small sigh, she resisted the urge to smooth her dress. When she'd been standing in front of her armoire earlier, agonizing over what to wear, the light summer-print sundress had seemed to strike the right balance between professional and casual. After all, they were meeting in a pub, not a four-star power restaurant. Now, however, it felt cute and flirty and that was absolutely the very last image she wanted to project. Wasn't it?

She found herself watching Reese's every move as she wound her way through the cluster of small pub tables. His belted khakis showed off his lean hips. But today he was wearing a pale blue cotton shirt with a button-down collar, still crisp even after a long day at work. The cut showed off the breadth of his shoulders. Had she noticed them before? And the way he'd rolled up the cuffs served to draw her attention to his forearms and hands. Big hands, she noted, as he downed a sip of ale.

Thanks, Alastair. The last thing she needed was to be thinking of Reese Chisholm as anything but a business prospect. Granted, he wasn't quite the aggressive corporate shark she'd found herself drawn to back in the States, but he was certainly Glenbuie's version of the same. She hadn't crossed an ocean to get tangled up with that sort again, no matter the variation. From now on, business was business. And only business.

"Well, there's the lovely lass now." Brodie lifted a hand and beckoned her to the bar.

Now that was the kind of man she should go for. He was a big, lovable hunk of a guy, fun and playful, easygoing and relaxed, everything she was supposed to be looking for. Of course, he was Kat's man now, and they were well suited. But surely there had to be more like him about. She'd heard about the youngest Chisholm brother, Tristan, sheep farmer and land manager. Low key to the point of being completely off the radar. Maybe she should wangle an introduction there. Talk about slowing down the pace. Just not Reese. The only corporate man within a hundred kilometers. And a prospective client, to boot.

Brodie pulled an ale for her and topped off Reese's before lifting them both in his wide hands. "Why don't you two take a table there around back and I'll have Marta bring you out some of her stew. She's made a buttermilk loaf to go with it that will suit you just right."

Reese finally turned as Daisy stepped up to the stool next to him. He didn't say anything, allowing her to decide. His steady gaze did that wobbly-knee thing to her. So she purposely glanced over to where Brodie had pointed.

"It would probably be easier to discuss this at a table," she said, "if you don't mind."

Since Brodie was already carrying their glasses of ale out from behind the bar, Reese merely nodded and gestured for her to lead the way.

Don't be nervous, she schooled herself. But she could feel him right behind her, like some sort of heat-seeking missile or something. *It's a business meeting. Focus on the bottom line.*

And not his bottom line, either, she thought, fighting a sudden urge to snicker. It was nerves, that was all. She always got fidgety, talked faster, laughed too much, when she was nervous. This meeting was important and she couldn't afford to get distracted like this.

"Here you go," Brodie said, arranging their glasses on the small, round table. "Stew will be out shortly. Make yourselves comfortable." Brodie winked at her, then cast a quick look at his brother. "You're having a drink and a bite with one of the prettiest lasses in town, the envy of all around you. Least you can do is smile."

Daisy flushed a little, wishing now that Brodie would go back to the bar. When Reese only managed a tight smile in response to his brother's teasing, she worried that he might just get up and leave before she'd even had the chance to discuss the Web site proposal with him. She quickly pulled out her chair before either Chisholm brother could reach for it, sitting down right away to encourage Reese to do the same.

"Loosen him up a little, Daisy, okay? The man doesn't understand the meaning of the word *relax*."

"I'm not sure you're talking to the right person," she said, with a quick laugh. She fussed with the zipper on the leather binder she'd brought with her, then, feeling Reese's attention shift to her, she tapped her palm on the cover. "Shall we get down to business?" she asked brightly.

"Would you like me to wait on the stew until you've had a chance to talk shop?" Brodie was still hovering.

"That sounds good," she said, then hazarded a glance at Reese. He was sitting casually enough, but there was something about his gaze that made her feel pinned. Her knees knocked together under the table, and she pressed her thighs together for good measure. Damn, but the man had presence in spades, and he wasn't even doing anything. Hadn't said a word yet, in fact. "Is that okay with you? Or would you rather eat first?"

His gaze narrowed there a bit, or maybe she'd just imagined it. Either way, she'd gone from feeling pinned, to feeling a little like . . . prey. Dear Lord, this was going to be a long meeting. Because it *was* a meeting. Not a date. Something she'd do really well to remember. To cover her reaction to him, and because she needed the fortitude, she picked up her ale and took a sip.

Reese finally shifted his gaze back to his brother. "Give us a few minutes, will you?"

Brodie grinned. "I'll give ye all the time you need." There was a definite undercurrent going on between the two, making Daisy wonder what they'd been discussing before she came in. "Just give me a signal when you're ready," Brodie added, then finally, mercifully, went back to tend the bar.

Which left her completely alone with his reserved, enigmatic older brother. Maybe she'd been too hasty in wishing Brodie gone. A buffer, even one as intrusive as Brodie, suddenly didn't seem like such a bad idea. She took another quick sip of ale, then put the glass back down and nudged it to the center of the table. After all but badgering his secretary to get him to agree to this, she'd been too nervous about meeting him to eat much today. She propped her binder in front of her instead. The last thing she needed was fuzzy thinking.

Pulling the zipper open, she resisted the urge to fidget in her seat. But she could feel Reese's stare drilling right into her, and it was disconcerting to say the least. He wasn't sipping his drink or looking around the pub. No, his attention was completely on her.

Sure, nothing to be nervous about.

It wasn't unusual in her former line of work for her to stand in front of a conference table filled with corporate bigwigs, all eyes on her, and give a solo presentation as smoothly and comfortably as if she was standing in her own living room, surrounded by friends. So why was she hyper-aware of being the focal point of his attention? He was just another prospective client. Yes, her first and hopefully biggest client, but the nervousness didn't feel all that business-related. Or she wouldn't have to keep pressing her thighs together, would she? Or worry that he was going to notice the fact that her nipples were standing at attention.

"I've given your proposal some thought," he said, rather abruptly.

His sudden comment after such complete silence startled her, and her half-open binder slid off the table into her lap. The contents came cascading out and slid across the polished hardwood floor. Both she and Reese moved to get them at the same time. For a tall man with such long legs, he moved quickly, crouching down beside the table as he reached for the scattered pages. Daisy had leaned down from her seat to reach what she could, then lost her balance a little. She over-corrected, grabbing for the table when her chair wobbled, and managed to pull the whole thing over with her as she slid from her seat . . . and landed right on top of Reese. Followed by the contents of both of their glasses of ale.

Other than the television over the bar, loudly broadcasting a soccer match, and the random clacking of a few pool balls, the rest of the noise in the pub came to an instant halt. Daisy could feel all eyes on them as she tried to scramble off of Reese. Her back was completely soaked, but at least she'd borne the brunt of the ale. Other than being knocked on his ass and having her sprawled all over him, Reese had come through it all relatively unscathed.

He grabbed at her arms, stilling her movements when her knee came dangerously close to changing that fact. "Hold on," he instructed her, then carefully shifted both of them so she could get her feet under her. "There you go."

Several other patrons had jumped up to help, one righting the table, another picking up their glasses where they'd rolled across the floor, and yet another helping Daisy to her feet.

She immediately reached a hand to Reese. "I'm so sorry. I—"

"Now, now, what is all this? I let ye come into my place of business to do a little courtin' and the next thing I know, you're tossing her to the floor." Brodie tugged his brother easily to a stand, then watched him with a broad grin as he brushed off his trousers. "Come now, Reese, I thought you had more polish than that. I know it's been a while—"

Reese's glare cut him right off, but not before laughter skittered through the avidly watching crowd.

Brodie turned to Daisy. "Can't take a joke, never could." He ran his gaze over her. "Och, look at you. A bit of a mess there. You want to go upstairs and—"

"I'll take care of her," Reese said, startling both of them, and a goodly number of the other customers as well if the looks on their faces were anything to judge by.

"I can take care of myself, thanks," Daisy said, clearly hearing the undercurrent suddenly flowing between the brothers and figuring it best to put a swift end to it. "I just need to—" she broke off when she looked down to find her notes and presentation information all stuck to the hardwood floor, sodden through with ale "—gather my notes," she finished lamely. "Bollocks."

Her very Scottish swearing in her very American accent made those around her laugh good-naturedly. And, most surprisingly, got a tiny crook of the mouth from Reese as well.

"I'll take care of your papers and such," Brodie said. "Why don't you go get cleaned up, then come back for some stew and we'll see what we can salvage from this date."

"It's not a date," Daisy muttered, but no one was listening to her.

Brodie was looking at Reese, but before he could say anything else, Reese was turning to her and taking her elbow in a gentle but determined grasp. "Let me walk you out," he said in a tone that brooked no argument.

At the moment, he wasn't going to get one from her. Even if his touch was warm, and his hand did feel big and wide and strong propping her up. And all those reactions she'd forgotten about for a moment came rushing back in, double time and double strength. She'd worry about that just as soon as they got out of the pub and done with being a public spectacle. She'd quite probably already ruined any chance she had to get Reese to take her seriously, but that didn't mean she wanted the entire village to think her a laughing-stock. Not if she planned on doing business in Glenbuie, any-way.

As soon as the pub door closed behind them, leaving them both blinking a bit in the sudden brightness of the late spring day, she extricated herself from his hold and stepped back. "I appreciate the assistance. And I'm so sorry I've made such a mess of this." She gave him a small smile. "I promise I usu-ally manage to conduct business quite professionally and with very little spillage."

Reese's mouth quirked at the corner again and she found herself staring. He really was arrestingly attractive, and with all that intensity, too . . . even if he wasn't her type. Well, not anymore, anyway.

"Accidents happen," he said, his deep voice so smooth, al-most melodic. "Let me walk you to your shop."

"I can manage. If you'd like to go back inside and talk to your brother, or—"

"No, I think I've given Brodie enough openings for one day. I'm certain they're all having a spot of fun at our ex-pense and I'd be loath to interrupt."

Her cheeks flamed. "I'm so sorry. I didn't mean to attract unwanted attention—"

He surprised her by letting out a short bark of a laugh. "You have little experience with village life, I take it?"

Her responding smile was rueful at best. "Very little. Guilty."

"If you're planning on residing in this one for any length of time, then you might as well get used to unwanted atten-tion right off. The term 'none of your business' does not apply here. Best to understand that straight off."

"So . . . you're not angry with me?"

"Of course not," he said, looking sincerely perplexed by the thought. "Why would you think that? It wasn't as if you did it on purpose."

"It's just . . . I'd all but badgered you into coming in the first place, and then—"

His deep sigh stopped her from going on and risking making things worse. If such a thing were possible. He said nothing, however, just braced his hand on the back of her elbow once again, and resumed escorting her across the square to her shop. "If you'd prefer, I can wait out here while you change."

"Wait?" She'd assumed their meeting was postponed. Indefinitely.

He held her gaze for an interminably long moment, then said, "Am I really as bad as all that?"

She frowned. "What do you mean? I'm the one that knocked you to the floor and got ale dumped all over us."

Rather than clarify, he said, "If you don't mind, I'd like to wait. I don't know you very well, but I'm guessing you are well prepared enough that you don't really need those notes."

"You still want to discuss—never mind," she said hastily. The man wanted to keep his business appointment and she was standing there second-guessing him? Was she crazy? "It will only take a second. Promise." She hurriedly unlocked the door and stepped inside the small vestibule. In front of her was the glass-paned door to the shop and to her left was a paneled door leading to the stairs up to her rooms over the shop. She debated a half-second on inviting him up, but decided he might take the invitation the wrong way. She'd done enough wrong already.

Not to mention the fact that she didn't need him prowling around up there while she was stripping off her clothes. She was having a hard enough time concentrating around the man as it was.

"You can wait inside the shop, if you'd like."

"That will be fine."

She opened the door for him, then turned toward the stairs. "I'll only be a minute."

"I'll be right here."

She stood there, but he didn't go into the shop. He was still staring at her. And she didn't go up the stairs, either. She was all caught up in staring back. The moment stretched beyond the socially acceptable, but neither of them made a move to break eye contact. Her thighs trembled a little as the silence continued . . . but it wasn't all that uncomfortable. Well, not in a bad way, anyway. *Laugh, say something witty, run up the damn stairs*, her little voice counseled. But the intensity in his gaze might as well have been a tractor beam for all the power she had to look away from it. "I . . . uh . . ." she finally stuttered.

He shifted an almost imperceptible space closer. But suddenly it was as if all the air had been sucked out of the tiny vestibule. "Do you need any assistance?"

Her entire body went on red alert. Had he really just asked her that? Really? Or had she just hallucinated what she wanted him to say?

Either way, she was in deep trouble.

Chapter 3

Dear Lord. Had he really just said that? Was he insane? Damn Brodie for provoking him, for putting thoughts of Daisy into his head that . . . well, okay, to be honest they had already long since taken up residence there. He'd spent the past fortnight trying to get them out, with a complete lack of success.

Now she was staring at him and he was wondering how to make her understand exactly what he'd been offering. Which he would, just as soon as he decided for himself. "Your dress . . . is soaked down the back." Something his entire body was quite well aware of at this point. Trailing behind her a few steps out of the bar had been pure torture. He told himself he was just blocking her rear view from the gawkers inside the pub, but that hadn't exactly kept him from gawking at the view himself, now had it?

The way the thin, wet fabric clung to her curves had already made him wish he hadn't been sipping an ale for the past half-hour before she'd arrived. He didn't need any less control than he already appeared to have. Seeing that dress all wet and plastered to every inch of her tight bum was like adding fuel to an already banked fire. One he was having an increasingly hard time putting out. *Hard* being the key term there.

"I thought you might need help, you see, with the buttons

up the back—" He stopped short and raised a hand between them to stall her response. "Right. Completely inappropriate. I didn't mean anything untoward." Which wasn't entirely true, as it happened.

Brodie's earlier ribbing at the pub echoed through his mind. Reese wasn't a social outcast, as his brother proclaimed; he was simply focused on getting his job done. So he was a wee bit overly work-oriented. He'd had to be for so long, back during those first years right after Finney died, maybe he'd forgotten how not to be. Brodie had pointedly asked him when was the last time he'd even thought about going out on a date, much less actually gone on one.

Reese had taken so long to think about it, his younger brother had laughed at him outright. Point to Brodie.

"I just thought," he said absently, his mind still going in circles, "with it being wet like that, it might be tricky . . ." He trailed off again, realizing he was only making it worse. "I'll wait in the shop."

He'd glanced down, not at all used to feeling quite so utterly foolish. When he glanced back up, however, it was to find Daisy smiling at him.

"No offense taken. I know you were just trying to be a gentleman."

She'd said it so matter-of-factly. As if never in a million years could she fathom someone like him making an advance. It pricked at him, made him want to prove her wrong. A reaction that, in and of itself, should have been a glaring warning sign. Maybe it was the ale lowering his defenses, but he doubted it. He'd grown up helping his grandfather run the distillery and he'd sampled more than his fair share of Glenbuie over the years, and knew his limits well. It would take more than a few sips of ale to cloud his judgment. What was it, then, that so provoked him when it came to one Daisy MacDonnell? Certainly not Brodie's pointed jibes—they were a common staple among all four Chisholm brothers, of one form or another. Well, three of them, anyway. No one teased Dylan overly much these days.

He'd only agreed to see her because he knew she'd persist in disrupting his carefully maintained schedule if he didn't settle her business proposition once and for all. And again, he knew he was lying to himself almost the instant he finished thinking it. He'd wanted to see her again from the very moment she'd exited his office.

"Would you . . . why don't you come up," she said. "I should have offered before. Excuse my poor manners, please." She smiled. "You've been nothing but kind, and I—I shouldn't make you stand around down here."

For some reason, this only served to irritate Reese further. Why in the world he wanted her to see him as some sort of dangerous threat he had no idea. It made absolutely no sense. And yet her sudden willingness to invite him up, clearly believing herself to be perfectly safe in his presence, made him feel somehow less than himself. Not that he wanted her to feel there was any danger to her physical well-being . . . but he couldn't help but wish she felt at least a tiny bit threatened by the more visceral reaction he seemed to have in her presence.

Before he could formulate a response of any kind, whether it be a tight refusal . . . or backing her up against the vestibule wall and seeing if she thought he was quite as harmless when every hard inch of him was pressed between those lovely legs of hers, she was unlocking the door leading up the stairs and beckoning him to follow.

"I can't vouch for the state you'll find it in," she said lightly, not a care in the world, followed by that musical laugh of hers. "I wasn't expecting company."

He could vouch for the state *he* was in, he thought, somewhat morosely as he trudged silently up the stairs behind her, watching her hips sway right in front of his eyes, unable not to, and finding himself not really caring at this point how rude it might be. He had no idea what was coming over him or why it was happening, but he decided right then he wasn't going to thwart it or shove it aside. Best to tackle it as he did any challenge when presented to him: head-on.

"Here we are," she said, pushing open the door at the top of the stairs. It was painted a shade of periwinkle blue that contrasted with her auburn hair perfectly as she leaned back against it to politely allow him entry in front of her.

It was all he could do to keep himself from pausing in the narrow doorway, his body filling almost the entire space remaining there. How easy it would be, he thought, to turn to her, press her up against that door, and—"Please don't let me keep you," he heard himself say, his tone so perfectly modulated when he felt anything but, he had no idea how he managed it. "I'm sure you must be uncomfortable." Lord knew *he* was. He shifted past her, part of him hoping she didn't notice the state he was in . . . and another tiny part of him wishing she would. What would she do if she knew the effect she was having on him? How would she react if she had so much as an inkling as to the thoughts that were running through his supposed you've-been-nothing-but-kind mind?

She smiled, her laugh self-deprecating this time and every bit as endearing. "Yes, there is a bit of a chill."

Maybe for her, he thought, feeling increasingly reckless, torn between being the gentleman he'd been born and bred to be . . . and the man who found his gaze drawn immediately to the front of her sundress, wanting to know just how chilled she was and uncaring what she thought of his less-than-polite perusal. He was leaning dangerously toward being the man who, when discovering her nipples were pressed hard against the thin cotton of her sundress, wanted to take them in his mouth and make sure their erect, tightly budded tips remained that way because of him, and not some aftereffect of spilled ale.

Why there was this need to claim her in some way, to make his mark on her, to feel this need to possess—Christ.

He abruptly swung around and pretended to look around her second-floor flat. It was much smaller than Brodie's, whose flat took up the entire second floor over the far more spacious pub. Having never been up here during the time Maude had owned the shop, Reese had no idea if Daisy had made her own imprint on it or kept it the way it had been decorated before. He didn't know her well enough to have any sense of what her style might be, or if the somewhat overdone theme of morning glories and lavender truly suited her. Somehow he didn't think so. "How are you faring here?" he asked, striving almost desperately for byplay that felt even close to normal. "You feel settled yet?"

"Mostly," she said, clearly no longer standing right behind him.

He turned to find her crossing the narrow living room area, which butted up with the kitchen nook that faced the rear of the building, heading to the only other door. Presumably that led to her bedroom. He resolutely refused to let himself imagine what it looked like. Hopefully like something an old maiden aunt would sleep in, if there was any mercy in the world. And yet, unbidden came the images of him tossing her straight on her back amidst chenille morning glories and lavender-scented pillows . . . and he was having no problem whatsoever being exceedingly turned on by the prospect. Maiden aunt be damned.

"I've spent most of my time focusing on learning how Maude handled the shop and deciding how best to start up my own business ideas. But eventually I'll work on making this my space up here. It's homey enough, but . . ." She let her words trail off as she opened the door.

Reese had a quick glimpse beyond, enough to note the walls were a pale lemon yellow, but couldn't see the bed or the spread across it. Not that his imagination required such actual facts.

"I'll be out in a moment." She waved a hand toward the settee and the one overstuffed chair and ottoman that comprised the living room arrangement. "Please, make yourself comfortable."

He was nodding agreeably, intending to do as asked, and yet his mouth opened and out came, "Are you sure you don't need a hand?"

This time she didn't brush off the offer with an innocent smile and a wave. Maybe because this time his offer hadn't sounded so innocent. But she didn't look annoyed—or worse, alarmed, either. She looked . . . well, confused, actually. Her gaze remained on his for a long, silent moment, as if she was trying to decide exactly what he was offering. And then she'd be annoyed or alarmed, most likely.

He should just brush it off, as he'd done before. She looked at him as a potential client, nothing more. Which was exactly when he realized what he wanted. He wanted her to look at him as if he had the potential to be more than a harmless business contact. He wanted her to look at him with the same intent and interest he was fairly certain she saw on his face this very moment.

"I . . ." She started, stopped. And the disconcertment on her face shifted a little as he continued to hold her gaze.

"Can I ask you something?" he asked her, unaware the question was coming until he'd given voice to it.

She went more still, if that was possible, but she'd yet to look alarmed in any way. "Okay."

"It's rather awkward, but I'd appreciate a straightforward response. And this is an aside to any business talk we have. I'm—there's just something I'm curious about, man to woman."

She frowned now, wary but clearly curious. "Okay," she said again.

"Before, down in the foyer, when you invited me up, you made it clear I don't make you feel threatened in any way." He quickly lifted a hand. "Which is good. I don't want you to ever feel alarmed in my presence, as you have no reason to be."

"Okay," she said slowly, then followed with, "but?"

He took a step closer without thinking, needing to see her eyes more clearly, and at a closer range. She could say anything, but the eyes always gave a person's true feelings away. At least he'd found that to be true in business. One assumed it held true in other situations. "I suppose I always fancied the idea—much as any bloke would, I guess—that, given the right circumstances, I could make a woman nervous . . . in a good way."

She held her ground. Her expression remained smooth. But her pupils dilated a bit.

Encouraged, he moved closer. "According to my brother, I'm far too much a gentleman, far too much of the time. And he likely has a point. It's just . . . I'm rarely provoked to be anything other than one."

He stopped a foot away from her. Her pupils had all but swallowed up the green of her eyes. And her nipples were still quite pointedly pronounced . . . whether from still being trapped in a wet dress, or because of his proximity, he had no idea. But he was going with the latter. He needed all the support he could get.

"So, what—" She paused to clear her throat, her voice having gone slightly hoarse. "What, exactly, is your question?"

He'd come this far. No point in sticking to hypotheticals now. "From the moment you walked into my office a fortnight ago, you've left me feeling somewhat . . . provoked."

Her eyes widened and her throat worked, making him want to press his lips to the side of her neck. He pushed on, knowing he'd never pursue this particular line of questioning with her again, if not now.

"Which I'm certain puts me in rather crowded company, as you've managed to turn a number of heads here."

Her cheeks flushed slightly and he'd thought it impossible for her to be any more beautiful. Or arousing. He'd been wrong.

"But it occurs to me now . . . that perhaps it wouldn't matter if I was provoked or not. Maybe women simply don't see me as anything other than a nice, polite chap who—"

She surprised him—shocked him silent, actually—by bursting out with a shout of laughter, then quickly clamping a hand over her mouth. "I'm sorry," she said, though it was clear she was anything but. "I wasn't laughing at you—I was laughing because . . . are you kidding me?"

Now it was his turn to frown, to be confused. "I assure you, I was quite sincere."

Which sent her off giggling again. "No, wait, don't frown like that." She grabbed his arm when he went to step away. "I'm sorry, really. I just . . . I can't believe someone like you, in your position especially, doesn't have a very clear idea of your impact on the opposite sex. I mean, you can be a little stuffy—"

"Stuffy?"

She blanched. "I'm sorry, that came out wrong. Maybe not so much stuffy as proper."

"What's wrong with being proper?"

"Nothing. It's just, you do come across as professional and all business, but you definitely—" She broke off, shook her head. "I know you said this is off the record, but I am seeing the cornerstone of my business plan going right down the tubes here. I should stop talking now."

"No, please don't." He covered her hand with his own, keeping its place on his arm. "I definitely what?"

She stilled, and looked down to where they touched. "I, uh . . ." She trailed off, then looked back at him. "You're really serious, aren't you? This isn't some kind of game?"

"What game would I be about playing? I'm all but surrendering my integrity here. It's doubtful I'd have anything to gain by asking such potentially ego-crushing questions of you."

She smiled a little. "It's the way you phrase things."

"What way?"

"Very . . . properly. Polished."

"I like to make sure my meaning is clear."

"It's an interesting mix, is all. That crisp brogue, and your—"

"My what?" he asked when she paused.

"Your intensity."

"My—you think I have intensity?"

She grinned. "Ah, yeah." She held her thumb and forefinger close together. "Just a wee bit."

He felt his body tighten again. There was a definite twinkle in her eye now . . . and it was most definitely directed at him. And he didn't think it was remotely business related. "And this intensity . . . it's a good thing?"

"You asked about women seeing you as anything other than a proper gentleman. You have this way of focusing on something quite intently. When that something is me—well, a woman," she amended, "then I think you can safely say she might feel a little . . . provoked. In a good way."

"And that's why you laughed?"

She cocked her head. "You really don't think you have that kind of magnetism?"

"Honestly, it's not something I thought much about until . . . well, until I met you. Brodie poked a bit today, and I suppose it's made me think. I do have a habit of focusing rather intently on one thing in particular. The distillery. And he suggested maybe I needed to spread my attentions around a bit. Then there you were, being quite provocative, although I'm certain it was innocently played . . . but you didn't seem the least bit affected by my reaction."

"What reaction?"

Had he been the rogue he claimed he wanted to be, he'd have pulled her into his arms and she'd have felt quite clearly the reaction he was having. As it was, he took her hand off his arm and turned her around so her back was to him. "Perhaps we should end this discussion now, before it does intrude on our business dealings with one another."

She went to turn, but he kept her firmly in place with his

hands on her shoulders. Once again, she stilled. And though he'd only intended to aim her at her bedroom door, now that her back was to him, the feel of the play of muscles in her shoulders, shifting through the thin cotton beneath his fingertips, made him wonder if there was such a thing as touching her impersonally.

"What are you doing?"

"Here," was all he said, as he pushed her hair over one shoulder. "Hold that."

She gathered her hair in one hand, then glanced back at him. "So does this mean we're going to have business dealings with one another?"

He didn't respond—he was too intent at working the damp fabric to release the top button of her shift.

She stilled, her breath held.

"Just getting the hard-to-reach ones for you."

She said nothing . . . but didn't move away, either.

Once done with the first, he attacked the second one, then debated on the third. He'd left the fabric clinging to her skin, not parting it, not tormenting himself more than he already was. And yet, there was her exposed neck, tilted so perfectly for him to access the tender skin with his mouth. Just one taste. He even found himself drifting closer, dipping his head just slightly, before pulling back. "There." With great effort, he dropped his hands. "You should have an easier time of it now."

She, however, did not turn back around. "Still the gentleman."

He let out a sigh. "I suppose I'm doomed."

She still didn't move. Neither did he.

"And this business talk we're going to have . . ." She trailed off, then was silent for so long, he finally prompted her.

"Yes?"

Once again she glanced back at him. In that moment, with her gaze intently on his, her dress half undone, and her hair moving in a curtain of silk back across her shoulders as she released it ... He was forced to curl his fingers inward to keep from reaching for her right then, and damn the consequences. Whatever they might be.

"What is your stance on mixing business with ... being provoked?"

At any other time, coming from any other person, the question could have only been interpreted as in invitation. An invitation to provoke ... and keep provoking. But there was a look in her eye, something almost wary, that made him wonder if perhaps this was a trick question after all. "I don't know," he answered honestly. "I've never had the occasion to give it any thought."

"Hmm," she said, giving him absolutely no indication of the murmured sound's meaning. "I'll be out in just a moment." And then she was gone and the door between them shut quietly.

Leaving him to wonder what in the hell had happened.

And just what the bloody hell he wanted to happen next.

Chapter 4

Daisy closed the door between them, then immediately slumped against it. Was he kidding? Back home, men in his position of power—even one without Reese's good looks and intensity—always had a very clear idea of their appeal and hold on the opposite sex. Maybe it was a Scottish thing.

She crossed her arms over her chest and shivered a little. Which had nothing to do with the damp dress, either. Just picturing the sincerity in Reese's eyes as he'd asked his questions made her body respond. No, he hadn't been playing any games. He'd said she'd provoked him. She rubbed her arms, and squeezed them more tightly against the ache in her breasts. He'd certainly managed to do that to her. How could a man like him honestly believe he didn't have the right kind of mojo to pull that off? What, were the single women of Glenbuie napping or something? Surely, even if he'd been too buried in his work to do the chasing, some bold lass would have given it a go her own self. He had to know that not only was his reserved nature an incredible turn-on, but he had the kind of intensity and focus that, if harnessed properly, could shoot laser beams or something.

The way he'd been looking at her as he'd asked her if he could be the kind of man who provoked a woman . . . And then, the feel of his hands on her, ever so lightly brushing her skin as he unbuttoned the back of her dress. It had been all she could do to stand there and not lean back against him, feel the length of his body bracing hers. Her gaze shifted to her bed, and her body quivered at the thought of the two of them there, naked, skin on skin, passionately entwined, rolling amongst the sheets and pillows, wrestling, teasing . . . Provoking one another.

There came a tap at the door at her back. She let out a little squeak of surprise and leaped away from the door, as if he could see her standing there, staring at the bed, fantasizing about the two of them together.

"Daisy? I'm going to step down to the shop, take a look about."

"Uh, sure. No problem. I'll be down in a minute." She immediately started peeling the sodden dress off, feeling foolish for giving in to her urges, even for a moment. He'd asked her a couple of highly personal questions, sure. And definitely there was some serious electricity bouncing between them. *Business, Daisy, stick to business.* She hadn't moved all the way across the Atlantic Ocean just to fall back into the same patterns she'd gotten herself into before. Reese Chisholm was her ticket to building a strong financial base from which to launch her small-business plan. She wouldn't make a fortune here, but she'd make a living and, more importantly, a home. In quiet, quaint, wonderfully off-the-beaten-track Glenbuie.

She'd find a nice local lad and settle into an easy, calm, relaxing relationship. No pressure, no high stakes. Given the fact that Reese had already bailed out and gone downstairs was proof he'd also thought better of instigating anything further.

And yet her gaze went once again to the bed. There was the critical difference this time, and it was the one thing she couldn't shake. Yes, Reese was quite confident about his role in his professional life, which he put first, investing the lion's share of his energies into it at the expense of a more fulfilling personal life. In that respect, he wasn't much different from the men she'd become involved with in the past.

Where he was different, however, was in his personal life. He was quite restrained there. Not taking advantage of his powerful position in any personal, private way. He was very focused on his job, but not because he wanted to improve his social standing, or gain power, or increase his financial net worth. He wanted his business to succeed in order to help his family, not for any personal measure of success. In that respect he was very different. Which led Daisy to speculate just what it would take to make a man like Reese take some personal time, maybe lose a little of that ingrained, controlled restraint. Her gaze remained fixed on the bed, the images flashing one after the other through her mind.

Reese, naked, all long and lean, sinewy and perfect, lying flat on his back as Daisy moved on top of him. Starting with his mouth, then moving down along his body, making his hips buck, eliciting guttural moans from somewhere deep in his throat. She'd slide down his body, run her tongue down the center of his torso, then take him in her hand, slide her mouth slowly down every rigid inch of his—

No. No, no, and no.

She yanked her dress the rest of the way off and tossed it in the direction of her hamper. No more carnal images, no more thoughts of exactly what she'd like to be doing to him in that bed right now. Or what she'd like him to do to her. She resolutely pulled a pair of crisply pressed, khaki capri pants and a short-sleeved yellow camp shirt from the towering walnut wardrobe that doubled as her closet. No more dresses around Reese. She'd be buttoned down and covered up and wouldn't give romping in the sheets with him another thought. Who the hell was she kidding? She slipped on her blouse, then slumped down on the edge of her bed as she did up the buttons. She really had to get a grip.

She'd come here to learn to relax. To find peace and embrace a slower pace of life. One that didn't involve eating antacids like candy, and where intimacy meant more than grabbing the occasional nooner with a power broker during her lunch hour.

Reese was off limits. Only his business was up for grabs. Nothing else.

She stepped into her bathroom and pulled a brush through her hair, then smoothed it back and clipped it at the neck. There. Very sedate. Quite professional. Almost schoolmarmish. There would be no more off-the-record chats with Reese. She would go down to the shop, then very carefully and precisely lay out her business plans, and do whatever it took to make him understand that refusing her services as a marketing and publicity consultant would be detrimental to his business and that of the residents of Glenbuie.

She sighed. "I'll be happy if I can get him to agree to let me launch a Web site for him." Which was her basic plan. Get her foot in the door, introduce him to the global world of the Internet, give him a taste of the kind of exposure his distillery could be enjoying, then gradually get him to let her overhaul his entire marketing scheme. Once the other residents saw what she was doing for the distillery, they'd surely clamor to have her help them expand their global presence as well. On a much more minor scale, of course, but one that would enable her to settle here quite comfortably. Not that running the stationer's shop as it was wouldn't provide her with a decent income, but she wanted to incorporate her own skills, do the things she loved to do. Just on a far more modest, down-to-earth scale.

With a determined smile, she squared her shoulders again and resolutely refused to so much as glance at her bed as she marched through the bedroom and across her flat to the stairs leading below. She'd get Reese's business. And that was all she was interested in getting from the man.

Really.

She found him downstairs in the shop, looking at a display of patterned envelopes by the front window. His head was bent and he appeared to be giving the arrangement the same kind of focused interest he seemed to give everything that crossed his path. Including her. She felt that shivery little rush of arousal again and very purposefully shut it out of her mind. "Sorry to keep you waiting."

He straightened and turned to face her, his expression unreadable. "Not a problem." His gaze stayed on her face and didn't so much as dip beneath her chin.

Of course, that was exactly what she wanted. That's why she'd pulled her hair back and dressed more conservatively. She was positively thrilled that they were back on a professional footing, and the awkward conversation between them was going to be pushed aside as if it never existed.

Now if she could only have the same kind of convenient amnesia about the electricity that had crackled between them upstairs. In her flat. Not a dozen feet away from her bed. Her big, empty bed.

"If you want to come back to my office, I can show you some of the other Web sites I've designed and we can talk a little about what kind of thing I'd have in mind for the distillery." She was already talking too fast and her voice was pitched higher than normal, but if Reese noticed, he didn't let it show. He merely nodded and fell into step behind her.

She crossed the small shop floor, wending through the narrow aisles filled with stationery, cards, notepads, journals, and the like, along with a variety of ink pens and marker sets, until she arrived at the set of paneled doors in the back. One led to a tiny bathroom, the other to her almost equally tiny office. With shelves lining one wall and a desk and office chair wedged into the corner, it was more a nook with a door, actually.

Something she became painfully aware of the moment he stepped into the small space behind her, all but filling up what little available room there was. Bad idea, she thought, her body already reacting to the proximity of his, clearly with a mind of its own, no matter what restrictions she tried to impose mentally. "Um, there is a stool just outside the door. Maybe if you want to slide that in here and . . ."

She heard him moving around behind her, but took that moment to slide into the chair facing her desk, which faced the back wall. There was a giant tackboard hanging in front of it, with a few photos that Maude had pinned up there, along with various articles and columns she'd clipped from the newspaper, all of them yellowed and faded. There was a dried rose with some baby's breath still entwined around it, tacked next to a picture of the shore. She hadn't removed any of Maude's memories or notes, but had merely made some room for her own. Notes, that is. She'd left all her memories behind, intent on making new ones here.

In the center of the tackboard was a flowchart she'd drawn up with a list of the various local businesses she intended to target, followed by a basic marketing plan for each. She wondered what Reese would make of it, and his prominent position at the top of the chart, but it would be too obvious to remove it now. And besides, she had nothing to hide here. Her plans were for the good of the town. And her own business, of course, but she hoped Glenbuie and its residents would come to embrace her business savvy as they'd seemed so willingly to embrace her.

She heard the scrape of the stool across the tiled floor and felt Reese angle himself just behind her right shoulder. It was imposing enough to be stuck in these small quarters with him after what had transpired upstairs. Having him in such an alpha position, his body seemingly surrounding hers as he leaned forward to get a better view of the monitor . . . well, it was nothing short of pure torture.

She moved the mouse and clicked on the Chisholm Distillery icon she'd created along with his file. *Pay attention to the monitor*. Not to the fact that Reese's body was emanating heat, and hers had somehow become a heat-seeking missile. "I've worked on a variety of accounts over the years that have successfully marketed products ranging anywhere from imported Scandinavian furnishings to a line of Japanese jeweled collars for your pet." She paused and delicately cleared her throat. Somehow her voice had gone a bit hoarse. "I initially worked on print ads and catalogue layouts, but eventually, as the Internet became an important tool in the global consumer market, I shifted my focus to building a Web site catalogue for my company that complemented the print, radio, and television ad campaigns for our larger clients."

"Sounds interesting. And complicated."

She tried not to shiver. His voice was so deep, so smooth . . . and so close. She wondered what it would feel like if he just dipped his chin slightly, and pressed his lips to that sensitive spot on the back of her neck. "It can be," she said, with a bit more forced cheer than absolutely necessary. "But the beauty of it is we can adapt each Web page to the needs of the client. Make it eye-catching, inviting, user-friendly, and, most of all, memorable. So that the person browsing your site thinks of Glenbuie first the next time they buy a bottle of whisky. Or, better yet, orders it directly on-line from one of your distributors. Or, one step beyond that, plan a trip to the Scottish countryside to tour the distillery in person. We can facilitate all of that very easily, in a single, unified site that will link—"

"We don't rely heavily on that kind of tourist market," he interrupted. "We're not close enough to the tour loop for that to be—"

"Nonsense. If people think you have something unique to offer, they will go out of their way."

"While I would like to think that the whisky that has been my family's pride and joy for close to two centuries is something unique, I'm afraid there are too many distilleries in Tayside alone to—"

"You are one of the only family-owned distilleries left in Scotland." She made the mistake then of turning to look at him. He'd been leaning down to see the monitor, so she found herself quite abruptly face-to-face with him. His gaze immediately shifted from the monitor . . . to her. She felt it like a physical touch.

"Yes, we are," he said, not so much as blinking. "But that by itself isn't such a big attraction."

"I, uh, it can be," she said, struggling not to just sit there and stare into his eyes.

Finally he shifted back in his seat, which, in a way, was worse, as now she had to stare up at him. And he was dominant enough at the moment.

"It may not be something that would attract the locals," she said, persevering. "But if you promote yourself properly to the tourist trade—"

"We've never really been after that market. We give tours, yes, but only as a standard courtesy. In the overall scheme of things, 'tis no' the focal point of my business plan."

He was such a clear speaker that his accent was all the more melodic for it. She could listen to him talk all day. And night. *Don't go there, Daisy.* "I'm not suggesting you change your overall business strategy. I'm merely saying that the expense of investing in an Internet presence would be far superseded by the potential returns. It might never be a focal point in terms of income, but it doesn't have to be that to still be a viable, cost-effective part of your business plan. Heightened visibility is never a bad thing."

He continued to stare at her, and the silence spun out for a long moment. There was still a tension between them, no matter that they were trying to pretend otherwise. Or maybe that was just her. He didn't seem to be having the same difficulty focusing that she did. He was probably thinking about her proposed business scheme . . . while she was still struggling mightily to keep from wondering what those hands of his would have felt like if he'd continued to unbutton her dress . . .

"I'm still not sold on the idea," he said abruptly, proving she'd been right. He'd asked one off-the-record question upstairs. Probably because she had the kind of sunny disposition that invited confidences. Yes, he'd admitted that he was specifically asking her, but he'd apparently put aside the whole provocation discussion when he'd left her flat for the business environs of her shop. It was only Daisy who couldn't shake the whole idea.

"What would it take for you to be able to give me a clearer idea of how the site would benefit my business?"

She blinked, thinking she hadn't heard him right. He'd been about to brush off her and her marketing proposal, she'd been sure of it. She quickly regrouped. "I can show you some other sites I've developed—"

"I'm not particularly Internet savvy. I don't know that it would make much sense to me to see other sites—"

"Well, it would give you an idea of what kind of interactive elements we can incorporate, the kind of design plans I would use. If you'd like, I could do a mock-up of something specifically geared to Glenbuie Distillery, but I don't have enough information at this point to really do it justice."

"What would you need for that?"

Her heart skipped a beat. He was considering it. Despite the complete lack of enthusiasm in his tone, he was really considering it. She had a toe in the door; now all she had to do was keep it there until she could wedge the rest of her in there as well. "I'd want to know more of the history and folklore surrounding both the area and the distillery itself. But mainly I'd need access to the distillery, all parts of it. I'll need to photograph everything, and I'll need a full tour. Someone, perhaps, who could explain the entire process in detail, in layman's terms, which is the same language I'd use on the site."

"Why would that matter to anyone?"

"Because people are a curious lot by nature. Designing a Web page is a little like telling a story. If you make it look and sound fascinating—and frankly, anything new can be fascinating if presented the right way—they'll be interested in it. They'll want to know. I'm not saying I'm going to exhaust anyone with a detailed manual on whisky-making, but the more I know, the more I have to work with."

He seemed to ponder that for a moment.

Not content to let him think on it too long, she plunged ahead. "If you could spare someone for just an hour or two, for a more detailed, behind-the-scenes tour, with a healthy question-and-answer session, that would be a good start."

"Start?"

"I'll need to know more about what you do, to know what kind of other information I'll want or need. After the basics, I'd ask that you let me wander around a bit—safely, of course—and take some pictures, get a feel for how the place operates on a normal day, maybe talk with a few of your people." She held up her hand. "I'd be very unobtrusive, I promise."

It was hard to tell from his enigmatic expression, but she got the impression he wasn't all that keen about having someone underfoot.

"Just a few days. Then maybe a sit-down with you to cover any final questions I might have. Then give me a week and I'll put together at least a basic idea of what to expect. We would then work together to develop it into something that you feel represents Glenbuie as you envision it. I've done some research on the other competing sites on the Internet and I think I could easily duplicate their traffic successes with your site, perhaps exceed them." She was babbling again. She took a short moment, breathed, and smiled. "And don't worry, this is all on spec. Nothing from you except some time and a little access. If you like what I come up with, we'll talk contract then."

"You sound quite confident."

Her smile grew slightly. "If I didn't, you'd never have given me this much of your time."

"Quite good at your job back in the States, I'll wager."

She felt her cheeks warm a bit. "I did okay."

He studied her for a moment. "I'm guessing that's an understatement."

She said nothing. Success had a different meaning to her before. But on any scale, yes, she'd done quite well for herself.

"So why relocate so far away? And pitch your lot with such a small village? What of your family? And your career? No matter if you have every one of us on your client list—I'm sure it won't match what you were accustomed to before."

"Maybe that's why I'm here. Because I don't want what I had before."

"What do you want, Daisy MacDonnell?"

Oh, there was a loaded question if ever there was one.

"I want access to your distillery so I can show you what I can do."

His eyes sharpened at that, and she wondered, for a moment, if he was as unaffected by her as he appeared to be. "Okay."

She'd already opened her mouth to rebut his reply—then the single word sank in. She snapped her mouth shut, then smiled. "Really?" She quickly regrouped. Never give a client a moment to doubt their decision. "I mean, thank you. You won't regret it."

There appeared to be an almost amused hint of a smile hovering around his mouth, the corners of his eyes. It was mesmerizing, really, that little hint. "Now that I've given you what you want, tell me the real answer."

"Real answer?"

"Why did you come to Glenbuie? Surely your life goal was not to create a Web site for some obscure, family-owned distillery. I know it was an inheritance that lured you here, but you could easily have sold that, remained in the States. But you didn't. You uprooted your entire life and transplanted yourself amongst strangers. Again, I ask, why?"

She cocked her head slightly. He wasn't making small talk.

He was hardly the type. In fact, he seemed quite serious. But then, when wasn't he? "Why does it matter?"

"I guess I'm curious to know what drives you. Success, clearly. I recognize that, as I see it in the mirror every day. But for that you could have remained where you were. Why here? Why us?"

His gaze settled on her then in such a way as to make her feel as if he could see straight through her. Or want to, anyway. It might have been business on the surface, but the way he held her gaze felt eminently personal and intimate to her. Foolish on her part, for sure, but it encouraged her to speak more freely, more frankly, than she otherwise might have. "I want a different kind of success. I don't have any real family per se. My dad took off when I was little and my mom passed away right after I graduated from college. So my career has been my partner in life, my haven, my security. But somewhere along the line, I let it become my entire life. I let it define me. All of me."

She paused, but he didn't say anything, encouraging her to continue. "I want a balance. I want a blend to my personal and professional life." She laughed. "I want a personal life, period. When I got the telegram saying I'd inherited this place from a relative I didn't even know I had, I decided it was a sign. That if I really wanted to alter my life drastically, a life-altering change was necessary. And I knew I could always go back. But from the moment I stepped out of the taxi into the village square, I knew I'd done the right thing. Glenbuie feels like the perfect place to find the new me."

He stayed silent for the longest moment, then looked like he was about to speak, but thought better of it. With a short shake of his head, he stood, pushing the stool back. "Then I believe you'll find what you seek."

Daisy impulsively stood as well, put her hand on his arm. "What else?"

He raised a questioning eyebrow in response.

"What were you about to say just now?" When he hesitated, she prodded him. "There was something else you were about to say, but you didn't. Come on. You've asked me some pretty personal questions."

He looked down at her, then sighed. "You came here to find balance. Yet, I've lived here all my life, and I haven't managed to find it."

"But you think I will?"

"I don't imagine any goals you set eluding you for too long."

Her lips quirked at that. "I'm not so sure that's entirely a good thing. All that goal-setting, I mean. Maybe I need to learn how to just let life happen. It's one thing to plan with business, quite another to plan out a personal life. It should be more spontaneous, more impulsive." The corners of her mouth lifted. "I'm still working on that part."

"Spontaneous," he said, his voice dropping to a deeper, softer note. "Impulsive."

Her heart rate kicked up a notch as his gaze dropped from her eyes . . . to her mouth.

"Perhaps," he said, slowly and quite intently, "we could help each other with that part."

"We could?" she asked, hearing the breathlessness in her voice and incapable of doing anything about it.

"Aye." Slowly, so slowly that she had plenty of time to deny him, he lowered his head to hers.

Her mouth went dry. The rest of her . . . didn't. "Reese . . ."

"I like to hear you say my name," he said. He tipped her chin up with his hand, then went about claiming her as if that very goal had been his sole desire, planned quite well and thoroughly. He started with kisses along her chin, then moved to the corners of her mouth.

She sighed and leaned into him.

"Like that," he murmured against her lips. "Just like that."

"Yeah," she said shakily. "Just like that."

Chapter 5

Reese took his time before finally claiming her mouth. She could have stopped him, could have kept things all business between them. It was well beyond him at that point. Provoked, indeed.

She hadn't stopped him. Nay, she'd sighed and leaned into him, that's what she'd done. And turned his world upside down, even as something had settled deep inside him.

Heaven she was, the taste of her. As sweet and intoxicating as he'd wagered she'd be. He'd spent more time than he'd care to admit over the past fortnight, imagining this moment. Never once truly thinking he'd take it this far. But what she'd said, about finding balance in her life, had struck a chord in him, in a way all the teasing in the world from his brothers never would. She'd changed her whole life to find something more for herself. Such bravery, he thought, and heart. Others might see such a move as foolhardy, but to him, she'd shown she had the capacity to stand up for herself, to put her needs first. A trait he, himself, did not apparently possess.

Until this moment. Kissing her was the most selfish thing he'd done in a long time. Possibly ever. There was no good reason to cross such a line, and plenty of bad ones. And yet there he was, taking her mouth like a man starved for it. And perhaps he was.

She moaned softly as he took the kiss deeper. He cupped

her face, tilted her so he could dip his tongue past those perfectly shaped lips into the decadent recesses of her mouth, and for all that was holy, she let him. Despite the difference in their heights, she fit him well, her body curving into his, making his scream more loudly with need. Heedless of the stool behind him, or the small confines of her office, he staggered backward, taking her with him as his back hit the door. Another groan, this one his, as her hands came up, braced against his chest. He'd thought perhaps nothing could top the taste of her, the feel of her beneath his hands. He'd been wrong. The feel of her hands on him threatened to unravel what little control he had left. Her living quarters were but a short jaunt up the stairs. All that softness awaited them if he only had the nerve to take them there.

At the moment, the animal she'd unleashed inside him would have been perfectly happy to have her right there, bent over the counter or up against the nearest wall. Naked, legs wrapped around his hips as he pistoned deep inside of her, their bodies glistening and—

"Hello? Daisy? Are you back there, dear? Halloo?"

Daisy went stock-still in his arms. The blood was pounding so hard in his ears, he didn't immediately catch on. "What's wr—?"

Then the voice drew closer. "I know the sign says closed, dear, but I saw the lights on and thought you wouldn't mind if I dropped in to pick up that adorable stationery set I was in here looking over for my niece. I need to get it posted tomorrow if it's to make it to her on time."

Daisy looked up at him with much the same look that deer get when headlights pin them to the middle of the road in the dark of night. Her cheeks were flushed, her neck and jaw slightly reddened from his attentions, her hair mussed as well, half out of her barrette. Any one of them a dead giveaway, but combined, there was no way she could brazen it out and not be the immediate talk of Glenbuie. Not after the ale stunt at Hagg's.

Reese pushed her back into the office before she could decide otherwise. "Stay here. I'll take care of this."

"You will? How? I mean—" She paused, shook her head a little, as if to clear it. He understood the need. "It's just—"

"Doris Granger," he finished for her. He'd recognized the voice. And the auld bat would love nothing more than to spread the word that Glenbuie's newest resident had been caught in her office juggling a little more than her books. "I can take care of her. Perhaps you'd like to step into the WC for a moment." He made a vague motion toward her head. "Fix your barrette."

Her hand flew up to her hair, then her cheeks. To his surprise, rather than scowl, she covered her mouth and snickered. "I don't suppose she'd believe I got into such a state unpacking the latest order of self-filling ink pens. Perhaps if I wedged a Styrofoam noodle or two in my hair."

Caught off guard by her amused reaction, he found himself smiling in return. Immediately they were partners in crime, rather than stuttering initiates. "Perhaps. But how would you explain me?"

The flush in her cheeks did deepen then, but her response was just as direct and frank as he was coming to expect from her. "I have no idea how to explain you. I'm still working on that one my own self."

There would be no dodging the awkward moment with Daisy. His respect for her grew. As did his smile. "I'd like to help you out with that. Give me just a moment, and I'll gladly return and provide more assistance on that matter."

She tilted her head, her smile growing bemused. "I wouldn't have thought you had a teasing side to you like this. I like it."

"I'll keep that in mind."

"Daisy? Are you back there?"

He shot her a quick wink, so completely out of character for him, he should have been alarmed. Except he was grinning like a loon and felt as if he floated out the door of her office on a cloud. Amazing what a kiss from a beautiful woman could do for a man's spirit, he thought. Even as he knew there was likely far more to it than that. Or could be, if he'd let it. She didn't seem opposed to the idea.

So many things to consider, his mind was racing in a dozen different directions.

"Reese!"

Daisy's voice hissed behind him and he turned back just before stepping beyond the first row of racks.

She made a motion of tucking in her shirt. He glanced down and realized his own clothing was somewhat askew. When had she tugged at his shirt like that? He quickly straightened things out and swore he heard her snicker, but looked up in time to see the door to the bathroom close. For good measure he raked his hand through his hair, took a deep breath, then squared his shoulders and moved to the front of the shop, prepared to do battle with the dragon for his fair maiden.

That thought made him smile a bit. Daisy MacDonnell was all woman, of that he had no doubt. Just as he knew she could battle her own dragons when need be. And possibly a few of his as well. So it was only sporting that he stepped in to help out when he could.

"Hullo, Doris," he said, announcing his presence as he stepped out from behind the end display on the middle aisle.

"Reese Chisholm!" Her gossip radar went on immediate alert, as he'd expected. She looked past him for a sign of Daisy, and was obviously disappointed. "What brings you in here?"

He could only hope she hadn't stepped into Hagg's at any point this afternoon and heard the tale of the spilling ale with him and Daisy. But Doris would have already mentioned that, were it the case. "Daisy is working on a marketing plan for the distillery, updating some of our publicity. We're neck-deep in a planning meeting at the moment. She sends her apologies—she's on the phone getting some cost estimates."

It was a wee white lie, but he felt it was necessary to expedite Doris's exit. "Is it possible you could come back in the morning when the shop opens again?"

The dour older woman studied him for far too long a moment. "Marketing plan, is it? What has that to do with running Maude's stationer's shop?"

"Yes. Perhaps you haven't heard," he said easily, knowing this would tweak Doris, who liked to pride herself on knowing absolutely everything. "Daisy was quite the marvel back in the States when it comes to things like that. She's looking to add that service to her shop here as well. Perhaps you and Fergus should consider consulting with her to see if she can do anything for your place." Doris and her husband ran the butcher's shop on the opposite side of the square. Fergus was notoriously tightfisted, and Reese doubted he'd avail himself of Daisy's services, but at the moment it was a much needed distraction and so he went with it.

Doris was clutching the stationery set she'd come in for. She stared at his guileless expression, apparently trying to figure out what wasn't right with his story. Admittedly, it wasn't a surprise that she thought it odd to see him here. He rarely did any shopping in town, usually getting his assistant Flora to help him out, or having Brodie pick a few things up for him. His needs were pretty simple. Given that he spent most of his time at the distillery, there wasn't a need for much.

"I do need to get this in the post," she said at length, motioning with the package in her hand. "Perhaps she wouldn't mind if I stepped back to her office and asked if it would be okay to take this with me and settle up with her tomorrow? She knows me well enough to know I—"

"I'm sure she does, and that's a fine solution," Reese said. Then, taking her by the elbow, he gently steered her toward the front door, thinking if he could get her outside and the door locked and lights turned off, he could possibly get back to Daisy in time to pick up where they'd left off. It should have unnerved him a bit more, the hunger and desire she'd unleashed in him. He felt like some kind of rutting beast all of a sudden.

And he couldn't seem to care much about thwarting it, either.

"I'll square it with her," he assured Doris. "Just come around tomorrow and all will be fine." He continued to nudge her forward, having to restrain himself from bodily ejecting her from the shop.

"Hello, Doris." Daisy maneuvered around one of the displays and met up with Doris and Reese as they reached the door. Other than a slight flush to her skin, she looked as fresh as usual. "Sorry it took me so long to get up here." She smiled at Reese. "Thanks so much. I can handle it from here. I'll get in touch with you tomorrow about . . . what we discussed. And to schedule a time for the tour."

Reese just stood there, dumbfounded. *He* was being herded out the door now? When had he become the dragon?

Daisy turned to Doris. "Meet me over at the register and I'll be glad to ring you up. I'll be just a second."

Doris was all smiles, so happy to have things go her way she barely gave the two of them a look. "Lovely! Such a nice girl."

She bustled over to the counter, and Daisy turned to Reese and gave him a rather conspiratorial grin. Which further confused him. Was he being given the bum's rush or what?

"I really appreciate you helping me out." She leaned closer, even as she shuffled him a bit closer to the door. "I—I think maybe we'd better—or I'd better—call it a day. I need to put in some time here tonight, in the office. Will you let me know when it will be a good time to tour the distillery?"

He didn't know what to make of her. Aye, he was out of practice, but he wasn't that far out that he didn't know a brush-off when he was on the receiving end of one. Perhaps he should have felt some remorse. After all, he'd pressed suit fairly hard back in her office, just minutes ago. But she'd responded . . . aye, how she'd responded . . .

Somehow he was back in the vestibule again. Once the door to the shop closed behind him, Daisy positioned herself in front of him so Doris couldn't see past his back to her. "Reese . . . about what happened . . . in the office—"

"No, that's okay. I understand."

Daisy smiled then. "Do you?"

This is why he spent all his time at work. Running a company with a few dozen employees on the payroll was far less complicated than understanding the inner workings of the mind of one lone female. "Perhaps no'. Enlighten me."

"When I said I was looking for balance between my professional and personal life . . . I didn't necessarily mean—" She stopped, her smile faltered. Then she sucked in a breath and shot him a smile that didn't quite reach her eyes. "I've mixed business with pleasure before and it's generally not done me any favors in the end. I—this is a bit different. Everything here is different." Her laugh was a wee bit self-deprecating. "You're most definitely different."

"I'm no' so certain I'm wanting you to explain that last bit."

She touched his arm, and her eyes warmed up as she stared up into his. "I just didn't want you to think . . . that what happened, in the office, had anything to do with my wanting you as a client."

Now it was Reese's turn to bark a short, surprising laugh. "I thought nothing of the sort. I'm afraid my ego is a wee bit shaky on this point, but trust me when I say, I was hoping your reaction to me was anything but mercenary in intent."

Daisy's smile grew. "Designing Web sites was the last thing on my mind when you kissed me." Suddenly her gaze sharpened and she looked past Reese's shoulder and gave a short wave and a smile.

Reese was beginning to have a strong dislike for Doris

Granger. "Perhaps it is best that we part, give each other—how do you say it in the States? Some space?"

"Space, yes."

"I'll be in contact with you, then. About the tour."

"Okay."

When he didn't say anything else, her confident expression faltered a bit. For the first time, he felt like perhaps they were back on an even footing, neither quite certain of where they stood. And, for the moment, that was enough for him. No sense in rushing anything. Though it would take a considerable amount of time, and possibly another ale or two, to erase the images he'd conjured of how he'd have liked this evening to go.

She turned then, pushed open the door to the square. "I'll hear from you soon, then," she said, all professional once again.

Reese couldn't see who might be milling about beyond the door, but he was quite certain he had an avid audience of one behind him. And he knew it was best, for now anyway, until the two of them had time to sort things out in private, to keep things just that: private.

So what impulse drove him to pause beside her, just before stepping outside, he couldn't have said. Not exactly. But pause he did, tilting his head just a fraction so as to keep his face averted from curious eyes, and lowering his voice so only she could hear him. "Were it not for potential spectators, I would be finding myself hard-pressed to allow even the tiniest of spaces to remain between us. For at least a lingering moment or two."

She stilled completely. He saw the pulse in her neck jump, and it made him want to press his mouth there.

"I've hungered for many things, most all of them having to do with keeping the Chisholm holdings afloat. I've rarely allowed myself to hunger for more personal wants." He shifted enough to snag her gaze and held it. "I believe that is about to change."

Chapter 6

"Meet me tonight at half past nine for your private tour. The employees entrance, around the back. Nothing will be off limits for your inspection. Questions and curiosity encouraged."

Daisy punched the button on the answering machine, but didn't play Reese's message again. Tempted though she was. His voice did things to her. "Everything about the man does things to me."

Nothing will be off limits . . .

She rubbed her arms, but not because she was cold. No, and her nipples weren't hard for that reason, either. Damn. Who would have thought proper Reese Chisholm could have such an improper streak in him? She grinned, unable to stop herself. Lucky her for discovering it. At least, she hoped she was going to get lucky. That had to be what he meant. Why else the after-hours tour?

She wished she'd gotten to the phone in time, talked to him herself. She punched the button and listened to the message again. It made her shiver in anticipation. Again.

It figured. She'd been sitting at her desk for the past four hours and the one time she got up to use the bathroom, the phone rang. She hadn't been expecting him to call so soon . . . certainly not tonight. So she'd been surprised when she'd played the message back and his voice had echoed through the small room. The small room where just hours before he'd kissed her speechless.

She sat down in front of her desk, but nothing on the monitor registered in her brain. Her thoughts were far and away from getting any actual work done. Which had been the case since she'd finally hustled Doris out the door. The older woman had managed to keep Daisy standing around talking for close to an hour after Reese's departure. Daisy hadn't really minded. One of the things she loved about Glenbuie was the slower pace and the family feel the tight-knit community had, and had begun extending to her as well. It really was exactly what she'd wanted, what she'd hoped for. No matter how gung ho she was about her business plans, Glenbuie moved along at its own pace, which was stubbornly slow. A pace she was getting used to . . . and finally beginning to enjoy.

Sure, the idea that everybody knew everybody's business took some getting used to, but it wasn't much different from working for a large corporation, really. Only instead of having her business conduct examined and analyzed, it was her personal life on display. Which hadn't been much of a concern, seeing as she hadn't had much of one.

Until today.

Her nipples tightened to the point of pain, and she pressed her thighs together as she thought about what she'd potentially started today. Or what she'd potentially let Reese start. All those lectures she'd given herself about building a personal life separate from her professional one were falling on deaf ears. Ears that only heard the echo of that guttural groan Reese had made when he'd taken his kiss deeper. Dear God.

Thankfully, Doris—one of the nosier gossips—hadn't really seemed to pick up on anything happening between her and Reese. She'd asked a question or two about the publicity business Daisy was hoping to launch, but steered their chat in other directions almost immediately. Daisy smiled, knowing quite well that Doris had been afraid Daisy would try to sell her and Fergus on her services. *If she only knew*, Daisy thought, *she could have relaxed.* Daisy hadn't lived here long, but even she knew better than to put the Grangers' butcher's shop on her list of potential clients. Even if every shop on the square hired her in some capacity, she doubted Fergus would follow suit. Still, she'd happily followed Doris's conversational lead.

She'd needed something, anything, to distance herself a little from what had taken place today. All of it, from the spilled ale, to the discussion up in her apartment, to the toe-curling kiss he'd delivered right before Doris's untimely arrival. She needed perspective, needed to put some distance between her still-raging libido and rational, common sense.

Daisy had no idea what to do about Reese Chisholm. Well, that was a lie. She knew exactly what she wanted to do about him, and that was drag him to the nearest available bed, strip them both naked, and get him to put his hands and mouth on her again. On every part of her, in fact. Lingering in certain places perhaps longer than others. For a man who professed to be all business with no social skills . . . well, he had skills, all right. In spades.

With a sigh, she shut down her computer. She'd spent the past few hours pretending to work on some details and ideas about the other businesses in the area she'd targeted after, she hoped, getting the distillery account. But she finally admitted defeat. The more she tried to shut Reese out of her mind, the more he invaded it. And now there was his invitation for tonight.

How would the village respond to an outsider pairing up with one of their own, especially when that one was Reese Chisholm? And if it ended up a fling, nothing more, then what? If she'd thought it was awkward when the man in question was a corporate peer, how much worse would it be when she had to live in what amounted to a fishbowl with the guy? And with his brother running the pub right across the square? She'd come here thinking she'd settle in, find her balance with the shop first—business was the one thing she understood—and let the rest of her life sort of figure itself out. So what did she go right out and do? Get the hots for the one guy she'd targeted to do business with. Who also happened to be the only guy in town who could be considered a high-octane executive. The Glenbuie version, anyway.

Relaxation was as foreign to Reese as it was to her. For all the reasons she'd come here, she'd be crazy to give in to lust the first time it tempted her. Most especially with him. To even consider going to the distillery tonight was the beginning of the end of her carefully rationalized life plan. She had to think beyond her empty bed upstairs, and how badly she wanted him in it, to the bigger picture. A far better idea would be for her to put her physical reaction to him in its proper perspective, then call his office number and leave a message saying she couldn't make it and would prefer something during the day. Reese was a sharp man—he'd get the message within the message. And if her swift turnaround on the subject of them continuing any personal liaison cost her the account, then so be it. From what she knew of the man, she doubted that he would be the punitive sort. He practically wore his integrity on his sleeve.

So, she thought, emitting a long, dejected sigh. It was decided, then. She'd end this before it went any further, return their liaison to a business-only proposition, and go back to her initial new-girl-in-town game plan. So what if he made her pulse jump like no one else ever had? So what if he looked at her in a way no one else ever had? So what if he had that rare combination of intensity and reserve she'd never seen before? She thought she'd been with enigmatic, charismatic men in her past, right?

But not one held a candle to Reese's controlled intensity, her little voice whispered insidiously. Not one had his innate ability to focus. Especially when that focus was on her.

Just thinking about that did make her squirm a little in her chair. *No.* She mustn't give in to that . . . that need to shiver whenever she so much as thought about him. In time that would pass. It was hormones talking. She'd been here alone for six months. It was natural she'd feel a bit needy. So her reaction to an alpha male like Reese was perfectly understandable. Hell, she'd be worried about herself if she hadn't reacted that way. Right?

She slumped down in her seat, dejected. The truth was, she could counsel herself until she was blue in the face. None of that changed the fact that, even though nipping this in the bud was the absolute smartest thing she could do, she wanted to go tonight. Badly. Wanted to see where this . . . whatever it was that had flared up between them, would lead. And the hell with the collective village opinion of her, the hell with keeping business separate from her private life, and the hell with not being able to hold steady to her hard-made decisions at the very first opportunity to fall right back into her old ways.

The real question was, which would she regret more? Falling off her self-imposed wagon? Or not finding out what she might have with Reese? No matter how short-lived?

Or incredibly hot.

"God, I hate this," she murmured. Before she could second-guess herself any further, or talk herself out of it—and into more trouble—she jerked up the phone and punched in the office number for the distillery.

After getting the canned recording, and honestly, she was going to have to mention that to him—he really could spruce that up a bit—she waited impatiently for the beep. Her heart was pounding and her palms were a bit sweaty. What was she doing, turning down a man like Reese? And potentially her biggest future account along with it? Despite knowing he wouldn't hold it against her, he wasn't exactly gung ho on the idea in the first place. Integrity or not, this could easily be the deciding factor, and she could hardly blame him if it were. Then the beep echoed in her ear and she scrambled to sound cool and professional with her message.

"Hello, this is Daisy MacDonnell. With regret, I can't meet with you at the requested time. Please contact me so we can set up a time most suitable to both of our schedules. Daytime would work best for me. Thank you."

She hung up, then immediately slumped over and covered her face with her hands. "You are such a moron." But, she hoped, this time a smarter moron. She wondered how Reese would take the message. She hoped he didn't think she was being coy, or playing some hard-to-get head game. She felt bad enough just jerking him around this much. It hadn't been intentional, though, which she'd make sure he understood when they did talk. Showing up tonight would have been essentially tacitly agreeing to continue to explore what they'd started today. Hopefully he'd make things easier and realize she'd had second thoughts and decided to keep things businesslike between them.

Out of habit, she turned back to her computer and was reaching to flip it back on again when she caught herself. It was late, well past any normal working hours. And there was absolutely nothing that required her immediate attention this evening. Talk about falling back into old patterns.

So she resolutely got up, flipped off the lights, and headed upstairs. To do what, she had absolutely no idea. She had Maude's ancient black-and-white television, with its hideous reception. A decent radio, but little patience to keep skimming for something decent to listen to. She had her own stereo and music, which had provided an almost constant soundtrack for her in the early weeks when she'd felt a little homesick in a strange, new world. She'd long since grown tired of them, but had been so busy familiarizing herself with the business and making her future plans that she hadn't gotten around to expanding her CD collection just yet.

There was always Hagg's, which had been her destination often as not when she was looking for something to do in the evenings. But after her disastrous late lunch there earlier today, she thought it best to steer clear for a little while. She climbed the stairs, thinking she could be having a social life right now if she'd taken Reese up on his offer to mix a little pleasure with their business. But no . . . And there would be no second-guessing now—she'd already cancelled on him.

"You really are a moron." But it had been the right thing to do. She knew that. Trudging up the stairs, however, she was having a hard time rousing any excitement for the evening ahead. She could kill some time folding the pile of laundry awaiting her. Then maybe she'd really get wild and read one of the murder mysteries in Maude's extensive collection. One thing she wouldn't do was give in to the urge to go back down to her office and work, so she'd feel productive. This was off-hours. She didn't need to produce anything. Hell, she could even flaunt convention and leave her laundry unfolded for another whole day if she wanted to. She could waste the entire remainder of her evening lazing around doing absolutely nothing. And learn to like it, dammit. She smiled a little at that as she let herself into her flat.

She flipped on the lamp by Maude's knitting chair and glanced down at the basket of yarn that was still tucked beside it. Maybe she should take up knitting. It would teach her patience and give her a much-needed hobby at the same time. She reached down, lifted out a soft spool of blue yarn, and rubbed it between her fingers. She glanced over at the ormolu clock on the mantel and saw it was closing in on nine-thirty. Yep, a whole evening ahead with nothing to do but sit back and relax and just enjoy the hell out of her brand new personal life.

Who was she kidding? "Yeah, well, at least you gave it a try," she murmured, then tossed the yarn back in the basket, turned, and walked straight out of her flat, not even bothering to flip off the light.

Ten minutes later she was right where she really wanted to be, and life plans be damned. She stood in front of the employee entrance to Glenbuie Distillery, praying Reese hadn't picked up his phone messages yet.

Taking a deep breath, she let it out slowly, then lifted her hand and rapped on the steel door. In addition to the old Renault she'd recently bought, there was one other car and two company trucks parked in the rear lot. Hopefully one of them belonged to Reese. She waited what seemed like an eternity, and had just about decided she'd blown the whole deal when the door cracked open.

It was darker inside than out, so Reese was totally cast in shadow, little more than a disembodied voice. "Change your mind?"

She flushed a little. "You got my message?"

"Aye. I was just locking up. In fact, if I hadn't seen you on the surveillance camera, I wouldn't have known you were out here."

He sounded quite professional, cool and distant. Maybe she'd already blown it and he was just being polite now. She really felt like the moron she'd accused herself of being earlier. He must think her a complete flake. She couldn't say she blamed him. "Do you—do you want me to go?"

He stepped back and pushed the door open wider. "We can still do the tour if you're up for it. Did you bring a recorder or something, to take notes?'

"What?" Still off guard, she stepped inside the building. He flipped a switch and the short hallway they stood in was immediately illuminated. She blinked a few times against the sudden brightness. "No, I, uh . . . I didn't." She definitely felt like an idiot. She'd rushed out of her apartment and raced over here, thinking about nothing other than seeing him again, about finding out what exactly was going on between them. For once in her life, business had been the very last thing on her mind. Quite naturally, given all her mixed signals, he probably had no idea what she was thinking.

If she hadn't been so mortified, she'd have laughed at herself.

When her eyes adjusted to the change in light, she finally looked at him, trying to determine if he was merely teasing her, or . . . or if he wasn't. She had no idea how to play this without further embarrassing herself, or him. So rather than play at anything, she simply came right out and asked him. At this point, what did she really have to lose? "I was under the impression from your invitation that, perhaps this was a more . . . personal tour."

Reese didn't make a move to leave, or escort her further into the building. She couldn't see beyond him down the hall—he filled her entire line of vision. He held her gaze quite intently. "I was under the impression from your message that you were no' so thrilled with that suggestion."

"I was perfectly thrilled, to be honest. But then I stupidly got to thinking and, well, it made me second-guess myself."

He shifted forward slightly, keeping her between him and the door at her back, with little space to spare. "That whole issue about mixing business with pleasure, you mean."

She nodded. "My goal here was to find a way to separate work from play. Or to find time to play at all."

"I don't believe these are work hours."

"But taking a tour, being here at all, is work-related."

"So would you rather I'd left a message inviting you to my place instead, then?"

She opened her mouth, then closed it again. He still hadn't come right out and answered any of her questions. "Is that what you'd rather have done?"

His mouth quirked a little at the corner, but his eyes were dark and enigmatic, difficult bordering on impossible to gauge. "You wanted to see the distillery. For business purposes, yes. And I'd like to show you the business my family has spent centuries building. For personal purposes. Because it's part of who I am." He made a short, almost self-deprecating snort. "Aye, perhaps too much, but I canno' change that fact. If you're going to capture the spirit of this place in order to effectively promote it, then I felt it was imperative that you see it through my eyes."

She was mentally scrambling to keep up. "And for that you felt we needed to do this after hours?"

"After hours there is less distraction and no immediate demands on my time, so yes, that was part of it."

"Part?"

"The other reason was maybe a little foolhardy on my part. You seem to bring out that side in me."

"Why foolhardy?"

He shifted closer still. "You invited me in today, gave me a glimpse of yourself, your private self. I liked getting to see that side of you, getting to know more about you. And so I was hoping you might feel the same. Sad to say, but this is my private self." He gestured behind him. "I thought to offer you some insight into me. Maybe help reduce the problem we both have about that balancing problem you mentioned earlier."

"That doesn't sound foolhardy to me. It sounds . . ." *Sweet*, she thought. And sincere. The latter didn't surprise her. Reese Chisholm was nothing if not earnest and forthright. But he was also edgy and enigmatic. Not to mention sexy as hell. *Sweet* hadn't been the first trait that had come to mind, or the second.

"I'll admit, I still don't know about the whole Internet thing. But I am curious to see what you'd do with it. More because I'm curious about seeing how you work, how your mind works." He smiled then. "I figured, worst case, the evening would be a personal bust, end up all business, but I'd get a Web site out of the deal, eh?"

She smiled at that, and began to relax a little. "So . . . you do want me to take notes, then."

"I dinnae think that will be necessary this evening." He reached out and tucked a strand of hair behind her ear. "Let me show you a little bit of my world. We'll start there. You can take notes next time."

Next time. Her heart began to thump, and her thighs trembled a bit. He hadn't called her here because he wanted to get her naked. Although she was fairly certain he'd given it some thought. As she had. But he was right—if that was all they were about, he'd have just invited her to his place, they could have jumped each other, and gotten it out of their systems. No, instead he'd offered to share a different, but perhaps more intimate, part of himself with her. He was serious about trying to figure out how to proceed with her, with . . . this. Whatever *this* turned out to be.

It should have unnerved her, or at the very least disconcerted her. She'd caved and given in to his request because he'd gotten her hormones hopping, yes. But she was also here because she'd been wrong in her initial assessment of what she'd live to regret. There was something about Reese Chisholm that was different from any man she'd ever met. And that something had called to something inside her that was new, and very different as well. That call was only getting stronger.

And now here he was, telling her he felt the same tug, the same pull. A shiver of awareness raced over her skin as his fingertips brushed along her cheek.

"Okay," she told him. "Show me."

Chapter 7

Reese was surprised he didn't lose it right then and there. *Show me.*

If she only had any idea what that quiet request made him want to show her. It took considerable restraint not to bury his fingers in her hair and drag her mouth to his. It still shook him, the primal way in which her very presence snatched at his control. Never had he felt so driven by impulses he had such little power over. His reaction to her should have made him run far and fast. Which had been precisely what he tried to tell himself to do when he'd left her shop earlier today.

And that argument had lasted all of the ten minutes it had taken him to get back to his office.

She'd apparently applied the same logic, or tried to . . . and had lasted only slightly longer than he had.

He'd spent the remainder of his afternoon wandering around the distillery in a bit of a daze, the taste of her still on his lips, the scent of her filling his head, the sound of her little moans echoing through his mind. He found himself wondering what she'd think of the place, seeing it through new eyes as he imagined showing her around, explaining the distilling process to her, the history behind it, the indefinable essence, the magic of knowing what to bottle and when. He tried to imagine what she'd make of it, how her creative mind would go through its own distilling process, taking the rather technical and not particularly seductive information and blending it with the history, the importance of what the Chisholm experience lent to the process, to the area, and blend it into a provocative on-line elixir intended to give Glenbuie whisky a global audience.

Although, to be honest, he spent more time imagining watching her, gauging her reaction to this vital part of himself, wondering what she'd think of it all. He'd been so distracted by it, in fact, that his stillman had been forced twice to ask him to come check one of the hydrometers. In the end, he'd extended the invitation for her to come by tonight, telling himself that until he did that and figured out this next step with her, he'd be useless.

Now that she was here, showing her around the distillery was the last way he wanted to spend the rest of the evening . . . and night. And to think he'd always prided himself on his patience. If Brodie could only see him now, antsy like a schoolboy readying himself for his first dance, he'd have a fine laugh indeed.

"This way," he blurted out, perhaps a bit more gruffly than intended, a wee bit embarrassed at realizing he'd been standing there like a dullwit, silently contemplating her for too long a moment. "To really understand the process, we should start outside. I wanted to take you out and show you the burn—pure spring water is a crucial part of distilling, and the water used matters in the end result. We've been distilling with water from that spring and brook for over two hundred years, long before this was a law-abiding enterprise. But it's too dark, so perhaps another time." He was essentially babbling. He never babbled.

"Another time," she agreed, and he could have sworn he heard an amused tone in her voice.

He opened the door at the end of the hall and took her elbow, guiding her around a corner, then through a large set of double doors. "It starts with barley. We malt our own." He glanced down at her, but quickly looked away. If he had

any hope of keeping even a semblance of continuity and co-
herence, he had to keep his eyes, and hands—he realized he
was gripping her elbow now and let it go—off of her. "Malted
barley is barley that has been soaked in water—"

"From the burn, I take it."

There was that amused tone again. He slowed a step. "Aye.
We soak it until the germination stage, then dry it slowly. The
starch in the barley turns to sugar, which is the first stage of
turning it to alcohol." He entered a large room and turned
on the overhead lights. "Here we grind the barley into grist,
then mix again with water. Our mashman—"

"Mashman?"

"Aye. He rules this particular domain. The temperature
must be carefully controlled. The grist is put in the mash
tun—" He gestured to the large vats lining the room. "And
the end result is called worts."

"Worts." She looked up at him. "I really should be taking
notes. There isn't going to be a quiz on this later, is there?"

Her smile eased a lot of the surprising tension and nerves
he felt, but jacked up a few other internal reactions. "It's a lot
to take in, I know. But not to worry—we can go over all this
again."

"Tonight?"

She held his gaze intently. But before he could decide what,
if anything, to do about it, she slipped from his side and
walked over to one of the vats. "How long does the whole
process take? From here to the bottle? I know it ages from
that point, but—"

"Actually, it ages in huge oak casks. The kind of oak used
is very important as it affects the final taste as well. We make
our own casks."

Her eyes widened. "Impressive. Actually, all of this is impressive, and I know we've barely begun." She crossed the
room toward him. "So tell me more about how it all began.
You said something about using water from the burn even
before it was a legal operation?"

He nodded. "Initially, two centuries past, there were over a dozen stills in this general area, all tucked away between burn and glen, amongst the rocks and such. And all run illicitly, as there was no way to pay the heavy taxes levied by the government. Young ladies from the village used to come up to the hills here and hide tin pots of whisky beneath their skirts and spirit them back into town."

Daisy laughed at that. "I've long agreed that ingenuity is the mother of invention."

"Aye, that it is." He found himself smiling as well. "Early in the nineteenth century, the heavy duties were lifted and Glenbuie obtained legal license to distill, as did a few others. However, ours was the only one that survived to become a legitimate concern. I'd like to believe it's because we've always strived to maintain the original methods, as much as one can, to maintain the quality even as we increased the quantity. We guard quite fiercely the specifics of our processes, not that there are any left in this area that care. We're quite on the outskirts of the more popular and larger concerns and definitely out of the tourist loop, as I've said. But we've remained a family-held business and I've no plans to change that fact in order to improve our bottom line. Finney and all the rest of my ancestors would collectively roll in their graves, right before leaving them to come haunt me."

She had gone off to stroll the length of the room, walking along the row of mash tuns, but grinned at that last remark as she wound her way back to him now. "I know this is everything to you, and I think it's all fascinating. Romantic, even, in some ways."

He gave her a look of disbelief, but she held up her hands. "I'm being quite sincere. I know the process itself is technical and dry, but there is a lot of the process that can't be defined or specifically spelled out. There is a magic in that."

"I agree. I suppose I was just a bit surprised that you see that, too."

"You talk of the burn and the land being part of all this,

land that's been in your family's hands for hundreds of years. Do you realize how few people can really fathom such a thing? Around here, perhaps, but think bigger, broaden your horizons. Or let me. If I can get the process detailed in layman's terms, along with the historical background of how it all began, and I'll need photos of all of it, including whatever you might have from the past. Also, pictures of the building now, the surrounding land, all so picturesque and beautiful, the village, too, as the distillery plays such a big part in its success, I—well, my mind is already spinning with the things I can do with this."

His mind was spinning, too. And it had absolutely nothing to do with something as banal as an Internet Web site. Her eyes were shining and her speech had picked up pace, along with the animated hand gestures and body language. She captivated and commanded his full attention.

"What?" she asked, a bemused smile curving her lips as she noticed he was staring. "Am I sounding like a hopeless optimist here? Because I am very much one in this case. It's a slam dunk, Reese, trust me. I know these things."

He wasn't quite certain what a slam dunk was, but assumed it was a good thing. "I was just thinking that you have as much natural enthusiasm for your job as I do mine. I find that . . . intoxicating."

She flushed a little, but her smile widened. "Good. Then maybe you're beginning to trust my judgment a little." Their gazes caught, and held a little longer. Then she cleared her throat and made a vague gesture to the room behind her. "So, what is the next step? The casks?"

He shook his head, but made no move to continue the tour. "That stage comes later. Much later." He, on the other hand, wanted to come a great deal sooner. Bloody hell, but starting this up with her tonight of all nights, after the afternoon they'd shared, had been a daft idea.

It was important to build the right foundation, handle these new feelings with care, and not to go blundering in, all rampaging libido and lustful urges. Perhaps he should have given himself a wee bit longer to cool off.

He should have headed home hours ago, taken a long shower—or a quick dip in the icy cold burn—and crawled into bed with some ponderous historical treatise or other. Anything to get his mind off of Daisy MacDonnell for a long enough stretch that his rampaging . . . well, rampaging lots of things . . . calmed down.

But he hadn't gone home, had he? He'd invited her here instead. So now not only had she invaded his thoughts, she'd invaded his personal space as well. The space most important to him, anyway. He'd never be rid of her now—she'd linger on in his thoughts ad infinitum. He'd picture her smiling face, hear her laughter echoing through the cavernous room, for some time to come, wouldn't he now?

"Lead on," she said brightly.

Eyes dancing, mouth curved ever deliciously so . . . he didn't want to be rid of her. In fact, he found himself craving quite the opposite.

"Is something the matter?"

"Loaded question, that," he said, the words barely more than a murmur.

She moved closer, so she could look up into his eyes. "I know this is a personal part of you and it means a lot to me that you're sharing it with me. I'm just having a hard time switching off the other part." She grinned. "Big shock, I know. But don't think I don't appreciate it on both levels—I do. I won't burden you with the dozens of questions popping about in my head, honest. I'll let you lead and just absorb as much as I can, but I'll want to come back when I can spend more time, maybe talk to the people who work here, get a few testimonials, maybe from the locals, too, and—" She cut herself off and let out a self-deprecating laugh. "I'm stopping, right now. Promise." She made a gesture as if she was zipping her lips. Which made his body twitch hard with the need to taste them again.

She was so animated, so certain of herself. Of him. He grinned.

"Wow," she told him. "You should do that more often."

He frowned. "Do what?"

"Grin. Flash those white teeth. It's . . ." She merely blew out a breath and shook her head. "*Lethal* is the word that comes to mind."

"I smile. Don't I?"

She gave him a rather pitying look. "You're quite serious, actually. But it's part of your edge." When he continued to frown, she bumped his elbow with hers. "Come on now, I didn't mean to make you self-conscious about it. You smile, yes. But that grin . . ." She shook her hand as if to say "shew." Then she reached up and pushed at the corners of his mouth with her fingertips. "It's no' so hard now, is it?" she said.

His lips twitched.

"See?" she said, in obvious delight.

He impulsively captured her fingers before she could pull her hands away. "You've a horrible Scots accent, you know."

"Have I no'?" she said, proving his point, then laughing at herself.

"I used to be better at that," he said.

"Well, yours might be a bit more on the proper side, but—"

"There's that word again." He shook his head. "I've no doubt you're right. But that's no' what I meant. I meant laughing at myself. You're right—somewhere along the way I've allowed myself to become far too serious a man."

"Maybe you've had to be. I can't claim to understand what it would be like to have the burden of my entire ancestry on my shoulders. I've only had to handle my own, and I didn't do so well. Brodie has told me some of what you all face with your property and the family holdings." She shook her head a little. "So I shouldn't tease you like that, but that's all it was, you know. Teasing." She smiled a little, even as he held her fingers still in his grasp. "Something about you provokes me."

He smiled then, and lifted her fingers to his lips. "You're like some kind of russet-haired pied piper, you know. You even have me believing in this modern virtual world. And I don't care a bloody whit about it."

Stung slightly, she pulled back.

"No," he said instantly, tightening his grip, pulling her closer. "I didn't mean it like that." He hated that he'd dampened even a flicker of the excitement that lit up her face. "I meant that if you can make even a doubter like me think that the arduous process of distilling malted barley into whisky can be made to sound like some kind of magical and fascinating subject to anyone other than a Chisholm, so that someone would willingly spend their free time reading about it, then I have no doubts of your ability to convince these supposed flocks of Internet wanderers as well."

She stilled, even as the energy emanating from her very being seemed to crackle in the air between them. "So, you're saying you'll let me do it then?"

He nodded. "Aye." His hands were already on her, having tugged her close by the elbows. "I'll allow you your access. You can hound my mashman and badger my still manager with your eager questions." He was certain they'd find her intrusion into their busy schedule as charming and undeniably appealing as he did. And if they didn't, well, they could answer to him.

"Oh, Reese." She flung her arms around his neck and hugged him. "Thank you. For trusting me."

He wrapped her in his arms, and couldn't recall a moment in his life when he'd felt so . . . weightless. An odd word, but it was the one that floated through his mind. As if the worries of the world were lifted and all was right and in balance, at least for that space in time when she was beaming at him as she was now.

"You won't regret it," she vowed. "I promise you that. We can sign a contingency contract based on traffic and hits-per-month, then—"

He silenced her excited chatter with a kiss. It was well beyond him then to stop. She'd have to be the one to tell him he'd crossed a boundary, that she wanted their liaison to be a professional one only. Because he'd discovered in the past fortnight, and most definitely in the span of the last hour, that he wanted far, far more where Daisy was concerned.

And though he'd certainly honor her wishes were that the case, he discovered something else about himself in that moment. All the parts of him that he'd invested in making Glenbuie whisky continue to be a success, for both family and the villagers, the drive he felt, the determination to succeed ... was now being channeled in a wider direction, with some of it circling back to him, to his needs, his wants. He wanted Daisy MacDonnell. And by damned he was going to fight for this with the same energy he'd bring to bear on anything else that mattered to him And she already mattered.

He wove his fingers through that glorious russet waterfall of hair and shifted her mouth so he could plunder it fully. She accepted him, allowed him in, with a satisfied groan that only served to wind him up further. "Daisy," he murmured against her lips, breathing heavily as he ran the edges of his teeth along her jaw. The very taste of her made him voracious with hunger and need.

"I know," she said, her own breath coming in short gasps as her fingertips dug into his shoulders. "It's crazy. But I don't want to stop this. It's different here. My whole life is different here. For the first time I feel like I do have a life. And—well, I want you in it. And not just as a client. I'd—I'd even give up the whole Web site idea if—"

"Nonsense. And maybe you need to think about this a different way. Things *are* different here. We can make time if we want to. But honestly? I dinnae want only one part of you. Who you are in here—" He tapped her forehead. "Your brilliant business mind, all that creativity, spark, and boundless energy for doing what you love, is also a part of who you are here." He pressed two fingers over her heart. "I wouldn't cheat myself by only wanting half of you."

Her eyes went a little glassy at that. "I never thought of it that way. I would have to say the same. About you. I can't imagine only knowing you away from this. It's the heart and soul of you."

He grabbed her fingers and kissed their tips. "I think perhaps I have a wee bit of room left over there."

She grinned again, and sniffled. "Yeah? Well, it's quite possible I might as well." She turned his hands and kissed his knuckles. "Maybe this balancing life stuff isn't so hard as I've been making it out to be. Maybe I was trying too hard to separate it so completely. I don't guess that would have really worked out." She grinned. "I'm a complete package. All or nothing."

"I want all." Then he swung her up in his arms, eliciting a squeal from her.

"We'll just have to make time away from our business parts."

He grinned. "Not a problem. I have a real thing for your personal parts, if ye havena' noticed."

She giggled. "Well . . . it's closing in on midnight, and here we stand, doing business. We're a hopeless lot, the two of us, aren't we?"

"At the time, it seemed the only way I could have any part of you, so I selfishly took it. And I'd be lying if I said I didn't have you here after hours because it was the only way I might get you all to myself again, even as nothing more than a business associate." He was already striding from the room, kicking at the double doors and swinging them both through them.

"I rather hope you don't carry your other associates around like this. Or kiss them breathless, either."

That made him smile. "I make you breathless?"

She laughed. "I know, the way I chatter on, that's quite a

feat." She tightened her hold on his neck. "But yes," she said more quietly, "yes, you do. And it's bloomin' wonderful."

She toyed with the edges of his hair, sending increasing ripples of arousal through him that threatened to undermine his ability to get her out of this building and off to where he wanted her most. In his bed. Beneath him.

"I could walk, you know."

"I rather like having you in my arms," he said, moving down the short hall now to the employees' exit. "I feel as if I've waited centuries to get my hands on you, and I'd like as no' to keep them on you as much as possible, if you dinnae mind."

She laid her head on his shoulder, pressed her lips to the side of his neck, right on his pulse. "No," she murmured, kissing him again. "I dinnae mind, a'tall."

He stopped just short of the exit and turned her toward the wall, pinning her there so he could lift one hand to her head and tip her chin up to his. "Come here," he told her. "I can't wait another second to—" And he didn't. His mouth found hers as if it had been its destination for years. She opened for him and he slid his tongue into her mouth, dueled with hers, then let her pull it deep and tight. As she pulled and suckled him, his hips moved of their own volition, pressing against her, the rigid length of his cock straining to be released, to be taken into her mouth just as his tongue had been, to be suckled just like that, in confines so tight and wet and—he growled and let her slip from his arms.

He shifted her back to the wall and pulled her thighs over his hips, pinning her there so he could bury himself, as much as he could, between her thighs. Now she was moaning, squeezing him tightly between her legs, driving him bloody starkers.

"Hold on," he commanded, wrapping his arms around her and swinging her from the wall. He pushed open the door to the back lot, not bothering with the lights or the locks.

"Where are you taking me?" She kissed the side of his

neck, then teased him with a light bite along his pulse, then another on the lobe of his ear.

"Not much farther than this parking lot if you dinnae stop what you're doin'."

She laughed against his fevered skin. "You mean this?" She nibbled the lobe of his ear, then ran her tongue along the outer rim. Then she dropped kisses all along his jaw, interspersed with more teasing nibbles. "Or this."

"You enjoy teasing, do ye?"

"Oh, aye, that I do," she informed him, her accent just as lousy as ever, and driving him absolutely mad with it anyway.

"Well," he said, crossing the lot and climbing the hill just beyond it. "So do I. We'll see how well ye like it then, when it's my turn."

The short hill was rocky but there was a narrow path, one he'd walked so many times since he was a wee lad, he knew it even in the dark. The moon was close to full and cast the glen beyond in an unearthly glow. He could hear the babbling sounds now, of burn running over rocks. Ahead, on the other side of the stream, was the dark shadow of a stone croft.

"What is this?" she asked, then squealed as he waded through calf-deep water without concern for clothing or leather shoes. "Reese!"

"Now ye've seen the burn."

She laughed and tightened her hold as she tried to turn and look over her shoulder to where they were headed. "Where—"

"This was the original legitimate distillery. Or a part of it, anyway, before my ancestors began building down below. We renovated it some time back, preserving it, thinking to add it to the tour, but I ended up renovating it again."

"Into what, an office?"

He stepped up on the small porch and slipped a key from the frame over the door. "No," he told her, pushing open the door. "As my home."

Chapter 8

Reese slapped his hand on the wall as he kicked the door shut and a small lamp illuminated the room, filling it with a warm glow. Daisy had little time to notice the interior of Reese's home, other than it was small, cozy. The main floor was one big room, much like a cabin, with a living area that opened up to a kitchen and dining area on the opposite side. A big potbellied stove was situated in the center of the room, where it could heat both living area and dining area. Beyond that, she saw little as he carried her straight to the spiral, wrought iron stairs that ascended to the upper floor at the far side of the room. "Hang on," he told her.

"Reese, your shoes. Your pants. You're tracking water—"

He silenced her with his mouth on hers, and she willingly sank into him. For a man who claimed to be all work and no play, he sure knew how to kiss. There was nothing tentative about the way he took her mouth, exploring, teasing, taking. He dueled with her tongue, coaxing her into his mouth, before sliding into hers. He groaned when she sucked on him, which made her squirm in his arms. Carnal images flashed through her mind, of exactly what she'd do as soon as she got him upstairs and naked. She wanted to make him growl, she wanted to make him buck his hips helplessly against her, she wanted to make him lose control.

And then she wanted to let him do the same to her.

The way things were going, she might not make it out of her clothes before climaxing. Wrapped around him as she was, she knew his body was lean and hard. Some parts more than others, she thought, tightening her thighs around him, pulling the rock-hard length of him closer to where she needed it most. She felt constricted by her clothes; so stuffy and hot, she wanted to claw them off. As he moved his attentions to the side of her neck, running his tongue along her pulse point, nipping her earlobe, then kissing her again, she wanted nothing more than to strip down and feel his mouth on every inch of her body, feel his skin brushing hers, tangle herself up with every lean, hard inch of him.

They topped the stairs and he flipped on another small lamp, but she didn't look around—her gaze was solely on him. She'd never seen anyone look at her the way he was right at that moment. Need, desire, want, all so focused, so intent. She shivered in anticipation, so very glad she'd reached for what she wanted. If her goal was to find a life outside of work . . . well, she doubted she'd be thinking of anything work-related for the duration of the time he kept looking at her the way he was right then.

"You'll have the grand tour later if ye want," he said, his voice roughened with need. "But no' now. I can barely take my hands from you long enough to gi' you yer balance." His accent was more pronounced now, his voice gruffer and not remotely polite or stuffy. The intensity only served to heighten her need further.

He shifted so she could unhook her legs and slide down his body, making them both groan a little. She wasn't sure her legs would support her at this point, she was so close.

He settled his hands on her hips, keeping her body up against his as she steadied herself. She reached for his face, to pull his mouth back down to hers, but he moved back, just slightly. "Yer sure o' this, Daisy? Sure of me?"

"I'd have stopped you long before now if I weren't. I know exactly what I'm doing."

"Ye need to know—you're no passing fancy for me. I dinnae believe in just carrying on for the sake of it. I should be courting you properly, doing this right, makin' ye see we can find a balance first, and—you're around me for five minutes and I can't think straight. I'm no' handling this properly and I shouldn't chance ruining anything by rushing—"

She grinned. "Reese."

"What?"

"Get me naked and make love to me properly. We'll balance the rest later."

"Dear God in heaven," he breathed, sounding so relieved. "I thought you'd never ask."

He'd been so confident, so certain, so assured in the way he'd literally carried her to his bed. She hadn't realized he'd been nervous or worried. That he had been, that he'd stopped long enough to ask her, when it was clear she wouldn't have stopped him from doing pretty much anything he wanted to her, made her heart swell, and tip even further in his direction. She stroked the side of his face, then curved a hand around the back of his head and tugged him down to her, while simultaneously unbuttoning his shirt with the other. "I'm asking," she said softly. "Take me to bed, Reese Chisholm."

"Och, Daisy, the things you do to a man." He pulled her into his arms, trapping her hand between them.

"The only man I want doing anything to me, is you."

He took her mouth again, only this time there was a fierceness to it, a visceral edge, as if he were claiming her instead of merely joining with her. His hands slid down her back, then up beneath her shirt as he took the kiss deeper.

She moaned at the feel of his hands against the bare skin at the small of her back. She pressed against him, wishing she was still straddling him as her hips were too far below his to match need for need. She yanked his shirt from his waistband, but he grabbed her wrist. She looked up him, surprised to find him grinning. He really should do that more often. It did things to her. Really amazing things.

"You said I should get you naked. I dinnae recall there bein' any talk of myself."

She smiled back. "I assumed that was understood."

He spun her around and laid her back across his bed. It felt like she'd fallen through a cloud. "Oh," she said in surprise, then followed that with a deep sigh of appreciation. "Wow."

One side of his mouth curved in a wicked grin. "And I'm no' even undressed yet."

She laughed, really enjoying this side of him. She hadn't thought she could feel any needier. She'd never been more wrong. "I was talking about your bed. It's the softest thing I've ever felt."

"I can but hope that's the only thing you find soft this eve."

She pushed up on her elbows and very deliberately let her gaze run over him from head to toe, and, with lingering appreciation, back up again. "I don't believe that will be a problem."

His eyes flared and she squirmed on the bed. She pressed her thighs together against the growing ache between them. He pushed his knee between her legs, parting them as he bent low over her, toying with the buttons on the front of her shirt. "I want tae see all of you, Daisy." He plucked her buttons open one at a time, pushing her shirt apart as he did.

Her hips bucked a little and her nipples were hard as rocks. Between the rough accent and the look in his eyes, she was all but quivering at this point. She wanted to grab him, any part of him, and put it where she needed him most. She wanted his mouth on her breasts and the rigidly hard length of him buried deep inside her. She groaned at the very idea, as he continued his excruciatingly slow removal of her clothes.

He released the front catch of her bra and bared her to him. The cooler air brushed over her hot skin, making her nipples tighten further. Her back arched of its own volition as her body tried to get closer to his touch.

"You're lovelier than I even imagined." He glanced from his approval of her bare breasts, to her eyes. "And I've imagined you plenty these past weeks." He pushed the flimsy bra and shirt aside, completely baring her to him.

She was trembling for his touch, so highly aroused the very air on her skin made her moan. "Reese," she pleaded.

"Oh, aye," he assured her. "A man could get drunk just on the vision of you." Slowly, so slowly she thought her heart might burst from her chest, so fast it was racing, he lowered his mouth to her. With the tip of his tongue, he circled her nipple, jerking a cry of pleasure from her. She reached for his head, wanting more than that teasing tip, but he swiftly pinned her wrists over her head with his hand. "Allow me this pleasure." He glanced up, his eyes almost completely black in the low light. "We've all night, after all."

She moaned and let her head drop back on the bed. Dear God, she wasn't sure she'd survive this slow, intoxicating torture. She was used to calling the shots. Men claimed they liked to be in control, but she'd never met one yet that minded a woman taking over and giving all her attention to his pleasure. In her past life, she'd always been pressed for time and found it saved a lot if she just took matters into her hands, as it were.

But now . . . here . . . tonight . . . She squirmed beneath his continued attentions. Relaxing was near to impossible in this situation. She wanted to urge him to go faster, to get on with it . . . and then he took her nipple between his lips and slowly suckled her, almost making her climax right then and there.

His groan of pleasure, almost a growl, as he continued his exploration, kept her from dragging her hands free and rolling him to his back. If she straddled him, she seriously doubted he'd stop her. She could quite clearly see the effect she was having on him, and—"Oh," she gasped, when he pulled on her nipple, then let it pop free. Only to make her gasp again when he did the same to the other. God, but that felt . . . "Ohh," she groaned, her hips moving again without her consent. Her arms went limp, her wrists his to control. "Don't stop that," she pleaded, when he shifted his mouth away. "That's—" It was her turn to growl when he again suckled her nipple. She'd never felt such a direct connection between them and the intensely pleasurable ache between her legs.

Assured she would keep her hands above her head, he slid his hand down her arm, then slipped it behind her back, arching her to him, so he could pull her bra and shirt completely off. He kept his tongue—and teeth—busy on the budded tips of her breasts, until she thought she'd go mad if he didn't pay attention to her—"Yes," she moaned as he laid her back against the bed, and let his tongue draw a lazy trail down the center of her torso.

She'd spent so much time imagining doing this very thing to him, she'd neglected to imagine what it would be like to be on the receiving end. It was doubtful she could have done it justice, anyway.

He toyed with her nipples, rolling their damp tips between his fingers, then shifted to unbuttoning and unzipping her pants. With little urging, she lifted her hips so he could slide them off. Her sandals fell to the floor along with them. All she had on was string bikini panties of pale yellow cotton, which he left on. Much to her initial dismay.

Soon, however, she found she didn't mind so much.

He pulled her toward him so he could kneel at the edge of the bed between her thighs. Her arms extended over her head and lay there, limply, as she focused exclusively on the delicious sensations he was creating by running his tongue along the elastic edge of her panties. Normally, by now she'd be dragging clothes off of her partner, in somewhat of a frenzy to get on with it. Said partner rarely ever minded, of course. There was always more work to be done, deadlines to be met. Pleasure was something scheduled in between client meetings and sales conferences.

At the moment, she couldn't imagine there being anything more important in her entire world than what Reese Chisholm was presently doing between her thighs. In fact, the only urgent thing about this moment was the anticipation of what else was to come. Mainly her, and soon, if— "Oh, please, you have the rest of my life to stop doing that."

She felt, rather than heard, him chuckle. He teased his tongue down the center of the cotton panel, then pulled it between his lips, soaking it further, teasing her through the wet fabric until she wanted to claw them off and let him finally, blessedly, get to where she needed him to be. In fact, she was lifting her hands to do just that when he pressed her hips to the bed. "Let me play," he said, glancing up at her. "I've waited too long for this. I dinnae want to rush."

Who could turn down such a sincere request? Not her, as it turned out. She let her arms go limp once again, then a split-second later arched her back sharply as she gasped when he pushed his tongue against her.

He slid his hands down her hips, and, with excruciating slowness, peeled the straps of her bikinis down with him. He kept his tongue pressed firmly against her as he slowly, oh so slowly, peeled back the damp cotton. As the night air brushed her damp curls, she bucked against his mouth, cursing the thin layer of cotton that still separated that devil of a tongue from her—"Yes!" She thrust her hips against him as he finally pulled her panties down enough to let his tongue slip up and over her, then plunge deeply inside of her.

She bucked almost violently as she climaxed instantly. Again and again, the waves of it rushed over and through her. She was reaching for him again, wanting him to slide up and push the best part of him into the now throbbing, wet, and waiting part of her. Once again, he stilled her by pinning her hips to the bed.

"Surely there is another," he murmured against the damp skin of her inner thigh.

"Another?" she asked weakly. She was still feeling the twitchy aftershocks of the first one. Usually she'd be well on her way to milking the one and only orgasm she was lucky to get for all it was worth, by taking her partner for his final, climactic ride. Meetings were scheduled. No time to tarry and linger. But she wasn't in D.C. anymore.

She was in the Scottish highlands. In a small stone croft. With a man who wasn't in the least bit of a hurry. Here it was, closing in on midnight. And there were no meetings scheduled, no early morning conference calls to take, no clients to pick up from the red-eye at the airport. In fact, the only thing she had on her agenda for the rest of the night, and quite possibly the rest of her life . . . was—thank you, God—more of this.

"Another," she repeated, then smiled like the Cheshire cat as she stretched and released a deep sigh. For the first time in her adult life, she felt well and truly at peace. "Why, I believe I will."

Another chuckle tickled her skin, making her twitch. He teased her with the tip of his tongue, softly, gently, building her up again. He drew fingertips across her stomach and up to her now neglected nipples. Toying with them again made her squirm. What he was doing with his tongue only heightened the sensation. He took her up slowly this time, let her roll her hips, find her rhythm with him. And just when she was close, he slowly slid his finger inside of her.

She gasped, and quite deliciously peaked all over again, squeezing hard against his finger, pushing up against his tongue, squirming against the way he flicked the tips of his fingers across one nipple, then the other. The waves rolled, and rolled, and she thought they'd never stop. She was still riding the crest when she felt him grip her hips and slide her back up the bed.

She hadn't realized her eyes were shut, her neck arched, until she felt his bare skin brush hers as he moved his body up between her legs. Her eyelids, so heavy now, opened to discover the absolutely brilliant sight of a very naked, very aroused Reese Chisholm. She was so drowsy, so sated, her body so sunken into the puffy down bed, she had to work to form words. "My turn," she mumbled.

He smiled. "You'll have your go at me, I assure you. But I'm not quite done with my turn yet."

"I wanted to undress you."

"The very next time I have clothes on, you have my full permission to take them off." He settled his weight between her legs and she could feel him so hard, the damp tip of him ready for her. "But I confess I don't plan on donning any for the foreseeable future."

"Brilliant." She groaned, bucking her hips against him, trying to get him to push every one of those brilliantly hard inches inside of her. "Good show."

He nuzzled the side of her neck, bit her ear, and the brush of the hair on his chest teasing her so sensitive nipples made her back arch again.

"Your accent needs a lo' of work, luv," he told her.

"So teach me."

"Come here," he said softly, but with a quiet urgency that had her turning her head and opening her eyes once again.

"What?" she said, his lips so close to hers now that when she spoke, they brushed each other.

"I just wanted to be looking into your eyes, the first time I did this." And with that, he gripped her hips, lifted her slightly, and drove fully inside of her.

His growl was low, long, and intensely gratifying. He stayed deep, pressing his forehead against her hair, his breathing uneven. "Bloody hell. I'm no' going tae last long, I'm afraid."

She wrapped her legs around his hips and pulled him even deeper. "So?" And she laughed as she began to move beneath him. "You in a hurry to go somewhere?"

He grunted, tried to hold back, but a split-second later he gave in and began to match her, thrust for thrust. "Nay. I'll be . . . right here . . . until ye kick me off."

Then he buried his face in the curve of her neck and took her with him until they were both panting and grunting, their bodies slapping together as they both went about staking their claim on one another. And that was exactly how she felt. Both taker and taken.

"Daisy," he panted, nudging her face back to his. They were both glistening with sweat, and he felt so incredibly good inside of her.

"Right here," she told him, staring into his eyes. And she realized right then that if she'd been looking for home, she'd just found it.

"Aye. And that's where ye'll stay, if I have a say in the matter." Then, as his back arched, he pulled her legs up higher and buried himself as deeply as he could, shuddering through a climax that rocked them both.

He gathered himself up and rolled from her, taking her with him, nestling her against his chest as they both stared blindly at the walls and fought to catch their breath. He toyed with the long strands of her hair, she stroked the crinkly soft hair on his chest. "What say tomorrow we take a grander tour," he said at length, his voice still a bit rough.

Fighting a yawn—when had she ever felt so replete?—she smiled and propped her chin on his chest. "What sort of grand tour? And would this be an after-work excursion? Because I have this new client, and I hear he's quite demanding."

He surprised a squeal out of her, rolling her swiftly to her back and pinning her amidst the pile of bedding. "Aye, that he is." He wiggled his eyebrows and it was so completely out of character with the man she had so swiftly fallen for, that she burst out laughing. He immediately adopted a mock wounded look. "A bloke could get a complex now."

She quickly reached up to stroke his face, knowing quite well that the smile now curving her lips was decidedly wicked. "The only complex you're going to have is figuring out how to juggle my demands with yours."

His eyes widened. So did his smile. "Really, now. You don't say."

"I do say." She slipped her hands down his back and over his buttocks. Finely formed as they were, she lingered there a bit.

He pinned her wandering hands back over her head. "About this tour . . ."

"I thought I was already taking one. And quite grand it 'twas."

"Yer accent wavers between Scot and a nice Irish brogue."

"I guess you'll have to work on me. It. I meant it."

"Sure ye did." He grinned, nipped at her bottom lip, then took it in his mouth, before slowly turning it into a long, savoring kiss.

She sighed deeply when he lifted his head, and stretched languorously beneath him. "I could get used to that." She bumped her hips up. "And this."

"Good. I don't fancy lettin' ye go anytime soon."

Any other time in her life, she'd have already been in the bathroom, washing up, gathering clothes, checking her Black-Berry. At the moment, she couldn't fathom why anybody would want to do something as mundane as think about their job. Ever. "So . . . about this tour . . ."

He rolled to his back and took her with him so she sprawled across his chest. "I was thinking perhaps we'd play hooky." When she raised her eyebrows, he mimicked her. "Aye, I know. Scandalous behavior for two such fine, upstanding citizens."

She pretended to ponder the idea. "Do you think the village will recover?"

"I'm fairly certain they will get on for a few hours without loading up on the latest stationery, and the whisky will age perfectly well without my constant attention." He reached up and kissed the tip of her nose. "At least for the length of a day, anyway."

"Oh, we're such rebels, aren't we?"

"It's a start," he countered.

She dipped down and kissed him. Hard. "And a damn fine one it 'tis, too. Where are we going?"

"I thought I'd take you out, show you the rest of the Chisholm property. Including the crumbling old manse that is our family estate. My oldest brother, Dylan, is in the midst of turning a portion of it into a bed and breakfast setup. A way to help defray the ever-mounting costs of maintaining the poor auld thing. I willnae vouch for his disposition. A cheery sort, he isn't. But he's had his share of troubles, so we leave him to it. I'd like to take you around anyway if you're game."

"Brodie has mentioned him, and the fledgling business. Of course I'll go."

Reese smiled. "Och, I can see the light dawning in your eyes already. I should have started with my youngest brother, Tristan, first, then. An artist's heart he has, but he's our farm manager by trade. He'll have nothing of interest for your businesswoman's soul, and you'll be safely mine."

"You didn't exactly make Dylan out to be a catch, you know."

"Trust me," Reese told her, "he's got that wounded warrior spirit that women love to take on, thinking they'll be the one to mend his broken heart."

"Broken-hearted? Is that why he's 'not a cheery sort', as you say?"

"See? Your heart is already tilting. What is it about—"

"We're nurturers by nature, Reese. We want to fix it and make it better."

"Well, you'll have your hands full enough fixing me," he said, rather gruffly, which made her laugh; then, to add insult to injury, she ruffled his hair and kissed him on the tip of his nose. "And as I was saying, if you're considering coming to him with a business proposal," he added, "well, if you think I was a hard sell when it came to convincing me of the lure of Internet marketing—"

"You weren't exactly hard." She pressed against him. "Well, except where you needed to be. "But don't worry, I have no intention of selling your brother on the merits of proper marketing and sales." She winked at him. "No' until I get to know him a wee bit better, anyway."

Reese rolled his eyes, but his smile was amused. "I've created a monster, I have."

"Oh no, you've tamed her, to be certain. And if it makes you feel any better, I'll send bottles of Glenbuie to all my friends back home for Christmas."

"Ye drive a hard bargain, lass."

Suddenly reenergized, she moved on top of him so she straddled his hips, making his eyes widen a bit when she pinned his hands to the bed. "We'll see about that."

He tipped his head back, closed his eyes, and let her have her way with him. "See, perfectly balanced we are."

"Aye," she said, leaning down and taking his mouth, before slowly fulfilling her every fantasy—and his, if the way he groaned and moved beneath her was any indication—as she slid down the length of his body, her tongue taking a slightly longer, more lingering path. He lifted his head and watched as she slid her tongue around him, then took him in her mouth and suckled him back to life.

"You have the rest of your life to stop doing that," he said, echoing her earlier claim.

"Deal."

Balanced, indeed.

NIGHT WATCH

Chapter 1

"Aye, aye. I've said I'll be there and I will be. Now let me get back to my sheep, ye auld sod." Tristan Chisholm stared out at the expansive glen, a stunning vista of the greenest grass to be found beneath the heavens, rolling endlessly before him like the most luxurious carpet. Dotted here and there with the burly white wool and black faces of his sturdy flock, taking their afternoon graze while he once again tried—and miserably failed—to capture the essence of the darkening sky with a stubby piece of charcoal and a dog-eared tablet of drawing paper.

The tall outcropping of rock atop the hillock on which he was presently perched was one of only a rare handful of spots on the hundreds of acres of Chisholm grazing land where he could get signal. Figures. He couldn't believe he'd gone to the trouble of climbing all the way up here with the intention of losing himself for a few hours with nothing more than pad and paper to record his thoughts . . . only to have his serenity rudely intruded upon by one of his brothers.

It mattered little that the reason for the call was a joyful one. Far be it from Brodie not to use the rare occasion of a conversation with the youngest Chisholm to point out his failures. Failures according to Brodie, anyway. *Ungrateful, the lot of them,* he thought grouchily. His brother would be lucky if he brought so much as a bottle of wine as an engagement present. Cocky bastard. How a fine young woman like Kat Henderson had ever agreed to latch herself to his miserable hide for all eternity . . . well, if Tristan didn't know better, he'd think she'd been sipping too much ale at Brodie's pub. Lord knows he'd have to be falling down pissed to even consider tying himself to anyone.

"I dinnae need to be scolded like a wet lad," he informed Brodie when his older brother finally took pause for a breath. "I'm perfectly capable of seeing to my own needs, carnal and otherwise, thank you very much. And ye wonder why I prefer the company of my flock."

He rolled his eyes heavenward when Brodie made the obvious joke, but didn't bother to rise to the bait. He was long since used to this treatment.

Sighing wearily, knowing he was more disgusted with himself, really, after another disappointing afternoon of trying to coax his muse to the surface, Tristan listened to Brodie continue his very amusing soliloquy on the state of his youngest brother's love life, or sorry lack thereof. He finally lost patience with both brother and the age of technology that made invading his privacy out here in the wilds as easy as punching in a few numbers into a plastic keypad. He didn't bother to ring off. He merely clicked his mobile phone closed and pocketed it. Handy thing, that little automatic OFF button. Let them call him a social misfit—he was perfectly happy with that moniker if it meant he got to stay out here, far away from the maddening crowds, aka his brothers and the other nosey villagers. If his siblings wanted their brotherly attentions reciprocated, they'd soon learn not to ride him every chance they got.

He stared down at the mess of charcoal streaks masquerading as the distant, late afternoon skyline and shook his head as he flipped the cover back over the pad. He'd thought perhaps returning to the more rustic rudiments of charcoal would free him up a little. Watercolors hadn't done it the week before. Nor pastels the week before that. He refused to even consider a pallet of oils. Autumn was turning the hills into brilliant rainbows of color, second only to the rebirth of spring for inspiring his artistic soul. Through at least half of his twenty-seven years, he had documented each of them in the way that moved him most. No two seasons, no two renderings, had been the same. He took great pleasure in finding something new at the turn of each and every season, each and every year.

For some time now, however, it appeared as if inspiration had finally deserted him. He couldn't even rediscover the old, much less tap into anything resembling fresh and new.

"Jinty!" Tristan whistled for his four-legged companion, then when the border collie pricked her ears and looked in Tristan's direction, he gave her the signal to begin rounding up the sheep. With Jinty barking and yipping as she raced to and fro, Tristan gathered up his things. He stowed them in his pack and began climbing down the back side of the rocky outcropping, before hiking around the base of it, back toward the glen. He was halfway down when he heard the first true grumblings roll across the heavens. It took another twenty minutes to hike the path that led around to the field where Jinty was still collecting strays and to regain a view of the setting sun on the horizon.

The encroaching storm wasn't so distant now. He'd gauged the front to be moving far slower than it was, which was unusual for him, as it was his business to be able to read those kinds of signs. It wasn't much beyond half past three in the afternoon, but this time of year it was full dark by five, and with the storm darkening the skies, that timetable would be accelerated. Apparently he'd been more distracted by the call than he'd realized, even as he admitted it was likely the frustration with his sketches that had caused him to lose track of time. Brooding again, his brother Reese would tell him. But Tristan didn't brood. Thinking, pondering, wondering, those things he did. Entirely different.

He whistled again and gave a sharp hand signal. Jinty shot

toward him, raced around his legs, then took off to her post on the far side of the field. Picking up the pace, he and the collie moved as a team, herding the small cluster of sheep he'd come up here to round together so he could push them back down the valley where they could rejoin the main thrust of the herd.

Lightning strikes streaked east and west through the rapidly darkening sky, but Tristan kept his steady pace. He'd get them back to the front fields before the worst of it hit, but he'd likely take a bit of the brunt of it himself before he saw the inside of his own four walls this evening. Ah well, it wouldn't be the first time. And there was nothing in his backpack worth worrying about preserving, that was for sure. A little rain might even improve his lines a little.

By the time he and Jinty had shuffled the stragglers through the narrow pass into the lower valley, it was dusk bordering on dark, and thin drops of rain began to spit from the skies above. Stacked stone fences sectioned off the valley floor like a giant game of tic-tac-toe. He shoved the gate closed behind him as he entered the first of several walled fields spread out ahead of him, each a good twenty acres square, content to leave the gang here for the night. He'd get them the rest of the way tomorrow.

"Come, Jint!" He slapped his thigh, then reached down to give her a good scratch as she fell happily into step beside him. The rain began to pick up pace, and so he did, too, jogging for the far wall, with Jint easily pacing him, racing to and fro, barking for the sheer joy of being alive. *Och, to have such a carefree heart*, he thought. The lightning strikes came closer together and hit closer to home. Thunder vibrated the very air around them. "Come on, girl. Let's get home."

Home was a large stone croft with a soaring, traditional thatched roof that required constant maintenance, but which Tristan had resisted replacing with more current textiles. He didn't mind the extra work. He'd often thought he'd been born in the wrong century anyway, a tenet also held by his brothers. Not that he didn't appreciate some of the more modern amenities, such as indoor plumbing and running water, but he liked the look of the place, knowing that those who had come before him had come home to much the same stacked stone gate, the same hand-laid stone walls, and the same thatched roof. All built by Chisholm hands.

It had been added onto over the past two centuries, as various managers and their families had lived there, and current amenities had been installed. It was a rambling, one-story affair, all told. The whole of the place currently housed three bedrooms, two full bathrooms and a half of another, an open living area complete with a large, peat-burning stove for heating, and an expansive kitchen with a rustic oak table suitable for at least eight people with room to spare, plus an outdoor oven pit as well. Tristan had created half of a second floor by constructing a loft space, which he used as his art room. He'd put in a skylight and a large inset window at the peak of the roof for light. Not that the loft had seen much use of late.

It was all far more than Tristan needed, but it was the manager's croft for a reason. Location and access. Tucked up against the rocky hills that framed the eastern boundary of the Chisholm grazing property, it looked out over the lower valley, which was marked with fenced-off sections of land, some dotted with smaller crofts that were leased out to farmers and other flock owners. It was Tristan's job not only to maintain the Chisholm flocks, but also to manage the leased properties and the concerns of all the tenants.

The far boundary of the lower valley was marked by the loch, which fed a narrow tributary that ran alongside the main road and helped to irrigate the crop fields. A single-track road ran between stream and field, and was the only access to the area from Glenbuie, the local village and home to the Chisholm clan for more than four hundred years.

By the time he and Jint scooted through the final gate and made their sprint across the last field heading home, the setting sun and the storm had joined to render the sky full black; no hint of stars or moon, making it nigh on impossible to see more than a scant yard or two in front of his face. But he knew this ground as he knew his own self and he navigated it easily.

Jinty had an even keener sense of where the best path lay, so he followed her lead, arms up to brace his face against the wind-driven needles of rain. She kept circling back to him, herding him home much the same as she did with the rest of her flock. It was raining hard now and he'd long since become soaked to the bone. As soon as he had Jinty fed, a long, hot shower was next on his list. Lightning strikes continued to light the black sky, and thunder literally shook the ground at his feet.

As he reached the steps leading to the back door and mud room, a loud, shrieking noise pierced the sound of the storm. He paused, but with the thunder and heavy rain, it was impossible to know what he'd actually heard. Typically the only sounds that floated through his valley, other than those created by Mother Nature, were the sheep baaing and dogs barking as they went about their chores. Whatever that had been didn't fall under any of those headings.

When the sound didn't repeat itself, he opened the rear door and shuffled inside, shooing Jinty in before him, then closing it with a heavy rattle behind him as the wind helped drive it shut. He'd go investigate if need be when the rain died down a little. Probably just a tree down and the wind having its way with the wayward limbs. It was amazing the odd echoes of sounds the valley and mountains could create.

The dog gave a good shake as Tristan dropped his pack and grabbed a towel off the stack. "Good work out there," he praised her. She wriggled under his ministrations, loving nothing more than a good towel rub. With another shake when he was done, she bounded from the room and set to prancing in circles in front of the kitchen pantry just beyond.

Tristan chuckled. "I'm coming, just hold up a minute." He

took a second to drag his boots and socks off, then peeled out of his sodden shirt and pants as well, leaving him in cold, wet boxers. "The hell with that," he grumbled, and dragged them off as well. One of the blessings of living out in the midst of nowhere. And he much doubted any of his tenants would be dropping by with a grievance this stormy evening.

Giving his own shoulder-length hair a good rub with a fresh towel, he shook it out much as Jinty had hers, then wrapped the towel around his hips as he padded into the kitchen. "What's on the menu tonight?" he asked her, as he opened the doors to the pantry and looked at the canned meat on the shelves. He dumped some dry kibble in her dish, the mere sound of which made her all but quiver in paroxysms of pleasure, then cranked open a can of corned beef and dumped some of that in as well. She worked hard, so if he spoiled her a little, well, who was to know?

She danced out to the kitchen with him and sat next to her water dish, tail going like a propeller against the hardwood floor. Tristan popped her dish to the floor and gave a dry smile as she dug in with gusto. If only it were so easy to please everyone who depended on him, he thought. "Cans of corned hash for all!" he announced with flair, waving his arm in a beneficent gesture in front of him, as if king to kingdom. Shaking his head at his own folly, he contemplated heating the rest of the can up for himself, then decided a shower sounded like the better option at the moment. Maybe if he felt half human, he'd find the energy to actually cook something up.

He paused by the peat stove and stuffed in a few fuel bricks, feeling a chill in the air that went beyond his damp, mostly naked state. Though warm enough during the day, the late October nights were considerably cooler of late. He wound his way through the living area toward the rear bedrooms. He'd converted the smaller of the two into his personal office—even though there was an outbuilding housing his official one, he liked being able to work here when he could—leaving the larger bedroom with the en suite bathroom for himself. There was another bedroom off the far side of the main house, with a second full bathroom wedged between it and the kitchen, ostensibly for guests. Though, over the years, it had housed only his brothers on the rare occasion that one or the other came out to share a bottle of the family whisky and opted not to head home until morning.

He was halfway through the front room when he noticed oddly angled shafts of red light piercing the rainy night beyond his front windows. Backtracking, he peered through the panes of glass, but the heavy rain made it difficult to see. Then a crack of lightning split through the gloom and he got a momentary flash of the track road leading to his house. And that's when he remembered the screeching noise he'd heard before stepping inside.

The red beams of light belonged to the brake lights of a small car, the rear of which was presently jacked up on the low stone fence that ran alongside the track road, next to the storm gully, which handled the overflow of stream water during heavy rains.

A second flash of lightning showed that those storm waters were rapidly rising. And that the front end of the car was already submerged.

Chapter 2

Well, won't I have the last laugh now?

That was the last thought Bree Sullivan had before she lost control of her car completely. She could see the headlines now:

INTERNATIONALLY FAMOUS AUTHOR SWERVES TO MISS SHEEP, DIES A WATERY DEATH BEFORE DELIVERING NEXT BLOCKBUSTER NOVEL.

Followed, of course, by the one millionth article explaining, in detail, why nothing she might have written could ever have hoped to match the phenomenal, best-selling, record-breaking sales of her first and only novel, *Summer Lake*, anyway.

If only she'd done something clever, like have six more connected books already outlined and ready to go, sales all but guaranteed. But no, the former small-town Missouri librarian hadn't thought ahead to her obvious future as a sudden celebrity. She'd totally failed to foresee that the entire free world would be rushing out to buy her first book, thereby turning her little world completely upside down. And silly her, she hadn't foreseen that she would spend a whirlwind ten months plugging her suddenly hotter-than-DaVinci novel on locations around the globe she'd never dreamed of visiting, while being interviewed by celebrity newscasters she'd formerly only seen on her television set. Where they'd been interviewing actual famous people. Not quiet little Bree Sullivan from Mason, Missouri.

Now, almost eighteen months after *Summer Lake* had first hit the shelves, she could hardly remember the woman she'd been back then. The one who'd led such a sheltered life that she'd been bowled over by an invitation to do a local radio talk show about her book. The same woman who'd all but swooned, certain she'd really hit the big time when she'd been invited on that local morning talk show in St. Louis. Sure, she'd dreamed of having some modest success, enough to hope that someday she could quit her day job and write for a living . . . but even her fertile writer's imagination hadn't extended much beyond that. Hell, she'd been thrilled just to see the book in print.

Then the invite had come to be on *The Dave Stevens Show*. Oh, wow, she remembered thinking, to be flown to the big city and be on national television? Well, her world just couldn't get any bigger.

Ha.

If she'd only known then what was about to happen, she'd have stayed in Mason and kept her day job. She'd have clung to her normal, middle-class, Midwestern lifestyle with every-thing she had. But no. Hot, edgy, controversial talk show host Dave Stevens had seen the local St. Louis spot and picked up a copy of her book. Hosting the first daytime show geared toward men, Dave had intended to use his ratings-grabbing, confrontational format to needle her about the value, or lack thereof, of sappy romance fiction. He would drill her on why women fell for such delusional claptrap, after which they'd give the men in their lives a hard time for not measuring up to the book's fantasy hero.

Only instead, when he'd read the book in preparation for the show, he'd shocked himself by liking it, and had ended up doing a twist on his own format by making himself the butt of his own confrontational style, putting Bree in the inter-viewer's seat—and grabbing the highest ratings ever for a day-time talk show. He'd ended the show by daring his male viewers to pick up the book and read it with a significant other.

"Guys, if you want to understand what women want—and trust me, if you want to get any on a regular basis, you do!—read this book. It's like an instruction manual for clueless men."

She couldn't have devised a more brilliant marketing cam-paign if she'd thought it up herself. Her publisher was over the moon, her agent immediately began to field offers. In less than one week, all hell had broken loose. *Summer Lake* sold faster than they could print and ship it out. It topped every best-seller list and stayed there. Going from the summer's must-read beach book, to everybody's book club pick for the fall, to the must-have stocking stuffer for the holidays. You weren't considered cool and in the know if you couldn't de-bate in detail which of the three lead heroines you most iden-tified with, or which of the three heroes you'd most like to sleep with. By spring, she'd been the subject of one of David Letterman's Top Ten lists, made the cover of *People* maga-zine—not once, but twice. She'd attended actual film open-ings in Hollywood and London, wearing clothes by designers she'd only read about, and had her book fought over in a much-publicized battle by two major studios for film rights, which had eventually gone for over seven figures, with all six lead roles claimed by the hottest reigning box office stars.

But no—for some silly reason, Bree had stupidly never foreseen that particular, mind-blowing, once-in-a-lifetime, winning-lottery-ticket-like future, and so she had only writ-ten a single, stand-alone novel, with no obvious follow-up spin-off. What *had* she been thinking?

And so the inevitable had happened. As the first anniver-sary of the book's release loomed, the paperback version hit the stands and renewed the buzz all over again. Everyone had been asking when the next book was coming out, but now the questions were impatient, edged with concern that maybe her success had all been a fluke. *Well, of course it had been a fluke,* she'd wanted to shout. So, at first she'd laughingly told interviewers that she hadn't exactly had much time to write lately, thinking it was nice that they were at least interested enough to ask. And, at first, they'd laughed along with her, all the while gushing over her overnight success story.

But now her diehard fans had turned into an unruly mob, with the press fueling the flames every chance they got, all demanding to know when—or if—she'd deliver the goods again. As if it were a given that she had a litany of blockbusters floating around in her brain, just waiting for the chance to get jotted down. Journalists began to speculate, quite nastily at times, that she would flame out as a one-hit wonder. Bree Sullivan Backlash erupted. As if she'd asked for the fame and the fortune in the first place! And now, by not feeding the hungry hordes, it was as if she was intentionally not making good on that unspoken promise.

She'd been hounded to the point of going into seclusion to avoid the inevitable cross-examination. So her publisher had happily taken up where the media had left off. After all, she had signed a deal for two books—which had thrilled her to no end at the time—and, dollar signs floating in their eyes, they would love to know when she planned on getting that next one turned in. Everyone wanted to cash in while she was still hot, everybody wanted a piece of her. None of this was exactly conducive to her creative process, which had abandoned her completely somewhere right around that St. Louis talk show a million years ago.

She fought to keep the car on the road after swerving to miss the sheep that had suddenly appeared in her headlights. But there was no saving it. The back end of her car slid from the road, slinging gravel and mud everywhere before plunging into a water-filled gully, which surged the back end up onto a low stone wall . . . and shoved the front end nose-down in the rushing water.

It all happened so fast. It was so dark, the wind so strong, the rain so heavy, that the whole event was a veritable blur to Bree. She'd been fighting unfamiliar terrain, the sudden loss of light, the ratcheting winds and pelting rain on one mountain curve after another. She hadn't even been aware she'd descended into a valley, so snake-like was the track road she was on, until the strobe-light effect of the harrowingly powerful, ground-shaking lightning strikes had illuminated a stretch of fenced-off fields . . . and what looked like a rapidly swelling stream. She'd made it across the single-lane bridge, but then had been plunged back into the worst of the storm.

Shoulders hunched, heart in her throat, neck long since gone completely stiff, it was almost a relief to have the battle finally over, even if it meant losing. Because, hey, by dying, she'd rob them all of the chance to continue the endless, nauseating speculation about what, where, and, most importantly, *when*, her next effort would finally appear. And it served the double bonus of saving her the global-scale humiliation and embarrassment of proving the gleeful naysayers right. Six months of staring at her laptop screen had produced exactly nothing. Nothing worth publishing, anyway. If only this particular solution didn't, by necessity, include the actual death part, she might have signed up right then and there.

Instead, she fought back, grappling with the wheel and stick shift, but a sudden overdose of adrenaline combined with bone-deep fatigue and abject terror served to rob her of whatever driving skills she'd managed to amass since going AWOL before dawn this morning and running away from her life. It had been hard enough in calmer conditions to sit on the right side of the car, keeping track of the brake, gas, and clutch pedals, using the regular arrangement of feet while shifting gears with her left hand . . . and combining all that with driving on the wrong side of the road.

She heard someone scream as the car screeched along the stone wall, yanking the back end up and sending her slamming forward as the nose end of the car was sucked immediately into the rushing gully waters. Only then did she realize, as the echoes reverberated through the interior of the car after the motor instantly cut out, that it had been her.

"S—seat belt," she stammered, her body beginning to tremble as the enormity of the situation began to really hit her. She immediately grabbed at the straps and began yanking, before finally getting a slight grip on herself and her rising hysteria. "Latch, unlatch it." Hoping the rational sound of her voice would calm her down, she tried to take a few deep breaths, but immediately began almost convulsively gulping air, as if her body thought the car was already filling with water and drowning was imminent. The belt mercifully popped free, which had the unfortunate result of plunging her chest-first into the steering wheel due to the steep forward pitch of the car.

She glanced wildly around the passenger seat of the rented car for her purse, her computer bag, as if those things really mattered at a time like this. Like she had anything on the computer worth saving, anyway. But they had been thrown to the floor on the passenger side, out of reach, the steep pitch sending them halfway up under the dash. The tiny two-seater had little room for maneuvering in general, but at its current angle, she had none at all. She felt the panic rise again as she tried the door handle and found it wouldn't budge. Electric locks. The windows were electric, too. With the motor dead and flooded, nothing worked.

"I was only kidding!" she shouted. "I don't want to die, dammit."

She was wrestling around in her seat, trying to push herself back with her legs so she could angle toward the door, try and see if there was any manual way to pop the locks. *Why-oh-why had she let her British editor talk her into renting such a teeny beast of a car?* She wasn't the hot rod type. Hell, she wasn't the type to jet set over to Britain and take up residence in a four-hundred-year-old manor house, either, the guest of a baron no less, in an offer of solitude to write her book.

Yeah. That hadn't worked out too well. Baron Farthingham

had let it slip that she was staying with him. At a grande ball, no less. By dawn the gates and walls surrounding the place had been besieged by press and fans alike. When she hadn't appeared to talk to them, the tabloids had taken up the gauntlet. And the Brits thought Americans were rude. She'd been shocked at some of the headlines:

BITCHY BREE BAGS A BARON!
ALL PLAY AND NO WORK EQUALS NO
BOOK FOR LOYAL FANS.
DIVA SULLIVAN TOO BUSY TO CARE?

She could only imagine what they'd say now. Maybe she wouldn't be quite having the last laugh after all. "It sure doesn't feel too funny at the moment," she said between gritted teeth as she tried and failed to pry up the little nub of a lock on the door.

A sudden pounding on the passenger window made her scream. And there was nothing ambiguous about who had made the sound this time. Someone was out there, in the storm-ravaged gloom.

A rescue! Oh, thank God.

Except, she was out in the middle-of-nowhere Scotland. Which pretty much described the highlands, as far as she could tell. Before the storm she hadn't seen so much as a red phone booth for hours. Who in the world would happen to see her car go in a ditch way the hell out here?

She looked at the window as her rescuer peered inside . . . and got her answer. A deranged lunatic.

She choked on a terrified scream as her throat completely closed over. Staring in at her was what appeared to be a very naked man, with long, wet hair plastered to his head and face in stringy ropes. A naked man with a very determined look on his face as he banged repeatedly, almost violently on the passenger window, shouting something unintelligible at her.

Death by drowning suddenly looked preferable.

Chapter 3

"Release the locks!" Tristan shouted again. One of the rear tires had ridden up onto the low stone wall, tilting the car at an odd angle, and burying the front end of the tiny sports car into the storm-filled gully. But with the force of the water pushing at the side of the car, it could go at any second, and when and if it did, it would likely turn over. And right onto him. The driver's side was propped up too high and too close to the wall for him to fight his way to that side, which left him here, dangerously downstream. And there she sat, like a fish in an empty bowl, waiting for it to fill up. Idiot woman would like as get them both drowned before he could get her out of there.

He tried the door, but it was still locked, so he banged on the passenger window again, motioning to the top of her windshield. "Unlock the top!" Between the wind and the raging rain, not to mention the windows being up and sealed tight, maybe she wasn't hearing him. But she was sure as hell staring at him. Why in bloody hell wouldn't she just put the damn top down and climb out?

It occurred to him that she might be hurt. For all he could see in the dark, the car hadn't sustained any heavy damage. The side closest to the wall was probably scraped up, given the screeching noise he'd heard, but it wasn't bashed in. It appeared as if she'd just lost control at the bend of the road and ended up sideways up the other side of the gully. Maybe she had knocked herself a bit senseless during the spin-about. What other reason would there be for just sitting there? She had no seat belt on, so maybe she'd hit her head on the steering wheel or side window. Of course, the fact that she had the little convertible roadster out in a storm, racing along single-track highland roads, didn't speak well for her being all that safety-minded in the first place.

She jumped suddenly and looked down, then began squirming in her seat. He couldn't see into the gloomy interior of the car well enough to know for sure, but he'd bet the water had just found its way in. She looked back at him, then down at her feet, then back at him, clearly panicked if the terror etched on her face was any indication. She seemed to be wriggling about enough to indicate she wasn't too severely injured. Surely she could get the damn top unlocked. If she'd been worried about what the rain might do to the exposed leather seats, the water coming in through the bottom of the car should erase that concern.

Again he pointed to where the windshield and canvas met and shouted, "Pop the locks!" He made flicking motions with his fingers, putting them right next to the glass in hopes she could see clearly what it was he meant for her to do. He was hip-deep, freezing cold water rushing around him, literally freezing his balls off, and the adrenaline punch that had sent him racing out here in nothing more than a damp towel knotted around his hips was beginning to level off to the point that he was well and truly feeling the effects of it. He was starting to tremble from the exposure, and his hands rattled a little against the windshield.

Lightning strikes continued to rain down at alarmingly close range, with the accompanying thunder reverberating through the ground moments later. And he was rapidly losing patience with his rescuee. If her antics were any indication, the water level in the car was rising rapidly. There was only one thing to do. He waded back through the gully, slipping in the mud and muck several times before getting back up onto the bank, losing his towel completely as he scraped his way to a stand. He didn't bother trying to get it back—there was no time. It was risky leaving her as it was, even if only for the minute it would take to get to the house and back. But he didn't see where he had much choice. He could hardly break into the car bare-handed.

He raced bare-assed back up the lane to the croft and let himself into the mud room, never more appropriately named as he was covered in it, and snatched his wet pants off the floor.

Jinty, excited by his sudden reappearance, barked in excitement, dancing around his legs.

"Aye, girl, aye, a bit of excitement out there." He gave her head a quick scrub, then grimaced at the muck he'd matted in her fur. He tried to pull on the pants, but they were so wet and his body so muddy he didn't have time for that battle. "Bollocks." He unclipped his knife from his pants before tossing them back to the floor, then grabbed his boxers instead and yanked them on, shivering as the wet material clung to even wetter skin. He'd catch his death saving her from her own. Idiot woman. Jinty raced to the door ahead of him.

"No' this time, sweet. I'll be back in a flash." And with that he took off around the croft and back down the lane. If she couldn't—or wouldn't—save herself, he had no choice but to do it for her.

Bree slumped down in her seat and let out a long, shaky breath when the lunatic banging on her window suddenly ran off into the night. Where the hell had she landed that naked men ran around in the middle of a storm? She immediately regrouped. She had no idea if he was going to come back, but she knew she had to get the hell out of this car. When he'd shown up, any thoughts of rescue had quickly fled with one look at him. He was clearly deranged. She'd thought maybe she'd be safer in the car than out. Her heart had about stopped when he'd tried the door, then banged on the window.

Then the water had come rushing in over her feet. Drown in her car . . . or escape into the clutches of a madman. Honestly, it was like a bad suspense novel. Who'd believe this? The storm and high winds raged on unabated, as did the lightning and the thunder. Even having nowhere to run, and a possible raving lunatic on the loose, staying inside the stranded car was no longer an option as the water level was rapidly rising.

"Calm down, take deep breaths. And think, dammit. Think." But all she could picture was the wild man outside her car, banging on her window and making obscene hand gestures. He'd kept stabbing his finger at her and shouting something she couldn't hear. She turned the key in the ignition to trigger the battery, hoping to get the windows to roll down, but nothing.

She pounded her fists on the steering wheel, frustrated, scared out of her mind, beyond fatigued. Not just from the storm, but from . . . well, her entire life. She let her head fall back. "Think, Bree. There's got to be a way out of this." She didn't have anything heavy enough to break the window with . . . except maybe her laptop. The water crept higher—it was up to seat level now, and she tried to pull her legs up, but she was trapped in the deep bucket seat with the steering wheel, stick shift, and door keeping her penned in. Why-oh-why had she listened to Dana and rented a damn convertible hot rod?

"Shit!" She looked up. "You fucking idiot!" She was sitting here, drowning . . . in a goddamn convertible. How had she let herself get so freaked out that she'd somehow become the embodiment of every stupid heroine she'd ever read about and hated? Christ, she deserved whatever fate was in store for her.

She reached up to release the locking mechanism . . . right as the wild man's face reappeared in the passenger window. She froze. *Shit, shit, shit!* But it wasn't until he pulled out the knife that she screamed.

A flash of lightning outlined him in a sudden burst of light, creating a strobe effect just as he swung his fist up, blade clenched in his grip, and brought it down, plunging it into the canvas roof.

She screamed again and fought to climb out from behind the steering wheel but she was well and truly trapped. The blade of the knife came through above the passenger seat, preventing her from reaching for the other lock. Not that she was interested in opening the top now . . . although he was coming in one way or the other, if the look on his face was any indication. The only weapon she had was her laptop. One good crack to the head . . .

Except it had been flung to the floor on the passenger side and was currently under water. Plus there was the little matter of a knife blade between it and her. Her attacker pulled at the blade and began sawing with it, ripping at the canvas. Bree plunged her arm into the water swirling up to her lap now and tugged off one of her shoes. Shaking hard with both the cold and an overdose of adrenaline, she took the sopping-wet shoe and began beating at the knife, hoping to make him drop it. Not that this would slow him down much, but then she'd at least have the weapon.

"Hey!" he shouted angrily, loudly enough so she could hear him clearly. Or maybe that was because there was now a gaping hole in the roof of her car. "What the bloody hell is wrong with you?"

What, she was supposed to let him destroy her car and attack her? Wasn't she already having a bad enough day? She just kept beating on his hand until he pulled it back out. With the knife, unfortunately. "I'm trying to rescue your wet, ungrateful arse and giving myself a nice case of pneumonia doin' it," he raged. "Maybe yer tryin' to kill yourself and I'm just getting in the way. So fine, fine." He lifted his hands as if in surrender.

"Saving me?" she shouted, her nerves so badly frayed at this point that she simply snapped. "*Saving me?*" With the knife safely removed, she reached out and popped the other latch, then pushed the top back far enough so she could climb out.

Freedom!

She used the steering wheel to pull herself onto the awkwardly angled seat, having to clutch at it to keep from falling. The rain beat down on her head and the heavy wind snatched at her hair, but she hardly cared at this point. She was already soaked to the waist, anyway. Standing up a little made the car list dangerously and sent her would-be attacker scrambling out of the way. He slipped and slid in the muck, so soaked and covered in mud already that she could hardly make him out. She glanced around, trying to figure out what her best bet was to get safely out of the car without sending it all the way over.

"Climb out the high side," he called out.

She looked over to find he was on the edge of the swollen gully. It appeared he wasn't entirely naked after all, but close enough. He had to be completely insane, regardless. Trying to save her. Right. Probably some dotty nutcase that lived in a cave in the hills or something and had seen her go off the road, figured she'd be ripe for the picking. Why else was he out in the middle of the night in his boxers?

"Are ye comin' down or are ye going tae stand about in the storm all night? The water didn't get you but the lightning still might."

Now that Bree knew she wasn't going to die, at least not immediately, she realized that once out of the car and on solid ground . . . then what? Where was she supposed to go? And what the hell was she going to do about the nutjob Scot, who, despite his claims, hadn't left her to do as she pleased? Even if he meant her no harm, and she certainly wasn't sure of that by any stretch, she didn't really fancy whiling away the nighttime hours with him until daybreak rolled around and she could see some sign of life she could hike toward. Maybe she could run, just flat-out run, find something to hide behind, or whatever. It was so dark now he'd never find her. Except he likely knew this area far better than she did.

"Come on, jump!" he shouted, pacing the side of the gully. "We could be inside and dry by now. Just wade around the front and I'll help pull you up the bank. You'll get yer clothes muddy, but there's no hope for that now, so no sense in worryin' about it."

He thought she was worried about her clothes? And why, suddenly, did he actually sound almost . . . normal? Wait. Had he said they could be inside? And dry? She swung her gaze around, looking for lights or a nearby house, but from her crouched position, clutching the steering wheel, the wind plastering her hair into her eyes, she couldn't see squat. She swung her gaze back to him. Did she dare even allow herself to contemplate—

"I'm no' leaving until you get out, but I'm not so sure what good I'll be other than gettin' in the way. I can't get around to that side, but if you get in and make your way around the front of the car, the water's only about waist-deep. Just take your time, go slow. I'll pull you out. But you need to get away from the car. Upstream."

He'd gone from raging attacker to cajoling rescuer. A new ploy, perhaps? Or had her fertile imagination just taken one look at a naked wild man and run with it? She could hardly be blamed, given the extreme circumstances . . . Could it be he really was a Good Samaritan? The whole situation was too surreal. Whatever the case, he wasn't going anywhere, and he seemed a great deal calmer now. And she had nowhere to turn.

What she couldn't do was stay crouched on the seat of her sportscar in a raging electrical storm one moment longer. So she made the split-second decision to work with him. If he thought she was being agreeable, maybe he'd let his guard down. She could use him to help her out, then take off at the first opportunity. She hadn't forgotten he was armed with a knife, but there wasn't much she could do about that at the moment. Maybe if he thought she wasn't a threat of any kind, he'd be lax enough so she could snatch the knife.

It wasn't much of a plan, but it was all she had at the moment.

"Okay," she called through the howling wind. "I'm climbing out the high side."

"Jump clear, use the car for leverage," he instructed, sounding tense but remarkably sane all of a sudden.

Balancing her weight by holding on to the windshield frame, she propped her foot on the skinny edge of the raised window, which was harder than it looked. She silently counted to three, then hoisted herself up and leaped into the rushing gully waters. The car rocked dangerously as she pushed off, but she didn't—couldn't—look behind her to see if it had rolled or not. She was too busy finding her footing in the water and muck. *You should have taken your other shoe off*, she thought as she stumbled and fought her way around the front of the car—which was still upright and partially wedged on the stone wall framing the opposite side of the gully. And she'd left the other one back in the car. Along with her backpack and her purse . . . and well, everything else she'd taken with her when she'd fled this morning. Smart. Real smart.

But there was no way she could retrieve anything at the moment. She was stuck out in the middle of nowhere, in a storm, with a half-naked man who may or may not be completely mad. No identification. She tried not to think about her laptop, presently in the watery grave of the car. Everything gone now. Not that there was anything to lose, really. She shuddered and it was only in part because of the murky water rushing around her waist as she continued with her painstakingly slow, slipping, sliding progress around the front of the car.

It struck her, though, even in the midst of her current situation, that instead of being horrified by the loss of her accumulated hard work, as she should have been, given the enormity of the consequences . . . she felt strangely freed.

There was a sudden large splash, and she looked up from

the slow, deliberate pace she was attempting, trying hard not to slip and go under . . . thinking maybe the car had come loose . . . only to find her rescuer presently wading toward her. As he drew closer, a particularly violent lightning strike illuminated his features.

She'd been so overwhelmed with her predicament, all she'd noticed before was that he was wild-looking . . . and mostly naked.

The unearthly white flash of light cast him in a rugged, harsh relief. His face was angular, his jaw a hard, square line. His eyes were bottomless pools of black, his long, dark hair plastered to his head and neck, reaching all the way to his shoulders. Broad shoulders, she noted. Muscular, in a lean, defined way.

He reached a hand toward her. She'd expected something broad, with blunt, work-roughened fingers. So the refined hand with the long, almost elegant fingers surprised her.

"Come, lass," he said, his voice roughly cajoling but impatient. He beckoned her with his hand. "I dinnae know about you, but I've had all of this wet I can stand for a night." He braced his weight, squared his hips, and reached for her.

She looked from his hand to his face, and back to his hand. Then he grinned. And it changed everything.

"No' to worry. Ye've had me in this water so long anything I have that might do ye harm is frozen."

She couldn't help it. She laughed. Not because he suddenly looked harmless. Far from it. No matter the fact that he was standing thigh-deep in water, bedraggled and shivering . . . this man would never look harmless. Not with a smile like that.

She laughed because this whole episode was so absurd that there was nothing left to do but laugh. "And if I don't get out of this water, I'll be too frozen to care what you do."

"Now that's the smartest thing you've said all night."

She could only hope so. She reached out and took his hand.

Chapter 4

Her hand was slender and cold to the touch. Not a surprise, given the circumstances. What was a surprise was the strength in her grip. Thus far, she'd struck him as an entirely helpless female—and somewhat flighty as well.

"Grab on to my wrist," he said, reaching past her hand to take firm hold of her arm. "Our fingers are too slippery."

Once he had a good grip, he didn't waste time. He turned away from her and began to guide her out. The sheeting rain and heavy winds hindered his forward progress, forcing him to duck his head down, barely able to see his way to the bank. The water was running higher and faster now, and it was so slippery and muddy he wasn't sure how he was going to get up and out again, much less pull her up behind him. But that was all he allowed himself to focus on. Not the droll tone in her voice just now, one that hinted that she was someone of far greater intellect than he'd originally assumed. Nor did he let himself think about her face, all pointed chin and angular cheekbones, with a veritable waterfall of hair billowing out about it, dwarfing her narrow features, even with the rain quickly reducing it to a heavy, wet mop. No, no point in thinking about her as anything other than a major pain in the arse. And an unwelcome intruder into his solitude.

It would only be for the night. He'd survive. By morning the flash flooding would have abated and they'd haul her car out of there and see what was what. He'd get Alastair to come take a look at it, tow it in for him. And yes, he'd offer to replace the canvas top, if the rest was salvageable. How was he supposed to know she'd finally figured it out? He'd apologize later. They'd almost reached the bank. Now that the car wasn't providing a breakfront for them, they were in the narrow section of the gully where the water was rushing unabated. With the wall lining the other side, there was no other choice but to find a way to crawl out this side. He scanned the edge for the least-steep angle out, but visibility was well limited . . . and it really didn't matter much at this point. He did look back then. "I'm going to lift you out first."

Her face was set in determined lines as she braced herself against the current, but she didn't argue. She simply nodded instead.

He braced himself as best as he could, then pulled her closer. "Hold on to my shoulders, and I'll give you a leg up and out."

She nodded again, then turned so the water came at her side and bracketed her legs in the muck before tentatively putting her hands on his shoulders. At no time did she so much as look at his face.

"Ye'll have to hold on better than that."

She did look up then, just as a particularly heavy gust of wind caught her back and had her clutching at his bare shoulders, her nails digging into his chilled skin. He found himself grinning and couldn't, for the life of him, have said why. "Better. Now up ye go."

He gripped her hips, trying not to note how trim she was, how lithe, as he bent his knees and lifted her up and more or less heaved her onto the bank. She grappled at the slick ground, scrabbling for a hold so she didn't slide back down again. He reached up and caught her foot and gave her an extra shove, sliding her chest deep across the grass and mud.

She grunted a little, but continued fighting for purchase, finally finding it and immediately climbing to her feet. She wobbled for a moment, but quickly regained her balance. She looked out and around into the dark of the storm, then looked back at him.

She wasn't close enough to read her expression, but Tristan could tell from the coiled tension in her body that she was thinking of running. Where to, he had no idea. Was she so afraid of him still? He had a flashback to the look on her face when he'd knifed the canvas roof. Perhaps from her perspective, he wasn't exactly a friendly face.

But before he could say anything to calm her down or reassure her—what that would have been, he had no idea—she turned back to him.

"Can I help you?" she said, yelling over the roar of the wind.

So. Well, then. He didn't know what to make of her.

"I'm fine," he said, then set about making his entirely graceless exit from the gully waters, which almost included the loss of what little modesty he'd managed to preserve during his rescue effort as he dragged himself up the slick bank. Mercifully he found purchase before his boxers were scraped clean off him. An instant later she was on her hands and knees in front of him, grabbing at his wrists and pulling with all she had.

The leverage was unexpected, and he'd just found a toehold and shoved with his feet. The end result was that he catapulted up the slope and knocked her clean to her back. Landing square on top of her.

She grunted, surprised by the impact, then turned her face to look directly into his. "Well," was all she said.

Again, his lips quirked. "Aye."

He rolled off her, managing to catalogue just how her body had felt beneath his despite the brief contact, not to mention the complete inappropriateness of such a thing. "Are ye okay?"

She sat up. "Define *okay*."

He laughed. "Come on. I've got dry clothes and a warm house just down the lane." He rolled to his feet and extended a hand.

She crawled to a stand without taking advantage of his offer. She started to brush herself off, then shook her head at the useless effort. The rain continued to beat at them and the wind snatched at her clothes and hair. "Th-thank you," she said, stuttering a little as she began to shake. Whether from the aftershock from the accident itself or the chilling effect of the water, he didn't know, but it didn't matter.

"I mean ye no harm. I live just down the lane and saw your brake lights streak across my front window. My family owns this property, far as you can see. I manage it. I'll take you into the village first thing. Beyond that, you're just going to have to trust me. There's nowhere else to go and it's no' safe standing out here any longer."

She studied him for a moment, then, crossing her arms across her chest, she looked back at the gully and her mostly submerged car.

"We'll get it pulled out tomorrow."

She nodded, rubbing her arms and shivering. She took a deep, shuddering breath and looked back at him. "Okay."

"You're not hurt, are you?"

She shook her head.

He paused, then turned and led the way at a trot. She stayed behind him, but said nothing else. He glanced over his shoulder every couple yards to make sure she was keeping up with him and hadn't had a change of heart and bolted across the field.

A minute later he was opening his gate and motioning her to the rear of the house. "Mud room," he shouted over the wind.

She didn't even hesitate, but put her head down and scurried around back. He matched her pace, both reaching the door at the same time. "I have a dog," he told her as they hunkered down. "Excitable, but friendly. Jinty is her name."

She just nodded with a jerk of her chin, shivering and shifting from one foot to the other while Tristan opened the door. He went in first, mostly to run interference. He corralled the dancing Jinty and herded her through the mud room door into the kitchen. "You can say hello in a moment," he told her, then closed the door between them, much to her whining dismay. "Sorry," he said, turning back to his guest.

She was standing in a growing puddle, looking anywhere but at him. *An odd one*, he thought. Forthright one moment, shy the next. He supposed being wrecked, stranded, almost drowned, then stuck in a strange man's house was likely enough to put anyone a bit off their stride, and decided to withhold further judgment. He pulled a towel from the pile and handed it to her. "Start with this," he instructed, "and I'll go see what I can round up in the way of dry clothes."

It was only then that he noticed her gaze had tracked to the pile of wet, muddy clothes he'd already left on the floor earlier. Which then led him to slowly glance down at himself. *Och, Christ.* And here he'd been thinking her a loon for not being able to rescue herself from her own car. In all the while he'd been freezing his balls off out there, not once had he stopped to think of the picture he was presenting. He'd been focused on getting her out safely and nothing more.

He shot her a quick smile as he snatched a towel from the shelf and wrapped it around his hips. "Perhaps I should see about dry clothes for us both. I apologize for my lack of modesty, but I'd just come in from the fields, caught in the same storm, and peeled out of that muddy pile. When I saw your car head into the gully moments afterward, it seemed best to make haste." He didn't bother to mention he'd been even less appropriately clad during his initial rescue attempt. Likely she'd seen him run bare-assed down the lane, anyway. Too late to worry about that now.

She'd wiped her face and arms with the towel he'd given her, and was presently wrapping the dry end around the length of her hair and squeezing the extra water out. All with her gaze carefully averted. But now she looked at him. "I'm sorry I've been so uncooperative and seemingly ungrateful. I'm not, really. I just thought you were . . ." She let the words trail off, obviously—if the slight color returning to her cheeks was any indication—realizing that whatever she'd been about to say might come off as less than gracious.

"A loon," he provided, easing her discomfort. He smiled as he took the wet towel from her hands and offered her another dry one. "Dinnae fash yerself," he told her. "You can hardly be blamed for drawin' that conclusion, now can you?" He scrubbed at his own hair and let his smile ease into a grin.

For a moment there, he thought he saw her lips twitch, but she was still shivering and trembling, so it was hard to tell. "Enough chatter," he said. "I'll be back in a moment. Use all you need," he said, motioning to the pile of worn, frayed towels stacked on the shelf next to the washer. "Those are for cleanup and the like, but they're fresh washed."

"Th-thank you," she said, her lips a bit on the bluish side. "I do really appreciate this."

"Not a problem." He slipped out of the room and headed swiftly to his bedroom, Jinty dancing at his side the whole way. "Aye, we have company. And I'll expect you to be on your best behavior." He realized he sounded almost jovial about the prospect, which wasn't like him in the least. But there was no denying the bedraggled woman intrigued him.

He gave Jint a quick scratch, then opened his closet doors and frowned. Jeans, trousers, work pants, a few pairs of summer shorts. There wasn't much in the way of anything that would fit her smaller frame. He rooted about and finally dug out a pair of dark-blue cotton drawstring pants that he'd had for ages but rarely wore. He grabbed a sweatshirt down from the shelf, then thought to toss an old Hagg's Pub t-shirt on the pile as well. A quick dive into his dresser produced a pair of heavy socks. "That should do. Come on," he said to the dog as he headed back out. "Might as well greet our new guest." Whose name, he realized, he hadn't bothered to ask as of yet.

He returned to the washroom to find her still standing

right where he'd left her, except she'd taken off her one shoe and was standing on several smaller towels in an effort not to drip any more water onto his floor than necessary. Both of them were covered with grit, grime, and mud. A shower was mandatory, but he didn't feel right asking her to strip down in here. "Follow me—I'll show you to the guest room. There's a bath, fresh towels, and soap. Not sure on shampoo, but I'll check. Take as long as you like."

"I don't want to track muck through your house," she said, and it struck him then that she was American. He'd been so caught up in the rescue process, he hadn't really paid attention to her accent.

"Och, no worries. This auld place has suffered far worse the last few hundred years and fared well enough. It'll survive a bit of grit and grime." He smiled. "Or a bit more, I should say." He gestured to his own less-than-shiny-clean self. He didn't wait for her to argue. He opened the door and let the dog romp into the room. She set to racing circles around his guest, tail whipping back and forth.

"This is Jinty, my sheep dog and all-around companion."

His guest didn't shy away from the dog at all, quite the opposite. She immediately reached for Jinty's ears and gave her a good scratch. "Hi, there. Good girl."

Jinty all but preened, quite pleased with the attention. Tristan found himself warming even more toward his guest.

"You've a friend for life now," he told her. "Come on, follow me." He steered her through the kitchen, into the living area, and turned the opposite way from his own rooms. "Guest room is here," he motioned. "Bathroom in here." He opened the door and stuck his head in. "I think you have what you need. Take as long as you like. I'm going to the opposite end of the house and take a shower myself. Make yourself at home when you're done. I'll find something for us to eat once we've scraped ourselves clean."

He held open the door and she scooted past him. She was a head shorter than he, and even with muck and mire, or maybe because of it, he found himself drawn to the unusual angles of her face. She had shadows beneath her eyes and hollows beneath her cheeks. Somehow he doubted those were just the result of this evening's adventures. Her eyes reflected a fatigue that went far beyond a single, difficult night.

"Thank you," she said. "I won't take too long."

"I've a water heater at both ends of the house, so take all you need. No hurry." He smiled. "It's no' like we have anywhere we have to be."

She tried to smile, but it didn't reach very far. He couldn't recall ever seeing someone who looked so . . . weary. Soul-deep weary.

He put the pile of dry clothes on the small towel stand beside the tub and left her to it. But even as he stood under the stinging spray of his own hot shower, he couldn't erase those eyes from his thoughts. It made him wonder what she'd been doing out here after all, racing around the countryside in that little death trap of hers. Maybe he'd been too quick to assume. Had she been running toward something? Running away?

Of course, he had no idea. But he couldn't look into those eyes of hers and make himself believe she'd just been happily out and about, only to find herself suddenly stuck in a storm burst.

No, there was a story behind those eyes.

He'd always been drawn to landscapes, wanting to capture the energy of nature in all her glory with nothing more than a pen or brush. But something about his guest made his fingers twitch with the need to draw, to sketch those eyes, that face, to ferret out her secrets and find a way to convey them to paper so as to have more than his memory to call upon when he thought about her.

He shook his head at the folly of that and turned his face toward the spray of water. One night. Then she'd move on. She wasn't going to linger under his roof.

If only he could be so certain she wasn't going to linger any longer in his thoughts.

Chapter 5

Bree carefully stepped into the high-sided, claw-foot tub and pulled the circular shower curtain around her. She groaned in deep appreciation the instant the hot water hit her skin. *I might never come back out of here*, she thought, as all the accumulated tension from the past several hours eased out of her muscles.

And if she stayed in the shower forever—or at least till morning—there was the added bonus of not having to face her rescuer again tonight.

She shivered a little, only this time it had absolutely nothing to do with being stuck in bone-chillingly wet clothes. Or no clothes, which is what he might as well have been wearing. *Jesus.* She had to stop thinking about him. She closed her eyes and ducked her head under the spray. But that only served to allow his image to pop up, fully formed and quite detailed, in her mind's eye.

Out in the dark, in the storm, he'd looked like nothing more than a crazed lunatic.

However, standing in his mud room, with nothing more than a towel wrapped around his lean hips and a grin on his handsome face . . . well . . . She twitched a little as she ran the washcloth over her breasts and belly, sensations that were definitely pleasurable as they skated across her skin. *Dangerous thoughts, Bree.* But, dear Lord, who wouldn't have

X-rated thoughts about a man like that? With those dark eyes, that long hair, a hint of a beard shadowing his jaw, and a bottom lip just made for nibbling on . . . not to mention the accent. Seriously, with the accent. He was every woman's Scottish hero fantasy come to life. He was certainly hers, anyway. The man cut quite the arresting figure, even in a towel.

She started vigorously scrubbing at her arms and legs. She was the one who should be arrested. She had no business thinking anything remotely of that sort about him. He'd raced out into a dangerous storm to rescue her, and what had she done but scream and beat at his hand with her shoe. Lord, but he must have thought her a completely brainless twit. She realized now, of course, what he'd been so wildly gesturing at. No wonder he'd looked so fierce and wild. Trying to rescue a woman who was drowning in a damn convertible.

She dropped her chin and let the water beat on her back and neck. She'd always thought she'd be calm and collected in the face of crisis, but no, she'd completely lost it. So what if she hadn't slept in days and was a little strung out? No excuse for the total loss of anything resembling common sense. She'd apologized to him, but of course that was hardly enough, considering.

She could offer him a monetary reward for his heroics, but something told her he'd reject that out of hand as a matter of pride, and might even be insulted. She'd have to figure out something. Just as soon as she found the energy to get out of this heavenly, steamy shower.

She massaged shampoo into her scalp and worked it through her hair, trying to focus on a plan of attack for tomorrow. She'd need another car, she'd have to decide whether or not to contact Dana, or anyone else, and let them know she was all right. She'd intended to do that once she found a place to stay—she didn't want anyone to worry. Not that she'd planned to tell them where she was, just that she was fine. She just wanted to drop out for a while, find someplace where nobody knew her, and be left alone to figure things out. But there had been no signal anywhere—then the storm had whipped up.

And once again, her thoughts drifted back to him. To his broad, sculpted chest, the scattering of hair dusting the taut skin, arrowing down his flat belly in a nice little line that went straight to—she cut herself off before she could think of how indecently his soaked boxers had molded to his body. He might as well have been naked, as she pretty much knew the contour of what lay beneath. And . . . well . . . she definitely needed to stop thinking about that.

Not that it helped. Her rampant thoughts merely hop-scotched to that moment he'd gripped her hips and heaved her up onto the bank. Granted, there was nothing remotely sexy about being shoved face first into mud and muck . . . but that hadn't negated for one second her surprise at his easy strength. He'd barely exerted himself. And those hands . . . she remembered being surprised they weren't broad and rough-hewn, as the rest of him would indicate. Long, tapered fingers . . . almost elegantly refined . . . and yet they'd dug into her hips with surprising confidence and power.

She absently slid her hands over her body again, then realized what she was doing and abruptly went back to rinsing the rest of the suds from her hair. With everything that had happened to her over the past year and a half, it wasn't any surprise she had lacked any kind of intimate companionship. Not that it wasn't available. As even a minor, flash-in-the-pan celebrity, she'd had guys all but throw themselves at her. She just hadn't wanted to catch any of them. Their motives were all suspect now. Besides, she'd been so overwhelmed with the whirlwind her life had become, that despite the fact that she'd long since grown tired of crawling into a hotel bed alone at the end of another exhausting day, it wasn't like she had anything left to devote to a relationship of any kind. And one-night stands were not for her.

All she'd wanted lately was to crawl into a cave somewhere, nurse herself and her creative spark back to life . . .

and write. Write something all for herself. With no expectations, no pressure, no deadline.

Ha. Fat chance.

But it was nice to know she had enough of something left
inside herself to react at all to the rather virile charms of her
rescuer. Any other time in her life, she might even entertain a
few impure thoughts of just how she could pay him back for
his troubles. She snorted and rinsed the last of the soap from
her skin. Yeah, right. Worn out, beaten down, and recently
hysterical, she was just certain he was all but drooling at the
chance to have her. Not that it really mattered one way or the
other. She might be world-traveled now, having hobnobbed
with celebrities and even dined with royalty. But when it came
down to being a woman, she was still a small-town librarian
from Mason, Missouri. And while not entirely the embodiment of the tight-bunned, and even tighter-assed cliché long
associated with her profession, she was hardly a wanton, either.
This was the first time that it had actually bothered her, though.

Sighing in regret, for that and the fact that her wonderfully
rejuvenating shower was over, she stepped carefully out of
the tub and grabbed a couple of towels. Heck, as many of
those as she'd gone through already, maybe she could repay
him by doing laundry for the rest of the night.

Which led her completely inappropriate thoughts circling
back to him, and wondering what he was doing right that
moment. Wrapped in another towel, slung low on those lean
hips? Or still in the shower, with all that hot, sudsy water
running down his chest, over that flat belly, only to get all
hung up on—Jeez, Bree.

She wrapped her hair in one towel and used the other to
dry off. She had to stop thinking about him like that. Really,
she did. In a few minutes she'd be facing him again and she
couldn't afford to be distracted by . . . well, by anything other
than sincerely thanking him for his help and offering to somehow repay him for his selfless kindness. She could not be thinking about the way that towel had clung so precariously to his

lean hips. And she definitely couldn't be thinking about how those soaking-wet boxers had clung to, and indecently outlined, every inch of his anatomy. Some inches more indecently than others.

She tried, and failed, to remember him as the crazy man she'd initially believed him to be, wildly gesticulating at her and looking so fierce. Instead, all she could remember was him turning to her in the middle of a deluge, extending his hand . . . and grinning. Her heart had literally skipped a beat. There he'd stood, mostly naked, long hair plastered to his neck and shoulders, grime and grit streaked across his wet and gleaming torso, with lightning dancing about the skies and thunder rocking the ground beneath their feet. All things considered, that smile should have made him look even more visceral and wild . . . and it had. But not in a way that had made her want to run screaming into the night. Quite the contrary.

He was completely different from any man she'd ever met. A rough-hewn Scot, tucked away far out in some rural landscape, doing heaven knew what to get by for a living. A man who, at the first sign of danger, had run straight at it without thought to his own safety or comfort.

Those wet boxers flashed through her mind again. She really had to stop that. And she would. Any second now.

Leaving her hair wrapped in a towel, she reached for the pile of clothes he'd brought. The first thing she noticed was how soft they were, well worn and laundered. Without thinking, she buried her nose in the soft cotton. Yes, it smelled like home. No artificial scents, just the aroma of fresh, clean air. He'd dried these outside, she'd bet on it, just as her mother had, and as she had, as well. Stupidly, it made her eyes well up. God, she missed her old life. The slow pace, the peaceful surroundings, the people who all knew your name and cared about you as one of their own.

She was just tired, she told herself, sniffling back the tears and putting the pile of clothes back down. She shook out the t-shirt and slipped it on. The shoulders were halfway down her arms and the hem fell past her hips. His broad chest and well developed shoulders and arms flashed through her mind. She rubbed the soft cotton on her skin, imagining him in this shirt, pulling it over his head and—

Right, right. She was stopping.

She pulled on the drawstring pants, then had to roll them down a couple of times on her hips to keep them up. The ends trailed past her feet, but there wasn't much she could do about that. The fabric was too loose and soft to be rolled up. She pulled on the thick socks and found herself relaxing into the soft comfort the clothes brought to her. It was too steamy in the bathroom to need the sweatshirt he'd given her, but looking down at the way the t-shirt hung on her bare breasts and detailed the very erect nipples she was sporting at the moment . . . she yanked the hooded sweatshirt over her head anyway. Or tried to. She'd forgotten about the towel wrapped around her hair. A minute later she was in a straitjacket of towel, hair, sweatshirt, and drawstring.

So, naturally her erstwhile savior and host chose that moment to knock. "Beef stew okay with you?" he called through the door. "I'm afraid the menu is limited."

Bree's response was a muffled grunt.

There was a pause, during which she managed to make things worse rather than better. Turning in circles as she fought with the sleeves and snarled hair, she managed to bang into the towel cabinet.

"Is everything all right?"

She didn't know whether to laugh or cry. At what point had her life gone from a Hitchcock movie to a Laurel and Hardy filmfest? Straining her neck in order to find a breath of available air, she called out, "I'm stuck."

She heard him fumble with the door. "Are you decent?"

Now she did laugh. Asked the man who had just spent the past hour running around quite indecently, she thought. "Yes," she managed.

Her face was completely swallowed in towel, hair, and sweatshirt, so she felt him enter the room, rather than saw him.

"Here, here," he said, laying a hand on her shoulder to still her movements. His touch made her jump, but not so much in surprise as in . . . well, as in she really didn't need to go there, now did she? Bad enough she was standing in his bathroom, wearing his clothes, and feeling every inch the naked woman she was beneath them, too. Then there was the fact that she had no idea what he was wearing . . . or not, as the case may be. More images she definitely did not need went floating through her mind. And to top it all off, he was touching her with such gentle confidence. Using those beautiful hands of his.

"Hold still." He tried to turn her with his hands on her shoulders, but she was so tangled, he opted to steer her around with his hands on her hips. She swallowed a little moan when he held her hips square, then tugged her a little closer. She could only hope he assumed it was the discomfort she was in, not the fact that his mere proximity was tangling her suddenly reawakened libido into far more complex knots than this sweatshirt-hair-towel combo could only hope to achieve.

"You've made quite a nest of it," he said, almost more to himself than to her. "See if you can slide your arm down a little—no, no." He stopped her movements by taking hold of one arm, then sliding his hand from wrist to bicep. If he had any clue what havoc his touch was wreaking with her senses . . .

He tugged a little. "Okay, I have hold of the towel and the shirt. All you have to do is move your hand a little and—"

She slid one arm free, and that gave her just enough wiggle room to get her other arm extricated. Suddenly loose, the sweatshirt tugged at her snarled hair even more as the towel fell mercifully to the floor. "Ouch," she said, wincing as she grabbed for the sweatshirt.

He did, too. "I have it now. Ye've only to hold still."

She did as he asked, trying hard to keep her restored line of vision aimed anywhere but at his chest, which was mere inches away. It didn't matter that he had on a t-shirt now. Her memory was quite fine, thank you very much, and incredibly detailed, as it happened. He worked to untangle the wet strands from the drawstring that ran through the hood of the sweatshirt. She found she was more than willing to let him toy with her hair as long as he wanted to. He was very gentle and she was rather enjoying the view, no matter what she told herself. She'd given up trying not to stare. It's not like he cared, or knew where her thoughts were going anyway, right?

"Och, but you have a horse's mane, that ye do."

How flattering. That was one way to cure her of her wandering imagination. If only it had worked. "Sorry to be such a pain."

"Dinnae worry," he said, in that smooth burr of his. "No extra charge for the second rescue. And I didn't have to risk drowning in anything but terry cloth and hair this go."

She felt her cheeks heat a little. "Not that you'll believe this, but I'm generally a very self-sufficient woman."

"Oh, I pass no judgment. You've had a hard enough time of it."

"You have no idea," she murmured.

His hands paused for a moment, then continued with the mission. "There," he pronounced, freeing her from the sweatshirt string. "All is good. Though it might take you a wee bit to get a comb through it."

She took the sweatshirt from him and their gazes locked for a moment. "It's usually a bit of a nightmare. I'm used to it."

He said nothing, just held her gaze, that slight half-smile of his playing at the corners of his mouth. "It's quite lovely, really. Worth the effort, in my book."

She was so caught off guard by the compliment she wasn't sure how to respond. He'd said it directly enough, with no real overtones, save that hint of a smile. Whatever the case, the moment ended when he broke eye contact to reach down and scoop the towel off the floor.

"I—uh, thank you," she stammered. Oh yeah, she was smooth. Dined with royalty, no problem. But couldn't untie her own tongue in the presence of a hot Scot. "I really do appreciate all you've done for me. If there is anything I can do—"

"Just come out by the stove and settle in, warm up. If stew is all right with you . . . ?"

"Yes, of course. I'll be glad to help do . . . whatever."

He cut her off with a real smile. "Grab a comb and follow me. I have a feeling I'm going to have the easier job at my task than you will with yours."

She found a comb, scooped up her dirty clothes, and followed him out to the main room. After insisting, he reluctantly let her take her things to the laundry room and load the washer. As she tossed his muddy things in as well, then added soap, she realized she was smiling. In spite of the earlier, harrowing drama, she was, to be quite honest, very content with her situation at the moment. Though not intentionally, it appeared as if she'd stumbled across exactly what she'd been looking for when she'd raced out of Edinburgh this morning, and driven headlong into the highland mountains, wanting only to get as far away from civilization as possible.

Well, she'd accomplished that. She'd landed in an alternate universe of sorts, where no one knew her name. No one cared what she did for a living. No one cared if she ever wrote another word. At least it felt that way at the moment.

It should have given her pause at the very least, stuck with a strange man in the middle of nowhere, cut off from everyone, not a soul knowing where she was. But it was that very notion that had her smile warming to something approximating an actual grin.

A taste of true freedom. At least for now. And for now, a taste was enough. More than she'd thought possible.

She recalled following him out of the bathroom and down the hall. Her gaze had been drawn to the jeans he was wearing . . . and how he was wearing them. Long, lanky legs that she happened to know were very nicely defined. His t-shirt had fallen in a straight sheet from his broad shoulders, left untucked at the waist. His thick hair was drying in long waves that reached well past his shoulders.

As alternate universes went, she found herself thinking the view from this one was pretty spectacular . . .

And she couldn't help but wonder just how long she could play at being Alice in her new little wonderland.

Chapter 6

Tristan paused at the door to the mud room and watched her for a moment, undetected. She looked completely ridiculous swallowed up in his shirt and pants. Her hair was a snarled mess. But she was smiling as she started the washer on its cycle, and seemed relaxed and content. And for whatever reason, that settled something inside of him. He wasn't used to having company and was generally quite satisfied with that status quo. So why the thought of having her here didn't bother him quite so much, he couldn't say. Especially given that she'd been nothing but trouble thus far. "You really didn't have to do that."

She jumped slightly at the sound of his voice, but her smile didn't falter as she closed the lid on the washer and turned to him. "It was the least I could do, trust me."

"Stew is heating. Why don't you come sit by the stove, warm up."

She picked up the sweatshirt and comb and followed him back to the living room. Jinty looked up from where she'd settled in the middle of the room. She thumped her tail, but went back to the chunk of rawhide Tristan had given her to calm her down. He motioned to the chair closest to the peat stove. "Here," he said, shifting the chair and accompanying footstool so they angled closer to the warmth of the fire.

"Thank you." She sat and went to work on untangling the snarls.

He watched for a moment, knowing he should make himself scarce and give her some space . . . but not particularly motivated to do so. "So, what sent you out into a raging storm in that little buggy of yours? Or did you get caught unawares?"

She paused for a moment, and he could see the mental debate she waged. So . . . there was more to the story then, as he'd thought. As it was, he was having a hard time matching the calm, seemingly level-headed woman who sat before him, with the panicked, borderline hysterical woman who'd been trapped in her own car an hour earlier. Perhaps she simply didn't do well under pressure, but his instincts were telling him otherwise. And the silent debate she was waging backed that theory. He sat on the end of the oak-plank coffee table and waited for her response.

"I definitely got caught unawares. But, I—my life has been a little crazy of late, and I was just trying to, um, you know, get away from things for a little while. I was still struggling to learn the whole shifting left-handed thing and driving on the wrong side of the road—then the storm just whipped up, with the wind and everything, and right in the middle of it a sheep jumped in front of my car and I lost control. Anyway, as I said, I've been a bit frazzled of late, and I certainly didn't handle the whole situation as well as I otherwise might have." She'd gone back to picking at the knots in her hair with the comb during her little speech, the most she'd spoken since they'd crossed paths.

And she carefully hadn't looked at him once, he noted.

So, she had been running from something. From her "crazy life." But it wasn't any of his business what that crazy life entailed. At least she wasn't the hysterical twit he'd thought her to be, and he should just be thankful that she'd be out from underfoot by morning.

As it happened, he didn't feel quite like that. It made him

think back to what Brodie had been teasing him about earlier today. Which now seemed a lifetime ago, given everything that had happened since. Thing was, he did like his life out here. He enjoyed the solitude and serenity. Not that he minded the village and the bustle and noise. On occasion. For very limited periods of time. He wasn't a hermit, but he didn't like to be in the throng of things. Nothing wrong with that. Out here he was left to his own devices, the king of his domain. He enjoyed dealing with the tenant farmers and handling their issues, as they were few and far between and generally left him plenty of time to herd the sheep, contemplate the world, and sketch and paint to his heart's content. If anything, he'd always assumed others would be jealous of his lifestyle, not the other way around.

Only Brodie had had one point. Companionship was something he missed. Specifically that of a female nature. But that was where things got tricky with the life he'd carved for himself. About the only female who was compatible with it, or would ever be, was Jinty.

Just then, his guest winced as she picked at a particularly bad snarl and he was reaching for the comb before he thought better of the gesture.

"No, that's okay," she said, automatically shifting away from him. Not alarmed, but not exactly comfortable, either.

He slipped the comb from her hands anyway and shook his own unruly mop. "I happen to have some experience with this and there have been more than a time or two when an extra pair of hands and someone with some patience would have come in handy."

She did glance up at him then, a hint of a smile on her lips. "You are blessed with more patience than I, and I can't blame that on ulcer-inducing stress or killer fatigue," she said, then apparently realized she'd let a little too much slip. But she didn't look away.

He held her gaze, and found himself imagining how he'd draw her. Pastels, maybe. Charcoal first, though, to get the feel of all those sharp angles. He wondered if her face was always so lean, almost hard at the edges, or if it was a result of that stress and fatigue she'd just mentioned.

He realized he could have continued to stare into those eyes, questions upon questions coming to his tongue, for an endless period of time before tiring of the view. So he nudged her shoulder and said, "Shift around, sit on the hassock here. Let me get the worst at the back." He pushed the padded footstool that sat between her chair and the coffee table more squarely between them. "You face the fire and let me work on the knots."

"You've done more than your share, and I'm already intruding on your hospitality. I—"

"Humor me. I don't often have company out here. It's just me and my sheep." As if sensing her exclusion, Jinty took that moment to thump her tail on the floor. Tristan laughed. "And my girl, Jint. But she's not much for chatting. If you'd like to repay me, not that you need to, but I wouldn't mind the conversation." He looked back at her—and realized he didn't know her name. He switched hands with the comb and stuck his right one out. I'm Tristan, by the by. Tristan Chisholm."

Instead of making her feel more comfortable, however, his overture made her go completely still. She stared at his hand, then at him. She glanced past him, taking in the room, looking for or at what, he had no idea, then finally back to him. "I'm Bree," she said, finally looking back at him and taking his hand in a quick shake.

The lack of a last name was so blatant it had to be intentional, but he let it go. She was a woman alone, after all, and it might have been simply a cautious move on her part. But it was harder than he'd have thought not to dig. His curiosity, now piqued, was only growing.

"Turn," he told her, deciding it better to let her dictate the course, if any, of their conversation. She hesitated, but when he smiled, did as he asked. He started working on the ends of her hair, his mind going a million miles a minute. For a man who lived in, and cherished, peace and quiet, it was taking an enormous amount of restraint to allow the silence to continue between them. Surprisingly, she broke it first.

"I—I really do apologize for . . . well, everything. You've done so much and, I just . . . you really don't have to do this."

"I dinnae mind," he said, never more sincere. "As I said, other than the occasional annoying visit by one of my brothers, I lack for company on a regular basis. So if I have to rescue a fair maiden in order to have a dinner companion, well . . ."

She made a sound that could have been a laugh, but it was so soft he couldn't quite tell. "Seems an extreme measure," she said, then added, "Just how far are we from the nearest town?"

Ah, so she was thinking of her safety, out here alone with him. He could, of course, reassure her all he wanted, but she'd either believe or not. He'd have to let his actions speak for him. Which made him work to hide a grin. At the moment, his actions had him playing with her hair and sporting the definite beginnings of a hard-on. Not exactly keeping a safe and respectable distance.

But what an amazing mane she had. Snarled, wet, it didn't matter. He wanted to sink his hands into it, to turn her to him and see if he could spark life all the way into the depths of those wary eyes of hers. He wondered what the fair Bree would say if she had any inkling of his thoughts.

"Glenbuie would be closest," he told her. "About a half-hour from here. My brother owns the pub there, Hagg's. Another runs our family distillery, located on the far side of the village from here. My oldest brother is presently turning our crumbling family manse into a bed and breakfast, in hopes of keeping it from disintegrating entirely."

She said nothing for a few minutes, so he continued to work his way through her hair. Then, finally, she asked, "And you?"

So . . . she wasn't as impervious as she appeared. Good to know. He was growing less impervious by the moment. Noticing things he had no business paying attention to, like the way her slender neck curved into shoulders that she held so carefully square. Or the way she kept her spine stiff and straight, as if she dared to allow herself to relax for one brief moment, something terrible might happen. Gone was that momentary peace he'd noted earlier, when she'd thought herself alone in the mud room.

"Aye, I tend to the family flock. I also tend to the needs of the farmers who lease out our grazing property. But their needs are minimal. Mostly I have the run of the land. Jinty and I, anyway."

"It sounds quite . . . solitary." She didn't say it in a condemning way. In fact, she sounded almost . . . wistful.

"Aye, that it 'tis. But I enjoy it. I fancy myself an artist from time to time, though no' so much of late. I seem to have lost my muse."

Now she did snort, but added no commentary.

He found he couldn't let that one pass so easily. "What? Is it me being an artist you find so unbelievable?"

"No, not at all," she immediately said, clearly not wanting to insult him. "It was a self-directed comment, trust me."

"Have you lost yours as well, then? What is it that your muse inspires in you?"

She held her tongue, but he was patient. She'd proven to have curiosity and he doubted it was her nature to be silent and withdrawn, as when she let her guard down, she was quite personable, even if only for a moment here and there. Those were glimpses of the real Bree—he'd bet on it.

"I'm a writer," she said, then almost held herself even more rigidly than before, as if waiting for an unseen blow.

He frowned now, unable to imagine what about the written word would inspire such trepidation. "A journalist?" he asked. Perhaps she'd written some volatile political piece or something.

"No." She didn't elaborate. When he didn't press, but simply returned to his task, she said, "Do you read much? Novels, that sort of thing?"

"No' so much novels, no. I enjoy history, books on art, farming, business."

She seemed to take that in. "Newspapers? Periodicals?"

She wasn't a journalist, so he wondered why that mattered. "The local village puts out a paper every Saturday, but otherwise, no' so much. My world is here."

She took that in, but added nothing. He finished with the section of hair in the back and paused. "Why do you ask?" It couldn't be helped. He had to know. "Are you in some sort of trouble?"

She turned then, looking over her shoulder at him. "Why do you ask that?"

He smiled. "Why do you deflect the question with a question?"

She said nothing, but twin spots of color bloomed quite becomingly in her cheeks.

"If you've someone after you and I'm giving you shelter, perhaps I should know about it. That's all. Not that I'd turn you out," he assured her. "But being prepared is half the battle."

"I didn't run away from any one person."

"Ah," he countered, holding her gaze, keeping his tone light. "But you do admit you've run."

She started to turn away from him, hide herself once again, as he was certain she'd been doing instinctively for some time now. Just as he was certain it was not her nature, and that in doing so, it had taken quite a toll on her. How he understood this, he couldn't pinpoint, other than that her eyes, her expression, spoke to him in a way that communicated more clearly her thoughts than others could with a whole dictionary of words at their disposal. Yet again, his fingers itched to grab pen and paper and begin trying to capture all that she was so silently, and yet so loudly, communicating to him.

"Does the name Bree Sullivan mean anything to you?" she asked, quite bluntly and abruptly, her tone both confrontational and somewhat wary at the same time.

"Mean anything in what way?"

"You've not heard of it, then?"

"Other than from you, no, I can't say that I have."

And in that instant, her shoulders slumped a little, the stiff line of her spine softened. She dipped her chin and if he wasn't mistaken, he thought he saw her jaw quiver a little. As if she was fighting tears, or some other wave of emotion.

"Hey, there, come now." Gently he took her shoulders and turned her to him. When she wouldn't look up, he used a gentle finger beneath her chin to coax her into it anyway. Her eyes were huge and glassy wet, her face so clearly weary and spent. "The day has taken a toll on ye, hasn't it, luv?" he said gently. "And here I've been badgering ye." It was clear there was far more involved than that, but he felt bad now for pushing, he who so prized his privacy. "Let me get some warm stew into you—then you can crawl in and sleep until you don't need any more."

"I—you—thank you," she stuttered, clearly embarrassed by her near-breakdown. There was a small sniff, then she pulled her chin from his touch and gathered her wits about her once more. "Maybe that's not such a bad idea. I'm . . . not myself. I'm sorry."

"Dinnae fash yerself, lass," he assured her. And the side of him that saw lambs into the world and cared for his flock, Jinty included, but rarely beyond, found itself extending to include her as well. She was most definitely a lost sheep. And for the span of this night, she was his to care for. "I think I've tamed the worst of it," he said, offering her back the comb. "You should be able to reach the rest okay."

She took the comb, her expression so grateful it made his heart ache a little. "Thank you. For—for more than you know."

"Come now," he teased, trying to give her space to recoup,

"we Scots are famed for our friendly hospitality." He smiled. "I canno' say the same for our food, though."

"I've had no complaints," she said, relaxing a little again. "I'm from the Midwest. Meat and potatoes are staples of life there. As far as I'm concerned, the simpler the meal, the better."

"The Midwest. Farming, perhaps?"

"Not my family, but yes. Missouri," she offered, when he didn't speak right away. "Small town. So I know how nice it is to have your peace and solitude."

"It's been some time since you've had that then, I take it?"

She didn't freeze up again, but the wary look made an immediate reappearance. "Yes. A very long time, it seems."

"So you crossed the big pond looking for it here?"

"Something like that."

"Not entirely successful, I take it. Given the flight today in your car."

"No," she agreed. "Not much luck at all. I'm not sure it's available for me."

"Well, you have it here," he told her. "Other than my annoying, probing questions, anyway."

"*You* have it here," she corrected him. "I'm just borrowing it for the night. But I'm more thankful for that one night than you can possibly know."

He held her gaze for the space of several long seconds, and then the offer was made before he could think on it a moment longer. "I've room," he told her. "And I dinnae think my peace and solitude will be shattered too much by the addition of another soul."

She turned, stared at him. "What do you mean?"

He hadn't planned this, had planned in fact to have her gone within twenty-four hours. But that was a lifetime ago, too. Before he was intrigued. Before he was entranced. Before his muse had made a very unexpected reappearance. "I mean, you can stay here. For however long you'd like."

"But I can't just—"

He cut her off. Because he'd seen that instant spark of hope in her eyes. And because he'd felt the same spark inside of him as well. He didn't claim to understand it, but he wanted the chance to try.

"Yes, you *can* just." He stood and extended her a hand. "Sometimes it really can be just that simple."

She looked at him, so wary, yet so obviously wanting to believe. When she put her hand in his and stood, he knew at once he'd been right. It really could be that simple. Just as he knew, and surprisingly accepted, that it was quite likely nothing was going to be simple, ever again.

Chapter 7

"Simple," Bree echoed. She wanted to laugh at the mere suggestion that anything in her life could ever be such again. But he was holding her hand, and looking into her eyes . . . and standing so close. It had been all she could do not to squirm the entire time he'd had his hands in her hair. If he had any idea the kind of thoughts she was harboring about him, especially when he'd been nothing but a gentleman . . . she wondered if the invitation to stay would still be open. "You don't know what you're offering. It isn't that simple."

"You're right. I don't know the whole story. I only know you have one. And that it seems as if you could use a break."

"You should know," she started, but he lifted his free hand, halting her.

"If you want tae tell me, fine. But don't feel ye have to. You're safe here, I can tell you that much."

"No one is after me, or anything like that." Well, the entire free world was hounding at her heels, but that wasn't quite what he'd been intimating.

He pushed the hair back from her face, and it made her breath catch in her throat. "You're runnin' from something, Bree Sullivan. I'm just offering you a place to stop for a bit and collect yourself. That's all." Then, as if realizing he was touching her with far more familiarity than he should be, he dropped his hand.

She almost sighed in disappointment and had to catch herself. He was right about one thing, she did need a break. She did need a place to stop and gather her thoughts, decide how she wanted to go forward. But while she'd expected or hoped to find some little out-of-the-way bed and breakfast or something, she hadn't quite counted on this. Much less him.

She was intensely attracted to him—there was no point denying that any longer. But now was not the time to be adding any complications to a life already far too complicated for one person to manage. Simple, he'd said. And yet she knew there was nothing simple about her life . . . or about this man. Staying under his roof might help her to solve some of her problems in the short term . . . but it would be sorely tempting her to create a few new ones at the same time.

"I'm an author," she said, quite abruptly. If she was going to stay here—and she realized even as the thought formed in her head that she'd already decided she wanted to—he had to know exactly what he was getting into. At least as it pertained to the life she'd led up until the moment she'd spun out into that gully. "I had a book out, about a year and a half ago, that sold very well."

She looked at him, waited to see if he put the name and the book together, but he simply continued to look at her. Could it truly be that she'd not only stumbled across a decent, generous man, but one who truly had no idea who she was, or anything about the phenomenon that *Summer Lake* had become?

"It did so well, in fact, that I became something of a celebrity. I haven't had much in the way of a private life ever since. And . . . and now the world is waiting for me to follow things up, and everyone is getting very impatient with me. Only . . ." She let the sentence drift, as the heavy weight of what awaited her out there lowered itself once again onto her narrow shoulders . . . and pressed heavily against her heart.

He tipped her chin up, and she belatedly realized they were still standing deep inside one another's personal space. And that she rather liked it. A lot. The part of her brain that was rational knew it was just a human reaction to something—or someone, in this case—providing much-needed shelter and comfort. But the rest of her, the parts that were trembling and quivering, knew she wanted to be far deeper in this particular man's personal space than she already was. And for reasons that had absolutely nothing to do with seeking safe harbor. There was nothing remotely safe about the way his mere proximity was tripping every sensory alert she had, and a few she'd had no idea she possessed.

"The expectations we put on ourselves are usually what doom us the fastest," he told her, his voice hardly more than a murmur. And then there was the way his gaze dropped to her mouth, before moving back to her eyes. Could it be he was having those same thoughts?

The very idea made her press her thighs together against the instant need that sprang to life between them. Ridiculous, really, to assume such a thing. Certainly, he wasn't having the same kinds of thoughts she was. She looked a fright and had been nothing but a nuisance to him.

"I canno' imagine having the weight of the world's expectations piled on top of my own," he went on.

His fingers traced lightly along her jaw. She went perfectly still. He . . . the way he was looking at her . . . had he seen something in her eyes? Was it wrong of her to want, almost desperately, for that to be true?

When she didn't move away from him, he slid his fingers beneath the weight of the hair on her neck. "But at the moment, I can only seem to think of one thing and one thing only . . ."

Her breath caught when he pressed lightly against the nape of her neck, tipping her head back.

"And what would that be?" she asked, amazed she'd found the words at all.

"Finding out what you taste like."

Her heart was pounding much as it had earlier, in the car, when she was trapped. Only now it wasn't in fear and trepidation . . . but the rather exquisite torture of anticipation. If she allowed herself to think at all in that moment, she'd pull free, push him away. He was certainly giving her plenty of time.

So she simply refused to think.

Life had been too hard for too long, and she'd felt so guilty for hating what, by all rights, was a fairy tale existence most people could only dream of having. But the truth was, she hated that life. She wanted to be left alone to write, to pursue the craft she loved without all the hoopla and pressure. Right now she didn't want to think about any of it. For far too long now, she'd felt very alone in a constant sea of people. Swimming in chaos and trying not to drown.

It had taken almost drowning for real for her to step outside of that chaos. And into the arms of the man standing in front of her. One man, surrounded by nothing but serenity and peace . . . even in the midst of a raging storm. He was like a life preserver being thrown right into her hands. She could hardly be blamed for wanting to grab on to it—him— and hold on tight. The rest could sort itself out later.

"So why don't you?" she told him, shocking herself, but the hell with that, too. "Find out, I mean."

"I shouldn't," he said. "The offer to stay was no' contingent on this, ye know that."

"So, if I asked you to stop, would you?" she asked.

He instantly started to lift his head, to pull back. Without thinking, she reached up and slid her hand into the thick mane at the back of his neck, not pulling him closer, but keeping him where he was.

"What if I'm curious, too?" she asked. "What if I've been thinking about this, too, ever since . . ." She broke off then, feeling her skin heat up. Images of him, soaked to the skin, all but completely naked, flashed through her mind, and she

realized that no matter how worldly wise she'd become over
the past year and a half ... in the ways that mattered at the
moment, there was still a lot of small-town librarian left in
her.

His mouth kicked up a little at the corners. "Ever since
when?" He shifted slightly, put a hand on her hip and held
her close to him without actually allowing their bodies to
make contact.

Just the way he moved, the easy confidence he had in the
way he touched her, moved her ... made the ache spread.
Words might be her life, but speaking them out loud to a
man who was looking like he wanted to devour her whole,
was suddenly impossible for her. She tugged his head a little
closer. "Since I had enough sense to know better ... and still
wanted to, anyway."

His eyes grew darker and his fingers dug into her hip as his
grip tightened. "I feel as if I'm taking advantage and I don't
do that."

Take advantage, she wanted to scream. Couldn't he sense
how rare it was for her to be reckless? She didn't want him to
be all reasonable and levelheaded, she didn't want to stop
and think.

"I know I shouldn't, but ... there's something about you,
Bree Sullivan. You've been through a lot."

"You have no idea."

"So, we probably shouldn't."

"Probably."

"Are ye tellin' me to stop, then?"

She gave him a slight shake of her head, her gaze never
once leaving his. "I'd really rather you didn't. I have been
through a lot. I feel like I've been living my life for a whole
lot of other people, because I feel I owe it to them for all
they've given me. Even if I didn't exactly ask for it, or expect
it. It's been a very long time since I did anything that was just
for me, and to hell with what everyone else wanted. I took
off this morning knowing I needed to get away, to stop the

world and get off, at least long enough to ask myself some hard questions about what I want, about what I need. And where I want to go from this point forward."

"So ye don't need me crowding ye, makin' demands—"

"What I need," she said, with surprising force, "is to do whatever I damn well please. I've been so micromanaged for so long, I don't even know myself any longer. I don't want to overthink things, I don't want to analyze. I just want to feel. I want to do what feels good and right and natural, without worrying to death about who might think what if I do this, or don't do that. I just want, for once, to follow my instincts and the hell with everything else."

He surprised her with a sudden grin that made his eyes twinkle in such a devilish way, she should have had immediate doubts. Yet, all it did was make her want him more. After all, if she was going to jump, she might as well jump big.

"If your instincts are tellin' ye to come after me, ye might be more battle-weary than ye think."

His teasing just made him all the more attractive to her newly discovered renegade spirit. He made it easy to respond in kind. "I don't know about that," she countered. "I think I'm getting a second wind."

"Are ye now," he responded, the twinkle still there, but his voice had dropped to a murmur . . . as his gaze once again dropped to her mouth. "I'll have ye know we're both playin' with fire here."

"I can stand the heat," she parried, secretly thrilled by her ability to do so. He called to something inside of her, and she discovered a side to herself she hadn't known she possessed. A somewhat playful, demanding spirit she could never have owned up to before. And she liked it. Quite a lot. Perhaps if she'd been more in touch with this side of herself, she'd have been more insistent about creating a better balance to her life in the past year or so, instead of being a doormat to everyone who made a demand on her time, feeling as if she owed everybody everything for the success they'd made her into.

He tugged her an inch closer. "I meant what I said," he told her, his tone a bit more gruff, and a bit more rough with need. "I'll stop if ye but give me the word. You've found yer haven, but that does no' mean ye have to let yer host—"

She took the final step and closed the remaining space between them, pressing her body against his. A small moan slipped out when she felt the proof of his desire for her pressing rigidly into her belly. "We're consenting adults." She looked up into his eyes. "I'm consenting, Tristan."

His eyes went even darker, if that were possible, and she felt him twitch, where he was trapped between their bodies. "I like the way my name sounds on your lips, with that accent of yours."

She smiled. "I don't have the accent, you do. In fact, it's probably the only reason I've fallen under your spell." He was so much fun to tease, and it came so easily to her, she should be shocked. And a part of her was. But it felt like she'd been set free, to romp and play and be completely herself without fear of reprisal, very public reprisal. No, this was private and personal and for no one other than the two of them, as it should be. It was intoxicating, to be certain. And far too much fun to waste a second worrying about whether she should indulge or not.

"Is that so?" He grinned again and moved against her, eliciting another little gasp of awareness from her. "I suppose we'll just have to see about that, now won't we?"

"I suppose we will," she breathed. And in that moment, the rest of the world fell away. For now, her existence was based exclusively on herself and Tristan, and the very private, exquisitely intimate world they were about to explore together. "So, what are we waiting for?"

Chapter 8

Indeed, Tristan thought. What was he waiting for? He'd given her every opportunity, hadn't he? She was correct—they were consenting adults. So why wasn't he carrying her off to his lair to have his wicked way with her?

He was so rock-hard with need he was in pain. He should be ecstatic to have such a delightful surprise drop literally into his lap. After all, she was just passing through. And more than willing to while away a little of her time with him. What wasn't to like? He couldn't have dreamed up a better scenario.

He looked down into Bree's eyes, alive now with desire. So thoroughly filled with trust.

It was that last part that was hanging him up.

Not that he couldn't be trusted. He was dependable and fair to a fault. And they'd clearly made no claim on each other beyond this storm-filled night . . . and whatever additional nights they chose to share beyond it. So why he looked into her eyes and felt . . . not guilt, exactly—he wasn't taking advantage of the situation any more or less than she was, after all. But . . . something. Something more, or perhaps different, than he should be feeling if this were nothing more than a simple roll in the hay.

There was that word again. *Simple.*

And that, right there, was the crux of it. She wouldn't be

simple. He already knew her life was being lived on a far grander stage than some rocky, highland acreage dotted with nothing more than heather and sheep. Which was fine by him, as he couldn't care less where life took her once she left here. Right?

Right.

Except she was smiling up at him, and he felt something shift inside his chest, in a spot very close to his heart. There was something about Bree Sullivan, something about the combination of her warrior spirit and her wounded soul, that reached a place deep inside of him. It made no sense—he hardly knew anything of her, really. But what he did know of her made him want to draw, made him want to create. It had been a very long time since he'd felt so moved, so truly inspired.

Och, he thought ruefully, knowing why he hesitated in carrying her off to his bed. She'd captured his muse's fancy, that was a certainty. But . . . the fear was, what if she went beyond that? What if she did what no one else ever had . . . and captured his fancy as well? Not that he was opposed to such a thing ever happening . . . he'd always assumed it would at some point. But as he was tied to this land, to his family's heritage here, and to the way of life he'd carved out for himself, he'd also supposed it would be with a local lass, someone well suited to highland life.

Not a Yank with no intention of hanging about.

And yet here she stood, tempting parts of him never before tempted. She was a dangerous one, if his clamoring instincts were to be listened to. He was borrowing trouble by just allowing her to stay under his roof . . . much less in his own bed. She'd hardly warmed his arms, and he already felt the pull. He'd yet to even taste her. It made no sense. And much as he wanted to blame it on long-overdue physical need, he knew the difference between wanting to rut for the sake of it, and wanting . . . something more.

It was his muse talking. Or that is what he tried to make

himself believe. He was feeling a connection of spirit, but that didn't mean he had to take it further. Like as not, they'd both have their fill of each other and be perfectly sated and more than happy to move on, leaving their time shared together as nothing more than a lovely reminiscence, something to be pulled out and remembered fondly at some future moment in time. His muse had been properly titillated, but his memory was the good and detailed one of an artist . . . he didn't need to keep her around for constant inspiration.

So stop being such a knobknock, he told himself. *Take her to bed. Bury yourself in her sweet, welcoming body, and dinnae think of naught else but her pleasure and yours. She wants it the same as you . . . what in God's name are ye waiting for?*

With perhaps a wee bit more intensity than intended, he tipped her head back and took her mouth with his. Mostly, initially, to get a move on before he could stupidly talk himself out of this amazingly fortunate set of circumstances. Any other man would have had her naked by now.

But the instant he tasted her, the instant he felt her body go soft in his arms . . . the intensity became quite real. Need for more of her, all of her, right this instant, roared to life inside of him with such ferocity, that that alone should have been warning enough. But he was all done waging battle with himself. He was committed to it now, and the only thing that would or could stop him would be her.

She was pliant in his arms, her mouth opening willingly beneath his, accepting him with a fervor almost as greedy as his. Stopping him was clearly something she had no interest in doing. So, have her he would. Thoroughly and well, until neither could catch their breath. And once they did . . . he'd have her again. The hunger she roused inside of him was that voracious a beast. Consenting adults, she'd said. And consent they both had.

She was a lithe, slender bit of a thing, he noted, as he hauled her body up against his. He buried one hand in that tangled mane of hair, keeping her mouth tipped perfectly to his so he could take it at his own will, his own pace. He wrapped his free arm around her hips, lifting her to the tips of her toes so he could fit himself where his body so badly ached to be. She moaned against his mouth, and he thought he might shoot off like a rocket right then and there. No, that is no' how this eve would play out. Not if he had a say about it.

Eliciting a surprised squeal, he bent slightly and scooped her up high against his body. "Wrap your legs," he murmured against her lips, lips that, in that moment, he thought he could explore for the remainder of his days and be perfectly content to do so.

She gripped his shoulders, digging into his skin as she hooked her heels around his lower back, grappling to stay up against him even as she continued to kiss him with everything she had. Something about that visceral need, the bite of her nails into his flesh, the simultaneous way she bit gently into his bottom lip, sent him stumbling blindly through the living room toward his bedroom, almost tripping badly over Jinty, who sprang to life behind them.

He managed to send her a hand signal, holding her where she stood. He heard her little whine of disappointment, but would gladly make it up to her later. At the moment, there was only one female he wanted in his bed, and she didn't possess four legs. Only two. And dear sweet Lord, the way they were squeezing his waist so tightly, he wasn't certain if perhaps he hadn't really died out there, after all. He certainly felt thunderstruck.

He kicked the door shut behind him, then turned and pressed her up against it, holding her there with his weight against hers . . . so he could bury his hands once again in all that hair. She made these soft, needy little whimpers that drove him wild. She let her fingers skim along from his shoulders to the nape of his neck, toying with strands of his own hair as she nibbled once again on his lower lip.

"You're making me mad," he murmured.

She pulled away slightly. "I'm sorry."

He laughed. "No' mad as in angry. Mad as in crazy." He nipped at her bottom lip—fair was fair, after all. "Wrap yourself tight," he instructed.

She hooked her arms around his neck and he spun them both around, and down onto his bed, so that she landed sprawled beneath him. His feather down duvet swallowed her up and she sighed in pleasure, then groaned in approval as he lowered himself fully onto her. He started to shift his weight off a bit, not wanting to smother her, but she immediately pulled him down and locked her ankles around his calves.

He grinned, gazing down into her beautiful, desire-filled eyes. "I like a lass who knows what she wants."

"Good," she responded tartly, tightening her hold, though her flushed cheeks and overbright eyes made it obvious to anyone paying attention that her bravado was hard-earned, that the journey she'd begun with him wasn't a path she'd taken often, if at all. And Lord knew, she had his full attention.

He wanted to devour her whole, to bury himself to the hilt inside of her petite, limber body, and piston himself into sweet oblivion. Given the way her hips were already moving beneath his, he was fairly certain this was her plan as well. So why he propped himself up on his elbows and slowed things down, he had no idea. Except rushing this just seemed a crime of sorts. There was so much to enjoy . . . and he knew better than to trust there would be time for that later. Later was unpredictable. Right now she was all his. And he wanted all of her he could have.

She reached for him, but he pinned her hands next to her head. Her eyes widened slightly, but in interest, not alarm. Her smile was both guileless and a wee bit challenging. How was it she could be both worldly and so sweetly naïve?

Pinning her arms with his, he framed her face with his palms, brushing his thumbs over the stark relief of her cheekbones. She'd been through an ordeal, that much was clear. Even if, on the surface, her life had seemed a fairy tale, he doubted the hollows beneath her eyes, the tautness of the skin stretched over her cheeks, was typical of the content Midwestern lass she'd been a scant few years ago. It made him want to care for her, see to it that she did right by herself, to provide safe haven for her and help her defend against those who would swallow her whole with thought only for their own gain. Insanity, perhaps, to feel such depth for what amounted to a total stranger. And yet she didn't feel like a stranger to him. It made little sense, but perhaps it wasn't intended to. It was as if she'd finally found her way here. To him. And he finally felt at peace, with her in his arms.

"Bree Sullivan," he murmured, thinking perhaps he *was* the deranged lunatic she'd initially feared him to be, after all. Had she but a single clue as to where his thoughts were at the moment, she'd be perfectly within her rights to run screaming right back out into the storm. And he wouldn't blame her. The very idea of her vanishing as suddenly as she'd appeared had him settling his weight more directly onto her, holding her beneath him, keeping her there, until . . .

"Yes, Tristan Chisholm?" she responded, interrupting his thoughts.

His body twitched—hard—at the sound of his name on her lips. It had nothing to do with her flat, American accent, and everything to do with the way the corner of her mouth kicked up as she said it, like she knew some highly amusing secret that she might share if properly convinced.

He wanted to know all of her secrets. Wanted to be in on every amusing thought that crossed her mind. Wanted to inspire a few of his own. "What is it you're doing to me?" he whispered, not realizing he'd given voice to the words until she wiggled her eyebrows and hips at the same time.

"I thought that was rather obvious." Her half-smile became a crooked grin. "Just how long have you been out here with your sheep, anyway?"

Her unexpected comeback elicited a quick snort of laughter from him. "Too long, to be certain." He pushed her hair away from her face, then traced her eyebrows with the sides of his thumbs before framing her face with his palms once again. So fragile, yet so sturdy. She'd let the world in, let them take too much, but she'd fought back, too. Her self-preservation instinct might have slipped a little, but it was there. She was strong, his Bree. At least for the moment, she was his. "Is that all it is, then? Accumulated need?"

"Is that all *what* is?" she asked, her eyes darkening with need when their hips continued with a rhythm neither could seem to control.

"This," he said, his own voice going hoarse as he moved between her thighs and pressed into her, as much as their clothing would allow. "It's insanity, really, the hunger you've unleashed in me. I've never all but dragged a woman to my bed."

"I don't recall you having to do much dragging. What with me clinging to your hips and all."

He grinned, loving her quick mind, her sharp mouth. "True."

"And I have a hard time believing you've ever had to coerce anyone out of their clothes and into your bed."

"You think so, do you?"

"An educated guess."

She was right—he'd never coerced anyone. But he'd never cared enough to, either. He'd always let things happen . . . or not. Never much caring, really. Tonight, however, he was fairly certain that he'd have done whatever was necessary to get her to at least give him a chance. "One could say the same of you," he parried.

She laughed. "One could. If one was seriously delusional."

"Come now." He gently raked his fingers through her hair so it fanned across his bed. It was a vision he'd take a long time to forget, if ever.

"I'm trying," she quipped, her cheeks going bright pink

even as she grinned and pumped her hips again, making them both groan a little.

"You're quite cute when you blush," he said, stroking his thumbs across her cheeks, then across her mouth, pressing against the fullness of her bottom lip until she parted them and bit at the tips of his fingers. His body leapt in response and he tried desperately to keep himself in check. "A saucy wench with a heart of gold, is what ye are."

Her face lit up. "Really? Saucy? Hmm . . . I rather like that description." She slid her ankle down the back of his calf. "Something about you makes it easy to be playful."

"I'm so very glad to hear that," he told her, never more sincere. He reared back onto his knees then, eliciting a quick frown of dismay from her. He leaned down and kissed it away, feeling starved for the taste of her after only minutes apart.

She sighed as he lifted his head, then pouted quite prettily when he sat back on his haunches. But she didn't move from where he'd had her pinned, her arms still splayed next to her head. With her dark hair fanned out on the white linen, her eyes all liquid with need, her skin flushed, her mouth slightly parted . . . his heart tilted dangerously and it was getting harder and harder to remember why she wasn't perfect for him. "You're stunning," he murmured. *And you're mine,* was the thought that immediately followed.

Inappropriate and certainly untrue, that he knew. And yet, the basic tenet simply refused to shake free.

He reached for the rolled-down waistband of the pants he'd loaned her and hooked his fingers inside, tugging lightly. She didn't immediately lift her hips, but if the way her eyes went all heavy-lidded, and the way she tugged at her bottom lip with her teeth, was any indication, she wasn't going to stop him, either. "Ye've seen most of me," he told her. "I want to see you."

He tugged gently but insistently until she lifted her hips, keeping her gaze tightly on his, but gnawing ever further on that bottom lip. Saucy wench indeed, but innocent as well. He hardly imagined she'd had no experience in these kinds of situations, but it was clear the worldly exploits that had come with the sudden fame of the past year or so hadn't jaded her to this particular form of interaction. Far from it, if the blush now stealing from her cheeks, down across her throat, and, he was fairly certain, clear to her chest, was any indication.

"Ye've naught to worry about," he assured her, sliding the soft cotton slowly down her hips. "You've but to tell me to stop and I'll—"

"I don't want you to stop," she said, and with surprising conviction. "I wasn't kidding about this . . . kind of thing not being a regular part of my life . . . but don't let my relative lack of experience slow you down." The crooked smile reappeared as she tried for insouciant . . . and missed by a mile. "Please."

Dear God, she was of a piece . . . and snatching up bits of his heart quite effortlessly in the doing.

"Your wish is my command," he told her, before finally breaking their locked gaze so he could look down upon the absolute loveliness that was her body as he bared her legs completely and tossed the pants aside. Straddling her ankles, he slid his hands along her calves, and up over her knees. Her neck arched, as did her hips, when his fingertips brushed along the sensitive skin of her inner thighs. "Lovely," he said. "Bloody brilliantly lovely."

He shifted down and moved between her thighs, sliding his hands to her hips, pushing up the edges of the long t-shirt, baring her to him even as he held her down to the bed, keeping her right where he wanted her to be. She bucked against him, but her soft moans were ones of pleasure. He pressed a kiss to the inside of her knee, then another one a pace or two higher, then another higher still . . .

She whimpered, her hips lifting, searching, reaching. "Tristan, I've never exactly done this sort of—"

He didn't want to hear what she'd never done, didn't want her to stop him now, to keep him from what he so badly wanted, what he knew she'd enjoy as well. "You will have now," he said, and dipped his head between her thighs. "And if you'll guide me, tell me what feels the best, I trust you'll want to again. And again." He brushed his lips across the soft curls at the apex of her thighs, then pressed a soft kiss there. "Promise."

Chapter 9

It felt a bit scandalous, the frank way in which he spoke about the things he planned to do to her . . . his certainty that she'd enjoy it. She was quivering so hard at this point, so on edge, he could breathe on her and she'd likely climax. Which was good, because as wanton as he made her feel, and despite the occasional quip thus far, she wasn't so certain she could be quite as direct as he was and tell him exactly what she wanted him to do . . . and where.

He pinned her hips down, and settled more contentedly between her thighs. She tried to relax, but her muscles were clenching to the point of pain. She wasn't overly modest, nor particularly self-conscious about her body . . . but the truth was, she'd never been intimate with anyone who, well, who enjoyed this particular kind of foreplay. She tried not to think about it, to just relax and let herself feel—

"Bree," Tristan said, his tone coaxing, his breath feathering across her oh-so-sensitive skin.

"Mmm," she responded, eyes closed, neck arched as she tried in vain to get him to ease his hold on her hips so she could lift up and press against his lips. Just one little teasing kiss . . . she was so close, if he'd only—

"Bree, look at me."

Did she really have to? This would be a lot easier the first time if he'd let her disassociate a little.

His fingers pressed more urgently into her hips, and he teased her by dropping hot, wet little kisses all along the insides of her thighs. So close, and yet just far enough away to drive her crazy.

"Tristan, please."

"Mmm," he responded, "so polite. Tristan, please what?"

He damn well knew what she wanted—she shouldn't have to say it. Without thinking, she lifted her head and looked down at him. He chose the exact instant they made eye contact to shoot her a wicked grin, then flick his tongue over her most sensitive spot.

She jerked hard against the feel of his tongue flicking at her, slapping her palms down on the sheets and grabbing on as she fought against the need to buck wildly against his mouth. *More. More of that,* she wanted to tell him. *A lot more.*

She was still watching him, couldn't look away. There was something downright primal about seeing him there. His eyes were twinkling with mischief and she wanted to be irritated with him for toying with a woman so obviously on the verge. But there was no denying it only served to drive her up even higher. She wished she could be more blasé about this, casually make her demands, but— He stopped her train of thought with the sweetest kiss, right where she needed it.

She gasped, trembling now.

"Tell me, Bree. Come on . . ."

"I—just, more," she managed. She let her head drop back, closed her eyes.

"Of what?" He kissed her again, so sweet, and so close, but it wasn't quite enough. "More of that?"

"Mmm." More of that would be really great, but she needed more beyond that, and he damn well knew it. She wanted him to use his tongue. But the words stuck in her throat. She could write this scene, quite graphically, with absolutely no problem whatsoever. Saying it out loud, however, to her lover was another thing entirely. *Her lover.*

She found herself looking at him again. His hands on her hips, his hair spread across his shoulders and her thighs . . . This man would be her lover. *Was* her lover. Kind, generous, fearless, playful. She'd dropped barriers for him she never dropped for anyone. He made it so easy, almost too easy. And now he was asking her to drop a few more.

In all the likely scenarios that had crossed her mind of where she'd end up when she'd left the baron's palatial estate this morning, none had come close to where she found herself at this exact moment. In a man's bed, with him taunting her toward an explosive orgasm.

"Bree?"

There was a note of question in his voice, as if he sensed the direction of her thoughts. He would stop if she asked. She knew that. No matter that she was a breath way from a screaming climax . . . and that he was rock-hard and likely dying for release himself. He must have felt the pull of her gaze as he looked up at her, eyes filled with desire, with need. For her. She felt like she'd been staring into those eyes for ages. He made her feel tended to, cared for. She trusted him, even though she knew quite rationally how dangerous it was to invest such a vulnerable emotion in a relative stranger. But he certainly didn't feel like a stranger at the moment.

In fact, from the instant she'd reached for his hand in the middle of that storm, he'd ceased to be one.

Yes, this man was going to be her lover. Her partner in rescue, and now her partner in pleasure. Did it matter if there was never anything else?

Kind, generous, fearless, playful. Those things she knew firsthand. She could most likely add *loyal, protective, honorable, and trustworthy* to that list. An ache of a different kind spread inside of her. The ache of wondering what it would be like to find out for herself if her instincts about him were right. He'd offered her his home as a haven. He'd offered her himself for her own pleasure. No strings. She called the shots.

What if she decided she wanted more?

"I want you to use your tongue on me," she blurted, propping herself up on her elbows. Suddenly, telling him what she wanted in bed was the least scary thing about what was happening between them. Or could happen between them. Had he any clue the dangerous turns her thoughts were taking, he'd likely regret ever rushing out into that storm in the first place, much less carrying her off to his bed. But it was almost impossible not to wonder. He made it impossible. And in her immediate situation, she could hardly be blamed for wanting more, now could she?

His eyes widened in momentary surprise at her blatant demand.

She smiled at him. Something about the way he so confidently commanded this situation made her feel inherently safe within it. As if she could do anything, say anything, and he'd rise—literally—to the occasion. His sense of play was equal to his sense of honor. He'd stop if she asked.

Just as he'd likely use that tongue of his on her all night if she asked him to.

"I want you to make me come." Her thighs twitched and she trembled as she moved against the hands that restrained her. "And then I want you to do it again." When he continued to stare at her, she smiled. "You said my wish was your command?"

He grinned then, and it was so wickedly perfect, she found herself laughing in sheer joy of the moment. Of finding the perfect partner in crime . . . or passion, as the case may be. "As it happens, your command dovetails nicely with my own wishes," he told her, then leaned closer, his gaze still locked on hers. "Like this, then?" he asked, oh-so-innocently. Wicked, wicked man that he was. He flicked out his tongue, expertly brushing over her, making her hips jerk hard, making her moan.

"Yes," she managed, sliding down so she lay flat on the bed once again. "Most definitely yes."

"Or perhaps this." He drew his tongue slowly over her,

then pulled her between his lips, gently suckling, then flicking his tongue over her again.

The sensations wound tighter and tighter, so close, so close. She wanted it to last, this exquisite pleasure. It was so good, too good. But he wouldn't let her. Not this time. He continued teasing, tormenting, until her gasps became whimpers, and her whimpers became moans, until she was begging him, with her body, with her words, to finish what he'd so brilliantly started. "Tristan, please—"

And please her he did, driving her over the edge with a series of tiny tongue flicks that had her swearing she saw stars as she came almost violently against him.

"Bree," he coaxed, once she'd stopped thrashing against him. "Bree, luv," he said, kissing her thighs, soothing her as she came back to earth.

Quite drowsily, she managed to open her eyes and gaze down at him. "Wow," was all she could manage.

He chuckled, and even that gentle vibration made her twitch and jerk as aftershocks of pleasure still continued to rock her.

She reached blindly for him, wanting to feel the weight of him on top of her, wanting him to fill the aching, desperately needy void inside of her that had yet to be met. But he nudged her hands away. "I'm no' finished with you yet," he warned her, all teasing smiles and devilish twinkle.

"No?" she asked faintly.

In response, he very gently, very softly, drew his tongue down over her, making her gasp and buck involuntarily. "No," he murmured. "Relax, let me have my fill of ye."

Well, when he put it like that . . . He followed up his request by continuing to caress her, gradually building her back up. She was deliciously relaxed now and a languid peace had spread its way through her. The intensity and need built slowly this time, her soft moans becoming more insistent as he brought her from one plateau to another. Her back arched almost lazily, but fully, as he drew her closer and closer to the edge. He kept her hovering there, a breath away, as her heart rate increased, her whimpers turned to growls, and her hips bucked with growing impatience, only then did he push one finger inside of her. She gasped sharply, clenched tightly . . . and came instantly. Muscles so aching with need clamped down on him hard, as she writhed beneath him and milked the orgasm for every last drop of pleasure it could give her.

The sensations were still shimmering through her in delicious little aftershocks when he finally drew away from her. She whimpered in automatic disappointment at his sudden absence, and fought to open her eyes, pull herself back from the foggy haze of pleasure she'd drifted into and focus on the moment. The fight was worth it. As she opened her eyes, she saw Tristan standing at the foot of the bed, slowly shucking his shirt and pants.

Splayed before him like the wanton, sated creature she'd so easily become, she took unabashed and quite avid pleasure in watching him disrobe. She'd seen him close to fully naked before, but it was nothing compared to now. Lit only by a small bedside lamp, the soft yellow light bathed his tautly muscled body in shadowy hues, highlighting every dip and curve so beautifully, she thought she could be content simply staring at him.

Until he slid off his pants, and she saw for the first time the full depth and breadth of his desire for her. Then she decided a far more up close and personal exploration was definitely going to be in order. "You're beautiful," she murmured, unaware she'd actually spoken the sentiment until he glanced up at her as he slid a condom packet out of his dresser drawer and tore it open with his teeth. It was hard to tell in this light, but he looked a little abashed at her blunt appraisal, and glanced away as he rolled the condom on.

"Are you blushing?" she asked, a very satisfied smile spreading across her face. She felt edgy and needy again, and liked the idea that he wasn't impervious to their byplay, either. She wanted him badly, and yet she found herself in no immediate hurry to speed things up. She understood now his desire to slow things down when he'd had his turn with her. His body twitched at her slow appraisal and her smile spread to a grin. Somehow she didn't think he was going to be any more patient than she'd been. Come to think of it, she didn't want to be patient, either.

"Perhaps I'm no' used to being looked at as if I were Sunday supper," he said at last.

She laughed, unable to remember a time when she'd felt this good, this relaxed, this happy. "Is that a bad thing?"

He crawled onto the bed and she shuddered in anticipation.

"I don't know," he said, his voice close to a growl. "Why dinnae ye tell me?" He moved slowly up and over her body, pulling one of her thighs up onto his hip as he did.

He lifted her up as he slid between her thighs, stopping just as he pushed against her. She wrapped her legs around him, keeping her hips tilted, wanting to push herself up onto him, but let him set the pace. Even if it killed her. She wasn't an aggressive partner in bed. Or she hadn't been. Tristan made her feel very earthy, intensely female, and definitely like his equal. He made her want to play, made her want to drag him down . . . and deep inside . . . and keep him there. For a very, very long time. *Forever* was sounding pretty good at the moment.

She'd come to her senses later.

He pushed one hand into her hair and cupped her neck, tilting her face to his. "Bree, luv, I wanted to take this quite slow, savor every bit of you . . . but I'm afraid my restraint is about worn through."

She nudged him closer by digging her heels into his backside. "Slow next time," she told him, her voice quivering right along with the rest of her body. He made it so easy for her to speak her mind, say the things she'd only ever let herself think. "Hard and fast now."

He didn't flash a grin as she'd expected. If anything, his

face grew more serious, his eyes reflecting a desire that should have overwhelmed her . . . but instead made her feel cherished and cared for.

"Bree . . ."

"I know," she whispered. "I know." She slipped her hand behind his neck and urged his mouth to hers. And as she mated her tongue with his, he pushed into her. She groaned, deep down in her throat . . . and felt something move inside her chest, close to her heart, as he started to move inside of her body.

The soul kiss continued as their bodies moved together, almost the more intimate of the two joinings. She felt his body gather, tighten, as he moved deeper, faster. She met him thrust for thrust, grunt for grunt, and when he finally came, they both cried out.

He gathered her close and buried his face in the curve of her neck, pressed his lips to the pulse point he found there, then rolled them gently to their sides. She felt thoroughly loved and wonderfully replete . . . which probably explained where the sudden lump in her throat came from. It had, after all, been a very long day, fraught with a lot of emotional highs and lows. It was only natural to feel a bit weepy.

Tristan shifted up, grabbed a couple of pillows and stuffed them under his head, then pulled her up next to him, cradling her in the shelter of his bigger, stronger body. Tucking her close, he pressed his face to her hair and slid one of his legs across both of hers. Never had she felt so cosseted, so cared for . . . so completely and utterly safe.

She pressed a small kiss to the center of his chest, then snuggled in and let sleep overtake her. She'd sort out the avalanche of emotions tomorrow when she was rested and thinking more clearly. For now, she was going to enjoy a night of deep, undisturbed sleep. In Tristan's arms.

"Thank you," she whispered, not sure he heard her, nor that she wanted him to. She didn't want to explain all the reasons she felt that way, most of which had very little to do with the physical pleasure they'd just shared. Because then she'd have to explain them to herself.

Tomorrow. She'd deal with everything tomorrow.

Just as sleep claimed her, she felt him smooth back her hair and press his lips against her forehead. "Aye," she thought she heard him murmur. "'Tis thankful I am, too, luv."

Chapter 10

They'd awakened at some point during the night and crept out to the kitchen, like two thieves in the night, whispering for no reason, only to have to stifle bursts of laughter and a squeal or two of surprise when one or the other would snatch the other close for a quick kiss or teasing squeeze.

Tristan had let Jinty out into the stormswept, early morning hours for a quick run while the two of them made quick work of the stew he'd left warming in the covered pot on the stove. Then he'd made her squeal quite loudly when he'd tossed her over his shoulder and taken her back to bed, where he'd stripped his t-shirt off of her and spent a delightful hour exploring her exquisitely sensitive nipples, then making love to her once more. He'd intended to go slowly, to savor it more, savor her more. But she'd surprised him and taken control, rolling him to his back, straddling his hips. From the moment she'd sat up, shaken her hair back, and grinned at him, he'd been completely lost. He gripped her hips and let loose, each of them taking the other for a wild, fast ride that left them both breathless and laughing in delight.

She was absolutely irresistible to him. He told himself it was simply because she was something bright and shiny-new to play with . . . intoxicating and initially addictive. But as he'd lain next to her afterward, watching her sleep well past the wee morning hours, he wondered about that. He felt as if he'd known her forever, his comfort with her was so utterly complete. It had been but one night . . . and he already didn't want to imagine a morning where she wouldn't be nestled beside him. He'd been alone thus far in life, and he was comfortable with that, but he'd never been lonely. When she left . . . he would be both.

Tristan shifted slightly in the armchair so the thin, early-morning light sifting through the window just behind him would illuminate his sketch pad somewhat more brightly. He didn't turn on the bedside lamp. He wanted to capture the sunrise precisely as it was, with the light gradually sliding across his bed, across Bree's body and face. His hands moved swiftly, with easy confidence, as he studied the tableau laid out before him.

He looked over the rough charcoal sketch, but even his overly critical eye liked what he saw. He flipped to a fresh sheet and began again, this time drawing her legs, tangled in the sheets, one foot tucked beneath her other ankle. He smiled, liking the fact that he already knew she liked to hook one foot over his ankle in her sleep and draw him close, keep him close. He'd awakened about an hour earlier to find her sprawled next to him, flat on her stomach, her face turned away from him . . . but hooked at one ankle . . . and with her hand comfortingly pressed to the center of his chest. He'd lain there for the longest time, thinking he rather liked the sensation of being claimed, liking that she'd felt proprietary about him, even in her sleep.

It should have made him feel cornered or trapped, which was typically how he reacted when someone got the least bit clingy. But those former someones weren't Bree Sullivan. With her, he wanted to be a marked man, wanted her to want him, wanted her to want more of him.

Wanted her to want to stay.

He continued sketching. Another of just her feet, one of her hand, clutching a fistful of bed linen. His body stirred, remembering what those fingers had felt like, clutching a fistful of his hair. He wanted her again. Had never stopped wanting her, even when his body was too spent to do anything about it.

He flipped another page and did a few quick studies of her face, not quite smooth or serene, even in sleep. He wanted to soothe away the last of those hollows, see the shadows leave her entirely. He imagined he would be able to recreate her face at will for ages to come, without ever having to lay eyes on her again, so permanent a mark had she made on him. He studiously avoided thinking about that day, the day that she'd leave here. Perhaps even today.

He absently rubbed at the spot on his chest, soothing the immediate aching sensation that very thought had incurred. For all that he was artist and dreamer, he was also a pragmatic realist. Flock owners, landowners, had to be. He'd already put a call in to Alastair Henderson's repair shop, leaving a message that he'd need the older man, or his daughter, Kat, to come out with their tow truck at their earliest convenience. He smiled a little, imagining his future sister-in-law's reaction upon finding a very tousled and happily content woman tucked away under his roof. She'd tease him mercilessly, for certain, then immediately hunt down Brodie to tell him all about it. But she'd also be sincerely happy for him. And it was that fact that had given Tristan what little peace he'd been able to scrape together about this whole ordeal.

He wanted Bree to stay. For however long she thought she could manage it. Sure, he knew he was only asking for greater heartbreak when the time ultimately came that she had to go. But he knew life was too short and too unpredictable not to cherish the things that made a man happy and fulfilled for whatever the duration of that happiness. It was something he'd tried to tell his oldest brother, Dylan, on several occasions. Not that he'd listened. He'd shrugged off his baby brother's insight, saying he'd dealt with his grief and had moved on with his life. Even though it was quite plain to anyone with even a passing knowledge of the tragic circumstances of Dylan's recent past, that nothing could be farther from the truth.

But his brother losing his wife so abruptly had only underscored Tristan's beliefs in holding on tightly and enjoying fully whatever life brought his way. He paused in his sketching and watched Bree snuffle softly into her pillow. She might only be in his life for a short time, but his heart had immediately recognized her as someone very special. He didn't bother to analyze it. A waste of far too precious time.

Yes, he'd shamelessly and selfishly do whatever he could to keep her here for as long as possible, if he thought she'd benefit by it in some way as well. If it was better for her to go . . . then he'd respect that. But she'd said herself she needed a safe haven, needed a place to step out of the insanity and regroup. He could give her that, wanted to believe that was why their paths had crossed, if for nothing else.

And Kat and Alastair Henderson could help him in that endeavor. He'd enlist their help in keeping Bree's identity under wraps, keep her from any unnecessary intrusion by the world at large. His village might be filled with nosey, opinionated busybodies who, in his estimation, spent far too much time concerned with the business of others . . . but they were also fiercely loyal and protective of their own.

And if Bree was in Tristan's care, then by extension their loyalty would convey to her as well. If he asked them to help him maintain her privacy, he knew they'd rally for him. It was one of the things he cherished about life out here. And they knew, each and every one, that he'd do the same for them.

He smiled a little, his sketch pad forgotten as he watched Bree begin to stir and stretch. Yes, he'd willingly endure endless ribbing from the same townsfolk whose help he intended to enlist, but that was part and parcel of the deal. The outside world would be persona non grata . . . but the gatekeepers would assume full access to this new chapter in his life. Payment for services rendered.

Tristan was surprised to discover that the prospect of being the focal point of village gossip for the immediate future didn't bother him so much. In fact, it shocked him somewhat to realize that he rather fancied the idea of taking Bree into Glenbuie, introducing her around. But not quite yet. He hadn't gotten his private fill of her yet, and he was feeling quite greedy and proprietary over her himself.

He slid the sketch pad to the floor and stood, stretching the kinks from his back and shoulders, having lost track of the hours he'd spent in that chair, capturing every detail of Bree for all posterity. Images that needed no recording as they'd be perfectly preserved in his mind's eye for the remainder of his days. Of that he was certain. And yet, it had felt so wonderful to translate those images, his view of her, to paper. He'd felt freed, his creativity finally unshackled and available to him again, to command at his whim. He'd never again take that gift for granted.

She rolled to her back, and the invitation was too much for him to pass up. He crawled onto the bed, stretching his body out on top of her, eliciting a surprised little grunt. Before she could fully awaken, he rolled to his back and pulled her across his chest, tucking her against him and hooking his legs around hers to keep her nestled atop his body.

To his everlasting pleasure, she immediately snuggled closer. "Mmm," she managed, then pressed a sleepy kiss to his throat.

"Hungry?" He'd already fed Jint and let her out for a run. His stomach had grumbled earlier, but at the moment he hungered for something else.

Bree wriggled on him a little, as evidence of his newly awakened hunger grew. "Is that a proposition?" she mumbled, yawning and stretching a little.

He groaned as her hips pressed against his, and had her flat on her back beneath him an instant later. "Would you like it to be?"

Her eyes blinked open, but took a moment to focus. She stared at him for a long moment, then her lips curved in a slow, sweet smile. "And here I thought coffee was the only thing that could perk me up first thing in the morning." She surprised him by coming very suddenly awake, pushing him to his back and straddling his hips. "Did I mention I'm a morning person?" She pressed her thighs against his hips and pushed down on him.

He choked a little as his body surged fully to life. "No, I dinnae believe so," he managed. "But I rather like that you are."

"Do ye now," she said, in a rather good imitation of his highland burr.

"Aye," he said, grinning and tugging her down on top of him. "Aye, that I do." He kissed her, and thought he could quite easily get used to this byplay being the start of his every day. All he had to do was convince her of that.

She tried to pull away. "I should brush my teeth and I likely look a fright—"

He kissed her soundly. "You're nothing but stunning to me."

She snorted, which made him laugh. He loved how unconcerned she was about herself. "Well, I'll feel better if I'm cleaned up a little."

"I can take care of all of those worries." He rolled up to a sitting position, making her grab at his shoulders. He tucked her legs around his waist as he swung his legs off the side of the bed. "Hold on."

She did without hesitation. "Where are you taking me?"

He kicked the door open to the bathroom. "Scrub my back and I'll scrub yours?"

"Heavenly idea," she said, kissing her way up the side of his neck, nibbling on his ear.

"We might only make it as far as the sink if you don't stop teasin' me."

She tugged his earlobe between her teeth, then ran the tip of her tongue along his jaw. "And that should bother me because . . . ?"

"I've forgotten," he admitted, letting her feet drop to the floor beside the tub so he could reach in and turn on the spigots for the shower. She slipped out of his arms when he tried to kiss her again, and stepped toward the sink, but he turned her right back into his arms. He gathered her close, kissing her until their smiles faded, and soft moans of need took their place as steam filled the air. "I'm no' sure I'll ever have enough of you."

Her arms tightened around his waist. "I feel as if I've awakened into some kind of fairy tale." She laughed a bit dryly. "And I was supposedly already having one of those." She smiled up at him. "I'm liking this one far better, if you don't mind my saying."

"I dinnae mind a'tall. In fact, I'm rather pleased." He pushed her hair back with fingers. "I'd like ye tae stay with me, Bree. For as long as life will let ye."

Her smile stayed, but her expression shuttered a bit. He hated being the one to do it, but it was a subject that needed broaching. He'd have much rather pretended that she had no other concerns, no other life, than one here with him. Which, of course, was the real fairy tale.

"We'll get your car taken care of," he told her, continuing to toy with her hair. "I've already placed a call to a friend in the village. They should be here sometime this morning. Is there anyone you should contact? Let them know you're okay?"

"One or two. I'll reimburse you," she said quickly. "I'm sure my cell is toast. As is my laptop and everything else I had with me." She didn't sound quite as bereft about that fact as he'd have thought.

"I'm really sorry about that," he said. "Don't worry about the calls. Your work—"

She rolled her eyes. "Trust me, drowning what little I'd managed not to already trash was a merciful death. I—I haven't exactly been coming up with . . . well, anything inspired of late."

"I can't imagine it wasn't brilliant."

She laughed and patted him on the chest. "Thank you for

that, my staunch and loyal supporter. Don't take this personally, but you have no idea what you're talking about. I'm quite capable of writing complete rubbish, I assure you." She shook her head. "Although at this point, to be honest, I'm so my own worst enemy, I couldn't judge the relative merit of anyone's work, much less my own."

"I can't pretend to understand the pressures put on you, but I do know the feeling of being abandoned by your own creativity." His smile was a shade wry. "I like to pretend I can draw, paint a little. Lately, a child with a pot of finger paints could do more inspiring work."

Her eyes lit up. "Really? Can I see some of your work? Do you have a studio out here?"

He thought about the sketch pad lying by the chair in the bedroom, and wondered how she'd feel about being his unwitting subject. "The loft is my studio of sorts, though I do most of my work outside. But trust me when I say I can produce rubbish quite easily as well."

She slid her arms around his waist. "Land manager and businessman. Shepherd and painter. A dreamer's soul in a workman's body. You're a fascinating man, Tristan Chisholm."

He felt his skin heat a little at her description of him. "Och, you're a romantic," he told her. "I'm no' so interesting as all that, tucked away from the world such as I am."

She rolled her eyes again, then impulsively kissed him hard on the mouth. "And you're not a romantic? Please. And I can't imagine anything more heavenly right now than being tucked away from the world." She laid her head on his chest. "I envy you your solitude and contentment with your life."

Share it with me, then, he wanted to say, feeling immensely more content with his life now that she was standing in his arms. It was premature, no doubt, to offer himself up like that. A week from now, a month, he could discover that she wasn't remotely compatible with him, or this life. She could be driving him straight out of his gourd. But oh, did he want the chance to find that out for himself. How else did one manage to know those things other than to try?

"My offer still stands." He nudged her chin up, looked down into her eyes. "And if ye think ye could work out here, I have a computer ye could borrow. Technology has invaded Glenbuie as well." He let the offer sit out there, his heart beating hard at the unmistakable leap of hope he'd seen in her eyes. An instinctive reaction that, one she couldn't have manufactured. It was almost too much to allow himself to hope for. He wanted it too badly, and he knew the folly of that.

And almost immediately, that hope in her eyes was extinguished, the shadows that he hadn't seen since yesterday returned. "I . . . you have no idea how attractive that offer is." She looked into his eyes. "Or how badly I'd like to take you up on it, for . . . for a lot of reasons, and not all of them having to do with writing. You've been . . . so much." She traced her fingers along his cheek and jaw. "More than I had any right to hope for, much less ask to keep."

"Bree—" he began, quite prepared to beg if it would get them both what they so obviously wanted.

But she cut him off. "I couldn't do that to you. You have no idea what you'd be asking for. I might be able to sneak off for a short while, but the world will eventually figure out where I am. As you say, technology reaches everywhere, even here. They'll find me . . . and the hounding will resume. That's why I ran away from Edinburgh yesterday."

"Sometimes small villages are better at keeping their resources tucked away from public scrutiny than big cities." He smiled. "Glenbuie managed to hide its illegal distillery trade for almost a hundred years, before they were finally able to make it a legal enterprise. It's our way to keep our treasures close . . . and our loved ones closer." He drew her arms over his shoulders and scooped her up high against his chest, so her face was even with his. "Stay, Bree. At least for now. If it gets untenable at some point, we'll deal with it then."

"You've really no idea what you're asking for, Tristan. Or asking your village to handle, for that matter."

"Then we'll go into town later and take it up with them directly."

She laughed. "What, call a town meeting?"

He grinned. "Share an ale at my brother's pub. Same thing, really."

She smiled with him, but there was a poignancy to it and his heart squeezed, fearing he'd already lost the battle, with the war soon to follow suit. "I'm not your village's treasure, nor am I a cherished loved one. In fact, I could be their worst nightmare when the vultures descend."

"Why don't you let me deal with that," he said. "Right now, there's soap and a washcloth callin' our names." She started to argue, but he was already pulling her into the shower with him. Moments later, they were both slippery with suds . . . and she was quite preoccupied with making sure every part of him was squeaky clean.

He was preoccupied as well, but only partly on the matter very literally at hand. Her ever so lovely and quite talented hands.

She'd given him the opening he needed . . . she wanted to stay. Now it was up to him to prove that her trust in him was well placed. He already knew he had the trust of his family and friends. He'd make this work.

He groaned as she stroked him, thought his legs might not support him. Then she was kneeling before him and examining her handiwork quite up close and—"Dear God in heaven. You've eternity to stop doing that," he said on a sigh of deep appreciation.

Aye, he'd find a way to make this work, or die in the trying.

Chapter 11

Bree was flipping through the sketch pad she'd found on the floor when Tristan came back into the bedroom.

"Alastair is here. You ready to go salvage—" He broke off when he saw what she had in her hands.

"I don't claim to know anything about art, but these are really amazing," she said, then glanced up to find him looking rather guilty. "It's okay," she reassured him. "I mean, it surprised me a little. No one has ever drawn me before. Awake or asleep." She flipped through a few more pages. "I wish I looked as good for real as I do in your eyes." She looked at him. "It's flattering. Embarrassing, kind of, but flattering. Were you going to show me?"

"Probably. Maybe." He entered the room and she handed him the pad with a laugh.

"Well, at least you're honest." She smiled at him and could see he was clearly uncomfortable. "Stop worrying. If anyone understands sharing something they've personally created with someone else, it's me. It's like stripping down in public, thinking about other people actually reading my work. Have you ever shown yours? In public, I mean?"

"No. I have my job to do here. This is just something I do for me."

She grinned. "There are days when I wish I'd kept mine in

my desk drawer, too. And I'm the last person who should tell you to share your talent with the world."

His lips quirked. "But . . ."

She shrugged, smiled sweetly. "I'm just sayin' . . ."

He returned the knowing look. "I hear you." He tossed the sketch pad on the bed and took her hand. "Come on, let's go see what we can salvage out there."

She sighed before she could stifle it. She really wasn't ready to face her life again.

He stopped immediately and pulled her close. "I know. I'm sorry you have to deal with it. And I'll pay to have the canvas repaired—"

"Please," she said, waving away his concern. "I'm sure that's the least of the problems with it. I had coverage, anyway." She looked past him out the side window, but that view didn't extend to the road out front. "I just . . ." She just wanted to stay here, in Tristan's farmhouse, with the stunning mountain and valley vistas right outside her door. She could understand why his creative talents were sparked by living out here. She had a feeling hers might be, too. She'd love the chance to find out.

"We'll deal with it," he told her. "One step at a time. Car first. Then whatever comes next. It will all get done in its own time."

She smiled wistfully. "You're so very pragmatic. I used to be. Somewhere along the way I lost that, lost my ability to focus on only the next thing. And instead I let myself get overwhelmed by everything all at once. It all seemed so beyond one person's ability to manage."

"Didn't you have help?"

"My editor, my agent, a publicist. But I felt beholden to them, too. And they had other agendas as well."

"What about family?"

"My parents are older, retired. I was a very late-in-life baby. When all the hoopla happened, they were hounded to the point of being in seclusion. I finally moved them all the

way from Missouri to a private resort community in Arizona."
She smiled. "My dad actually loves it down there. He's learned
to play golf and almost has my mom convinced to join him.
It's turned out okay for them. The rest of my town, though
they support their own, were happy to see me go, I'm sure."
She smiled a bit sadly. "I don't want to do that to you or people you care about."

"One step at a time," he told her, then kissed her on the
corners of her mouth, before groaning a little and pulling her
close for a deeper kiss.

She was sighing when he finally lifted his head. "You're
just saying that because you're enjoying the perks of having
me here."

He slid his hands up her waist and ran his thumbs across
her nipples, making her gasp. "You are perky, and I won't
deny I'm enjoying it. But I'm also a grown man who knows
his surroundings . . . and knows what he wants." He nudged
her chin up when she glanced away. "I want you to stay here.
I want a chance to find out."

"Find out what?"

He grinned. "How long we're both going to enjoy you
staying here."

She laughed. "I wish it were that simple."

"I know you might have a hard time believing it, given
what you've been dealing with . . . but sometimes it can be
easy." He took her hand, tugged her to the door. "Come on,
Alastair is waiting." He looked back over his shoulder. "One
step at a time. Deal?"

She couldn't help it. He was like a Scots pied piper. And
she wanted to follow him anywhere. "I'm trying."

"Wow. You get to look at this every day?" Bree topped the
rocky outcropping, breathing a bit heavily. Even though she'd
been out walking the moors of the loch with Tristan every day
when he came in from the fields, she hadn't gone out to run
the sheep with him until today. She didn't have her highland

lungs quite yet, but for this view, she'd willingly work on it. She'd been here, with him, for two weeks now. It felt like a lifetime . . . and it also felt like time was ticking way too fast. Not that there was any reason for her to leave just yet. But there was an impending sense of doom she couldn't shake, though she'd done a pretty good job of pushing it to the background.

That first morning, she'd contacted her agent, who, together with her publicist, had put the word out that Bree was stepping out of the spotlight to work in seclusion on her next release. Which, as it turned out, was actually, finally true.

There was magic here. She'd felt it that first day, and it had only grown stronger the longer she stayed. She wasn't sure if it was the utter privacy, the stunning vistas right outside her door . . . or the cocoon of emotional security that Tristan had so effortlessly woven around her. For a man with an artist's soul, he was incredibly well grounded. Just being around him extended that sensibility to her. She only wished she'd met him sooner, but perhaps the old adage was true: all things happened when they did for a reason. Perhaps it was only now, at this point in her life, that she would truly appreciate this newfound gift in her life.

Tristan had talked with Alastair the morning they'd towed her rental car out of the gully. It had been a total loss, so rather than drag it into town and provide a trail for any diehard member of the media hell-bent on finding out where Bree had run off to—though she'd told no one, not even her agent—they'd tucked it away in one of the shearing sheds for the time being. She'd deal with it later. At the moment, she had no intention of going anywhere that required transportation. She was quite happily stranded and perfectly content to remain that way.

Alastair and Bree had hit it off immediately—it was impossible not to love the old Scot. He was charming, and soon to be part of the Chisholm family when his daughter wed Tristan's brother Brodie the following spring. He had vowed to keep her whereabouts and identity to himself, and made it clear that whenever the time came for her to surface, the village would rally around her and do their best to protect her privacy. They had little patience for rudeness, he informed her, and a great deal of respect for people's right to lead their lives as they saw fit. The fact that Tristan was obviously sweet on her wouldn't hurt her stock, either, he'd added with a wink.

Alastair, along with two of Tristan's brothers, Brodie and Reese—who threatened to show up every day, but who had so far left them to their peace—were every bit the shining knights Tristan had sworn they would be. Each had worked in their own way to assure her they'd watch her back and make sure she had the room and space to simply exist for the time being. Her faith in basic human kindness was making a remarkable comeback. She felt closer to the woman she'd been back in Mason, Missouri, than she'd ever hoped to be again.

She hadn't been into the village just yet, but Tristan had already warned her that while the world at large might be leaving them alone, the price to be paid would be having the village assume complete proprietary rights to their budding relationship once they came out. She assured him that small towns were small towns . . . and that she rather liked the idea of being adopted into the bosom of his. Small fishbowls she could handle, because the underlying motivation was affection and respect.

Which was what was making her so nervous. The longer she stayed, the more deeply involved she was becoming. Okay, who was she kidding? She was head over heels already, and every new thing Tristan introduced her to made her fall that much harder. It was scary how much this place suited her, soothed her, settled her soul. And how much the man himself did the same for her heart.

Scary, indeed.

Because something this good couldn't last. It just couldn't. She'd learned over the past year or so to stay perennially braced for the next wave to thunder over her. The minute she let her guard drop? Pounded straight into the beach.

But as the hours turned to days, and the days to weeks, she wanted desperately to allow herself to believe her own personal paradise might stay intact.

Tristan stood behind her and wove his arms around her waist. "I was thinking maybe we'd work up here sometime later this week. It's getting a bit brisk, the closer we get to November, but if we time it for midday, it might be worthwhile."

He pressed a kiss to the side of her neck, and she reveled in that shivery sensation that shimmered through her every time he touched her. "I'd like that."

He slid his hands under her shirt and skimmed them up over her breasts. She pretended to smack at his hands. "Right in front of the flock? What kind of example is that setting?"

Tristan laughed. "You're kidding, right? I've had to watch these guys mate for years. They owe me." He nuzzled her neck, and toyed with her nipples. "If it bothers you, I'll stop."

She leaned her head back against him. "Have I stopped you yet?"

"Hmm," he said, and she could feel him grin against her skin. He nipped at her ear. "Makes me wish I'd brought a blanket."

She smiled and tipped her face to the sun. "Me, too," she said, sighing as he turned her in his arms. "Next time?"

"You know I always like the sound of that."

Yes, she did. One thing she'd learned about Tristan was that he wasn't afraid of asking for what he wanted, or making his needs known. He made her feel wonderfully desirable, and desired. And without being pushy or clingy, he made sure she knew where he stood. He wanted her here, wanted her to stay.

He kissed the tip of her nose, then the corners of her mouth. "Will it bother you if I draw while you try to work?"

"If we bring a blanket next time, I can't promise either of

us will get much work done," she told him, getting better every day about telling him what she wanted, too.

"I'm going to have to teach Jinty to fetch, that's all there is to it," he said. "She'd have the blanket here in no time."

Bree laughed. "And you tell me I'm the impatient one." That was another thing she'd learned about him. The man enjoyed taking his time. It wasn't taking her quite as long to learn that letting him was always a good thing for her.

"So," she asked, "am I going to be the subject this time, or are you going back to landscapes?"

He'd given her carte blanche to go through his loft and she had marveled over the absolute power and drama of his work. Much to her dismay, he'd reiterated his lack of desire to show his work, but she felt it was a shame not to share his talent with others. So she'd tacked a few watercolors up in the corner of his loft that she'd sectioned off as her work-space. He hadn't minded, so she figured maybe eventually she'd convince him to frame a few properly and hang them in the house . . . and who knew—if that went well, maybe eventually Brodie would hang one in the pub, or Reese could mount one in the reception area of the distillery. Far too soon for her to be pushing him like that . . . but the ideas were there anyway, in the back of her mind.

He was trying to get her to narrow her focus, to worry more about her own needs than those of every other person on the planet. And he'd made remarkable inroads in a short time. So maybe she'd get him to expand his world just a teeny tiny bit and let others enjoy the fruits of his artistic labors. They were too stunningly beautiful not to share.

"Maybe I want a chance to combine the two," Tristan said. "Although you're a lovely landscape all on your own."

She laughed and tugged his head down for a long, hard kiss. "You flatterer, you."

"I think you almost believed me that time." He turned her back around so they could both look out over the pastures below. Jinty was barking and moving back and forth, keeping the strays in line. He propped his chin on her head. "So, what do you think? Are you game to try?"

She knew he was talking about working up here, but she couldn't help but expand that to include the life she was slowly embarking on here.

"Yes," she said, "yes, I am." She thought about what it would be like, spending the occasional afternoon up here, working peacefully side by side. It was a way of life she could never have imagined . . . and one she badly wanted a chance at keeping.

She'd rediscovered herself here. She'd been writing longhand since starting back on the book. Not having to stare at a computer screen had also been freeing to her. She hadn't intended to start at all, actually. Tristan had encouraged her just to relax and be, to walk the moors, settle in and not push herself. And maybe it was truly giving herself that freedom that had had her itching to get back to work. She'd been standing by the window in his loft the day the story idea had hit her, almost fully formed. Instinctively she'd grabbed one of his sketch pads and begun furiously making notes, getting down as much information as she could.

She'd been both jubilant and emotional when she'd finally come up for air. She had begun to think that part of her was well and truly dead. She wasn't even sure it was a good idea, but she was excited by it, and that was more than she'd had in a long, long time. She hadn't said anything to Tristan about it, not wanting to jinx it until she'd looked at it again. Besides, it had only been one day, albeit a momentous one.

But the next day when he'd headed out with Jinty, she'd climbed up to the loft and begun putting together a more detailed outline. Which had led to actually beginning to write the opening pages of the book. And that's how he'd found her late that afternoon, sprawled in front of the window, with barely enough light to write by, but writing furiously, as if it might disappear on her if she didn't get it all down right then.

He'd flipped on the soft track lighting overhead and waved

her to continue working when she'd startled at his sudden reappearance, long since lost to what time of day it was. She'd smiled at him, he'd winked at her. They'd celebrate later. Then he'd done the perfect thing . . . he'd moved to one of his easels, and begun quietly working himself, sketching her. She should have felt self-conscious, and initially she had, but she was soon pulled back into her story, which was all but gushing out of her. And sharing that moment with him was celebration enough. Although the bottle of wine and bubble bath he'd drawn for them later that night had been pretty special, too.

She sighed and tugged his arms more tightly around her waist. "What did I do to deserve this?" she murmured.

He didn't question the track of her thoughts—he rarely did. They had a rhythm that was natural, easy. She cherished it already.

"It's no' about deservin'," he told her. "It's about allowing yourself the right to live life as you please. On your own terms."

If anyone understood the value of that, it was the man currently holding her in his arms. And it was his innate strength that gave her the courage to voice her biggest fear. "I want to. But for a long time now, I've felt like I owe a lot of people for my success, that I had to somehow repay them for supporting my work so spectacularly. They just want more, and it should be flattering. It *was* flattering. But it was also enormous pressure. I didn't want to let any of them down."

"Ye wrote them a good story, Bree. And they enjoyed it. Ye didn't demand success, it came to you for work already well done. Ye may owe your publisher another story, but you dinnae owe them or anyone yer soul."

"They'd believed in me, and I didn't want to disappoint."

He turned her in his arms, looked steadily into her eyes. "Who did you write that first book for? Not for them. They didn't exist yet. You wrote it for you. And that's the only person you should ever write for."

"You make it sound so simple."

"It can be. We're proof of that, don't ye think?"

"I want to believe that. I truly do."

"Then take hold of it, and make it be what you want. You get to say. No one else." He smiled. "Well, save for me, anyway."

She didn't smile in return; instead, she grew more serious. "But what if—"

"Och, Bree, ye can't 'what if' yer life away." He framed her face. "Do you want to be here? With me? Write your stories, enjoy your days?"

"The nights aren't so bad, either," she quipped. But he wouldn't let her dodge. Now he was serious, as serious as she'd ever seen him. "Okay. Yes. Yes, I want to be here. With you. And I'm excited about what I'm writing when I never thought I would be again. Yes, you're right, I'm finally writing for me. But I am afraid. How petrifying do you think it is to know the whole world is going to judge the book, and me, and quite publicly. I'd think you of all people would understand. For the same reason you don't share your work. You don't want to be judged and found wanting."

He laughed outright at that.

"What?"

"I don't share my work because in my case, it truly is for me. I honestly dinnae care what others think. But then, it's not my lifeblood like writing is for you."

She had other ideas about that, but one battle at a time. "I'm trying to let that fear go, really I am. I am writing, and I am finding the joy again. But the pressure is there, the expectation. I can't hide here forever. I will have to face it at some point. When or if the book ever finally hits the stands, you, your friends, your family, everyone in the village, they all might have to, too."

"Then they'll have to decide how to handle it, won't they? You're doing it again, living for others. It's no' selfish, Bree, to put your needs first. You're not neglectin' anyone, you know. It's no' your responsibility to oversee how your career affects every living being. It's sweet and wonderful that you care, and they'll all know that about you, as I already do. You live here, you write here, and you can be published again here. We're all adults and we're all in this together. We'll figure it out."

"It's not that easy."

"Most things worth having aren't. My brothers and I have held on to property that has been in Chisholm hands for centuries. It hasn't been easy, but it's worthwhile. Because the alternative is untenable." He framed her face. "That's how I'm comin' to feel about you. But you have to feel that about yourself, your work, too. I'll fight for you, Bree. But you have to learn to fight for yourself, or no one can help ye."

She held his gaze, feeling the truth of his words clear down to her soul. "I guess, the more I have, the more I risk losing. And it scares me, to care that much again. I don't want to risk losing any of this."

"All of life is risk. So you do what you must to hang on to what you have, to what you want. It's all any of us can do. Ye can't live waiting for the other shoe to drop."

"But—"

"No buts. Do you want what we've begun here to continue, Bree?"

"Yes," she said immediately.

"I do, too. I want you here. I want you in my life. So we go from there. What comes our way, we deal with when it gets here. You've made me as aware as possible of what's out there, and we've done our best to protect ourselves. Beyond that, we live for now, not in fear of then. We live for us. No' them." He kissed her, so tenderly it made her heart melt. He pressed his forehead to hers and wove his fingers through her hair. "Trust me, Bree. But more importantly, trust yourself."

He was so certain. Of course, he had every right to be. His whole life had been led on his terms. He took care of business and those he loved, but he made no apologies for living in a manner that made him happy and gave him peace. So . . . what made her happy? What gave her peace? The answer, as it turned out, was rather simple indeed.

"I feel like I'm meant to be here," she told him. "With you."

Tristan smiled. "Then stay. That's all you have to do."

Simple. So simple. And maybe, just maybe, it really was.

Epilogue

It was a beautiful, late-spring afternoon. The sun shone through the stained-glass windows of the abbey, cascading a rainbow of color across the excited, chattering congregation.

Tristan stood at the head of the aisle, his hands behind his back, palms sweating. The pews of the centuries-old Chisholm family church were packed with smiling, happy faces, all eagerly anticipating the momentous occasion.

Brodie glanced past brother Reese, his best man, and shot Tristan a grin. "You look like ye've had a taste of bad meat, lad. I thought I was the one who was supposed to be nervous."

Tristan looked at his brother, the groom, who, from all appearances was relaxed and quite delighted by the impending event. "Why aren't ye?"

Just then, the double doors swung wide and Kat Henderson stepped through the church doors on Alastair's arm. She was an absolutely stunning vision. "That's why," Brodie whispered, voice tight, eyes a wee bit glassy. "Because I'm no fool. I know I'm the luckiest man on earth."

Tristan did smile at that. "You do have a point." He felt the hairs lift on his arms as organ music swelled inside the small family abbey, and Kat began her walk down the aisle. His heart picked up speed and he glanced behind him, at

Dylan. He was glad their oldest brother had consented to taking part. It had been three years now since Maribel had passed away and he'd come home to Glenbuie. Well past time, they'd all thought, for him to join the land of the living again. They'd all done their best to encourage it, but with little success. But standing in a chapel for a wedding . . . well, that tied itself to memories that no number of years could erase, and they'd have each understood if he'd begged off. Tristan had taken it as a hopeful sign when he hadn't.

Tristan's gaze shifted across the aisle, to Kat's two attendants. The maid of honor, Daisy MacDonnell, was a vision her own self, and soon to become Reese's intended. His brother had confided that he'd only put off asking because he hadn't wanted to overshadow Brodie and Kat's joy, along with the rest of Glenbuie, in the planning of their wedding. Daisy's eyes were misty as she watched Kat's measured procession toward the altar, and Tristan knew she'd make an equally stunning bride. And that Reese was also a very, very fortunate man.

Daisy had made a huge impact on the village with her business acumen. The Web site she'd constructed for the distillery had not only increased their sales internationally, but had created quite a stir village-wide with the throngs of sightseers who were now flocking to Glenbuie, both for a tour and taste of the family whisky, and also to enjoy the village itself. She'd woven together a ring of connected Web sites for many of the village shops, all extolling the charm and endearing ambience of the town square. The family would benefit further from her creative genius when Dylan finally opened the bed and breakfast. She'd cross-promoted it on the Web ring, and he was already booked for the season.

Which led his gaze to Kat's other attendant. Bree. His pulse bumped up a little faster, as it always did when he looked at her. Seven months had passed since she'd stepped—or swerved—into his life, forever changing it. And him.

"And here I thought the bride was supposed to be the most beautiful woman in the room," Reese whispered in his ear.

"Oh, she's stunning enough, she is," Tristan said, never taking his eyes from Bree.

"We're a lot, aren't we?" he said with a light chuckle, his own gaze clearly on Daisy. "Do ye think the village can take so many Chisholm weddings in such a short period of time?"

Tristan glanced back at him. "How many?"

Reese grinned. "Are ye tellin' me you're not contemplating dropping down on one knee yourself?"

His hands shook a little. "I'll gladly wait my turn."

Reese just smiled and shifted back in place. "Perhaps I should wager on that."

Tristan wisely said nothing. Bree had finished her book just last week. The entire village had celebrated the joyous occasion. They'd long since adopted their new resident author as one of their own, and considering they'd each done their share to protect her privacy as the media had eventually discovered her whereabouts and descended en masse, they all felt a bit proprietary of both her and the book itself. Bree had happily obliged and throughout the nightlong celebration had made certain they knew, each and every one, what their support meant to her.

He was so proud of her, so in love with this amazing woman, he'd had to bite his tongue to keep from begging her to marry him right then. He hadn't. Partly out of respect for Reese's plans, but mostly because the completion of her novel was cause all by itself for a joyous celebration.

He was willing to wait until the moment was all theirs.

Standing where he was now, however, the enormity of that moment truly sank in and took hold. Yes, it made his heart pound; yes, it made his palms sweat. He was rarely nervous, but admittedly, the idea of standing before the entire village and watching her walk toward him down that very aisle . . .

Bree looked up just then and smiled at him. Just for him. And he thought about all she'd handled, all she'd overcome, the leap of faith she'd taken, both with him and with herself.

Kat arrived at the altar, and Tristan watched as Alastair gave her hand over to Brodie, who quite eagerly took it in his own, anxious to declare himself to her and begin their new life together.

His gaze went back to Bree. He wanted that. He wanted to declare his commitment to her. Only not here. He wanted to do it outside, on the land he'd also committed himself to. He wondered what Bree would say about taking their vows high up on their rocky bluff. A small, intimate gathering, with just his brothers, their wives, her parents perhaps, standing in attendance. They could celebrate all night in the village afterward if she wanted to.

He listened as Brodie and Kat repeated their vows, unable to tear his gaze from Bree's. And he realized he'd marry her in the middle of a crowded train station if that was what she wanted.

His hands stopped trembling. His palms stopped sweating. The only thing that mattered was that she say yes. All he had to do was ask her. She chose that moment to wink at him.

Simple, really.

Here's a look at Lori Foster's
"Playing Doctor" in
WHEN GOOD THINGS HAPPEN
TO BAD BOYS,
coming next month from Brava.

With an indulgent smile, Axel Dean watched the young lady exit the room of suffocating, overbearing people. Damn, she was sweet on the eyes. Tall, nearly as tall as him, with raven black hair and piercing blue eyes and an air of negligence that dared him, calling on his baser instincts, stripping away the façade of civility he tried to don in polite company.

Her straight hair skimmed her shoulders, darker than his own, blue-black without a single hint of red. It was so silky it looked fluid, moving when she moved, shimmering with highlights from the glow of candles. The white catering shirt and black slacks didn't do much for her figure, which he guessed to be slim and toned. She didn't have the lush curves he usually favored, but what she lacked in body she made up for in attitude.

And attitude, as he well knew, made a huge difference in bed.

As a waiter passed, Axel plunked his empty glass down onto the tray and headed for the sliding doors. He hated uptight formal affairs that being a doctor often obligated him to attend. That didn't mean he had to linger. That didn't mean he had to mingle.

Especially when more enlivening entertainment waited outside.

Making certain no one paid him any mind, he slipped through the doors and onto a wide balcony lit by twinkling lights that mirrored the stars in the evening sky. He waited, saying a silent prayer that no one followed him. Every time he attended a gathering, women hit on him. And that'd be fine and dandy by him, given that he adored women, but not within his professional circle.

He absolutely never, ever dated anyone in his field. Not even anyone related to someone in his field.

Despite the martial bliss of both his brother and his best friend, he had no intentions of settling down any time soon. That being the case, it wouldn't be wise to get involved with relatives, friends, or associates of the people he worked with. Walking away could cause a scene, and then the entire situation would get sticky and uncomfortable.

There were plenty of women who weren't interested in medicine, like secretaries, lawyers . . . or caterers.

He'd been prepared to be bored spitless tonight. Then he'd seen her hustling around the crowded room with robust energy. At first he'd assumed her to be a mere waitress for the catering company, but given how she performed each and every job, from putting out food to collecting empty dishes to directing the others, she might actually be the one in charge. Given her air of command and confidence, he figured her to be in her late twenties, maybe early thirties. Sexy. Mature. Flirtatious.

His heartbeat sped up, just imagining how the night might end.

When no one followed, Axel went down the curving wooden stairs to the garden paths behind Elwood's home. The pompous ass loved to flaunt his money, and why not? He had plenty to flaunt.

Spring had brought a profusion of blooming flowers to fill the air with heady scents. The chilly evening breeze didn't faze Axel as he searched the darkness for her. Then he saw a flare of light, realized it was a match, and made his way silently toward her.

She had her back to him, going on tiptoe to reach the top of an ornate torch anchored to the ground and surrounded by evergreens. Just as the wick caught, Axel said, "Hello."

She went perfectly still, poised on tiptoes, arms reaching up to the top of the torch. Slowly, in an oh-so-aware way, she relaxed and turned to face him.

Don't miss Amy J. Fetzer's,
PERFECT WEAPON,
available now from Brava!

He smiled slightly as his gaze traveled over her face, the fall of her dark hair, just noticing the gold flecks in her brown eyes. Her expression was at once innocent, and sexy. A hell of a combination. Jack wasn't much on centerfold types, pretty was good, but most times, after a couple months, he didn't like what he found beneath. With Syd, he already knew what lay beneath, besides a wicked sense of humor.

"Well, don't just jump to answer. Take your time."

"I'm thinking a kiss will never be enough," he murmured, lowering his head.

"I'm so wide open to suggestions it's pathetic."

His dark chuckle rumbled in the hallway an instant before he laid his mouth over hers. Something unfamiliar crackled through him. It wasn't instant, it'd been there, waiting—in that place he'd packed away most of his emotions, the need to link himself with her when he'd been solitary for so long. He kissed her and kissed her and somewhere in between, the barrier broke, poured like water from a shattered dam.

Sydney felt it, a difference in him. Patience turned possessive, as if he was staking claim, that he knew she'd deny him nothing of herself. She wouldn't. His hands splayed her back, driving up her spine as his warm mouth rolled back and forth over hers. She felt his restraint, his need to crush and take.

Her brain went fuzzy, her thoughts centered on only one thing. *More. I want more with this man.*

Jack gave. "You know where we're going." It wasn't a question.

Yet her answer spoke when her tongue slid into his mouth, in her hips rising to mesh with his. Jack nearly roared, letting go a little more. His hands mapped her contours and she moaned, a delicious little sound that nearly tore through his restraint.

Impatiently, he backed her up against the nearest wall, devouring her mouth as his hands plowed over her body.

She winced and jerked back. "Ow, sorry, oh, that stings."

He looked down at her leg. It was bleeding again. "Oh, hell. Sorry, baby. Let's have a look now. Have a seat in the kitchen, the light's better."

Almost robotic, he turned away, and went deeper into the house. She stared at his back for a second, too turned on to move.

Then he called out, "And take those pants off, too."

She smiled. "You're always telling me to do that." She went into the kitchen and slipped her jeans off.

He came back with a large plastic toolbox. "And you keep doing it. What's that say?"

She sat at the kitchen table in panties and a T-shirt, peeling the layers of gauze. Her breath hissed.

"Stop that before you tear the skin," he said, and she looked up. He tugged her to her feet, gripped her at the waist, and lifted her to the counter. She gasped at the cold stone under her bare skin.

"Do you always just do what you want without asking?"

He looked chagrined. "By your leave, ma'am, I'm not used to waiting to take action."

"That just excites me all over. Bossy men, who'da thunk it?"

He snapped on latex gloves. "Wiseass." He carefully cut the bandage away and started cleaning the wound. It was bleeding at the point of impact, but the rest was dried and sticky.

He wasn't all that gentle and Syd smacked him on the shoulder when it hurt too much. "Ease up. I'm not a Marine, ya know."

"Oh, I know." He winked, then rummaged in the large kit. He snapped the cap of a small plastic tube with a needle on the end. "This will help."

"Is that necessary?" Though it felt on fire right now.

"Unless you have an amazing pain threshold, this is really gonna hurt. Too much blood is caked on the wound. There could be fibers from the jeans in it, glass. It did pass through the window. And who was telling me about how fast germs multiply?"

She gestured for him to keep working. "You could have stopped at fibers."

"I have to open it back up."

"Gee, no stick to bite? No whiskey?"

"I have morphine."

She shook her head. "Go ahead." He injected the topical anesthetic, then while he waited for it to take effect, he laid out his bandages.

Syd grabbed a stack and with some antiseptic, cleaned the couple of cuts on his jaw and neck. "They aren't bad. But you have flakes of glass only a shower will clean."

"We can try that later."

"We?"

He slid her a dark sexy look that liquefied her muscles. "Nothing gets past you, huh, Einstein?"

"Not unless I want it to. And I could jump on you right now, boo-boo and all, like an undersexed teenager."

"Undersexed?"

She lifted a bottle from the kit, read the label. "Antibiotics? Prescription?"

He got the message. She didn't want to discuss her sex life. Fine with him. His mind was already on that lacy bra he'd bought and how it looked on her—because the transparent panties were just about driving him nuts as it was.

"Rick's a corpsman, Navy."

"I thought he was a Marine."

He soaked a cloth in the sink. "Might as well be." He hesitated for a second, in voice and moves, then said, "He found me in the mountains."

Sydney felt oddly privileged. The tiny piece of him made her feel closer to him. Rick had saved his life. "I should thank him for that. But I swore an oath."

He glanced, flashed a smile, then applied a wet cloth to the wound, softening the dried blood. He blotted and rubbed, taking tweezers to pluck out debris. "This will burn," he warned and drizzled hydrogen peroxide on it. He blew and blotted again, but when she didn't utter a sound, Jack looked up.

She sat perfectly still, gripping the counter ledge, her lips tight. Yet tears cascaded down her face.

"Aw, honey I—"

"Keep going, please."

He felt helpless, a first in about a dozen years. Silent tears were a powerful thing to see, and he hated causing her more pain. She'd had enough for someone who didn't wear Kevlar to the office. She bit her lip, swallowed hard, trying so hard not to sob, and Jack leaned in and kissed her, focusing everything into it, a slow molten roll of lips and tongue. She responded instantly, and he felt a tender ache in his chest when she cradled his jaw and took control. It was an eating kiss, as if her pain flowed through it, almost dark and ravenous, and when he pulled back, she looked more exotic than before.

"It still hurts like hell." She sniffled.

"I was trying to take your mind off it."

"And that's all you came up with?" Her fingers dribbled down his chest to his jeans.

Christ, the woman was going to make him an idiot. "Give me a minute, I'll think of something else." Jack went back to cleaning the wound down to the tissue. It bled again.

Syd wanted to cry like a baby, but what good would it do? She stared at the long, narrow gouge, seeing exactly how close they came to dying today. She'd have a permanent reminder of how precious life had become.

"I know it looks bad," he said, "but it has to heal from the inside out. It's broad enough that stitches would just make the scar worse."

"The scar's the least of my problems."

He covered it with antibacterial ointment, then bandaged it. He sat, and propped her leg on his shoulder to wrap the ace around her thigh. "Bad fashion statement in a bikini?" He secured it, then pulled off the surgical gloves.

"As if. You do not want to see this body in a bikini." She was glad to think of anything but the pain right now.

His gaze lingered over her. "You underestimate yourself, Einstein." He kissed her bandaged leg.

"I rarely do, Jack. I know my weaknesses." She slid her leg off his shoulder, and for a moment she just stared. "Algorithms, English Lit, loading i-Pods . . ." Suddenly, she gripped handfuls of his bloody shirt, yanked. "And right now—you."

Her mouth covered his in a swoop of heat and put every seductive nuance into it. There wasn't much information in her past to gather. She'd spent her adult life getting her doctorate or using it. But she tried.

And she was winning.

Jack felt like a puppet being played and he let her. Her life was in shambles and she wanted control, wanted to command something and he let it be him. She teased, drawing back and making him chase her, then erotically licked the line of his lips before she pushed her tongue between. A hot, desperate need riddled him down to his heels as she kissed him. He wanted her, right now, on the counter, and the image made his dick like lead in his jeans. When she broke the kiss, it was to peel off his shirt. Her hands scraped over his skin, and she dragged her tongue across his nipple, then suckled.

It left him trembling, his head thrown back, and he gripped

her hips, wedging closer. His hand slid upward, under her shirt, shaping her ribs, teasing the underside of her breasts cupped in a lacy bra. Her kiss intensified.

"Keep that up, Marine. Please."

He drew off her shirt, his lip quirking at the pink lace bra. A quick flick and it was falling. Jack swept it away. His gaze rolled down her body, and everything between them seemed to go still for a moment. By increments she leaned closer, her nipples grazing his chest. That first press of flesh to flesh held a sort of euphoria, crossing the line of intimacy. Jack had helped a lot of people, rescued many, killed to save them, but nothing compared to the single moment when you invited someone this close. He fought for patience when he was craving her like air, his body flexing with need. Although Syd might have a mouth on her, he sensed this was a brave thing to do.

She was still, waiting for his touch, watching his hands come toward her and when they did, Syd experienced something close to nirvana. She covered his big hands and arched and Jack kissed her and kissed her, loving her moans, her eagerness.

He wouldn't last long.

Take a peek at
Katherine Garbera's
BODY HEAT.
Available now from Brava . . .

Andi straightened and caught him staring. Tuck shrugged. He was attracted to her and wasn't even going to pretend he wasn't. Everything about her turned him on.

Suddenly all the confidence he'd seen seemed to drain away. She held the can out to him and hurried behind her standard issue desk. There was something different in her body language now. This wasn't the same woman who'd joked with her men about strippers.

He hooked his ankle over his knee. Popping the tab on the top of the can, he took a long drag hoping the icy beverage would cool the heat of his body. The heat that was being generated by the woman sitting across from him—eyeing him warily.

He held the Coke can loosely in one hand trying to look as non-threatening as possible. But he wanted her and he knew himself well enough to know that he wasn't going to back away without a fight, or watching her and waiting for everything to click into place.

As an arson investigator he had to be intimately aware of human behavior. The subject had always intrigued him. He'd never met a person who he hadn't wanted to figure out. Find out why they behaved the way they did. It was the same techniques he used to find arsonists.

He just had to figure out what the turn-on was. Why they were drawn to fire. And what they hoped to get out of it.

Shamelessly, he used the same techniques with women. And nine times out of ten it worked. Of course, that one time when it didn't work, had served to keep him humble. He knew on one level that he didn't know everything about women or about human nature. But he'd been willing to turn failure into success.

"Why are you staring at me?" she asked, her voice dropping an octave.

"I like the way your mouth looks," he said, his own voice sounding deeper and huskier than normal. Damn, this woman made him hotter than he'd been in a long time. And, honestly, she wasn't doing anything other than being herself. He didn't understand this attraction to her but he knew himself well enough that he didn't question it.

"You are making me uncomfortable," she said, chewing on her lower lip. "And I don't like it."

"Your mouth is making me uncomfortable." She wasn't helping him get his mind back on business. "And I do like it."

"I can't be responsible for your fantasies," she said, in a way that made him realize that this was a woman at home in the business world but not one-on-one with a man.

"Yes, you can." She was solely responsible for those fantasies. He'd never had this problem on the job before. But if she nibbled on her lower lip one more time, he was coming across the desk and tasting her mouth for himself.

"Why? If I was a guy sitting here you wouldn't be having those fantasies would you?" She sat up straighter in her chair and that fire that he'd seen earlier was back.

It was there in her eyes. She had the kind of passion that most women were afraid of. And he knew she was afraid of it too, but when she felt threatened it came out with her temper.

"No, but neither of us can change the fact that you are a woman. One I can't help but notice."

She opened one of the files on her desk. "Well, stop."